PRAISE FOR

Praise for *INVISIBLE LINE*
(Previously published as CYCLING TO ASYLUM):
Longlisted for the Sunburst Award

"Prescient a decade ago, pressing now. *Invisible Line* will take you to the lowest darkest places, then fly you up into the air and scatter you into joyful molecules."

> RICH LARSON, AWARD-WINNING AUTHOR
> OF *CHANGELOG* AND *YMIR*

"One of the best books I read in 2014. . . . Couldn't recommend it more."

> FABIO FERNANDES, EDITOR OF *WE SEE A DIFFERENT FRONTIER: A POSTCOLONIAL SPECULATIVE FICTION ANTHOLOGY*

"That the characters stay with you long afterwards testifies to the depth of Sokol's vision and authentic voice. This is a memorable novel by a new Canadian writer."

> NEW PERSPECTIVES ON CANADIAN LITERATURE

"*Cycling to Asylum* defies the strictures of genre, crossing borders geographically and metaphorically."

> CORA SIRÉ, AUTHOR OF *SIGNS OF SUBVERSIVE INNOCENTS*

"Su J. Sokol's eloquent prose takes us through a fascinating near-future landscape that is uncomfortably familiar. The distinctive, vivid voices of her characters make *Cycling to Asylum* a joy to read."

CAPITOL LITERARY REVIEW

"Plenty of storytelling to enjoy. . ."

QUÉBEC READS

"STOP whatever you are doing now and READ THIS NOVEL!!!"

TIMOTHY CARTER, AUTHOR OF *EPOCH*

INVISIBLE LINE

INVISIBLE LINE

BOOK 1

SU J. SOKOL

FLAME ARROW PUBLISHING

ALSO BY SU J. SOKOL

Five Points on an Invisible Line (2025)

Run J Run (2019)

Zee (2020)

This book is dedicated to the memory of my father, David J. Sokol, who taught me to love reading and to question authority.

Su J Sokol

When I see an adult on a bicycle, I do not despair for the future of the human race.

H.G. Wells

AUTHOR'S NOTE ON CONTENT

Invisible Line is a work of hopepunk, exploring themes of solidarity, activism, love, and community. Hopepunk is also a genre that looks at marginalization and oppression, violence and struggle, and as such, often includes depictions of some darker experiences and realities. In this novel, some of these depictions include: scenes of police violence (some on page and some in flashback); suicidal ideation; rape/sexual assault (some implied or off page); flashbacks concerning torture; and PTSD.

Along with these darker elements contained in the story, there are also comic, loving, and exciting moments, as well as scenes of pure joy. I intend for the reader to leave this tale with hope and a taste for continuing the fight for social justice.

Su J. Sokol

BOOK ONE: PEDALING

CHAPTER 1
LAEK

'm counting American flags. Eleven regular-sized, five minis, three hanging sideways, fascist-style. A giant one suspended from a thick metal pole in front of the bank. And the two hanging from either side of the police car just ahead. I stop counting. Quickly switch lanes. *Keep pedaling, Laek. Just keep pedaling.*

I continue north on Fourth Avenue. There's no need to check my screen or project a holo map. I know where I am. I know what time it is. My body can feel these things. So I sense that I'm not going exactly north, but more northeast. The convention is to say north, though, because of how the grid runs in this corner of Brooklyn.

My bike is moving fast. Slicing through the heat. Sweat streams down my shirtless back and under my arms. I don't mind the sweat, the heat, and besides, it's only 91 degrees. Not too bad for 6:58 a.m. on a late March morning. A heavy truck rattles by. I feel a whoosh of hot air as it whizzes past me, inches from my left elbow. I hold my ground. A car comes up on me from behind. Sounds its horn. Does it think I don't know it's there? That I can't feel its heat on my bare neck? My eyes dart between the traffic on my left and the double-parked cars on my right, alert for opening doors. I've only been doored once, the slight asymmetry of my handlebars a constant reminder.

The sour stench of garbage combines with the delicious aroma of fresh muffins. Owners of local diners and bodegas are neutralizing alarms, unlocking gates, and resetting their holo-boards. Unhoused people still asleep are pushed away. Some with kicks and shouts. Some with phaser rods. A rod is raised. I slow, body taut, ready to intervene. It's lowered. I move on.

I fill my lungs with the early morning air. Reach my arms above my head. The wheels of my bicycle vibrate on the warm pavement and, like a tuning fork, I respond with a sure, steady hum deep inside me. I stretch my gaze west, towards the piece of sky that's visible beyond the urban landscape. There's a green-ish-brown stain around the edges, but it's still beautiful, still fills my heart with the hope I always feel looking at the morning sky. Like the City's beginning again. Like something good could happen.

At Ninth Street, I turn left towards the Gowanus. Once in Red Hook, cut off by the expressway, the walls of the neighbor-hood close in around me. I coast to a stop in front of my school. Dismount. We've started a new unit in ninth grade history: Citi-zenship, Patriotism, and the Social Contract. Should I mention the new anti-immigrant laws? Should I mention flags?

I slip on my shirt. Bound up the broad concrete stairs with my bike. Inside, I notice a new security guard. I hesitate. Then give them my best smile. They don't ask for my wrist to scan my Uni. Relieved, I dig my hands deep into my pockets. Disappear into the distortion field of the elliptical security booth. I hold my breath as currents of metallic, tangerine air surround me. Once I'm through security, I exhale slowly. Walk down the hallway towards the teachers' lounge. I roll my bike beside me, the sweat drying under my shirt.

In the classroom, I get to work activating new holographic images. A security gate appears across the door. Stern-faced offi-cers blink into existence. I add teeth-baring dogs. They snap at the air, barely restrained by their uniformed handlers. Nearby, I place other holos. Unified National Identity data being imbedded in wrist chips. Oaths being sworn. People marching. At the back corners of the room, adults and children of various nationalities, their possessions on their backs, wait patiently. The line of refugees disappears into the horizon. At the last minute, I add American flags of all types and sizes, waving disjointedly.

My ninth graders begin to file in. Some seem excited, their heads whipping around. Others are looking down and clutching their school screens tightly. I begin class, hoping I haven't overdone it. Even after turning the lesson into a game, with the apples I've brought for prizes, a few of my students still sit in their seats, fidgety and tight-lipped.

A few minutes before the end of the period, when I've given out apples to most of the kids in my class, I smile at Sasha and ask, "Who's hungry?"

"I am," Sasha answers timidly.

"But he hasn't even answered one question!" Marcus complains.

"He's *hungry*," Inez says. "You already had an apple on top of your big-assed breakfast."

Before Marcus has a chance to retaliate, I put my hand on his shoulder and squeeze.

"It's a good question the two of you raise. What's more important in deciding who gets an apple—whether you're hungry or whether you answered the question right?"

Hands dart into the air and I watch the fight resolve into an intellectual debate.

After a few minutes of discussion, I say: "OK, a good start. I want you all to think more about it while you're doing the homework assignment I've beamed to your screens."

I toss an apple to each student who hasn't received one yet, starting with Sasha.

"You have enough for everyone?" Marcus asks, surprised.

"Of course I do. I love you guys too much to short you on apples."

At lunchtime, I head over to the teachers' lounge.

"There's coffee," Erin says, pushing dark bangs from her eyes as she studies her screen.

"Think I'll pass." I look around the teachers' lounge. "You seen Philip?"

"I saw him earlier, why?"

"He's meeting with his ex tonight. Still trying to convince her to take him back."

"Dana will never take him back."

"Yeah. That's why I want to talk to him."

"He'll only get mad at you, Laek."

"I don't want to see him hurt again."

"You can't keep him from getting hurt."

She takes a gulp of coffee. Grimaces. Returns to studying her screen.

"Is that sour look from the coffee or what you're reading?" I ask.

"They've changed the English Comp exams again. Do they want these kids to fail?"

I bend over her chair. "Talk about a moving target. Want to raise it at the union meeting?"

"Maybe. You're lucky you teach history. At least the past isn't subject to change."

"Guess you never heard of revisionism."

"OK, you have a point."

"Seriously, Erin, you know how to teach English. You don't have to jump every time the current admin wants to try out the latest regressive educational theory."

"And you need to be more careful, teaching a subject that's so politically sensitive. We're scrutinized enough as it is."

"I'm teaching the required curriculum," I tell her.

"I heard that for the citizenship unit, you were talking about civil disobedience."

"They asked me about it. Wanted me to take them to a demo. The parents of a student apparently saw me at one. I had to explain it was too dangerous."

"They also said you told them that borders aren't real."

"Where are you getting this?" I ask her.

"Don't worry about it. The students think you're hyper, as they put it."

"Well, it's not what I meant, exactly. You know there are kids in my class who are undocumented. I wanted them to know they're safe in our school. And that having docs and having human rights are two different things."

"But borders exist," she insists.

"Ever think about borders when you were a kid? I did—a lot. Maybe because of how much my mom and I had to move around. When we crossed into a new state, I'd stare at the road. Try to find the thick black line I saw on the map."

Erin smiles but doesn't say anything.

"Yeah, someone eventually explained that the lines on the map weren't there in real life. Not between states and not between countries, either. It got me wondering. If borders are imaginary lines, why can't people just step over them?"

"But you know the answer to that, Laek. You're an adult now." She says this like my transformation into adulthood happened just yesterday. As though I wasn't a man of thirty-two, only one year younger than her.

"It's not about being grown-up. I still wonder about this. And about what kind of world we'd have if that were allowed."

"But in the meantime, we need to teach about the world as it *really* is," Erin insists.

"A bitter duty, sometimes."

———

Grabbing my bike at the end of the day, I spot Philip on his way out.

"Hey, when are you going over to Dana's? You have time to grab a beer?"

"Yeah, I'm not supposed to pick up Kyla before six. Dana needs me to take Kyla to daycare tomorrow. Do you think she might ask me to stay for dinner?"

"I don't know. Did she say anything?"

"No. Maybe I should bring a bottle of wine, just in case."

"That's a strategy, I guess. Any other ideas on how to approach things?"

"Well, I was thinking about getting down on my knees and begging. But that hasn't worked especially well in the past."

"Ah, Philip."

"Don't give me those sad puppy eyes, Laek. I was only kidding. Mostly."

"Now here's an idea. You can find someone who actually appreciates you."

"She's the mother of my child. How easily could you give up Janie?"

"If it were best for her. . ."

"Tú no entiendes. How could you? Janie would never leave you."

Maybe not. But there could still be a reason to give Janie up. Reasons related to her safety. And the safety of our kids. Philip doesn't know why I've needed to think about this. And burdening him with that information won't make him feel better. Instead, I try to find some words for him. But there are no words, because beneath it all he's right. Just imagining a life without Janie makes me ache inside. So I wrap my arms around my best friend instead. He hugs me back, then pushes me away awkwardly. "We'd better hurry."

It's almost time for the first of the three sequenced ultrasound alarms. At least judging by the way the guards are hurrying everyone through. I've been on school property only once when the first alarm went off. The bursts of sonic sound are only supposed to bother kids and teenagers. I still ended up with a pretty bad headache. I've never been on school property for the third alarm. It's at a high enough decibel level to be classified as a sonic weapon.

Philip's on foot so I walk my bike. We take a shortcut through the Red Hook Projects. Entering them is like being swallowed up by some beast. The jutting buildings like jagged teeth around a big hungry mouth. I stop at a sign: "Welcome to Red Hook Houses West—Another Successful P2 Partnership!" Public-private partnership, sure. Half the windows are boarded up. Playgrounds looking like battlegrounds. I stop reading signs. Read graffiti instead. "Forced implants = slavery." And below that, in thick red paint, "Fuck the fazer." I wave to a few students before cutting north. We emerge two blocks from our favorite local pub, The Look and Hook.

We each order a Brooklyn Brown. One is enough for me. I want a clear head for the union meeting. Philip orders a second round. I pour half of mine into his glass while he's in the men's room. When it's time to go, I wish him luck with Dana and head to the union meeting.

In downtown Brooklyn, I tense up. Holo-ads, loud and lurid, assault my senses. I ride, head down, until the approach to the Brooklyn Bridge. Standing on my pedals, I glance over my left shoulder, take a deep breath and go, crossing five lanes of busy traffic to arrive at the narrow, curved path at the far left of the bridge. A chorus of horns and a heartbeat later, I'm on.

The bridge is a transfer point between two realities. I move away from the bustle of downtown Brooklyn—poor, ordinary, and mostly non-White—towards an island of wonders and riches held by a very few. Below me, the newest zip-and-soar yachts mix with older ferries and sailboats. Above, mini-balloons hover and swoop, a colorful counterpoint to the security drones. Yet here in between, on the Brooklyn Bridge bike path, time is frozen. Everything still seems possible. I reach the midway mark, now finished with the long but modest climb. I roll with a crowd of cyclists past the spiderweb cables. I've passed the point of no return.

In Manhattan, I glance out at the bubble dome being built around the business district. Then imagine the swarms of heavily armed cops and private security surrounding the construction. Gliding down the ramp off the bridge, I veer right, happy to be going north instead. I slip into the uptown traffic. Quickly pass the courts and then Chinatown. Zigzagging around the cars, it's not long before I'm at East Fourteenth Street trying to catch a view of Union Square Park, a place steeped in fascinating labor movement history. I hope this might inspire us tonight. I take a left onto Broadway. Look for somewhere to lock up my bike.

There's an air of excitement, like before a good fight. It takes twenty-five minutes to make my way to Erin with all the people who stop me to talk. The eleven officers enter the hall together. A hush settles over the packed assembly and the two-way holo-chatter goes silent. I listen to the president speak. It's mostly leadership spin. I zone out until a teacher from Queens stands up to oppose legislation that would lower the age to twelve for mandatory iris scanning.

"Requiring this at sixteen is bad enough. Can't they have some time to be kids before their personal info is spread all over the national security database?"

I listen to her words. Childhood memories try to creep into my head. It's difficult to breathe. I push myself to my feet, applauding to hide my discomfort.

Erin's watching me with concern. I smile. "I'm just a little tired," I tell her.

"Nightmares again?" she asks.

I shrug instead of answering.

"Close your eyes for a few minutes. I'll let you know when we get to the important part."

I shake my head but lean back anyway. The presentation consists of glossed-over proposals for givebacks. I try to listen but despite myself, I feel my eyelids close. Soon I'm walking the midwestern drylands. The odor of dust and ozone is suffocating. A sudden rainstorm. Water pouring down, filling my mouth and nostrils. Then it's not a rainstorm because I'm inside and strapped down to a board. I can't breathe. I jerk myself up and cough.

Erin's hand is on my shoulder. "I think you might be getting sick," she says.

"I'm OK." I try to shake it off. The discussion has moved to proposals for privatizing services for special-needs students. Virtual-only classrooms. AI mentoring models. I drift off again.

I wake to Erin telling me that they've beamed the proposals. I begin to read. Halfway through I see it, buried between the "no strike" clause and the "duty to report." I grab Erin's arm. Show her the section. While she reads, I beam a message to our coalition. Confusion moves like a wave across the room. Zion, the delegate from the Music and Arts School in Boerum Hill, asks, "Does this mean what I think? They can't expect us to turn our students in to Immigration."

Some chapter leaders stand, try to ask questions. They're cut off. Discussion of this item has been reserved for the legal subcommittee. We're told that a newer version of the text will be beamed for next meeting. I look down at my screen. The proposals have been deleted at source.

After the meeting is over, our coalition briefly discusses how to respond, but everyone's exhausted. It's decided that a plan of action is premature before the subcommittee report. We disperse, but I still feel worked up. I lean against the building. Stare off at Union Square. There's some commotion. I walk to the corner of Fourteenth. Cross the street. An unhoused person is being forcibly removed from the park by two cops. I step out from the darkness, am seen. The cops' grip on their arm loosens. I decide it's time to go home.

I find my bike where I parked it. Unlock it from the pole. Enter the codes to release the handlebars and brakes. I stow my stuff, get on, and start riding down Broadway. I'm thinking about the meeting. About possible organizing strategies. Half a dozen blocks from my starting point, I wait at a red light. It turns green. A car arrives on my left. I roll into the intersection just as the driver turns right—directly into me!

Swerving, braking, and skidding, I stand up on my pedals and, feeling the heat of the car just inches from me, I smack the hood hard with the palm of my left hand. It screeches to a stop. I clear the intersection. As soon as I'm across, the car jerks forward, disappearing down the block. I shake my head. Continue on my way. Not two blocks later, a gunmetal grey car —one of those models resembling an armored box—cuts me off and stops, blocking my path. The driver opens his passenger window. I lean over my handlebars.

"Can I help you?" I ask, trying to control my frustration. Behind me, horns are blaring as drivers steer around us. The person in the gunmetal car ignores this, looks me up and down and says: "You just went right through a red light."

"I did not. I stopped. The driver of the car turned into me without even looking."

"You think you own the road, don't you? Goddamned bicycles."

I wonder where all this road rage is coming from. Maybe they were caught in the Bike Strike this past weekend. I start to respond, angry myself, when they show me their ID. Shit, he's a cop.

"Off the bike. Pull it over."

I examine his car. It's unmarked but through the open window I see the special screen, the scanners, other police tech. My senses sharpen. I follow his instructions, mind racing for ways to defuse the situation. He leaves the motor on. Activates the blue light hidden in the roof.

"Bare your wrist. Keep your other hand in plain view."

I slip off my wrist band and extend my arm to him. I try to act casual. Will myself to keep my hand from shaking. "Listen, I really don't think I went through the red light. I'm sorry for my reaction, though. It's been a long day."

"Are you armed?"

"What? No! I'm, I was just on my—"

"Up against the car."

Quickly, I assume the position, hoping my cooperation will cool his temper. Instead, I realize I've made a big mistake.

"Done this before, haven't you?" He sounds satisfied and excited at the same time.

I try to push my brain into a higher gear. "I watch a lot of real crime drama. You know the one with the tall blond policewoman who's partners with that guy—"

"Shut up and don't move."

He begins to read the text that's come up on his screen. My heart is racing. I need to know what he's seeing, but it's impossible from my angle. Scrolling down with his thumb, he turns to me. "Maybe I should take you downtown, run your Uni through the big federal database. Then we'll have a nice little chat, just the two of us."

My mouth gone dry, I don't reply. What has he noticed? I've tried to stay off the grid as much as possible. Used my Uni only when absolutely necessary. Up until now I haven't had a real problem. Even when I made my application to teach in the public school system, everything went smoothly. Making good on the assurances I'd been given about how my Uni was altered.

I watch the cop carefully. Try to calculate my next move. I'm leaning forward against his car, seemingly calm, but the muscles in my arms are tensed, ready to push up and away, my legs set to spring and run. How long would it take for me to reach my bike, to mount it and flee? On my bike, I could go places it'd be hard for him to follow—the sidewalk, against traffic, into narrow alleys. But there are no narrow alleys in this part of town. Realistically, I have little chance of evading him for long. He has my ID on his screen. And if he'd intended to take me in, he'd've simply done it. Not bothered to threaten me with it. If I run, he'll take me in for sure. Even knowing this, I want to flee so badly it takes every ounce of my strength to remain here, posed against his car, wondering what's coming next.

He stops reading. Approaches me. He's not carrying handcuffs. But he's strapped a phaser stick to his belt. He begins by sliding his hands down my arms and checking my shirt pockets. I try not to flinch. He stops. Puts his hand flat against my chest.

"Scared, aren't you?" he asks in a low voice.

"No."

"Your heart's going a mile a second. What are you hiding? Tell me."

"Nothing. . . Well, I'm a teacher. I guess you saw that on the screen?"

"So what."

"I can get into trouble, maybe lose my job."

"Yeah, I bet."

"They're very strict at my school." This is not a total lie.

"I had a teacher once who told me I'd never amount to anything."

"That's terrible."

"You talk too much. Shut the fuck up."

He continues his search, his hand still on my chest, like he wants to monitor my heart rate. His other hand slides down my stomach to my belt. Then down my back. I know he doesn't actually expect to find a weapon. Otherwise he wouldn't perform a pat-down in such an unorthodox way. As he's guessed, I've been searched before. So what's his game?

He's now moving his hands very slowly below the back of my belt. I'm wondering how long he's going to leave his hand on my ass; then he slides it between my legs and to the front.

I jerk my body back, away from his hand, feel my shoulder make contact. He grabs me and slams me hard against his car. I feel his phaser stick across the back of my neck, my face and windpipe crushed against the metal as he lurches at me from behind.

"Like it this way?"

I feel his hot breath against my ear. Struggle to turn my head to the side. I suck in some air. Breathe out, "Fuck you." He takes his phaser stick from my neck and smacks me on the hip. The volt sends an agonizing spasm of pain down my left leg and across my crotch.

"Or you can taste my stick." He prods me with it from behind.

I don't trust myself to speak. He waits, then hauls me up by the back of my shirt.

"Spread'em. This time don't move."

I do as he says. He continues from where he left off. I will myself to be perfectly still as I picture my fist smashing into his face. No, I despise violence. But as the search goes on, similar images keep coming into my head. I try to push them away. I concentrate on taking deep, even breaths. If I have to feel this cop's hands on my body for much longer, I don't know how I'll control myself. No, I've gotten through worse. If this is all he's after, I'm pretty sure I'll be allowed to go home in the end. Home. I focus on that instead. Home and keeping my family safe.

He removes his hands. Tells me I can get up. I push myself away from the car and start to turn around, not looking at him. He grabs me and throws me against his car again, smacking my forehead against its thick, hot metal.

"Did I tell you to turn around?"

When I don't answer, he gives me another jolt from his phaser. I barely keep to my feet, but I won't give him the satisfaction of seeing me on my knees.

Then he tells me to open my belt.

CHAPTER 2
LAEK

'm walking the streets of New Metropolis. Everything's sketchy, blurry. Faded street signs, hard to make out. I haven't been here since I was young. Since before I met Janie. But I came here a lot when I was a kid. When I first invented this place. I focus hard, recalling details. The grid reforms around me.

A purple flower bobs in the light wind. I kneel down and caress its velvety petals with my fingertip. Inside the dome where The Community lived, there were no flowers. Not in the middle of the drylands. We were hidden beyond the drought farms, the burnt-out towns. Under the dome, we had our own weather. Artificial lightning. Thunder so loud, my ears pounded with pain.

I check the street sign against my memory of where I am in New Metropolis. In our domed community, none of the streets were named. It didn't matter because there was no way out. No way to even dig down below. I know because I tried. He said it was our duty to stay inside. Where our environment was a weather experiment. Where a deal with the government kept us fed. And off the grid. And under the power of one powerful man. How bright my mother's eyes burned when she looked at him. But his eyes looking back were so cold.

New Metropolis has real streets. I named them all when I was eight. I wander over to the central square. Let the water from the fountain run over my hands. I try to wash the dust from my face, from my neck. But it's not dust I see mixing with the water. It's blood.

I shove my hands into my pockets. Can I feel my hands? I make them into fists. The nails dig into my palms. Keep walking, I tell myself. It's safe here. No one can find you. No one can hurt you. Let your mind drift from your body. Your body's strong. It can take care of itself.

I allow myself to run through the streets of New Metropolis, looking for other people. I don't like to be alone. All that time in the Thinking Place, in that small, locked room. I tried to make them talk to me. When they left me food. Everyone was too afraid to disobey. And my mother? Maybe she didn't know. Maybe she didn't really know what went on.

New Metropolis has lots of people. I recorded all the demographic data. Created political parties. Held elections. I built schools and big green parks. And lots of playgrounds. I go to one now. See an empty swing. I sit down and start swinging. I go higher and higher, pumping my legs into the air. I can feel my pulse beating in my head, my breath tightening, but I push through it, push until I'm free. I decide to keep swinging until it's over. I swing for a very long time.

———

I land hard. His voice has pulled me out, back to the streets of New York. Telling me, for what's clearly not the first time, that I can get up and get the hell out of here. That he's decided to let me off with a warning. I close my belt. Notice the bright red marks on my palms.

I continue my ride down Broadway, shaking my head to clear

it. It feels like hours have gone by. I see it's been less than twenty-five minutes. I ride slowly, stopping at each light. I look over my shoulder, check the traffic in all directions. Even normally, I'm an unusually conscientious cycler. Most people who commute by bike don't follow all the traffic rules, written and designed for cars. But I prefer to follow a rule when there's no good reason not to. Breaking rules has been necessary enough in my life. I stop my bike, confused. Where am I?

I see the sign for Great Jones. I'm tempted to go down to Mott Street, access the narrow twisty lanes of Chinatown. There, I could shake anyone who might be following me. But I have a better idea. One that doesn't involve me going anywhere near One Police Plaza. I ride all the way to Bowery, then find the Manhattan Bridge bike path.

Biking across the East River, my mind keeps going back to Broadway. My body bent over the police car. I pull myself away. Focus on the ride and my surroundings. It's hard to keep it out though, so I'm halfway across the river when I wonder about the remark the cop made about his teacher. Did that really happen or was he playing me, even then? I try to put him out of my mind but I keep feeling him behind me. *Pedal*, I tell myself. *Just keep pedaling*.

Once in Brooklyn, I take Flatbush all the way to Grand Army Plaza. Make my way into Prospect Park. I take the circular Park Drive, not slowing on the long climb. When I get back to the place where I started, 3.35 miles later, I begin again, this time faster. I go around a third time. Remove my shirt. I breathe in the darkness, grateful for the broken street lamps.

I let myself drift into a cycling zone. Round and round. Faster and faster. Each circuit gets easier. How many times around have I gone? Six, no, seven times. That's more than 20 miles and I'm not even winded. But, as I look down on the screen of my bike to see how fast I'm going, I suddenly realize how long I've been riding in circles and that it's almost 1 a.m., the park curfew. The Prospect Park Southwest exit comes up and I take it, like a kid stuck in a revolving door who finally stumbles, dizzy, into the street.

I'm OK now. I'm covered in sweat and my body aches, but I'm relaxed and calm. Empty of emotion. Ready to move on. I pedal home. Wipe the sweat off my face with my shirt.

I carry my bike downstairs to the basement apartment. Hang it on the hook mounted on the wall. I peel off my clothes, dump them in the bin, head for the shower. I turn on the hot water and step under before it's hot. I shut the water, soap up, vigorously cleaning every surface of myself, every crevice. I rinse with the still-cold water coming out of the hot tap. I soap up and repeat the process. The water's begun to get warm, quickly turning hot. I let it run over me for as long as I can stand it.

I step out of the shower. Pat myself dry. Walk down the hall. I check on Siri and Simon. All is quiet. I enter my own bedroom and slip under the sheet. As I review the events of the day, it's only then that I begin to tremble. Bitter anger, terror, exhaustion, I let it all pour through me. Almost instantly, Janie wraps herself around me. My tremors slow, then stop. I lie quietly in her arms. She asks me what happened, if I want to talk. I say no, that I'm OK. For once, she doesn't press me and I'm grateful. Then she kisses me, opening her lips against mine. I kiss her back, then turn away, telling her I'm sorry, that I need to sleep. She says it's OK, that she's tired too. She snuggles up against me and I feel safer, her breath soft against my neck.

A long time later, I'm still awake, struggling to keep my thoughts from slipping backwards. I give up trying to sleep and instead think about the next day's classes. The week's lessons have already been planned. Tomorrow's subject: the social contract.

CHAPTER 3
JANIE

My heart wakes before my head, alerting me that something's wrong without telling me what it is. I glance over at Laek sleeping, his long arms and legs sticking out from under the sheet, and the memory of our fight last night comes flooding back. Shit! Did I really tell him to fucking grow up and live in the real world? Laek, of all people, with the childhood he had? I saw the hurt look on his face, and when the hurt changed to anger.

I watch him sleep for a few minutes. Laek's eyelids seem almost violet under his thick, dark lashes. He looks so peaceful, innocent—a dramatic contrast to the set jaw and scalding eyes of last night. Maybe he didn't mean the things he said either.

The morning already feels hot and airless, so I peel the sheet away from my damp skin, wondering what time it is. I grope the side of the headboard. A radiating sun holo, followed by text, takes form just above my knees: *6:02 A.M, 94°, Alert Level ORANGE.* The display doesn't disturb Laek. A marching band parading across our bed probably wouldn't wake him either. Maybe his ability to sleep deeply accounts for why he seems to need so little of it. Then again, he doesn't always sleep well. I think about the nightmares he's been having recently, ever since he came home late from that union meeting a few weeks ago.

A wave of protectiveness douses the last flames of my temper. My anger is quick to ignite and burns hot, but never lasts long. Some say it's my red hair, but I think it's more how I do everything fast. Quick to anger, quick to forgive. In other words: next, next, next. Or maybe that's a bit simplistic. I also hate being at odds with people, especially people I love.

I think how when Laek came home that night, shaking from head to toe, I reacted instinctively and took him in my arms. I understood he was in no shape to talk. Well, mostly I understood, because for me, being in no shape to talk would have meant either I was unconscious or my tongue had been cut off. But people are different and sometimes Laek doesn't like to talk. What he needed then was physical comfort. I start to reach for him now but pull my arm back. If only it were so simple.

On my bike ride to work, I chew over all the possible reasons that Laek still hasn't told me what happened. After what we've been through together, how can he not trust me? I listen to the background music of dissonant honks, screeching brakes and rumbling motors, and murmur "Fuck you, fuck you, and fuck you too," as a series of drivers nearly kill me while I go around the double-parked cars. I burn two consecutive red lights, then adjust my mask while I wait out the next one, drumming impatiently on my handlebars. I'm stuck behind a family box vehicle painted a hot pink camouflage and emitting a "baby on board" holographic bumper sticker right over my face. Could there be another reason Laek hasn't confided in me? I weave around the monstrous pink car, trying to make some progress, but I'm getting nowhere. I'm not getting anywhere in my analysis either, the same questions cycling around in my head.

During the rest of my bike ride, I review the facts of my three cases, rehearsing what I plan to say in court. I'm on autopilot and don't consciously focus on my surroundings again until I roll off the Brooklyn Bridge bike path into Manhattan. At Foley

Square, for good luck, I glance up at the majestic Federal Court-house followed by the State Supreme Court. These buildings are surrounded by an uneasy mix of City cops and private security, as well as concrete anti-terrorist barricades posing as works of art.

I continue up Centre Street to arrive at my destination: 111 Centre, the hideously ugly office building that's home to the New York City Housing Court. If it weren't for the metal fence surrounding the whole thing, it would be a place where people could keep out of the rain.

Urban myth has it that before the fence was constructed, people who were unhoused used to shelter themselves against this very building where, in all likelihood, they received their eviction orders. Then one day, the City was planning some kind of victory march downtown. Lots of press was expected, so a general cleanup order was given and the unhoused, along with the garbage, were carted off. The fence was constructed, suppos-edly as a temporary measure, but has stood here ever since, mute testimony to the City's intolerance of irony.

Waiting to be checked in by the court officers, I look over at the non-attorney line snaking out the door. I wonder how many litigants will lose their cases on default today because they didn't factor in enough time for security.

My third case is the most difficult—an eviction of a tenant living in public housing. Before "the Projects" were privatized, these hearings were nothing more than rubber stamps. At least now the landlord can be forced to prove its case, just as any private landlord would be.

I slip in just before the second call of the calendar. My client is sitting in the last row. I can tell she's relieved that I'm at least dressed up and wearing shoes and that my hair's tied back into a tight bun of curls instead of spilling out all over the place.

The judge makes us go out into the hallway to see if we can settle. My adversary, Eric Broder, is strutting around in his shiny black shoes, saying I'd do well to tell my client to accept the offer he's made—permanent exclusion of her eldest son, James, from the apartment building and grounds, in default of which, she and her three younger children will be evicted from their home. "Management's agreement with the City requires zero-tolerance drug policies."

This is bullshit, as we both know, but I have to at least go through the motions. "At sixteen, James is still a minor," I point out, "and the alleged drug sale is for such a minuscule amount he'd've made more money selling his old screen games."

"The amount doesn't mean shit under the law," Broder responds.

"Look, even if my client were to agree to exclusion, how's she supposed to enforce it? Suppose James comes onto the property to visit his friends or see his siblings in the playground? Let's talk about something less draconian, a probationary period, for example."

"Zero tolerance, that's it."

"There are three younger children in this family, all in local schools, and there hasn't been a single complaint against any of them."

"Your client should have learned to control the oldest one, and anyhow, if this is how he turned out, the other three will probably end up the same. Who asked her to have four kids on the government's tab? Last time I looked, abortion was still legal in this state."

I'm through with this conversation. I look him straight in the eye. "Ready for trial," I say in the same tone of voice someone would say, "Fuck you," and this is exactly how I mean it. I turn my back on him, walk into the courtroom, and catch the judge's eye, giving her a subtle shake of the head. I don't know who's less interested in trying this case today: the judge, my adversary, or me.

I slide into the smooth wooden bench and tell my client what happened. She asks me what to do. I explain that it's her decision, but the worst thing would be to agree to something, then violate the agreement. She'd be out on the street in a second flat that way.

She sighs. "We have to fight it, then."

The court officer calls us up and Broder presents his case. Then it's my turn to speak.

"Your Honor. This is Grace Johnston, the respondent." I nod towards my client.

"Pleased to meet you, Your Honor, ma'am," she says.

"Ms. Johnston has been a tenant of the subject premises for fifteen years, is a member of the tenants' council, and a volunteer at the on-premises Senior Center. She's raised four children in this apartment, including James and his three younger siblings." I then list them all by name, age and year at school. "Grace Johnston is a model tenant, never late with her rent, a good neighbor, and aside from this one incident, there've been no other complaints against the family. If necessary, my client is ready to go to trial and will demonstrate that she's never permitted drugs in her home and that anything illegal that James may have done happened outside of the project grounds and was a one-time occurrence."

"That being said, Your Honor," I continue, "I have just this morning received unfortunate news of developments on James' criminal case. It seems he's been found guilty. I'm beaming the decision to your screen and counsel's screen now. James is sure to get a minimum ten years' imprisonment—that's mandated now, is it not, Mr. Broder?" I ask, turning to him. Before he has a chance to answer, I continue. "Given these facts, I'm not sure what point would be served by a stipulation of exclusion nor a decision on this matter. The situation has evolved beyond that now. James won't be seen on the premises for some time, and the remaining occupants, Ms. Johnston and her three young children, have done nothing to merit eviction."

My client is crying quietly beside me as what I'm saying begins to sink in. I take one of her hands and squeeze. "But if opposing counsel has nothing better to do, we're ready for trial right now. We'll see what the police have to say about James' activities and, in particular, *where* they took place. They're outside waiting to testify, I assume?" I glance over my shoulder and then back at Broder. He doesn't answer.

"Are your witnesses here, Mr. Broder?" the judge asks, raising her eyebrows.

"Your Honor, I can have them here by this afternoon. And I can present the rest of my *prima facie* case this morning."

"That's not acceptable. Your case was scheduled for 9 a.m. It's already been adjourned twice on your application. I have other matters in the afternoon. And I agree with respondent's counsel that there's little point in all this. You seem to have your exclusion. Unless you have allegations against. . ." She looks down at the file. "... Ms. Johnston and her other children?"

I consider pointing out that no such allegations have been made, but I keep my mouth shut. When things are going well, the best thing to say is nothing.

"No, Your Honor," Broder concedes.

"In that case, I will consider a motion to dismiss. Or would you prefer to discontinue?"

Broder looks like he's swallowed something bitter, but discontinuance is a better option for him. "Fine, Your Honor, a discontinuance without prejudice to bringing a new case."

"Of course. I believe the next one is yours as well, Mr. Broder?"

My exit cue. "Thank you, Your Honor." I put my arm around my clients' shoulder. "Come with me to the women's room," I whisper, leading her out of the courtroom. I take her to the elevator to bring her to a bathroom on another floor of the building. Satisfied that none of my adversaries are in one of the stalls, I turn to her.

"I'm so sorry you had to hear the bad news about James like that."

She leans over the sink. I'm afraid for a minute that she's going to throw up, but she just splashes some water on her face.

I look away, keeping myself busy by reading the old-fashioned electronic message board which warns us not to drink the tap water.

"Listen," I continue. "I may have made it sound worse than it was in front of the judge, so. . . well, talk to James' lawyer, he'll explain. Also, there's this new program I know about for youth offenders. Very small, experimental only. But not military, don't worry. Here, hand me your screen." I beam the information to her. "Speak to James and his lawyer and if there's interest, you have the contact info. You can mention my name."

"Thank you." She takes her screen back and clutches it tightly. "Can I go home now?"

"Of course. Be sure to contact me if there's anything new."

"Thank you so much, Ms. Wolfe."

"Janie. You promised to call me Janie. I'm glad I could help."

I watch her leave the bathroom, head held high and back straight. No, she'll never call me Janie. I wash my hands, but it doesn't wash away my feeling of shame. I don't think I'll ever get used to the need to play with the truth in the work I do, but I have no real moral qualms about it. Not how I do it, anyway, never actually lying, merely presenting my clients' situations in a way that encourages a more just result.

What I do feel bad about is how, standing in front of the judge and that fuck Broder, I gave the news of James' verdict, with his poor mother standing there, totally unprepared, knowing that she'd be shocked and heartbroken and react exactly as she did. Even if it was to help win her case, it was a heartless thing to do. Consciously or not, Grace Johnston can't help but keep her distance from someone like me who can be so cold and calculating, and I don't blame her. One more pyrrhic victory under my belt.

I arrive at my office in Bushwick, the upset stomach I always have before court replaced with the slight tension headache I always have after. I wave to Alma at reception and place my wrist in front of the scanner. I push the high-security door open and head for the shoddy stairwell. Magda hears me coming down the hall and invites me into her office, asking me how it went. I tell her about court and then ask what she's up to.

"Trying to resolve a few of my older welfare cases, but it's impossible. Mira, Janie, you've got to hear this." She touches her call screen. After a couple of rings, a computerized female voice comes on, saying:*"You have reached the Office of Employment Assistance, Training and Disability Support. Please enter your party's code by voice or touch now. Para continuar en español..."*

"Employment assistance and training?" I snort. "Another new name for welfare?"

"Yeah, *EAT DIS!* is what we're calling it."

"Oh, that's great," I laugh.

"Wait, though, listen."

"If you are calling to report a welfare fraud, please enter one. If you are calling to terminate assistance or because you have found a job, please enter two. If you are being sanctioned and wish to arrange compliance, please enter three. If you are looking for daycare, please note that all waiting lists. . ."

I begin my own set of choices: "If you want to be fucked in the ass, please enter one. If you want it in the mouth, please enter two. If. . ."

"Stop, stop," Magda begs, laughing helplessly. "No really," she says, terminating the call. "It's not funny. I keep finding myself bounced to the AI agent with the most limited repertoire of responses. Not only that, but if your voice is too deep, the system doesn't even recognize the speech. Javier over at East Harlem had a client who had to talk in falsetto the whole time."

"That's bizarre."

"Yeah, it's probably the number of voice templates they used in designing it. That's what Sara thought. Saved money that way, I guess."

"Or maybe they did it on purpose to discourage men from applying for welfare."

"You have a diabolical mind, you know that?"

"That's why you love me. Hey listen, we should probably get back to work. But how would you and Sara like to hear some music tonight? "

"Any band I know?" she asks me with a smile.

"Yeah, my group's doing a gig in North Bushwick. It'd be nice to see a few familiar faces in the crowd. Or any faces."

"Is Laek coming?"

"He was supposed to, but now. . ."

"Did you two have another fight?"

"How come you and Sara never seem to fight?"

"Oh we fight, all right, but neither one of us likes to go to bed mad. So someone always gives in, and then the other one apologizes too. Making up is always nice."

"If it were up to me, I'd never go to bed mad either. Maybe it's a girl thing."

"Hmm, I'm not so sure about that."

"Maybe it's just that Laek and I are so different."

"Different how?"

"Well, you know, he's a guy, I'm a woman."

"You're teasing now."

"He's tall, I'm short. . ."

"Janie, you are positively obsessed with your height. But seriously, I think the two of you are like peas in a pod."

I shake my head. "Come on, you know my quick fuse and total lack of patience. Meanwhile, Laek's so Zen it's scary. And he's so. . . so in the present physical moment. Half the time I have no fucking idea where I am in real-time/space. I mean, even now, I'm still picturing what happened in court and at the same time thinking about tonight, the music we're going to be playing. I should be here, in this conversation with you."

"You're here too, don't worry. And of course you and Laek are different. I mean, Laek is. . . no offense, but I don't know anyone who's quite like Laek. The important thing is that you both have the same values. And that you actually *follow* your values, all the time. You take this for granted, but to the rest of the world, it's striking. I mean, look at me and Sara. I'm a welfare lawyer and she's a wetware engineer, working for a company profiting off of other people's genetic material. At least you two don't have to argue about the value of your work."

"Maybe that's not enough."

"You're just going through a rough patch. Didn't you tell me that something was up with Laek?" I nod. "And anyhow, values are not all you have in common."

"What else?"

"Music. You have the exact same taste in music, which is pretty remarkable, given how eclectic your tastes are."

"Hmm, maybe there's hope for us after all."

I return home late after the gig. Laek's lying on his stomach asleep, the sheet crumpled around his hips. I touch the smooth skin of his back lightly, but he doesn't stir. I get into bed beside him and inhale his scent in the bedclothes—warm and sweet, like soap and clean cotton and something else, distinctly him. I lie awake for a long time, finally falling asleep, exhausted, and all night long, over and over in my head, I hear the songs we played that night.

In the morning I wake up early, feeling as though I haven't rested. Laek is still sleeping deeply, but during the night he's turned to face me, his knee resting heavily on my calf and his hand lightly touching my shoulder. He's done this unconsciously in his sleep, without thought or intention, but even so, I decide to take it as movement in the right direction.

CHAPTER 4
SIMON

Before daring to escape The Cube, I make sure to turn myself totally invisible.

I breathe in a bunch of air and tell my heart to beat slower and quieter. Then, I make my head disappear. Next, I go down my body and do the same thing to each part of me, all the way to the tips of my toes. When I'm finished, I lift up one foot and put it down softly, then spread out my arms. Nothing. I'm like smoke. The air passes through me.

I walk to the door and, quick as invisible lightning, I'm out of The Cube and into freedom. The darkness is heavy as a weighted blanket. I slip through it like a phantom.

I'm in the long skinny hall. The wood feels smooth under my feet as I slide along it. Before long, I've made it to the big screen. I sit down behind it. Even though I'm invisible, I still try to make myself as small as possible by folding my legs up and scrunching my shoulders together. I know not to use voice activation. Instead, I touch the screen and make the contrast as low as possible. Luckily, I have super-powerful eyes—which is also how I spied the password a few nights ago from all the way across the room.

I bring up the program, narrowing the wrap-around holo to

the smallest scatter. Just like I feared! There's been a catastrophic collapse of the ecosystem in the area I've been monitoring. The animal populations will be doomed if something isn't done. It's up to me to save them.

Scanning the regions bordering this zone, I find a safe refuge. I do some calculations. I could reroute the watering stream *this* way, to the north. I work on other calculations. If only I could be there, in my physical body, in the here and now! I would jump onto the back of the one I call Darkeyes and ride him to safety. The others would follow for sure.

I'm totally into the problem, creating a probability graph above my pentagon of constraints, when I hear a small noise on the other side of the room. I freeze. My fingers are still reaching out towards the screen and my body is surrounded by the glowing blue of the holo-images. I'm scared to breathe, even to think too loud. But it's too late. I've been found.

"Simon!" Mommy lets out a big whoosh of air as she says my name, making it sound like it has three syllables. "What am I going to do with you? Do you have any idea what time it is?"

"It's 4:12 a.m.," I tell her, but this seems to make Mommy angrier. She walks up to me and puts her hands on my shoulders. Even though I'm nine and Mommy is a grown-up, she's only a few inches taller than me. But somehow she seems a lot bigger.

"Why do you do these things, Simon? You'll be exhausted at school!"

"The animals are dying. I need to save them." Saving the animals is more important than going to my stupid school where Keri's there to trip and push me and my teacher won't let me draw and I have to show my steps for math even though I don't have any steps. The only thing good about school is seeing my best friend, Henry.

"Are you talking about that silly game again? You're supposed to be taking a break from that. How did you get the password?"

"It's not a silly game. Animals are really dying. I saw on the newsfeed."

She sighs and speaks more calmly to me. "It's true that there are animals in jeopardy, but not the animals in your game. The newsfeed is about *real* animals in the actual physical world."

"The animals I'm trying to help are the same animals as on the news. The same *species*." I pronounce the word "species" carefully, so she can see I know what I'm talking about.

"Yes, but the animals in the game aren't real—*really* real—even if they're *based* on real-live animals. It's just a *simulation*, you know, a sim."

"They look the same as the animals on the newsfeed. And act the same."

"Simon, don't you know the difference between real and pretend?"

I don't answer. Of course I know what is the difference between something real in the here and now, and something that's made up. But what happens when a real thing is shown on my sim? Isn't the thing it's showing still real, even if what you're looking at is not the thing in the here and now? That's not the same thing as a completely made-up thing, like a unicorn or something. All I know is that real animals are really dying in the real world, just like in my sim.

Mommy is looking into my eyes with her own eyes like she's trying to beam her thoughts right into my head. But I don't get what she's saying. How are the animals on my sim different than the animals on the newsfeed? I'm sure the stuff I'm doing could help them. But whenever I argue with Mommy, I always lose. I mean, she's a lawyer, so arguing's what she does at her work, and she's really good at it. Her words always sound better than mine, but does that make her right? Something's either true or not, no matter whose words sound better.

"Janie, is everything OK?" I hear Daddy ask from down the hall.

All of a sudden I'm very tired and my chest is starting to feel tight, the way it does when I get an asthma attack. "Mommy, can I go back to bed now? I don't feel so good."

Mommy still seems mad. But then she looks at me and all of a sudden she seems sad instead. I think she's sorry she yelled at me. I go over and give her a big hug. She hugs me back and says she'll come and tuck me in.

So that's how I find myself back in The Cube after my big escape, tired but not beaten.

CHAPTER 5
SIRI

When Mommy comes in to tell us to get ready for school, I'm already awake. She leans over the bottom bunk to wake Simon. He mumbles something about being tired and not wanting to go to school. Simon's so lazy. He always falls asleep at least an hour before I do and now here he is asking to sleep more! If it were up to me, I'd never sleep at all. That way, I wouldn't miss anything. I can't wait until I'm older and can stay out hyper-late. Twelve is at least into the two-digits and next year I'll be thirteen: an official teen-ager.

In my drawer, I find my two new bras. Most of my girlfriends have bigger boobs than I do—mine are only small bumps—but I convinced Mommy to buy me these, telling her they'd protect me when I was playing sports. They're sports bras actually, but one of them is kind of pretty with some lacy stuff on the straps. I'm not much into fancy clothes, but my friend Katima said I need to have at least one nice one just in case. Just in case of what I'm not sure, but it seemed like good advice.

I grab a baseball jersey and a pair of shorts and go into the bathroom to pee and wash up. Before putting on my socks, I wiggle my toes, admiring the turquoise glow-in-the-dark polish that my friend Sierra painted there. I can't let Mommy see or she'd strip it all off, claiming it was toxic and acting like I was being poisoned through my toenails.

I tell Simon it's his turn in the bathroom, then put on the friendship bracelet Michael made me. I'll probably end up spending most of the weekend at his place as usual since Michael's mom asked me to help out with Michael's little brothers. I also told Michael I'd braid his hair, since Rebecca doesn't know how. I think if you're White and end up having kids who are Black or biracial, you kind of have a moral obligation to learn how to do Black hair. But it's hard to hold it against Rebecca. She can't help it that she's so disorganized and doesn't know how to do practical stuff. Anyhow, I don't mind helping. Rebecca's nice and treats me like I'm her own age.

I put my ear piece in, pull my baseball cap over my eyes and grab my screen. Finally, I fish my mitt out from under my pillow and put it into my pack for practice later. I've been having to use my own regular glove to play catcher, which is usually OK except when the coach's son pitches. He throws hard. He can't do any other pitches, though—like curve ball or change-up. I can do four different types, but Coach didn't choose me to pitch. David, Michael's dad, said he'd help out this year. Maybe he can convince Coach to let me try out pitching.

I peel my batter's glove off my hand and take a peek. I wear the glove all the time now, even when I sleep. There's a bluish bruise in the middle of my palm, crescent-shaped like the top of a baseball, and it doesn't hurt so bad when I wear the glove. Plus, Mommy and Daddy would never let me keep catching if they saw my hand.

Mommy's pushing us out the door—we're running late as usual. She hands Simon his lunch. I already told her I don't want one because I plan to get pizza with my friends. Mommy's lunches are embarrassing—way too healthy-looking with her fruits and veggies and tofu nuggets. Someone always teases me and then I want to chuck the whole thing.

Once on the street, I start jogging. Simon's lagging behind so I yell at him to come on. We arrive at the R train station and there are two cops standing by the entrance, checking everyone out. They smile down at us. I take Simon's hand and smile back.

As we're going through the old turnstiles, I hear the screech and loud clacking sound of a train coming into the station. I know it's our train and not the one going the other way because of the direction of the hot wind hitting my cheek. "Come on!" I shout to Simon. "Let's go for it!"

As the train rumbles to a stop, I peer into the subway car that's next to us and see that it's mostly empty—a bad sign. If Mommy and Daddy were here, they'd pull us over quick to a different one. I try to do that with Simon, but he's already going through the doors as they slide open, trying to beat me inside. No choice; I have to follow him.

The only one in the car is this old person who I think is unhoused. I peer at them sideways with my eyes slitted like I don't care, even though the person looks really sick. They're wearing a torn and faded long-sleeved shirt with old-fashioned buttons, but half of them are popped off, and you can see their chest, which is skinny, and their stomach, which is kind of droopy and puffed out at the same time. Their skin looks grey-colored and dusty. They have white curly hair on their head, in their beard and coming out their ears. Their face is a mess with eyes that are, like, half open and half closed. I think they're kind of asleep. Worst are their feet, which look all puffed up and oozy and have rags wrapped around them.

Simon has backed up as far away as he can get from the person, and he's staring with his eyes all big and his mouth open, exactly the way you're not supposed to act when you're on the subway. Why doesn't he know anything? I tell him that it's impolite to stare, so he looks down at his own feet instead, frowning.

"Get ready," I say to him. "When the doors open again, we're running for the next car."

We do, but the next car is packed with a gazillion people also trying to avoid the unhoused person. And the air-conditioning is only half working. Plus, my head is under someone's armpit. Gross! This is worse than being in the other stinky subway car. At least there's only a few more stops before we get out.

Fourth Avenue—time to change for the F-train. The doors open and people pour out. The doors stay open and we hear an announcement, something about a police action. We're walking to the stairs when we see four cops stampeding by with their gear towards the car we'd first been in. Maybe they'll take the unhoused person to the hospital. I watch the four cops go into the subway car. Then, one of them takes a phaser stick and smacks it down hard against the wall, like, two inches from the unhoused person's head. The poor person jerks up then slumps down to the ground all quivery-like.

"Let's go," I say to Simon, grabbing his arm. "We're gonna be late!" Simon acts like he's frozen in place, staring at the scene. I practically have to pull him up the stairs, but not before I see a second cop raise his stick up above the unhoused person's body. I don't hang around to see where it lands this time.

We wait on the platform upstairs for the F train for long enough that my heart slows down most of the way. I feel a little sick. I turn to Simon and say, "Don't tell Mommy or Daddy what happened."

"Why not?"

"It'll only make them upset. And then they won't let us take the subway anymore."

"But. . ."

"No listen, they'll make us take the bus instead, which means getting to school twenty-five minutes early. I don't know about you but no way I'm doing that. It'd be hyper-embarrassing, like I can't wait to get to school or something."

Simon nods but he looks unsure. I know how he feels because I feel the same way inside. Maybe we should tell Mommy and Daddy what happened, but I don't want to, and not just because of what I told Simon. I guess I feel kind of ashamed. Maybe they'll think we should've done something. If Mommy were there, she would've helped the unhoused person and Daddy would've stood up to those mean cops. But all I wanted to do was get away as fast as I could and forget the whole thing. Only problem is I can't. I keep on seeing the person's scared face and the way they tried to scoot away on their behind. Worst of all, I keep on seeing the phaser stick go up in the air and then, even though I didn't see this part, I keep seeing it smash down hard on their body.

CHAPTER 6
LAEK

The back courtyard behind our apartment is nothing more than a tiny concrete lot. Still, this bit of outdoor space makes our basement apartment a precious find. I look at Janie's geraniums. Her stunted tomato plants. Simon's antique rocking horse. Siri's sports equipment.

It was Siri and her sports that finally made me realize that I needed to tell Janie what happened. Last night I woke up, chest constricted in fear, to Siri's sobs as she cradled her hand. Siri, who didn't even cry when she'd dislocated her shoulder in the first grade. I carried her in my arms to the hospital, eyes straining for bus headlights. The doctor found two breaks in the bones of her hand. Almost called in Child Protective Services. Siri'd been living with this pain, day in and day out, continuing to play baseball. I asked her why she hadn't said anything.

My daughter explained it to me, voice earnest and sure: "Sometimes you have to take a hit for the team, Daddy." She'd given other reasons as well. That she didn't want to complain. And that she didn't want to get anyone in trouble. Not the boy who kicked her hand with his cleat so she'd drop the ball. Not her coach, who made her play catcher with a regular glove because he kept forgetting she was a lefty. She kept quiet because she's a team player. She kept quiet because she's a girl and couldn't appear weak. She kept quiet because that's what victims do.

What I told Siri was this: Sometimes we keep secrets and tell ourselves things about why we're doing that. It's not always the whole story.

When Janie comes outside, we sit on the small iron bench chained to the wall. Her eyes are so open and trusting, I falter. Tell about the union meeting instead. Janie's outrage warms me.

"Are they fucking serious? Agree to report your students to Alien Defense and Security?"

"I won't do it," I say simply. "But there's more. . . more that happened that night."

I begin with the unhoused person who was thrown out of Union Square Park. And then my bike ride home, what happened with the cop. When I'm done, I find myself standing, looking down at the ground, arms folded across my chest. My heart is beating hard. Janie doesn't say anything, so after a moment, I force myself to look at her.

She's gone pale. Then a flush of color creeps up her neck and into her cheeks. Her small fists clench and unclench once. She's sitting very still, tightly controlled.

I haven't yet brought myself to meet her eyes. When I do, I let out a breath I didn't know I was holding. All the walls that had built up between us during the last few weeks drop away. Janie's thoughts and feelings are plainly written on her face. And there's no disgust or even pity there. All I see is compassion and understanding. That and a fierce love.

She gets up and walks over to me. Gently takes me into her arms. When I respond, she hugs me hard. Tells me she loves me and that she's sorry. I wrap my arms around her, pressing her head against my chest. What was I waiting for all this time, closed up tight and feeling so alone? Then I remember part of my concern.

"Please don't do anything crazy," I say.

"Look who's talking! No, listen, I only want to speak to someone at the Law Guild. My friend Roberto. Don't worry. I'll keep it general."

I nod. I trust her.

Then she surprises me by saying, "There's a concert in the park tonight. Let's go with the kids. I'll pack a picnic supper."

CHAPTER 7
JANIE

There's a knife in my hand and I'm cutting with it. I slice through the slightly elastic red skin into the white flesh beneath. The apple falls in pieces before me. My knife is not very sharp, but that's OK, I don't mind pushing hard with the blade. In fact, I would like to push harder. What else can I cut with my knife?

The sandwiches have already been cut into quarters. I'll make two more sandwiches and cut them up too. Laek will be hungry, but I'm not sure I'll be able to eat at all. Carrots! I seize a thick one in my hand, peel its skin and chop it up violently.

I am not a pacifist. I think I'll finally have to admit this to myself. I'm not one in my heart, anyway. Laek, on the other hand, is a pacifist through and through. I go along with him, actually agree with him, pushing away my baser instincts. I think that he's much stronger than I am. He's certainly more stubborn. Stubbornness takes a certain strength, doesn't it?

The cherries are purple-red and juicy. It's because we have cherries that I thought of the picnic. I take them out of the bag, wash them and begin placing them in a plastic container, counting each one. Thirteen, fourteen, fifteen. . . twenty-four, twenty-five. . . forty-seven, forty-eight, forty-nine. . . I don't know why I'm counting the cherries. It's a strange habit, like the way I count off the seconds while filling a pot of water. Maybe it's a way of passing the time, and the fact that my mind can't bear to be still. Right now I'm filling my head with numbers and cherries to avoid thinking about other things.

The four of us bike over to the park, Laek in the lead with Siri sitting on his back rack, her good hand holding on to his seat. I'm nervous about her riding like this, but Laek and Siri only laugh at me.

When we arrive at the park, there's a long line to get into the concert. The whole area is gated off and they're forcing this huge mass of people to enter in one little trickle so that our bags can be checked by security and a "voluntary" donation solicited for the free concert series. I look up at Laek and he says, "Come on." We get out of the line and walk onto the path instead, away from the bandshell. This will be fine, better in fact. We won't be able to see the band but we should still be able to hear the music.

I let Laek choose the spot. I would have selected a spot closer, but he tells me not to worry because the wind will be blowing in our direction, bringing the music with it. I believe him, though I have no idea how he knows these things. I lay out the picnic and everyone digs in. Michael and some other of Siri's friends find us and we share our food with them. Laek eats two and a half sandwiches and finishes everyone's leftovers, and I just eat cherries.

Laek and I listen to the music together while the kids descend on the cookies. It's getting dark. I put my arm around his waist, sliding my fingers under the hem of his t-shirt while he drapes his arm around my shoulder. His skin is warm, almost hot, reminding me of the way sand on a beach retains the heat even after the sun has gone down. He seems relaxed now, tired maybe. He's been getting to bed later and later these past weeks, working on some mysterious research project.

When there's nothing but cookie crumbs left, Siri and Simon come over to ask about joining a big game of capture-the-light-flag.

"How long would it take?" I ask.

"Long, 'cause it's a tournament. Please, Mommy. It's not a school night or anything."

"Yeah, OK. But be careful, Siri, careful with your hand. You too, Simon."

"There's nothing wrong with my hand," Simon says.

"No, I mean just be careful. Show me where you're going to be."

Siri points to a field some distance off. I can see the disembodied light bracelets and necklaces of the kids playing. "OK, have fun."

I watch them run off with Michael and the others.

It's peaceful here, especially with the kids gone to play, but I feel a little strange. Maybe it's the music. There's an odd quality to how the wind is bringing over the individual notes, like they're not quite blending together but simply overlaying each other. Meanwhile, my brain is doing that weird thing it does sometimes—assigning colors to certain sounds.

Laek's lying on our picnic blanket with his shirt off and bunched behind his head. I'm anxious to join him, to feel his smooth, hard chest under my fingertips. I finish cleaning up and organizing our things and finally feel I can relax.

I rest my head in the crook of Laek's shoulder. His breathing is deep and regular. I think he's asleep. He opens his eyes, though, smiles and starts kissing me, at first very gently, his lips barely brushing mine, and then with a growing hunger. My response is immediate. I feel like a stream where the huge rock blocking my fast-moving watery flow has finally been dislodged.

I place my hands on his face, stroking his slightly rough cheek and his smooth forehead. How I love Laek's body, the contrasts of hard and soft I find there. I touch his silky dark hair, run my hands down the sleek skin of his back, take his velvety earlobe into my mouth; then I squeeze his round biceps, press myself against his muscled legs, his hard cock. His body is like a mirror to his nature. When I touch the softer parts, I think of his gentleness, his sweet, almost naive goodness; his hardness reminds me of his remarkable strength and resilience.

My face buried in his neck, I inhale his familiar scent, my mouth finding that downy spot behind his ear. I kiss him every-where like I can't get enough of him, and I can't. With each caress, the ache that's been building inside me all these weeks lessens, but my need for him grows. I don't want to wait until we're home, and why should I? And I don't care that we're in a public park. It's dark and the kids are far off, involved in their game. If people happen to pass close by and see what we're doing, let them. I think with fury of all those who must have gone past Laek in the middle of Broadway as he was sexually assaulted by a cop. So let them walk by now and get a glimpse of what sex looks like when it's an expression of love instead of someone getting off on having power over another human being. If they can pass by that other scene, unashamed, let them pass by now too and get their fill.

CHAPTER 8
LAEK

I stretch out onto my back. Janie's close by, busy at something. I put my hand behind my head and watch. She's bent over the remains of our picnic. I'd like to get up and kneel behind her. Cup her breasts in my two hands and rub against her. I don't think she'd be annoyed with me. But I also know she won't be relaxed until she finishes whatever it is she's doing. So I'll wait. I'm patient, I don't mind. Maybe I'll close my eyes. Patience is easier that way.

It's hot. I take off my shirt and place it under my head as a pillow. With my eyes closed, I can focus on the music. It's beautiful and eerie. There's a light wind coming in small gusts. I feel it on my skin. It seems to bring snatches of music with it.

I'm almost asleep when Janie lays her head on my shoulder, sighing as she settles in. I turn on my side and kiss her. She tastes like cherries. I lick her lips, taste her mouth more deeply. She responds with caresses, gentle touches. She's kissing me all over and I lay back, totally happy. I feel loved and safe. I wrap her up in my arms and legs. I want to see if I can hide her completely inside my own limbs. Now no one can see her or get at her. This makes me feel safer.

We're soon covered in sweat. She pushes gently against my

chest with her hand. I release her and she rolls over onto her back. She's wriggling out of her underpants. I'm surprised, but totally into it. Next thing I know, she's sitting on my thighs, opening the front of my shorts. I don't need a second invitation.

The rhythm of the music is beating from inside of me. It's pushing everything else out. Everything except Janie's lips and hands, the softness of her curls, her slick sweat, her smell and taste. I feel the music in my blood, in my bones, and it's Janie, the music is Janie. Her fingers are stroking my skin, making me permeable again, letting the pleasure enter me. It builds and builds and when it can't get any bigger, it crashes like a wave over all of my senses, leaving my vision blurry and my ears ringing with clear high notes.

After, we lie quietly together, with me still inside her, one hand tangled in her hair, the other on her breast. Her foot is resting on my calf, her fingers playing silent music on my hip and ribs, her lips blowing softly against my throat. I want nothing so much as to stay here like this forever, the music surrounding us, the sound of the kids playing in the distance, the soft breeze caressing our skin, our bodies at ease on the warm earth of the park.

Janie begins to slowly move away from me. It's so hard for her to remain still. I'm too tired to speak but my thoughts are loud in my head and they're begging her not to move, to stay close. Then, as if in answer to my silent plea, Janie stills, looks deeply into my eyes. I gaze back at her for as long as I can, but my eyes are beginning to close. I finally let go.

The next thing I know, I'm in New Metropolis. I've somehow brought Janie and the kids here with me. We're all holding hands. Walking through the streets I know so well but have always, up until now, wandered alone. All at once, we arrive in a part of the city I've never seen or known. But this is impossible. I created New Metropolis, didn't I? The kids laugh and pull me along after them. I try to follow but the scene is breaking apart. I open my eyes to Prospect Park.

I sit up, stretching. Janie's sitting a few feet away from me, her arms wrapped around her knees. She's wearing shorts now and a thin, old top—her Bread and Roses t-shirt. When did she have time to change? The music is finished for the evening and the people at the bandshell are packing it in. Time to leave. I love this park so much. I'm not ready to go. I wonder if we could stay here tonight. Maybe we could live in the park. With his asthma, it would be healthier for Simon than our basement apartment.

I go through the logistics in my mind. The type of tent we'd need. The other necessary supplies. How we'd bathe. Whether we could risk living in a community, or whether we'd need to be on our own to avoid harassment and eventual eviction by the authorities. Janie likes camping. Living that way isn't something she'd see as practical, though. Of course, I've personally lived in far worse conditions than sleeping rough in a park. As for Siri and Simon, I'm sure they'd both enjoy it. Well, Siri might have some objections. Not knowing what to do about inviting friends over. Things like that. I laugh, knowing my thoughts are bizarre.

"What's so funny?" asks Janie.

I hesitate, thinking of how to put it. Janie doesn't wait for my response. Instead, she tackles me, trying to pin me down by my wrists.

"I swear, Laek, if you ever so much as think about keeping anything from me again, I'm gonna beat the crap out of you."

I was about to tell her what I was thinking, but wrestling is more fun. I let her pin me to the ground. I've forgotten how strong she is for her size. I have to make a real effort before I can reverse our positions. All of a sudden, Simon's there, yelling that he's going to save Mommy. He jumps onto my back, his skinny arms and legs struggling for purchase. I collapse in mock defeat, but then Siri jumps in, saying she'll save me from Simon. We're soon like a pile of puppies. Then Janie starts fretting about Siri's fractured hand. I pull both kids onto my lap. Subdue them with big wet kisses on their heads.

"OK, time to go home," Janie announces. The rest of us sigh and start off towards our bikes. The kids run ahead.

"So what were you laughing about before?" Janie asks me.

"I was wondering if maybe we should live in the park."

We've caught up to the kids now. Simon and Siri are both talking at once about their game. Simon begs his sister to let him tell it since he was the one who captured the light-flag. She says OK but not to leave her part out. So Simon begins the tale. He includes every single thing that happened. No matter how insignificant. This is Simon's way of telling a story. It's as though his almost perfect memory means he has no ability to distinguish between important facts and inconsequential details. I look around for Janie, who's lagging behind.

"Janie, you coming?"

"I think I may have left something." she answers. "But don't wait. I saw Magda, so I may stop and chat. I'll meet you back at the apartment."

The rest of us head home. Both kids laugh and talk the whole way back.

"Tonight was fun, Daddy."

"It was the best night ever," agrees Siri.

I feel the same way. Tonight is a memory I'd like to save for myself. For a day when I need something warm and beautiful. Where will I keep this memory safe? I need a receptacle. Something small but strong. And then it comes to me. An acorn. I visualize it in my mind. Hard and smooth and light brown between my fingers. Its intricate, perfect cap. Inside it, I'll place the taste of cherries, and of Janie's lips; the smell of grass and earth; the feel of my beloved's body around mine; the strains of achingly beautiful music riding to us on the warm, light wind; the sound of the children's laughter. I hold on to this image and wait for Janie to get home.

CHAPTER 9
SIMON

"Once upon a time, the Bicycling Family decided to go on a new adventure.

Mommy's been telling us these stories since I was little. The Bicycling Family is Stardust, who's really Mommy, Ocean, who's Daddy, Dandelion, who's Siri, and Panther, who's me. I know they're not really us but when I was little I thought they were and that someday we'd go on biking adventures just like they do. In tonight's story, Ocean's in the lead, biking up a big hill while Stardust watches everyone's back. There's a beautiful meadow with wildflowers.

"Were there animals?" I ask.

Mommy says yes, like I knew she would. I cuddle under my sheet and listen to the rest of the story. Siri tries to pretend she's too old but I can tell that she likes the story too.

"Dandelion and Panther helped Ocean make a fire. He was cooking dinner. Stardust carved a wooden flute. They had a concert, with the wind playing music on the family's water bottles. All the animals came over to listen. When it was bedtime, the family got into their tent. A long ride was planned for the next day, so it was important for them to get plenty of rest.

"Was there a storm?" I say. I love stories with storms. Plus, when the Bicycling Family goes to bed, that means the story's over, but I want Mommy to tell more.

"Yes. A big one, and loud, and wild. Ocean was a little scared, but tried not to show it."

"How about Stardust?" I ask.

"I don't know." Mommy says. She looks worried about something, but when I'm about to ask her what's wrong, she continues the story. "So everyone cuddled together and Ocean wasn't scared anymore. Eventually, the storm moved off to the south. The day would be clear and beautiful tomorrow, since they were traveling north."

"And what happened the next day?" Siri asked.

"Tomorrow is for tomorrow. But to give you a clue, there'll be games with interesting new friends, fat concord grapes on a vine, and beautiful animals. Good night, my loves."

"Goodnight, Mommy," we both say.

I don't want to fall asleep yet. Siri's still awake too, probably writing in her diary. I can see her glow-light shining on the ceiling. I wonder if we will actually in real life take a trip like in Mommy's story some day. I know it's all made up but I still think it could happen, maybe in a parallel universe or something.

I think about tonight in Prospect Park. It was the music that helped me capture the flag. After I got caught and put in jail, Siri came and rescued me and the music sounded exciting and loud. Then the music changed. It was in a new key and had a different pattern and everything, even though it was still the same song. That's when I decided to do something different too. I split off from Siri. The kid who was chasing us went after her. No one was paying attention to me. I was near the border, almost safe, but instead of crossing over to our side, I turned around and went after the light-flag.

My head's getting sleepy and mixing everything together. We're riding our bikes towards a gigantic light-flag. We don't need to steal it 'cause it's not a flag anymore. It's a big, bright, beautiful light. Then my bike turns into a panther and my whole family's with me. All the kids who were playing are there and all kinds of animals too, and I can't remember anymore who was on which team. We're just together, playing in the light.

CHAPTER 10
SIRI

Before I start typing, I touch my scrambler icon—a baseball next to a dandelion. This way the entry can only be read with my special decoder.

Dear Diary,

Tonight was the best night of my life. It's funny how things work out sometimes. All week long, my hand had been killing me, especially since the game on Saturday. When I found out at the hospital that my hand was broken and I wouldn't be able to play ball for two months, I was angry, sad, and depressed. (See, Ms. Althea, I am writing about my emotions, just like you told us in class.) I wanted to say Fuck! Shit! Goddam it! the way my mother curses when she's mad. I'm allowed to write these words in my journal if I want to. I can edit them later if I decide to share this entry but I don't think I will. Edit or share, I mean.

Anyway, just when I thought that I would be sad

for the whole rest of the school year at least. Daddy said I could go to camp for both months instead of only one. The whole summer for playing baseball and hanging out with Michael! So OK, here it is, I will admit it and write it in words. Michael and I kissed. The first time, I wasn't sure I liked it. He didn't ask me or anything, he just did it. I think that's better because I like when people have their own minds and dont always have to check on what everyone else thinks first. I kissed him back, to get even. The third time was the best. Both of us were ready. He put his hands on my waist and I liked the way his lips felt. They are not too thin and not too thick and not too hard and not too soft.

After we kissed, I ran back to where everyone was. No one seems to have noticed that we were gone for a few minutes. Michael went to talk to his mom and when he came back, we started another game on different teams. We didn't act any different with each other. The only thing was when it was time to go home, it was like his eyes were saying "I will miss you and you are special to me."

I am not going to tell anyone about what happened. I don't want everyone to say "I knew it" or "I told you so" and talk about us behind our backs. I don't want people to be giving me advice, or my mom to want to "have that talk" with me. I just want to be left alone. That is part of the reason I'm so happy about camp. No one there will know us. We can do what we want without feeling like everyone is watching and talking about us. I will have two months of baseball and being with Michael, without my parents and brother and without Michael's huge crazy family either, even though I love them too, almost like my own family.

So that's it, today's entry. It's pretty exciting so I need to have a good ending. I know, I will end with a moral. The moral of this story is: Sometimes something that seems bad can end up being good. Also, you don't always know how a story is going to end.

CHAPTER 11
LAEK

From the hot, still air of the street, the air-conditioning is like a splash of cold water on my face. I stand at the entrance. Absorb the scene. The three-dimensional quality of the holos is surreal. Almost hallucinatory. The experimental music Philip's pumping through the space sharpens this effect. I watch our students dance. Their limbs appear and disappear in multi-colored flash. The holos create portals and different backgrounds. There's almost a sense of time travel. The urge to dance grabs me by the throat. I want to join my students. To disappear. To reappear. To let the joy of the music, of letting go, move me through time and space.

I resist. I'm here to chaperone. I'm a teacher. But what have I taught? Are these kids ready for what awaits them? For what they'll find outside the protective walls of our school? My eyes scan the crowd. Even fewer have made it to graduation day than we'd thought. The dropouts are doing mandatory military— fodder for the war du jour. Those who aren't in jail. As for the students who stay in school, can we continue to offer a safe haven?

During the evening, I feel out the other teachers about resisting the new immigrant reporting requirements. Some of them seem to be on the same screen with me and Erin. Others just want to go along with the leadership. It's as though having taken the risk of teaching at an alternative school, they've used up all their independence. No will left to oppose authority any further.

When it's time to leave, the kids file out in twos and threes, most to continue celebrating through the night. I stand outside with the other teachers in a receiving line to wish our new graduates well. I nod and smile, shake hands if they're offered. What I want to do is take them in my arms. All of them. Hold them and keep them safe.

The students are finally gone. The teachers who still remain drift inside, chatting. I don't join them. I try to push away the darkness taking hold of me. I see Philip standing outside with his back against the building and walk towards him. I stand beside him and lean against his shoulder. Philip is six foot three, a couple of inches taller than I am, and huskier. It's comfortable standing like this with my shoulder just below his. He glances over, takes one look at my face and wraps his arm around me protectively. A little of the darkness recedes.

"What's the matter, Laek?" he asks me, squeezing my shoulder hard.

"I just wish there was something more we could give our students."

"Something more than an education?"

"Yeah. Some kind of magical protection, maybe."

Philip laughs and squeezes my shoulder again. Erin comes over to join us. I lift up my other arm, inviting her into our huddle. I feel better now, a friend on either side of me.

"What's going on?" asks Erin.

"Just Laek, wishing for magical powers."

"Forget magical powers, I can't even give them a hug for good luck. What sort of society do we live in where hugging a kid on graduation night is seen as inappropriate, even dangerous?"

"It's prom night, not graduation night," says Erin, who's a stickler for this type of thing. "And you know very well why these rules exist. Yes, they're a bit exaggerated, but you've had enough problems with student crushes. You can't afford to be slack about this."

"I don't think I'm slack, but. . . What do you guys do? I mean to avoid crushes?"

"Well," answers Philip, acting as though he's actually thought the question through, "I wear extremely ugly clothes. You could borrow some if you like."

I laugh. The real reason Philip doesn't have this problem is that he just doesn't notice when someone has a crush on him. His messy break-up with Dana has left him with such low self-esteem he can't even imagine anyone, let alone a student, looking at him in that way. He's actually a good-looking guy. Being a bit of a quirky intellectual only adds to his charm.

"What about you, Erin?" Philip asks. "You must have them lining up at your door."

"It's simple. I give them no encouragement." I begin to say that I don't either but she cuts me off. "I mean none *whatsoever*, Laek."

"What do you mean?" I ask, a little defensively. "I'm not doing anything to—"

"It's your smile. The way you smile at your students when you're pleased with them."

"So now I'm not allowed to smile either? What am I supposed to do, glare at them?"

"It's OK to smile but. . . How do I put this? It's *how* you smile at them. You have a devastating smile when you're happy or pleased. It's hard to resist."

Erin smiles too, but it's true her smile can be distant. But I don't have a chance to respond because just then I see some-thing, someone, and it's like a ghost has walked over my grave. I go very still. He's some distance away but I can feel him meet my gaze. I watch him nod. He turns towards the section of the docks that was never redeveloped. He stops once more to beckon me. I turn my head before anyone notices what I was looking at.

"Listen, I need some air."

"I thought we were going to get a beer," Philip says.

"Chris is meeting us," Erin adds. "I know he'd like to see you."

"I can meet you later," I say quickly, trying not to look towards the docks.

Erin seems a little disappointed, but Philip takes her by the arm, pulls her along. "You know where we'll be—at The Look and Hook, OK?"

I wait until they're out of sight and begin walking towards the docks. I go north. Leave the lively commercial section of the Red Hook waterfront district. After a while, I reach the dead-end alleyway where I saw him disappear. The street leads to a small lot hidden behind some long-condemned industrial buildings. The lot shelters a group of people without housing. A couple of wild dogs prowl restlessly. I smell some cook fires, no longer lit. Piles of junk sit on patches of yellowing crabgrass.

Slowing down my pace, I suddenly feel conscious of my exposed skin. The back of my neck tingles. Am I being watched? I look around discreetly. Everybody seems very much in their own world. Even the man sitting on the dock waiting for me.

I look up suddenly to see the Statue of Liberty out in the bay, unnaturally large and bright. The majestic woman of the harbor is gazing directly at me. There's a combination of pity and disappointment in her eyes. Broken phrases from Emma Lazarus's poem jump into my head. *The conquering limbs astride from land to land. The teeming shores. The tempest-tossed homeless.* Whose limbs? Whose shores? Whose homeless?

I walk to the end of the dock. He's sitting close to the water, his back to me. I sit down beside him. Without looking away from the water, he gives me his sign. I nod my head but don't give him mine. I haven't used that sign in fifteen years and won't show him what I use now.

When I knew him, he was a vigorous, wiry man in his mid-forties. The oldest among us, but strong and tireless, full of life and humor. The man beside me looks older than he could possibly be. I've never seen anyone sit so still. His eyes are the same, though, bright and lively. I steal another sideways glance. He looks like any unhoused person. Is this a disguise? He certainly smells like he doesn't have a place to shower. So many questions go through my head. I'm tempted to wait him out, see what he has to say, but this seems pointless. Plus, I need to hear his voice. So I blurt out the first thing that comes to mind.

"How did you find me?"

"It wasn't hard."

I wait, but he says nothing more. "Why are you here?"

"To tell you that. That it wasn't hard. To find you, I mean." Silence again.

I'm not in the mood to play this game, so I say to him, with more anger in my voice than I intend, "I thought you were dead."

"Yeah, well, sorry to disappoint." My face snaps towards him as though I've been slapped. He looks away. Was that remorse I saw on his face for a moment? "Look, I didn't think it would be wise to contact you too soon after what happened, even though I knew you'd be concerned, would no doubt assume the worst. Then I lost track of you—a good thing too." He looks up now. "But you've been careless recently. That can be dangerous."

"I'm fine," I say curtly, suddenly very angry at his presumption.

"Yeah, you look good, Laek. You've made a nice life for yourself—teacher, father. Cute kids, by the way. And Janie's good people."

"Don't talk about my family." I say this coldly, but what I feel is fear. Just as he intends. "They have nothing to do with. . . with before. I have a new life. Family, friends. Real friends."

He looks at me with a smile that's half mocking, half indulgent.

"Yeah, your friends at school seem nice. I saw you over there with them earlier. They don't know much about your past though, eh?"

I don't answer. I feel cold inside, but at least my brain is sharper. The way it was before I got so complacent. Thoughts of a beer with friends are far, far away. I look him full in the face.

"Been spending some time in Canada?"

"Yes," he admits without hesitation. "You were always good with accents, speech patterns. I was in New Brunswick, other places. A person can still lose himself over there."

He stops, but I don't say anything. I'd rather keep him talking, see what he's up to.

"Things have gotten interesting up north," he continues. "Like Montreal, declaring themselves an international sanctuary city. They've gone a lot further than other North American cities that've tried this. Not surprising maybe, with the province's history. The independence movement and so on. Well, I'm sure you know all about it, being a history teacher."

He pauses, gauges my reaction carefully. I bring my knees up to my chest and fold my arms around them, a look of polite disinterest on my face. In fact, the topic has fascinated me since reading about it in *El Nuevo Ciudadano del Mundo*'s international edition.

He continues. "They're doing their best to be not only an political refuge but a green, solidarity city. But with the United America to the south, and the current Canadian government the U.A.'s biggest lackey. . . I'm sure it's a lost cause. But still, maybe your type of thing. You'd have to learn French but learning a new language has never been difficult for you."

"Are you done?" I ask.

"I thought we could chat about a few other interesting places in the world. Evaluate the chances of getting a European passport. Discuss certain promising Latin American and African states. And which regions to avoid at all costs. Although again, with your background, you could probably teach me a few things."

"You may find it's harder to manipulate me now than when I was younger."

"I should hope so!" he says cheerfully. Then he changes his tone again. "Look, Laek, I'm not trying to manipulate you. I'm trying to get you to see something. It's not the same thing."

"Yes it is. It's exactly the same thing."

"What would you have me do, then?"

"I don't know, Al. Maybe just say what you came here to say in simple, clear words. Then you can pop back out of my life again."

"Fine. How's this? I believe your ID will soon be compromised and that the government's going to find you. I think you shouldn't stick around to see if I'm right, that you should go underground or, if you can, to another country. With your family, if possible. Clear enough?"

"So I should take my family. . . or leave them. Whatever, right? Just disappear. Only thing is, I've been fine all these years. Sure, I've had to be careful, but I'm more or less living in the open, leading a pretty normal life. I'm a teacher, for fuck's sake. I practically work for the government. But you come out of some hole after sixteen years and tell me it's no good. That I have to go into hiding." I unclench my fists, surprised at how furious I am. "My ID isn't even fake. Not strictly speaking. It uses my real iris scan and DNA print. That's what I was told."

"Yes, thanks to your age and that cult you grew up in, you weren't in the system yet, so we could do that. That doesn't mean they can't track you now, though. There's the little matter of the biometric data they took from you while you were in custody. You remember that, yes?"

Yes, Al, I remember when they grabbed me, my face still bloody and swollen from the beatings, and forced my eye sockets against their scanners, three of them holding me down while I twisted and kicked. And the dozens of times they came for tissue samples, frustrated at their inability to find a match in their database. They took a good deal more flesh and fluids from me than they could possibly ever use. Yes, I think we can safely say I remember all this. The question is why Al is forcing me to recall these details. Because he never does anything without calculation. Is it so I'll be angry? Afraid? Whatever it is he wants me to feel, I'll try hard not to feel it. Not out of stubbornness, but because otherwise, I won't trust the conclusions I reach.

"Yeah, I know they got my data and could possibly match it to my ID. Even with the hack that was done. But that's why I hardly ever use my Uni. I never received government benefits. I don't have a credit card or a high-rail pass. I don't travel. Don't go to the doctor. Don't even go shopping, except for food, using cash. I hardly use my personal screen—just for emergencies. I don't even have a fucking bank account. My salary is deposited into Janie's. People probably assume I'm too incompetent to manage my own finances."

"But Laek," Al says gently, "that creates its own red flags. Such light use of a Uni isn't normal. And even with minimal usage of your ID, there's still a build-up of discrepancies. Over time, it's almost inevitable that these discrepancies will be found, traced. Especially now that better auditing programs exist."

"I did what I was told. I thought I was being safe."

"Whoever let you believe that there was such a thing as safe? Look, forget the technical details. All you need to understand is one simple principle. Any system, no matter how good, can be hacked. This is how you've been able to live in the open all this time, yes? But this principle applies to the hacker's system as well. And not only can it be hacked, it can also be bought and sold. Or simply given away."

Here we are finally, back to the subject of betrayal. The elephant in the room. But as much as I don't want to go there, not again, I can't seem to keep myself from asking.

"But why would anybody do that, and now, after all these

years?" I'm ashamed at how young and anguished my own voice sounds.

He doesn't answer. I sense that maybe he's through trying to convince me of anything. So I go quiet too. I let myself think in careful, little chunks of memory about our tight group. And all we'd hoped to accomplish in the short time we had before we were arrested so many years ago. I think about "Papa Al," and his role in all that. I bow my head, pressing my face into my knees. The memories overwhelm me.

After a moment, I feel him lightly place his hand on my head. He begins to stroke my hair. I tolerate it, even though it feels like he's put his hand inside my chest and is squeezing my heart. I close my eyes to this pain, to the memory he's awakened.

And suddenly, he has both of his hands around my throat, his thumbs pressing down firmly against my windpipe.

I tolerate this too. It feels about the same as it did when he was stroking my hair. After a few moments, he releases me, sounding disgusted. "You trust too much. You always have."

I don't answer but open my eyes to gaze out at the bay, at the statue. After a long while, I look back to where he was sitting, knowing he's gone. Satisfied, I look out at the water again. I try to order my mind. I can still feel his ghost fingers in my hair. Just like I felt them that afternoon, in the police van after the raid.

I'd been alone in the house where we'd all been living off the grid. The others had been due back hours ago. I was on edge. Should I stay put or should I flee? When the terror squad finally burst in, wearing full riot gear, I was almost relieved that I didn't have to make this decision anymore.

They started off by trying to convince me that there was no harm in my telling them everything. That they already had the names and identities of the others and were only seeking confirmation. That everything could go relatively easily for me, given my youth, if I cooperated. Then they claimed my friends had already betrayed me. Why was I trying to protect them? I'd been trained to expect these kinds of mind games. I knew they were lying. Even so, I was self-aware enough to realize that I wasn't good at this sort of thing. So I decided to cut it all short by spitting in their faces. Of course they beat the crap out of me after that, but at least I wasn't worn down and confused by hours of their psychological warfare.

I didn't tell them anything. Not even my name and age. I remember feeling proud of this, when suddenly Al burst into the room. My first, childish, reaction was one of relief: Al would know what to do. That lasted a few seconds until I realized not only did this mean that he was caught too, but that things were about to get worse.

Al shouted at them to leave me alone. That I was only a kid and didn't know anything. I was surprised at this behavior. Didn't he realize they'd use this against us? For that matter, why didn't he know not to come in to begin with? He must have seen the unfamiliar vehicle or other signs that all was not well.

Sure enough, one of them grabbed me around the neck and held me while another federal agent shoved a gun between my legs. He threatened to blow my balls off if Al didn't give them a complete list and last known whereabouts of everyone staying in the house. I called out to him not to tell them anything. That I wasn't scared. This was a lie, of course. The gun was huge and when the bastard shoved the inch-and-a-half-wide muzzle tighter against me as though he were about to shoot, I pissed myself in fear. I was fifteen at the time, and up until that moment, I'd thought I was pretty tough.

Al gave them all the names. All but two, but at the time, I didn't notice the missing ones. The agents laughed at us. Said they'd captured the rest of our group already. That we'd betrayed our friends for nothing, repeating again that they'd betrayed us too, and that we were all cowards. When they loosened their hold on me for a minute, I threw myself at them, hoping they'd kill me. Anything but live with what just happened, with my weakness, and what Al did as a result. They didn't kill me though. Only beat me until I was unconscious. That didn't take too long.

I started coming to when they threw us into the back of their van. I saw it was true that the others were already taken. They were handcuffed to the floor of the van. I didn't realize right away that two of us were missing. The same two Al had neglected to mention. So I didn't come to any of the obvious conclusions. In any case, I was crying so hard I could barely see. Al had pulled my head onto his lap and was attempting to clean my face off with his shirt so I could breathe more easily. Covered with blood, mucus and tears, it was a pretty impossible job. He gave up at some point. Simply tried to hold me as still as possible with one hand, while the van swerved towards our destination. With his other hand, he was stroking my hair, trying to comfort me. He kept repeating in a soft voice that it was OK, that no one had betrayed anyone. That he'd been tipped off and knew who'd already been taken, had only given those names. That there was no point in letting me continue to be beaten.

I wouldn't accept what he was saying. How could he have told them anything? I knew it was all my fault. There were my friends, handcuffed and helpless. Even me, barely conscious and with my right arm broken in the beating, even I was tightly bound in handcuffs. How then was it possible that Al's fingers could be in my hair, his other hand holding tight to my shoulder? Why was he the only one not in handcuffs?

I sit for a while now thinking about these things. Events I'd thought I'd worked through long ago. And then I think about what Al told me today. When your head, your heart, and your fears are telling you different things, which one do you believe?

There's no movement on the water or in the air. The unhoused community is mostly asleep. Even the wild dogs are quiet. It's a very still night. I think I'll stay here for a while, quiet, immobile, like everything around me. There's a peace in this stillness. But then I feel a small vibration on my left leg. It's my mini-screen. I'm getting a message. Strange, because I thought

I'd turned the communication function off. I pull it out of my pocket and look at it. A message from Erin, asking where I am. But from Chris's phone. Chris, the cop, my good friend's husband. Whom I like and trust. Could it be they have an override device? No, this is simply paranoia.

I stare at the screen. It's blinking at me, demanding a response. I have no response. How I hate these technologies, tracking and trapping us, making us sick. I stand up and toss the screen as far as I can into the river. I watch with satisfaction as it soars through the air, high up. It makes no sound as it hits the water, sinks. A stupid thing to do, maybe, but it's worth the momentary feeling of release it gives me. I decide I'll get some air like I'd said I would some hours ago. In a different lifetime.

CHAPTER 12
JANIE

Before 2:30 a.m., my body knew it was too early to start worrying. After that, though, it was like an internal alarm had gone off, screaming and wailing. Now I'm wide awake, heart pounding, as I look at the empty space beside me in our bed.

There's a good likelihood that Laek went out for a beer with Philip and Erin. It's good for him to relax with friends after the emotional roller coaster he experiences at the end of a school year. I try to go back to sleep but it's no good. I decide to call him even though he'll accuse me of babying him. There's no answer. He's probably turned the thing off like he often does.

I read for a while, but can't get into it. I think about cooking something, but I don't want to wake the kids. Instead, I plug myself into some music. I put on something soothing, but that makes me want to scream with impatience. I probably shouldn't be plugged in like this anyway. How will I hear Laek coming down the stairs?

I decide to shower. I've been sweating a lot and my sweat smells like fear. Maybe if I shower the smell away, I can feel more normal. Right now, I'm sick to my stomach and my head feels like it's stuffed with a hive of tiny buzzing insects. This could simply be lack of sleep.

I get dressed, make our bed and look at my screen again. Nothing. I check Siri's baggage and go through the camp packing list once more to make sure we haven't forgotten anything. I've already done this about ten times.

It's 7:30, time to wake Siri up. I've gone from fear to fury. When Laek does get home, I've decided I'm going to kill him. That will solve my problem once and for all. He should be here, helping me get Siri ready for camp. She's going to be gone for eight fucking weeks, the least he could do is be here to see her off. Yes, I'll kill him and then I won't have to be sick with worry wondering if he's lying in the street somewhere dead.

I'm able to keep this feeling of anger going until Siri asks me where Daddy is, at which point I feel like the ground has dropped beneath me and that all is lost.

"He's a bit late coming in, sweetheart," I say. "I'm sure he'll be here soon."

"Late coming in from where?"

I'm thinking about how to answer this when my mini-screen alerts me to a text message. I see that it's Erin. She's asking me if Laek got home OK. I walk into the bedroom, telling Siri to shower and get dressed since Michael and his parents will be here soon. I tell my screen to dial Erin and I'm soon facing her holo.

"Hi, Erin. Actually, Laek's not home yet and I'm a little worried." Nothing like gross understatement.

"Did he call?"

"No, but you know how he is about using his screen. Did you all go out for a beer?"

"We had planned to. I mean, Philip and I went, and Chris. Laek was supposed to meet us, but he never came." She pauses. "But I don't think you should worry much."

"Why not?" It comes out sounding like a challenge, but I'm not looking for an argument, just a reason not to worry.

"I think Laek may have been upset about something I said."

"What did you say?"

"You know how sensitive he can be, especially at the end of a school year. We were talking about student crushes and. . . anyway, he said he needed some time to himself and would meet us, but since he never showed up, I'm wondering if he's still upset."

"Maybe. At least it's some explanation. Though I don't get why he's still not home."

"Well. . . I'm sure everything's fine. Do me a favor and let me know when he shows up?"

"Sure. And thanks for checking in."

"Oh, Janie, one more thing before you go. . . Chris wanted to talk to Laek about the demonstration today in downtown Manhattan. Were you planning on going?"

"Laek was, yeah, but since Siri's leaving for camp today, I thought I'd stay home."

"Well, maybe Laek shouldn't go either. Chris wanted to pass on a message to sit this one out. He has some information. It could be. . . a bad situation."

"Bad how? Is Chris going to be on duty at the demo?"

"Bad, like dangerous. I don't have the details. But no, Chris won't be there. He's actually calling in sick. That alone should tell you something."

"I understand. Thanks. And thank Chris for us."

"I will. And don't forget to ping or message me. And Philip too."

I walk into the kitchen to make breakfast. I have a spatula in my hand when I finally think I hear something. Laek walks in the front door, closing it behind him quietly. I just look at him, my spatula suspended in the air. He seems a bit drawn, but otherwise in one piece.

"Are you OK?" I ask.

"Yeah."

That out of the way, I ask him where the hell he was all night.

"I'll explain, don't be angry. Here, let me do that, I'm supposed to cook today." He walks over and tries to take the spatula from me.

"Get your hands off my fucking spatula." I raise it like a weapon. Laek freezes. I stare at my upheld kitchen utensil and carefully bring it down to the frying pan, blowing air out through my closed lips before speaking. "Siri's supposed to be leaving for camp in less than half an hour. She'll be gone for eight weeks. Did you even remember?"

"I'm here, aren't I?"

"Couldn't you have at least messaged me?"

"I lost my screen."

"Lost it how?"

"I threw it into the river." He says this as though it's the most natural thing in the world.

"Threw it into the river," I repeat. "Could you fucking explain that, maybe?"

"Can I explain later? Please, Janie, I need a shower."

I open my mouth to argue but think better of it. I'd rather talk about this after Siri's left for camp. "Fine. If you want to shower before we eat, you'd better hurry up. Siri just finished up in there."

I put breakfast on the table as Laek comes out of the bathroom, hair wet and wearing clean shorts and a white t-shirt. He seems refreshed, smiling and joking, and looks way too good to have been up all night doing who knows what. Simon comes out in his pajamas, sleepy-eyed and somber, probably thinking about his sister being away at camp all summer. Soon Rebecca and David arrive and we chat for a few minutes while Michael helps Siri with her luggage.

"Thanks so much for taking Siri to camp for us," I say.

"Don't be ridiculous," Rebecca replies. "We're taking Michael anyway, and besides, Siri's practically a member of the family. I'll call you later."

"Great, thanks." I kiss Siri good-bye and warn her to be

careful with her hand. Laek hugs and kisses her too, telling her to have fun. Finally, Simon gives her a sad, awkward hug. Siri musses his hair and tells him that she'll bring him home a souvenir.

After they've left, Laek takes Simon to his friend Henry's house. When he returns a short time later, he asks me to sit with him and I do, though I think that our conversation would go better if I could keep my hands busy. I'm not as angry as I was, but I'm still in a state where I fear I might jump down his throat at the slightest provocation. I'm seriously having trouble imagining how it's something other than thoughtlessness that could have resulted in him staying out all night and never even trying to send me a message.

But that reminds me of something. "Before we begin this conversation, you need to check in with Erin. And Philip too. I wasn't the only one who was worried."

"Could you do that for me?"

"Oh, right," I remember. "Your screen is at the bottom of the East River."

"Technically, it's not the East River at that point, it's—"

"Do you really think I give a crap which river it's at the bottom of? I'm not planning on swimming over and fishing it out now, am I? You can use the house screen to call."

"Please, Janie, just do it for me, OK?"

"Fine," I say, exasperated. I send off a quick text to the two of them. "I'm listening—get on with it already." I settle down on the rocking chair across from him.

"I was waiting for you to send it."

"Believe it or not, I can listen to you while sending a simple message."

"I want you to be fully focused. Not sending messages or whatever."

"You were the one who asked me to send the message."

"This is getting us nowhere. Turn off the screen, OK?"

"Erin said that you argued?"

"Argued? No, not really. It happened after. I saw someone. A man."

"Yes?" I respond. He waits, glances at the screen. I lean forward and turn it off.

"A man from before. From before I knew you."

"What do you mean? An ex-lover or something?" I'm trying to be casual. I know Laek has had a lot of lovers, men as well as women, but he's never mentioned anyone in particular and I've honestly never felt jealous about his other relationships.

"No, nothing like that. I mean someone from my. . . group."

He's fingering his wristband. A new one, but it looks old. Where could he have gotten it in the middle of the night? "Oh." I sharpen my focus. "What happened, what did he say?"

"Well, the long and short of it is that my ID could be compromised."

"How does he know this?"

"He didn't give me all the details, but the fact that *he* was able to find me."

"Can they be interested in you after so long? You were just a kid when all that happened."

"There's the fact of my arrest."

"Fair enough," I make myself say. I don't know why I'm questioning him on this. I've heard of activists involved in the same kinds of things Laek was involved in, who've since been found and arrested. And some who've simply disappeared. I just can't help playing devil's advocate. Maybe because I have a sharp uneasiness about where all this may be heading.

"But Laek, you told me that your ID was pretty solid. It was good enough for the Department of Education and they aren't slack about their background checks."

"I said the same thing. But what he told me makes sense. That there'd be better tracking programs now, and. . . it's like I'm pushing my luck. I guess I realized this danger myself. It's why I use my Uni as little as possible. It's why. . . it's why I let that cop. . ." Laek pauses and looks down, wrapping his arms around himself like he does sometimes when he's feeling vulnerable. That gesture, more than anything he said, makes me want to go over and hold him. But I don't.

"I know. I'm not doubting any of that. It's just. . . I mean, what are you thinking of doing?" My heart is pounding and I have that weird déja vu feeling. It's like I'm following a script with a bad ending that someone else has written. It makes me furious.

"Maybe we could move away. Start over," Laek says.

I'm still experiencing the déja vu, yet this is not what I thought he was going to say.

"Move where? Wouldn't it still be simply a matter of time until they found you?"

"I'm not talking about moving to another city or state. I mean leaving the United America."

"Leave the country? Where would we go?"

"Well, I had this idea. . . Do you remember the article in *El Nuevo Ciudadano del Mundo—The New World Citizen*? About how Montreal had declared itself an international sanctuary city?"

"Yeah. You were intrigued by the title: 'The New Metropolis, in English, right?' But you're not thinking of us moving up there, are you?"

"Why not?"

"Well, for one thing, would we be safe? From what I've heard, in the mainstream media anyway, it's some large-scale socio-political experiment. A few months from now, the Royal Canadian Mounted Police could gallop in, arrest everyone and shut the whole thing down."

"The movement has municipal authority on its side as well as provincial support."

"Are you fucking serious about this idea? No way. It's crazy."

"What's so crazy about it? Why are you reacting without thinking about it?"

"I'm not the one who isn't thinking here! What, we just slip across the border, hoping they'll let us stay? And. . . what about the fact that we don't speak French? I couldn't practice law in that jurisdiction, and you couldn't teach. How would we earn a living?"

"These are all small, temporary problems. We could learn French and we could see what it takes to get licensed in our fields. It's not that big a deal."

"Not that big a deal? I've never managed to really pick up Spanish despite the fact that I've been working with Spanish speakers my whole adult life. Even if I could learn French and pass the bar, I'd have to argue my cases in a second language. Can you imagine that, trying to advocate for the underdog in a second language?"

"You could do it."

"Laek, my way with words—English words, that is—it's my only weapon. It would be like trading in a sharp, shiny sword for a rusty kitchen knife."

"I wouldn't want to face you with a kitchen knife either." Laek gives me one of his smiles.

"Don't smile at me," I snap at him. "I can't tolerate that right now. How can you drop this on me? Casually suggest we leave our whole life behind, friends, family. What about the kids?"

"The kids'll be fine. They'll adjust."

"Like you did?" I'm being mean when I say that, but fuck it. I didn't have kids so that they'd suffer but "grow stronger for it." Laek may have survived his own screwed-up childhood and emerged as a good and somewhat sane person, but it wasn't without scars.

"What I want is for the kids to grow up with their father. Is this too much to ask?"

I collect myself. He's being emotional but I need to get him to look at this rationally. "Of course not, but this guy from your past, is he the one who put this idea in your head? About leaving the country, about going to Montreal?"

"Kind of, but I'd been interested in Montreal even before we spoke."

"Laek, do you trust this man? Does he have your best interests at heart?"

"No. Yes. Janie, stop cross-examining me. I hate when you do that."

"You still haven't told me why you threw your screen away."

"Erin called. Well, Chris actually. But I thought I'd turned that function off. I got paranoid. Especially just after talking about the government tracking me down."

"Oh, remind me later to tell you something. But Laek, listen, did it occur to you that maybe you'd made a mistake? That you left the communication function on?"

"It's possible, but I don't think so. Still, I agree, what I did was a bit impulsive."

"Maybe this whole plan is a bit impulsive. Kind of like pitching expensive tech into the river. What about all we've tried to achieve here, for our kids, for. . . for the community?"

"Aren't you sick of putting band-aids on huge gaping wounds? Because that's what you're doing. What we're all doing here, those of us who are doing anything."

"That's not fair. My work is important. I'm keeping people in their homes, off the street."

"For how long? Until the next case? Maybe they won't get to you in time for the next one. Or be too sick from all the other impossible problems in their lives that you can't solve."

"If you think putting down my job and making me feel like shit is going to make me want to go away with you, you should probably rethink your strategy."

"Janie, I have no strategy."

"Maybe that's the problem."

"Stop," he says, raising his voice. "You're purposely twisting my words around. Can you listen and try to understand what I'm saying for a minute?"

I unfold my legs and begin rocking in my chair, gesturing for him to continue.

"Just once, wouldn't you like the chance to be a part of something new?" Laek asks, leaning forward towards me. "Some-thing that could actually be allowed to succeed? Here we are, putting our fingers into little holes in the dyke when the whole fucking thing's coming apart. We think we can't take our fingers out, but all we're doing is allowing the pressure to build, not accomplishing what needs to be accomplished, which is rebuilding the dyke. But they won't let us near there. And, they've taken all our tools away. So we're scraping with our fingernails, banging our heads against the wall. . ."

"OK, Laek. Enough mixed metaphors. I understand what you're trying to say. We all feel this way sometimes, but what choice is there? We can't give up. We have to keep fighting the good fight, even if we feel we can't succeed in our lifetime. There's no such thing as utopia. If you're hoping for that, forget about it."

"I'm not talking about utopia. Just something a little less awful, maybe."

"I love New York. The whole rest of the country can go to hell for all I care, but this is my city, in all its awfulness. Maybe you can't understand that, growing up like you did."

"Yeah, you're right," Laek says bitterly. "I guess it's different for me since I never had a place I could think of as home. Until I came here, that is. Where I've lived for fifteen years with you and the kids and all our friends."

"It's not the same thing; I've lived here my whole life. How can you expect me to just leave, swallow everything you're telling me without question? You've been thinking about this all night, while I've been worrying about you all night."

"If you were worried about me, you wouldn't give me such a hard time. You'd understand why we have to do this."

"How dare you accuse me of not worrying about you! After the night you just put me through? At least give me a little fucking time to absorb it all!"

"Fine. Take all the time you need. I gotta get out of here, anyway."

"Where are you going?"

"To the demo, remember?" Laek starts for the door.

"No, wait, Laek. That's what I needed to tell you. Chris says not to go."

"Chris?" he asks, in a strange tone of voice.

"Yeah, he said we should stay home, that something bad is going to happen."

"Did he say what?"

"No, he wouldn't give details."

"Well fuck that shit," Laek says angrily, walking towards the door again.

"But wait, what about what Chris said?"

"If something's happening, he should be warning everyone, not just me. Are you suggesting I sit at home and do nothing? While our friends are putting themselves on the line?"

"Not exactly, but Laek, listen, if you're in more danger now, wouldn't it be wise to lay low for a while? At least until we sort out what's going on, what we need to do?"

"While others take risks for the things I believe in? You want to stay here? Fine, but don't ask me to sit things out. I live my life the way I think is right. I can't tolerate anything else."

"All I'm asking is for you to skip one demo, not give up your life as an activist. You just got home, you've been up all night. You'd do better to take a nap."

"Are you seriously suggesting I should take a nap after telling me what Chris said? Without even giving my affinity group a heads-up? What if something happens to them? How could I live with myself?"

I sigh. What can I say? He looks at me and waits, but I'm out of arguments. So he walks out, closing the door behind him.

What if I had begged him, said please don't go—stay home just this once, for me? Would he have stayed? But I know that particular set to his jaw. And earlier in the conversation? I don't know, but I'm realizing how much simpler things would have been if my first suspicion had been true, if the man who sought

Laek out last night had been an ex-lover rather than an old comrade.

It takes me about two seconds to decide that the one thing I absolutely cannot face right now is another long wait at home worrying about Laek. So I decide to follow him to the demonstration. Rebecca and David will call tonight, and if anything comes up before, there's nothing I can do from my apartment that I couldn't do outside.

Before heading out, I consider calling Philip. Sometimes he can talk sense into Laek when even I can't. But it's too late for that anyway—Laek's already on his way to the demo, with his screen at the bottom of the river. So instead I call my friend Roberto from the Law Guild and explain what's up. He agrees to arrange for more legal observers and then go with me to the demonstration. I grab my wrap-around tinted glasses, a mask, a protective cap, and a bottle of water, and put them in my pack. I leave the apartment only fifteen minutes after Laek.

CHAPTER 13
LAEK

On my ride to Manhattan, I keep forcing myself to slow down. I haven't slept in thirty hours, but there's this manic energy inside me. I feel nervous. Edgy. Maybe I should pull over. But I feel like if I stop, I'll do something crazy. Like pick up my bike and pitch it through a window. Yeah, like that window I'm passing now, the army recruitment center.

I think I'm just angry. Not at Janie, though. Frustrated with her, yes. But she's just another victim, reacting the same way I did. Upset at the messenger bearing bad news. And she's scared. I am too. I don't know what to do, what will happen. Maybe there's no way out.

I'm not even upset with Chris. I speed up again, standing on my pedals and pushing hard up the Brooklyn Bridge bike path. I imagine Chris as a little boy. Blond, tow-headed, toy-tech attached to his belt, running after bad guys, pretending to have superpowers. But he ended up with a gun instead. And a phaser stick. I'm still thinking about Chris when I arrive downtown. I'm looking at all the cops. I've never seen so many. Are they like Chris? Do any of them actually dream of saving people, of bringing justice? If I could only see their faces, maybe I'd know. But they're wearing masks. And riot gear. Yet there's no riot.

Some are on horses, some on motorcycles or zip-cars. Some are on foot wearing white shirts or business suits. Those are the ones to be most scared of, but I'll admit it, I'm scared of all of them, of this whole scene.

I lock up my bike but I don't know where and how to enter the demonstration. There are barriers and blockades everywhere. It's like trying to break into jail. How would you do it and why would you want to?

I walk all the way around Bowling Green, passing the Customs House. Across from this, the entrance to the Bowling Green subway station is being guarded by two cops. They aren't letting anyone in or out. I hear the younger cop telling an angry commuter, "I can't answer that question. I'm from Brooklyn."

I pass an old-fashioned pretzel cart and make my way north around the huge bronze sculpture of the charging bull. It's closely guarded by a whole phalanx of cops. Including one planted right behind the bull's ass. If Janie were here, she'd laugh and say that this is a metaphor for what our country has come to. At the bull's head, a number of police buses covered in tech are parked, waiting to receive demonstrators who are arrested. This is less funny.

Finally I hop over the fence to enter Bowling Green Park. Walk towards a sign I saw for Brooklynites for Peace. I spot Leslie and Bernard from the neighborhood.

"Laek!" Bernard shouts. "Is Janie here?"

"No, not today. Is this where the main contingent is? I'm looking for my group."

"I think there are more demonstrators at Zuccotti Park," he answers.

"You know they cancelled the permit for Battery Park at the last minute?" Leslie asks.

"Yeah. Listen, I heard some stuff," I tell them. "We're gonna need to be especially careful today. Maybe you can spread the word to be alert for trouble. Don't let anyone provoke you."

"Hah, as if! We've been coming out to these demos and occupations from before you were born," Leslie says. "You be careful too, darling. We'll spread the word, don't worry."

I hop back over the fence and walk north. Broadway is practically impassable. I go west one block onto Greenwich Street, then cut back east. At Zuccotti Park, I stand across the street in front of the World Trade Center Memorial Headquarters. I scan the crowd, hoping to find my affinity group. At the same time, I'm automatically estimating the number of demonstrators. To later compare to police and media reports. The usual formula of half the organizer's estimates and six times the media estimates works almost every time.

A private security agent comes over, asks if I'm here to visit the Headquarters. I tell him I'm here for the demonstration. He tells me to get the hell away from the building. I give him a long look before crossing the street. I've actually been to the Memorial Headquarters. Took the kids. I figured they might learn something about an important part of this city's history. This country's too. But it was mostly a tourist trap. I wonder what it was like here, pre-9/11. It's hard to pinpoint when New York changed from a relatively open metropolis into a tightly controlled and policed city. The replacement of regular neighborhoods with gated communities definitely came later. That's been well documented. But the history books don't answer my real question.

In the park, it's the usual multi-issue circus. I study a spinning holo-map of the world showing countries occupied by U.A. troops or corporate security forces. A dove animation is flying to each place and making the troops disappear, to scenes of cheering crowds. Right next to the group with the holo are two middle-aged demonstrators carrying a cloth banner with a simple handwritten phrase: *Delete Invasive Technologies*. I zigzag around them to join a contingent in body paint playing a game of leap frog. Each time they leap, they shout a different phrase: "Jump over racism." "Leap over xenophobia." "Fly over genderism." I join them for a while but my eye is drawn to a large photo-board flashing a series of still photos. They're of people being tortured. With captions indicating where the photos were taken. I recognize the names of some of the more well-known "terrorist prisons." And of local immigration detention centers. The captions explain the type of torture being used. My eyes glide over this. I don't need explanations. But it's hard to look away from the photos themselves.

The crowd is growing, making movement difficult. I push into the center, lose myself in the chanting, swaying, jostling mass. This usually energizes me, but today it has the opposite effect. I feel lost, oppressed, shaky. Like I'm a marionette standing in the middle of some lifeless show, going through the motions of hope when hope is already dead. A wave of fatigue hits me and I think about sitting down in the middle of all this. Maybe sleeping. To wake up someplace where the slogans have come to life, or brought our society back to life. Or maybe not wake up.

I see a group of people in masks dressed in red body armor and make myself start moving again, as far as I can get from these hired agitators. While demonstrators can't even use poles for their signs, the group in red are being permitted to carry stickball bats. If only I could find and warn my affinity group, I'd go home. Maybe I should check further downtown again.

Back at Bowling Green, things have gotten more tense. There's an announcement to clear the streets or prepare to be arrested. No one knows where to go. Most of the side streets are blocked off, and cops on horses are surrounding the park. More and more people arrive every minute. There won't be enough space to hold everyone. It's a scene of utter chaos.

At Battery Park, there's a line of cops in riot gear carrying micro-netting. They're standing shoulder to shoulder on State Street, blocking entry to the park. I stay wide of them and walk towards Battery Place, away from the policed zone. I follow it to the piers. There, I enter the park from the back, where tourists wait to take the ferry to the Statue of Liberty. I skirt the old castle, which served long ago as an immigrant processing center.

Looking east, I take in the scene. It reminds me of some sick hunt. People have been lured inside, trapped, and surrounded. Now the hunters are closing in with their nets and weapons. I watch a cop trip a demonstrator whose wrists have already been zip-tied. Nearby, another cop is pulling someone across the pavement by their hair. To my right, a group of demonstrators sitting back to back are being kicked apart and roughed up, then systematically cuffed and dragged out of the park. Others have their faces pushed to the ground with a knee in the middle of their backs. All this is happening towards the front of the park, while at the back, it's a regular tourist scene. Like two separate realities.

Which way to go? Looking ahead, I notice a pair of lone individuals who seem familiar. Maybe members of my group? As I get closer, I see they're two kids from my ninth grade social studies class from last year. They're backed up against the low chain fence surrounding the memorial sculpture. Two cops are standing over them, one with a raised phaser baton.

Without stopping to think, I shout out, "Hey! What's going on over there?"

"Don't approach any closer," one of the cops says.

The other says, "These anarchists were resisting arrest."

The two students are dressed in a patchwork of flags from a variety of long-defunct nations. They may look like dangerous anarchists to the cops, but to me, they just look like kids. All dressed up and looking for something to believe in.

"They're high school students," I say in a calm voice. "They were in my history class. Fari, Nina, stand up and show the police officers that you don't mean any harm."

They stand slowly, holding hands. Even from here, I can see they're shaken, scared. I keep walking forward with my hands in plain view.

"We. . . we weren't doing anything wrong," Nina says. "We want to go home now. We didn't know we weren't allowed in this park."

"Please," I say quietly, looking directly at the two officers. "Please, just let them go."

One of the two cops looks at the other, expression uncertain. The other one shakes their head once, quickly, and the first one hardens their gaze.

"This is an illegal demonstration and everyone here is subject to arrest," the second one says, "and that will include you too, Mr. Teacher, unless you clear out right now."

I move sideways, taking their gazes with me. "You kids remember the class trip I took you on? A whole crowd of tourists are there today. You should take a look. . ." And then all at once I run at the cops, full speed, shouting: "Go! Go!" at the top of my lungs.

Both cops turn their full attention to me, one of them raising their phaser stick as I sprint towards them. Before it hits me full force across the chest, I have the satisfaction of seeing Fari and Nina already rounding Hope Garden, soon to mix with the tourists getting on the ferry.

I'm on the ground but I don't remember falling. I've lost some time, I think. I stay very still, moving only my eyes. The two cops are some distance from me, speaking to an officer wearing a white shirt. I lift my head carefully towards the sky and see a small self-propelled camera floating above us. I hear some strange music. It sounds like the circus.

I try not to breathe much, though I'm not sure why. There's a taste of metal in the back of my throat. I turn my head and see the eternal flame of the 9/11 memorial. I try to crawl closer to it, hoping it will warm me. I'm so cold. But there's no warmth coming from the flame.

I tilt my head backwards. See a gingko tree. Simon's favorite. This type of tree survived the bombing of Hiroshima. I push myself towards it. It hurts so much that time slips again. I'm leaning against the tree, one hand touching its bark, the other wrapped around my own chest. The tree feels warm against my back. I close my eyes, hoping the urge to breathe will pass quickly.

CHAPTER 14
JANIE

Roberto's already on the platform when I arrive at the Atlantic Avenue station.

"Thanks for coming with me," I say, giving him a peck on the cheek. I fill him in on what happened, switching to a kind of code we use to discuss these things. I don't need to give a lot of explanation. We've talked about Laek's situation before. I'm thinking of one particularly memorable law school night getting drunk in the Lower East Village. But he does have a question.

"This, uh, old friend of his, had Laek mentioned him before?"

"Not by name. But there's someone he talks about when he's in a particularly dark mood. I think it's the same guy. . . Where's that fucking train already?"

"It's the weekend."

"The thing is," I tell him, "I don't completely trust this guy. I don't think Laek does either. But it's like he has some kind of weird loyalty to him."

Roberto looks like he wants to say something, but we hear the train arriving. When we're inside, I steel myself before finally asking the question: "What should I do?"

He looks at me grimly and says: "Take Laek and get the hell underground."

I grip the pole hard and push back a feeling of panic. "And the kids? What about them?"

"You know, chiquita, there are families who'll help out in these situations."

"No. Absolutely not. I am not giving my kids to anyone for safe-keeping."

"I understand," Roberto says immediately. He looks at me and then down again. "You don't need to go anywhere yourself, you know. You could be with the kids while Laek. . . goes somewhere to wait this out. You'd get hassled, of course, but you'd probably be alright. And who knows, things may change. With another election in less than two years, maybe—"

"Stop. You know that's bullshit. This isn't something that changes from administration to administration. Things get worse, then get worse again, maybe with bits of less horrible shit in-between. That's what we've lived our whole lives." I'm shaking with rage.

"I'm sorry, Janie." He puts his hand on my arm.

"No. It's just that you don't understand. No one does. I couldn't. . . I couldn't ever. . ." I take a deep breath. "Can I tell you a story? About how I met Laek?"

Roberto tells me he'd like that, so I tell him how I saw Laek for the first time when I was volunteering with a group working for the rights of the unhoused in Washington Square Park.

"He was working with the group too?"

"No, he was a street kid. It was right after he'd come east. He was still off the grid."

"Really! I'd assumed you'd met at NYU. He went to the teacher's college, right?"

"Yeah, but that was later, when I was at NYU law. This was when I was still an undergrad. Laek was only sixteen at the time. Anyway, I offered him a sandwich and talked to him about his legal rights, options, safety. You know the rap. He thanked me and offered me some of his own food. I remember, it was fruit and nuts. I thought to myself, I can't take this kid's food, it's probably all he has, but some instinct made me accept his offer."

"And?"

"And I was rewarded with the most gorgeous, sweet smile I'd ever seen. I think I fell in love with him at that moment. We ended up talking for hours, and when they threw us out of the park for the night, I asked him if he had somewhere to sleep."

"Talk about bringing home stray cats."

"I was living with a bunch of other kids at the time. One more body wouldn't have been a big deal. And I would have let him stay in my room."

"That's our wild Janie, stray cats in your bed."

I laugh. "I wasn't thinking that, really. OK, maybe a little, but mostly I just wanted to help. Anyway, he turned down my offer, but I could tell he wanted to stay. At the time, I thought it was pride." I pause. "I didn't see him again for three months."

The train is now moving at a slow crawl through the tunnel to Manhattan, but thankfully, the next stop is Bowling Green.

"I looked for him on and off after that, first in Washington Square Park, asking the old folx who play chess there if they'd seen him. When it started getting colder, I began checking all the parks in the East Village. There are so many, and even the tiniest ones are gated! I eventually found him, not far from where I was living."

"What happened?"

"He was in bad shape. I don't mean physically. He seemed. . . I don't know, like he was waiting to die. I asked if something had happened. He didn't respond. I remember offering him a candy bar. He just wrapped his arms around his legs and rested his head on his knees."

"What did you do?"

"I did what I always do in situations where I'm unsure. I talked. And then I talked some more. I told him about myself, about school, my family, but mostly I talked about ideas—like fighting injustice and making the world a better place. He didn't say anything, but I could see he was listening. Finally, even I was talked out."

Now I figure is the moment when Roberto will make some joke about how he can't imagine me ever being talked out, but instead he waits, looking at me with a soft expression on his face. I squeeze his hand.

"It started getting late, and dark and cold, but I still sat by him, not knowing what I could do but not wanting to leave either. Then he finally spoke."

"What did he say?

"He said something about how I should leave now unless I planned to stay forever."

"So you stayed."

I nod, closing my eyes, remembering that moment like it was yesterday. Laek had looked at me, lifting his hand slowly through the air until it was just touching my cheek. Then, he gently outlined the shape of my face, saying 'It's a heart,' in a voice that was so tender that even now, sixteen years later, remembering it sends chills down my spine.

"And then?" Roberto prompts.

"And then, he laid himself down and went to sleep. So I lay down too, but I wasn't used to sleeping rough and it was pretty cold that night. Finally, I drifted off. When I woke, Laek had his jacket and shirt over my shoulders and his bare arm wrapped around me."

"Wow. So how did you get him inside?"

"It took a while. I learned why he wouldn't stay in my apartment. He was terrified that he'd somehow bring disaster down on all of us, something he believed had happened before with his group. But being all alone was literally killing him. Laek's need for community, love—it's like food and water to him, absolutely essential to his well-being. That's why. . . it's why I'm so scared about what's going to happen now, about what we should do."

As I'm trying to articulate this, the ventilation cuts off with a sudden loud huff, followed by the lights, air-conditioning and electricity. Seconds later, the electricity comes back on and the train slowly begins moving again. We hear some squeals over the antiquated sound system, followed by an announcement in a computer-perfect voice: *Attention passengers. This train will be bypassing Bowling Green. Next stop, Wall Street.*

"Shit!"

"It's OK, Janie, we can get off there. It's not much further."

I wait to hear if they're going to give an explanation for why the train isn't making its usual stops. Maybe they'll blame it on "a sick passenger"—which usually means a suicide or an unhoused person being thrown off the train—or maybe on "technical difficulties"—which can cover anything from a water main break to a fire on the tracks to a broken door. But what they say is "police action." This announcement fills me with more dread than ever before. Especially when the train passes Wall Street station, horns blaring, without stopping there either.

Attention passengers. This train will be bypassing Wall Street and Fulton Street stations. Next stop: Brooklyn Bridge.

"Oh fuck, oh fuck," I say, walking around in circles. Roberto takes my arm firmly and leads me towards the back of the car to be closer to the southern-most exit. Time seems to crawl as we slowly pass Fulton Street with the doors closed. If we're not allowed to exit, at least let the train zoom by. Instead, it's as though the locked-in passengers are being teased with a slow-motion view of each inaccessible station.

When we arrive at Brooklyn Bridge, we burst out the door and up the stairs, weaving our way through the crowd. Roberto's on his mini-screen, getting an update on the situation. We decide to check Zuccotti Park first, since it's closer. When we arrive, Roberto puts a legal observer badge around my arm and activates it. I climb up on one of the low walls surrounding the area and survey the crowd, trying to spot Laek.

"How was he dressed? Is he carrying a sign?" Roberto asks, looking around.

"A plain white t-shirt, tan shorts. No sign. But forget what he's wearing. Just look for a tall, dark head that's moving. Laek never stays in one place. And you know how he walks. Very energetically, almost like he's bouncing."

After a few minutes of craning my neck and jumping up and down, I haven't found Laek and I'm ready to move on. It's true that it'd be easy to miss him in this crowd, but I can't stay put. There's a feeling of dread steadily growing in the pit of my stomach. I pull on Roberto's arm and we jump down from the wall.

"Let's head further downtown. Any news from the legal observers?"

"They're reporting arrests and the beginning of some trouble near Bowling Green."

"How are the arrests going down?"

"With lots of force and violence. And new tech is being used. A kind of disruption field."

Walking south, we're stopped three times by cops who laboriously check our legal observer IDs. At Bowling Green, I see Peg and Melo from the Neo-Anarchist Scatter Band. Peg has her tuba and Melo has a holo-drum suspended from a silk scarf around his neck. Behind them I see the other members of the band, about two dozen in all, dressed in a variety of colorful costumes and trailed by their usual coterie of fans and press, including floating cameras. This whole scene, shaped into a cutting-edge sound art experiment, is sure to make it to the international entertainment feeds by midnight. The musicians, with their excellent access to the press, are being left alone by the cops.

"Has anyone seen Laek?" I ask as Roberto talks on his screen.

"I did," Melo says. "Walking around Battery Park. He was moving pretty fast."

"How long ago?"

"Fifteen minutes? I'm not sure."

Roberto comes running over, a little out of breath.

"I think we should head to Battery Park."

"What's happening?"

"They're surrounding the demonstrators with micro-netting and closing in. It's being described as a free-for-all."

I'm walking towards the corner of State Street and Battery Place when I suddenly have an idea. I run back to Peg. She agrees to talk with the others. After she's left, I back up a few paces to try to see over the heads of the cops. A free-for-all is an apt description. I start crossing the street when my eyes are drawn to a figure moving towards the front of the park. He's far off but there's something deeply familiar about the way he moves. I cross the street quickly and join Roberto in trying to enter the park, but we're rebuffed by the solid line of riot cops. We flash our legal observer IDs but are told to move on.

"Who's the officer in charge here?" Roberto demands. No one responds right away, so Roberto holds up his screen to show that he's recording the exchange. "I promise to have every one of you brought up before the Special Civilian Board if you don't call the officer in charge right now. The Singh Decree obligates you to give legal observers access to the scene."

I let Roberto handle this and walk off along Battery Place, trying to peer between heads in the line of cops. Yes, the person I saw walking must have been Laek because I see him now, closer, talking to two cops. Suddenly he's running towards them. What the hell's going on? One of the cops raises his phaser stick at the same moment as a big white-shirted cop walks into my line of vision. I move sideways, craning my neck, just in time to see Laek go down. I open my mouth to scream but what seems to come out of my throat is the full blast of sound that can only be the Neo-Anarchist Scatter Band. Then all twenty-four of them march by, plus press, hangers-on and four more legal observers who've arrived.

As the band makes their way along Battery Place playing post-modern circus music, complete with whistles, drums, accordions, and a surreal holo-surround, a few cops break formation to watch them. I see my chance and, heart pounding, dart through their lines towards where I saw Laek fall. I don't wait to see if anyone follows me, but am comforted by the sound of the band's music close by. I glance back quickly and catch a glimpse of Roberto, also in the park now and talking to the white shirt in charge.

I fall to my knees beside Laek. He's propped up against a tree and seems out of it. I can't tell how badly he's hurt, but he's clutching his ribs with one hand and holding onto the tree with the other. His breathing is shallow.

"Laek, are you OK?" His eyes aren't even tracking me. I put my hands on either side of his face and say his name again. This time he looks directly at me. His eyes are full of pain.

Roberto's at my side now and tells me we have to get Laek out of here as quickly as possible. I look around to try to figure out where to go. The whole park is a scene of violence and chaos, the marching band adding a bizarre soundtrack that seems strangely fitting. Everywhere the band goes, whatever's happening comes to an abrupt halt. This is fortunate because nothing that's going on in this park is good, nothing but the band's music and the magic it's performing.

"Do you think you can stand?" Roberto asks Laek.

"... don't know." Laek sounds breathless and weak. Roberto and I help him up, but he cries out in pain and would have fallen if we hadn't been holding him up.

"Grab onto me," Roberto says to Laek. "I'll support your weight. Try to keep your legs moving as best you can. Janie, stand close to him on the other side. OK, which way?"

Roberto surveys our surroundings and starts walking towards Battery Place in the direction of the nearest exit. It takes us forever to walk the short distance out of the park. Roberto's looking more and more panicked as he glances behind us, as though he expects to be stopped. He pulls Laek's arm more firmly around his shoulder, taking most of the weight of him onto his own back. Laek is slumped over and stumbling, his breathing more and more irregular.

"We should call an ambulance," I say, but there's a cab just ahead at Greenwich. A cab could be faster. I tell the driver to take us to the Downtown NY Workers' Hospital north of here.

In the cab, Laek is seated between us, breathing with his mouth open and holding his ribs. Each time the car swerves or stops or starts, Laek can't keep himself from letting out a gasp of pain. I wrap my arms around his shoulder, hoping to stabilize him. It's not working very well. Roberto's supporting Laek on the left side, speaking a non-stop stream of comforting words— that we're almost there, that he'll have help soon, that it'll be OK, all the while belying these assurances by looking as grim and worried as I've ever seen him.

CHAPTER 15
LAEK

'm bound hand and foot, the cuffs digging into my wrists and ankles. The Room is up ahead. I twist and struggle, trying to get away. They subdue me with more blows. Drag me down the corridor. Taunt me, saying that it's time for my shower.

I'm in The Room now. Fish Man is looking at me. His skin is too white. His lips are fleshy, and his eyes, cold and dead-looking. He watches as they tie me down to the board, my head hanging back below my shoulders. Fish Man bends down over me. Calls me Young Mr. No-name. Asks me if I have anything to tell him today. I can't tell him anything, not even my name, because by now, I don't remember it.

They put the wet cloth over my face. Pour the water. I hold my breath for as long as I can. Soon I'm struggling, sucking at the cloth, as water instead of air enters my mouth, my throat, my lungs. They remove the cloth and I try to breathe. Retch and cough instead, acidy liquid dripping from my lips. Before I can even get a full breath in, they do it again. And again, and again.

This time, I think I finally understand. It's me who's Fish Man, or Fish Boy maybe. *Please let me up*, I think. *I can tell you my name now.* I know they can hear me think sometimes. That's why

I try to keep my thoughts quiet. But today I want them to hear. So they'll take the cloth away. *Let me up. MY NAME IS FISH BOY!* But they don't hear me. I know what I need to do. I have to become a real fish boy. So I suck the water into my lungs eagerly, seeking the oblivion of deep, dark waves. Only my plan doesn't work. They pull the cloth from me, sit me upright, pound my back so that the water comes up. I cough, my lungs on fire, burning me from the inside. The pain is unbearable. Please. Let me swim away.

I start coughing and wake up in my hospital bed. It's seventeen years later. I'm covered in sweat and shaking, and I discover the pain from my dream is real. There's a terrible burning, crushing agony in my torso. Just trying to breathe makes me feel like I'm going to pass out. I don't know what's worse—the pain or the feeling that I can't get enough air.

There's a small screen at the foot of my bed showing the time. It's very early, barely morning. There's a button for summoning a nurse, voice controls for adjusting the bed. I choose the latter. Get a little relief by repositioning myself. Whatever they gave me for the pain—morphine probably—has pretty much worn off, but I need to wait as long as possible. I'm not being brave. Morphine almost killed me once, but the hospital would have no way of knowing this. The most interesting parts of my medical history won't be found in any public records.

There's another control. For the screen at the foot of my bed. I pick it up. Watching the screen might distract me for a while. And I want to see what the news is saying about the demo. It asks me for permission to charge my account. I see it's actually Janie's account. I feel reassured, just seeing her name.

I scroll down. The options are limited, mostly mindless entertainment. Reality shows, cooking, virtual travel. The only newsfeeds are for local coverage. As though local news is safer somehow. It doesn't take long to find coverage of the demonstration. The reported number of protesters is a fraction of my own estimates. They're talking about a large number of arrests.

Showing scenes of vandalism and violence downtown. The police blandly looking on in the background. Well, why shouldn't they? The vandals are probably on the same payroll. Not much play is being given to the issues raised by the demonstrators. The fact that the City pulled the permit at the last minute isn't even mentioned.

I flip through other newsfeeds. Watch scenes of arrests being made. The pain in my ribs is getting very bad again, the relief of changing position wearing off. I make myself wait a little longer before asking for pain medication. Meanwhile, the voice-over on the screen is talking about protestors resisting arrest and clashing with the police. All I see are peaceful demonstrators tripped, pushed and dragged. Do people really watch these images and believe what the voice-over is telling them instead of their own eyes? I mute the sound. It's making me too angry.

I'm flipping back and forth between images, when I decide I've reached my limit. The pain is so bad, each time I inhale or exhale is an ordeal. I've decided to call for the nurse when I see a familiar image on the screen. It's the group I saw sitting back-to-back in Battery Park. I would be walking a little west of there. The camera moves away as the protestors begin to be dragged off. I see a familiar figure. Roberto! And Janie just to his left, now disappearing off the frame. Then I see a chilling sight. It's him. The cop from Broadway who sexually assaulted me. Wearing a uniform that marks him as a high ranking officer in the anti-terrorist squad. He turns, faces the camera. He's looking straight at me as he smiles. Then he turns left and frowns, to where I saw Janie standing a second ago. My heart freezes. Janie. He's looking at Janie.

I watch the coverage at double speed through to the end to see if there's anything else with that cop or with Janie. Nothing. I replay the earlier sequence. And then I replay it again, to see if maybe I was mistaken about what I saw. It's looping now. He stares at me. Smiles. Looks at Janie. Frowns. I keep watching it. I can't stop.

The control drops down out of my hand. Without thinking, I reach for it. Agony fills me. I pass out. I wake confused, trying to remember what I was looking for. All I know is that I need to warn Janie. I try to get out of bed and wake up on the cold floor. I can't breathe. I pass out again.

When I next wake, I'm back in my hospital bed, a mask on my face and something attached to my arm. When I inhale, it feels like my insides are being torn apart. I hear myself moan. My doctor's talking angrily to someone. He turns to me and speaks in a gentler voice.

"Easy does it. You had a fall, but it's OK now. We've raised the morphine dosage. Try to take good, slow breaths. I'm going to take the mask off." He removes it. "How are you doing?"

"It hurts." I shiver.

"We can raise the dosage a little and then we'll see. That's why it doesn't pay to try to be heroic with these types of injuries. You just end up paying for it later. Take a breath. . . Good."

"Janie," I gasp.

"She'll be in later. It's still early in the morning."

"Please. . ."

"Just a few more minutes, you should feel some relief. Try not to move."

I can't stop shivering. I close my eyes, but it doesn't help. In my head, I keep on imagining Janie at the mercy of that sadistic cop. I open my eyes. I have to do something, but I can't think. The doctor's talking to me again.

"Laek, I'm going to leave you for a few minutes to talk to another doctor about your pain medication. Meanwhile, I want you to try to relax. As soon as the pain has receded enough, you'll be able to sleep a little. I'll be back, just lie still."

I nod, still shivering. He puts his hand on my shoulder, then leaves. Good. I need to be alone. To plan what I have to do. But all I can think of is how, despite everything, I've done exactly what I've always dreaded. I've brought trouble down on Janie.

I'll have to flee, go underground. Or leave the country

without her, without the kids. It's the only way they'll be safe. But even with me gone, they could find them. Like they'll find me. I should leave the hospital now, hide. I try pulling myself up and it's then that I notice the strap across my shoulders, across my hips too. I'm tied down, like a prisoner. I fight the rising panic, try to breathe like the doctor told me, but I can't get enough air. I struggle against my straps, ignoring the pain. If I fell off the bed again, I wonder if it would kill me. An idea enters my head. If I were dead, they'd eventually leave Janie alone.

My thoughts are going round and round. There's no way out. I can't put her in danger. The pain is dulling now, my limbs and my mind growing slow and heavy. I have to decide, before I can sleep. Go off the grid. Or flee. Each choice has its own risks. My breathing is slowing. I remember this feeling well. This oblivion. I'm not afraid of it. No, it draws me deeply.

I close my eyes. I'm in Prospect Park again. Siri's explaining something about baseball to me. "Sometimes, there's more than one way to make the out, Daddy. Like when there's a runner on third, and the batter hits a grounder to the shortstop. You could throw home, but that might not work—there's no force play. Or you could throw to first, which wouldn't be as good as making the out at home, but you'd be surer to succeed. Coach says you always need to go for the sure out, not the best out."

I know what the sure out is here. But no, I've already decided. I'll go underground again. . . or maybe flee the country.

As I fall deeper and deeper into a profound sleep, my mind is still struggling with making the best decision. But my body has already decided. It will take the sure out.

CHAPTER 16
JANIE

This time, when Dr. Metcalfe called to ask me to meet him downstairs, I put him off. Each time I've met with the doctor, the news has been worse. The first day at the hospital, when I learned that seven of Laek's ribs had been broken, I felt like I'd been kicked hard in the stomach. The doctor had reassured me, saying that Laek was young and strong, that the tear in the lung had been repaired, and that the internal organ damage would all heal in time. Then, when Laek fell out of bed, Dr. Metcalfe told me it was a minor setback. Instead, Laek had to be heavily sedated and later took a turn for the worse. The third long conversation was scarier, because it was obvious that the doctor was concerned, even though he claimed that developing pneumonia is not uncommon with these types of injuries. During our latest conversation, when Dr. Metcalfe spoke to me about morphine tolerance and addiction, I could see that he'd left behind his earlier optimism about Laek's recovery.

I sit beside Laek and take his hand. He lies motionless under the sheet, head turned away from the door. His skin, ordinarily warmer than mine, is cold as ice. His breathing is slow and shallow. I put my hand on his cheek, but he doesn't stir.

I will not give in to despair. I won't.

Maybe if I could warm his hand, it would be a good sign. I put it in between my own, smaller, hands. His fingers are long and slender. A beautiful hand, really; he could have been a pianist. As much as he loves music, Laek doesn't know how to play any instruments. I rub his hand up and down, in long, slow motions. I put his hand against my breast, my cheek. It already seems warmer. I rub it some more, kiss it, put one of his fingers into my mouth, suck each finger in turn. My saliva is hot, wet. I dry his hand on my shirt. It's definitely warmer now, even a little pink.

I look at Laek's face, searching for some reaction or change. Does he feel that his hand is warmer, that I'm by his side? I sense something behind me. Dr. Metcalfe's standing by the door, a sad smile on his face. Has he been standing there, watching? I can't bring myself to be angry at him. Blaming the doctor would be convenient, but I honestly can't reproach any of the treatment decisions he's made, and I can tell that he, too, is deeply upset by Laek's deteriorating condition.

"How does he seem to you?" Dr. Metcalfe asks.

"Aren't I supposed to be asking you that?" He doesn't respond. "I'm scared."

"Yes. He's not doing well. Failing, in fact." Strange choice of words. Like Laek got a bad grade on his midterm or something. Can he retake the test?

"We can't give up." I hold Laek's hand tighter.

"I'm nowhere near giving up. Laek's the patient I think about when I leave the hospital each day and wake up each morning. I've read everything in his medical file—which isn't much, by the way—examined his case from all angles, done research. I'm not telling you this so you'll be grateful or have false hopes. Or even so you'll decide not to sue me."

I smile at his attempt to joke. "So why are you telling me this?"

"Because I've reached a certain conclusion, or at least I strongly suspect something, but I want you to understand it's after giving it a lot of thought." He looks over at me and I nod for him to continue. "The injury that Laek has suffered, I don't want to understate it, yet as bad as it was, well, he's young, unusually healthy and strong. So why isn't he recovering? Why is he getting weaker instead?"

"Well, there was the fall." I wonder why I feel like arguing with him.

"Yes, but how did that happen? It's strange that, as painful as it was for him to move, he managed to throw himself out of bed."

"I don't know. But the pneumonia—you said that can happen sometimes when there's a bad chest injury, that secretions can get stuck in there and cause infection."

"That's why we increased the morphine level so he could cough. And then did it again when his tolerance went up. How quickly this happened—it tells me certain things."

"Like what?"

"That he's used morphine before, a lot of it. And that there are many things that have happened to Laek—medically—that aren't in his file."

I don't say anything.

"So the other conclusion I've reached, or rather, the question I'd like to ask. . ."

He stops and looks at me and I suddenly feel even more afraid. "What?"

"Janie, do you think it's possible that Laek. . . that he doesn't *want* to recover? That. . . Do you know, for instance, is there any history of mental illness or depression? Any suicide attempts, talk or thoughts in the past of killing or hurting himself?"

Though I didn't see this question coming, in all fairness, it's a legitimate question. I stroke Laek's hand, finally turning it palm up, to gently caress his wrist with my thumb. His bracelet tattoo

—is it a vine of thorns or barbed wire?—doesn't completely cover the long white scar. That scar has been there since before I met him and I've often wondered what could have left such a thick, ragged line.

Even at nineteen, I knew what I was getting into when we held each other in that small park on Avenue D by the Projects and I was caught by the intensity of the play of light and dark in his eyes. It was probably a conceit on my part, thinking I could hold all that darkness back, away from Laek. Still, I can't keep myself from protesting.

"You don't know him, what a joyful person he is. The smallest thing—like a beautiful sunrise, a surprising act of kindness—practically sends him into a state of ecstasy. He glows, and his smile. . . And he never sweats the little things. Sure, he gets sad sometimes. He's just more sensitive than other people. But he has me and his friends, so many friends; and he loves his work, his kids. . . If you knew how much he loves his children, what a good father he is, you wouldn't, you wouldn't suggest. . ."

"Janie, I'm not suggesting anything," he says gently. "I'm only asking, because if there's a psychological aspect to Laek's case, a mental health aspect, there may be other approaches we should be taking."

I close my eyes, feel the tears that had been welling up fall down my cheeks, as I remember the last thing Laek said to me before he had to be so deeply drugged that we could no longer hold conversations. *I'm sorry, Janie,* he'd said. *Please forgive me.*

"What kinds of approaches?" I ask the doctor. "Our daughter, she's away at camp. Do I need . . . Should I make arrangements to have her sent back home?"

"There's a little time before you need to think about that. There are still things to try."

As he speaks to me about his ideas, one thought keeps repeating in my mind. That promise I made to Laek in the park sixteen years ago that I wouldn't leave him. But now he's leaving me. For a moment, I'm filled with anger, and it's such a relief from the fear and despair that I hang on to it as long as I can. But then another thought enters my mind—that he hasn't actually left me, that he's only lost. A strange thought—Laek, who never gets lost in the physical world, who's always there to help me find my way. Now I have to find him, find him and bring him home. Wherever home ends up being. Because I know now I failed him in not seeing that we could still be home together somewhere else. I lift Laek's hand to my lips, kiss it on the wrist. It's still warm.

I talk to the doctor about my own ideas and he approves. I call Magda and tell her which photos of the kids to bring from the apartment and where to find my old acoustic guitar, the wood mellow and smooth from my student days. I can't go and gather these items myself because the most important thing I've been given permission to do is to stay in this room with Laek day and night until, one way or another, he leaves it.

We've also decided to decrease the amount of morphine. Controlling his pain is medically necessary, otherwise he won't be able to breathe deeply and clear his lungs, but the dosage is now so high that it could backfire into respiratory depression. It was a hard decision, but decreasing the morphine is the path of hope. And if pain is needed to pull him out of whatever oblivion he's sunken into, so be it. We're fighting for his life.

————

We're alone now, Laek and I, the photos by his bed, my guitar in my arms as I strum softly. I'm finally seeing the first signs of the decrease in the morphine as he rolls his head from side to side, his breathing more labored. I pull my chair closer and take his hand in mine.

"It's OK, baby, I'm here." He settles down, seems to fall back into that state that looks more like a coma than sleep to me.

Time passes and he's still lying there, cold and lifeless. I need to do something, to break through somehow. I get up and look out into the hallway. The hospital seems abnormally quiet, the lights dimmed. I take off my shoes and slip into bed with him. I wrap my arms around him, heedless of hurting him. If only I could warm him up, help him to feel that he's not alone.

I stroke his hair, kiss his face. I should leave him in peace. This is crazy, climbing into his hospital bed as he lies here so badly hurt. I try to imagine life without him. My stomach twists with the thought of so unbearable a loss, my insides loose and jagged with pain. I can't stop the tears so I press my head into the crook of his neck, wetting his cool skin. I lie there crying, my body against his. After a time, I doze, exhausted from the vigil and the crying and feeling some comfort from his body close to mine. I wake a few hours later and reluctantly leave the bed. He seems warmer, but no closer to consciousness.

It's starting to get light outside. I hear activity in the corridors —the night life of the hospital is at a close. It feels like the end of a kind of purgatory. I pick up my guitar and begin to strum it softly. The music I'm playing is soothing, but maybe soothing is not what's needed. I think for a minute, choose one of my group's own tunes, rebellious and angry but also filled with hope. I play, loud enough for him to hear, but not loud enough to disturb the other patients.

I look up. Diffused sunlight filters through the institutional windows. I keep playing, watching Laek. A small horizontal rectangle of sunlight stripes his face. He stirs, turns his head. I'm by his side in an instant. I rest my hand on the far side of his face, to keep it turned in my direction. I take his hand and start speaking to him.

"Laek, listen to me. I know where you are. You're trying to go to New Metropolis. But we have to go together. I've worked it all out. We're gonna go, I promise, but you need to wait. The kids and I, we're coming with you. Wait for us, please. Come back."

He tries to turn his head away but I hold it, willing him to open his eyes, to look at me. I feel him squeeze my hand, watch him struggle for a deep breath. Then his eyes open. My own fill with tears. I let him pull his hand from my grasp. He lifts it up the few inches to my face.

"Janie." He moans softly.

"I'm here. It's OK."

"Don't. . . don't let him get you. I saw him. . ."

"Shh. It's OK, baby. You're safe."

"Janie. . . Can't let him. . ." He starts to close his eyes again.

"No! Stay with me now. Don't close your eyes." I hold his face firmly in my hands, my own face close to his. His eyes fly open again.

I keep talking to him, encouraging him to take deep breaths. He tries to fill his lungs, shudders with pain. I cradle his face, gently but firmly preventing him from turning away.

"Please, it hurts. Let me. . . Let me go. . ."

"No! I will never let you go. Now breathe!" He does, but his eyes flutter as he starts slipping away again. I hold his head, talk to him more about the plans we need to make.

"It'll be after Siri is finished with camp. We can all go up and get her, then continue north. But you need to start getting stronger, getting better. We can't make it without you. I don't know the way. We'll be lost." Laek starts to tremble.

"Keep breathing, baby. You need to keep trying to breathe."

"I couldn't, I couldn't bear it. . . I saw him. . . and I thought. . . you'd be safer. . ."

"I can't lose you. You need to understand that. I can't do this without you. All the light would be gone, all the music. Please Laek, we promised, we promised to stick together."

He puts his hands over his face, trying to hide his tears. I pull them away.

"It's OK," I whisper. "You can let go. I got you."

He cries for a short time while I hold him, then his body relaxes. His breathing is still shallow, but regular and stronger. I pull the blankets over his shoulders, smooth his hair. His eyes snap open again.

"Janie." he says, sounding scared and very young.

"I'm here. I'm not going anywhere."

He relaxes again and falls into a deeper sleep. Something about the sequence of the words I spoke tugs at my heart—a kind of déjà vu, like something right has come around again, full circle.

CHAPTER 17
SIMON

never thought I'd be sick of pizza. Ever since Mommy's been staying at the hospital with Daddy and I been staying with Henry, it's all I get for dinner. I guess it's 'cause Henry and I both like it and his mom's not used to cooking vegetarian.

"Aren't you hungry, honey?" Henry's mom asks.

"Not really."

"You'd tell me if you weren't feeling well, Simon?" I nod. "Or even if you're just. . . homesick, or need someone to talk to?"

"He's got me to talk to. Don't be all worrying, Mom. Come on, Simon." Henry pulls me by my arm and we race downstairs to the playroom.

"Listen, little brother. . ." Henry calls me that sometimes, even though I'm only eleven months younger. He says I could be his younger brother in real life because eleven months is more than long enough to grow a new baby. "I got something you need to hear. About your daddy."

"What? Tell me!"

"I know what happened. It was a cop who done that. Beat him with a phaser stick."

All of a sudden I have a stomach ache. I pick up one of Henry's hyper-battle droids.

"Put that shit down, Simon, it's for babies. I thought you should know what happened, that they did a beat-down on him. Even with him being White and all."

"There are lots of Black cops too."

"Stop acting like you ignorant when you ain't. You know how it is, or ought to. Don't matter the color of the cop, just the color of the one getting beat."

"How do you know what happened?"

"Remember when we were doing homework and I had to pee? I heard my mom talking to my dad."

"Did she say. . . did she say anything else?"

"Like what?"

"Like was he gonna die or something."

"Nah, your daddy's too tough for that."

I reach for the droid again, but pull my hand back. "Let's play holo-cube."

"Not yet. We got some preparing to do if you wanna avenge your daddy. But first you gotta take care of your own self."

"Whaddya mean?"

"I mean Keri. Showing him you ain't gonna take his shit no more. Then after that, you'll be ready to go after the ones who hurt your daddy."

"I don't know."

"Look, first we'll work with these weights. Here." Henry hands me one and he takes the other for himself. "Over your head like this. Fifty times each arm."

I copy Henry. The weight doesn't feel heavy until you been doing it for a while.

"This is boring, Henry."

"No pain, no gain. Don't you want to do right by your daddy?"

"My daddy doesn't believe in violence."

"Well violence sure do believe in him."

I'm not sure what to say to that so I keep on with the weights.

"Anyhow, the question is what *you* believe. Should people just get away with shit?"

"No."

"Well, then. And you don't mind violence when we're playing The Game."

That's true, but the violence in The Game isn't real. Can't I like pretend violence and still not like real violence? "I like the music in The Game," I tell him. "It puts me in the right mood."

"I can put that music on if you want. It's a real band—Fight Frenzy. You know them?"

"Uh uh."

With the music on, it's easier to keep doing the exercises. I'm thinking, Fight Frenzy, *fight frenzy*! I think of other "f" words like that: fury, furious—that's how I feel when I think of what happened to Daddy. And fear. No, I can think of better words with "f." Like "fist," which I'll use to punch, and "fangs" to tear. Freak, faint, fall, fire, fever. Phaser, like in the cop's phaser stick. But that's not spelt with "f." Except on graffiti or holo-art— "Fuck the fazer"—you see that a lot. And just "fuck" too, which means have sex, but people use it as a curse word. Like my mom. Fuck, fuck, fuck. How could they have hurt Daddy like that?

Henry puts his weight down. "Lemme feel your muscle now." I make a muscle. "Good. You're skinny, but strong. You can whip Keri's ass. OK, time for battle practice. I got the new zeta version."

My parents would never let me play The Game if they knew about it. I feel a little guilty but mostly I'm excited. I walk into the shadowy holo-chamber the screen projects and put on my game bracelet. I do a fighting stance and make a fist with the hand that has the bracelet.

"Ready, little brother?"

"Ready."

Suddenly it's like the whole room has gone dark. It feels real even though I know it's the holo-wrap. I see Henry's game persona next to me carrying his weapons—a flying, spiked energy ball in one hand and a poison scythe in the other. He looks like himself, only taller and with bigger muscles, and his face is older. I don't know what I look like—Henry says like me, but leaner and meaner. I'm carrying my usual light laser and also a full-throttle repeat-action phaser gun. Henry's on a flying motorcycle and I'm riding my familiar. He's a giant equibeast with long, sharp white horns, dripping fangs and armor plates under soft black fur.

We ride down an alleyway with broken glass and twisted up metal. I lift my light laser and circle it in the air so we can see. Out in the distance are plasma deserts where different alien armies are marching around. Farther off, I can see the digital debris mountains.

Henry starts an attack right away. His energy ball takes a piece off the first guy's head. Some of the guy's brains fall out, but he's not dead yet. Henry always starts up too soon. When the guy is close enough, I slice his whole head off with my light laser.

"Hey, that one was mine!" Henry complains. "You go after those others."

I gallop over and do a bunch more head shots using my light laser. Soon about six heads are on the ground in front of me, some of them still moving their lips and screaming. Henry flips his light ball towards a group of five who are running together. The ball has a delay-charge, and I watch it explode. Body parts fly out in all directions. The ball returns to Henry's hand like a boomerang. I use my phaser gun on about a dozen zombies, aiming for the middle and seeing if I can cut them all in half. I'm sick of head shots.

I see another phalanx of enemy creatures. They're right in front of us in no time flat and I have to use both my weapons at once to keep them off me. When I've destroyed the closest ones, I look over at Henry again. He's killed most of those around him and is messing around with the ones who are left by slicing off different parts of their bodies. I see cut-off hands and blood spurting out of wrists. The hands seem to be waving at me.

Suddenly, I hear my familiar let out a shriek. It sounds like something between a human scream and a horse's neigh. When I wasn't paying attention, someone slipped in and attacked him. There's a long lance pushed halfway into his chest, between the armor plates. I slip off his back, dropping my weapons, and try to pull it out. He screams and screams.

"Simon! Watch out!" But it's too late. They're on top of me and I'm dead from four different lethal wounds.

The lights come back on. Henry's pulling my bracelet off. He looks disappointed.

"Last time we got to level six," he says. I look down, but he puts his hand on my shoulder. "It's OK, little brother. The new version's probably harder. We'll do better next time. Anyhow, we gotta go. It's time to play some B-ball."

I put on my sneakers as Henry talks to his mom.

"I don't want you staying out too late," Henry's mom says.

"Don't worry, we're just gonna play basketball with some friends from school."

"Alright, but be home in an hour and a half. Set the alarm on your screen, Henry."

"Yes, Mom."

I'm dribbling the ball around my legs. I ask Henry who's coming to meet us.

"Just some kids."

"But who?"

Henry steals the ball. I take off after him.

And stop dead. Keri's waiting for us on the court.

"I'm going back."

"No. This is your chance. What did you think we were training for?"

I follow Henry onto the court. We choose up teams. Me and Henry and Khalil are on one team, Keri and Darwin and Frank on the other. There are two girls playing so we each get one. We get Dre, who's short, but that's OK 'cause she plays better than Shawna.

Keri takes a three-point shot to decide who gets possession. He misses, the ball rebounding wide off the rim. I catch it and Henry says I should shoot for our team. I take the shot and swish, it goes in. Yes!

"No good, your foot was on the line," Keri says, grabbing the ball from me.

"Was not!"

"Was too. Ain't I right Shawna?"

"Uh huh."

"It was not! I checked and everything. Right, Henry?"

"I wasn't watching."

"You calling me a liar, Simon-Says?" Shawna walks up to me, hands on her hips. "I saw your own big foot right on that line."

I look at Henry, who shrugs.

"Huh, thought so. Go ahead Keri." Shawna turns her back on me.

Keri takes the shot. This time it goes in, and since it's break-the-ice, they get to start.

We play a zone defense, but they're playing us person-to-person. I manage to score off Darwin, but then they do a switch and now it's Keri who's taking me. I try to take a jumpshot and Keri pushes into me from the front. I fall on my butt.

"Foul!"

"You fell on your ass on purpose."

I look at my teammates. They're looking down or away, except for Dre.

Henry says, "Let's keep playing," and slaps me on the back.

Shawna gets a rebound and passes it to Keri. Henry charges him and steals the ball right out of his hands. He dribbles out, then back in. I try to get his attention to send me a pass, but he's dribbling all around, hogging the ball. Keri goes after Henry, double-teaming him, and now I'm completely free. I jump up and down, waving my arms. Finally, Henry feeds me the ball. I drive to the basket for a left-side layup. Keri charges into me from behind and I fall down hard on my knees. The ball goes flying out of my hands.

"Foul!"

"That wasn't no foul."

I get up, dust myself off and notice that my knee is scraped.

"Look! My knee's bleeding."

"Ain't my fault you went and hurt yourself."

"You pushed me from behind! Henry?'

"Uh huh." But then Henry just folds his arms across his chest and looks at me. It's like he's saying, "So do something about it." And then, in case I didn't get it, he puts his fist into his hand and lifts his chin towards Keri. I look around and everyone's waiting to see what'll happen, except Dre who's looking from me to Keri like she wants to do something. But I don't think she will. I wonder if people were around when Daddy got beaten up by the cops. I wonder if anyone said anything or tried to help him. Maybe everyone was too scared. I feel scared but angry. Mostly, I'm tired of this.

I walk over to Keri. May as well get it over with. Like magic, all the other kids make a ring around us. It gets darker, like in the holo-chamber when we play The Game.

"So what are you gonna do about it, freak? Go crying to your mama and daddy?'

I think about Daddy as I listen to Shawna's mean laugh. It's been so long since I've seen him. I clench my fist like in The Game, raise it up. I think about how my poor equibeast got killed when I let myself be distracted. I focus totally on Keri's face and punch out hard and fast.

Keri's on the ground. His head is bent down over his right hand, and when he looks up, blood pours out from his nose. His hand is like a cup. When he flattens it out, the blood he's already caught there drips down his wrist. He looks at his hand, looks up at me, then runs off the court. Everyone else is, like, frozen in place. Finally, Henry walks up to me and puts his arm around my shoulder.

"You did good. He had that coming." But then he whispers into my ear: "But why'd you hit him in the nose like that? You may've broken it."

"Are we playing any more ball?" Darwin asks.

Henry looks at me. I shake my head.

"We're gonna take a break," Henry says.

The kids leave one by one. I walk up to the basketball hoop and lean back against the metal pole. Did I break Keri's nose?

"I wasn't aiming for his nose," I tell Henry.

"What were you aiming for?" he asks.

"Nothing. The middle of his face, I guess."

"Well, that's where the nose is, egghead."

I remember how it felt when my fist went into him. It wasn't like in The Game. It was. . . I don't know. Less big and bright and loud, but, like, more real. I slide down to the ground, my back to the pole, and start crying. Henry sits down next to me and pats my back.

"Hey, come on, its okay. What are you crying for? It's not you who got hurt."

But that's exactly how I feel. Only it's a hurt you can't see, an inside hurt that pokes my stomach each time I remember how it felt when my fist went into Keri's nose. And when I think of Daddy in the hospital, his bones broken on purpose by a cop.

CHAPTER 18
LAEK

I hear Philip's voice move down the hall as he jokes with one of the nurses in Spanish. I smile. Push myself up a little in bed. A spasm of pain rolls across my chest. I fall back, nauseous and shaky. No, this visit is a mistake. I look at the timer. Not at the clock. Twenty-four minutes. The time remaining before my next dose of M. When Janie and the doctor asked me if I felt up to visitors, I thought I'd finally get to see Simon. But both of them agreed it was too soon for that. Now I know they were right. How am I gonna hold it together for the next twenty-four minutes? And with a visitor watching, asking me how I am? Even Philip, who's seen me when I'm not at my best.

"Hey, Laek," Philip says, entering. He approaches my bed, holding up his fist. I tap it gently with my own. A wave of pain crashes down my right side. I make myself very still. Will my face to remain blank. After a moment, I glance at the timer. Twenty-three minutes.

"How you doing?" he asks me, with an uncertain smile.

I wipe my runny nose with my sleeve, not knowing how to answer. Philip chews on his lower lip. Looks at me again. I make an effort.

"It's good to see you, Phil."

"I would have come sooner. Right away, if I'd been allowed. . ."

"No, better later. I wasn't fit company. Still not, actually." I smile to take the sting out. Try not to look at the timer again.

"Don't worry about it. You're not here to entertain me. If anything, it's the other way around. . . Everyone's asking how you are."

"I guess you'll tell them." I'm now covered in sweat so I tug at my sheet.

"Are you hot? Can we lower the temperature in here?"

"Don't bother. Three seconds from now I'll be shivering. It's just one of the symptoms. Of morphine withdrawal. Like the runny nose." And my irritability.

I look at the time again. Twenty-two minutes. Right on schedule, I start shivering. Philip helps me cover up again with the sheet. My muscles spasm. I curl up on my side. My breath comes short and quick and my trembling makes every nerve of my body vibrate with pain. If Philip wasn't here, I could go away into my mind for a few minutes. But a small voice in my head, Janie's voice I think, reminds me that this would not be a good idea. Even for a few minutes. The spasm passes. I push myself painfully onto my back again. Take some deeper breaths like the doctor told me. Phil's hand is on my shoulder, his face creased with concern.

"I'm OK. . . I'm OK," I say. I try to pull myself together. He checks the timer.

"Couldn't they . . . There's only around twenty minutes to go. I could ask the doctors to give you the dose early."

"That would just fucking send me back to square one." I don't want to snap at him like that but all of my bones and muscles ache. Not just the ribs, but the pain there is especially excruciating. This was a mistake. We should have timed the visit better. Nineteen minutes.

"I have something for you," Philip says after a moment. "It's a get-well card, from everyone at the school. It's made of real fiber. There's a hand-written message from each of us." Philip holds the card up for me to see. It's covered in hand-writing.

"Can I hold it?" He hands it to me. "You must have spent a fortune on this."

"It's no big deal. The hard part was finding everyone to sign, with school out."

I look through what's been written. "Where's your message, Phil?"

"Down here," he points. "It's in Spanish. Wouldn't want you to get rusty."

I read: "El pueblo unido jamás será vencido." The people united will never be defeated. Beside the message is a pen drawing of two fists touching inside a heart. It's hard not to smile.

I read through some of the other messages. It suddenly hits me that I'll probably never see any of these people again. Not even Erin. Especially not Erin. I take a deep, shuddering breath as another crushing wave of pain goes through my body. I drop the card. I don't see how I can even take it with me. It's too big. My eyes fill with tears. I don't let them spill. I try to fill my lungs with more air but it hurts too much.

"Can I do anything for you, mi broki?" he asks me gently. He's placed the card on the table by my bed. Now his hand is suspended over my shoulder, like he's afraid to touch me.

"You have your knife, maybe?" I suck in some more air. "We could rub it across my throat a few times. . ." I press my fists against my eyes, waiting for the pain to pass.

Philip doesn't answer. After a few minutes, the wave recedes again. I take my fists away. Philip's looking straight at me, unsmiling.

"Don't talk like that," he says.

I swallow. "I don't with the doctor. Or with Janie. It would hurt her too much."

"I'm glad you feel that you can joke about killing yourself in front of me." Philip's voice is intentionally bland, but there's an edge of anger too. I think I've hurt him.

"I'm sorry, Phil. I'm really sorry."

"It's OK." He stands up and walks to the door, peers outside, then comes back and sits. "Look, say what you need to, get it out. Whatever you want to use me for. I mean it. If I can do something for you that your doctor and Janie can't, well, that's why I'm here."

I feel ashamed. Philip looks at the timer again. I won't look this time.

"Listen, Laek, it's not that much longer. Maybe you can take my hand, squeeze hard when the pain is bad. I know that probably sounds kind of useless. But you could squeeze very, very hard. You won't hurt me and maybe it could help you bear it a little."

In answer, I reach for his hand, squeeze with all my strength. I watch his face. He doesn't flinch, though the way I'm gripping his hand can't be comfortable. I couldn't do this with Janie.

"Squeeze back," I tell him. "Just like I'm doing. Give back what you're getting." He does, and it pulls me out of the rest of my body. I concentrate on our hands, back and forth, back and forth, like a forceful message. We do this for a while, not speaking. I lose track of time, trying to live inside the rhythm of it. After a while, I look over at the timer and see the digit has turned to zero. A rush of warm pleasure courses through my veins. I let my breath out slowly, my body heavy with relief.

"Thank you. Next time. . . Next time you visit it'll be better. I'll even save you my lunch. I can't hold it down, but I'm told it's good quality for hospital food."

Philip gives me a small smile, but his face is tight with suppressed emotion. "If you really want to thank me, you'll give me the name of the pendejo who did this to you. Then I'll find a use for my knife."

My pulse races. His anger seems barely under control. It warms me. And terrifies me.

"No. Please, don't even think about it. Promise me."

After a moment's hesitation, he says, "As you wish." This retreat into formality is reassuring. When Philip's angry, it's his way of signaling capitulation.

I'm sleepy now. With the morphine in my system, I might be able to doze off. Philip must sense this because he asks me if I want to close my eyes, try to take a nap.

"Yeah, maybe. You probably need to go, anyway."

"No, I don't have anywhere I have to be. I'm just taking Kyla to the park after this. She's having a great time downstairs playing with Simon."

"Simon? How is he?"

"Oh, he's fine. You'll see him yourself soon, don't worry. . . Listen, Laek, I have an idea. I could tell you a story—to help you fall asleep. I'm getting pretty good at that, with Kyla. I know, a story about my love life. That'll definitely put you right to sleep."

I laugh a little. It's worth the twinge in my ribs to laugh with him. "Sure, I'd like to hear what's going on with you. Gone out with anyone new lately?"

"I had a date this weekend. Just wait, I'll tell you about the whole evening and your eyes will be closing before you know it."

Already, my eyelids are heavy, even though I'm very interested in hearing about Phil's date. I struggle to stay awake, at least for a few minutes, but there's something about his voice, steady and familiar, that relaxes me as the morphine fully takes hold. I listen to him speaking, try to concentrate on the words, but they take flight in my mind. I'm losing the train of events. . .

He's stopped talking now. I don't remember when the story ended. I feel him take my hand and I watch, eyelids drooping, as he leans down over me. My eyes are already closed when I feel his lips gently brush my own.

CHAPTER 19
JANIE

The family waiting area of the hospital was obviously not built with pacing in mind. I push past a row of chairs affixed to the floor and around a pile of dingy plastic toys. Where is Philip already? We'd agreed to half an hour max for the visit, but he's been up there now for at least fifty minutes. I thought he'd understood how important it was not to tire Laek out. Physically, Laek's not ready for visitors, but the doctor and I agreed that it was something he could benefit from psychologically. With Laek, the psychological trumps the physical.

Finally, I see Philip coming around the corner.

"You've been up there nearly an hour. I thought we said. . ."

"He was asleep most of the time. I was just sitting with him. At least, after the first twenty-four minutes or so."

"Twenty-four minutes?" I ask.

Now Philip's a few paces away from me, looking around the waiting area for Kyla, who's playing hide-and-seek with Simon. Close up, I can see how red Philip's eyes are and that he's been crying. My anger drains out of me.

"It's OK. He's doing so much better now," I tell him.

I'd hoped this would cheer him up, but instead it makes him

start crying all over again. I put my arms around him, feeling inadequate to the task, with my head barely reaching his chest.

"How could we have come so close to losing him?" Philip sobs. "You poor thing, what you've been through. And dealing with it all alone."

I lead Philip to some chairs where we can keep an eye on the kids. What I'm thinking is how we can be leaving friends like this, and without even a word of warning or explanation. But no, all my needs, all my hopes, everything has shrunken to a tiny little point. Laek: alive, safe, well. Together with the kids. Period. Anything beyond that is a luxury I can't afford to think about. Even friends. I'm done being greedy, with taking anything for granted. And true friends will understand why we had to keep our plans a secret.

Philip is wiping his eyes roughly with the heels of his hands. I give him a tissue.

"Can I visit again?" he asks. I'm not sure what to say. It will be increasingly difficult to hide our plans from Philip, the more we see of him. I stall.

"How did the visit go? How did he seem to you?"

"It was hard, I won't lie. He doesn't like other people to see him hurting."

"No, he doesn't," I say.

"But I think he was glad to see me. He shouldn't be allowed to feel too alone. You know how he is. It's not good for him."

And suddenly I can't do it. As much as I fear for Laek, I just keep picturing Philip when he learns we've left without even a good-bye. Because the thing is, when I look into Philip's eyes, red from crying, from the pain of seeing Laek suffer, it's like a mirror. It's one of those things that once you see it, you wonder how you could have missed it before. Their physical closeness, the emotional intimacy—even for best friends, I'd known it was unusual. And the way Philip's eyes always track Laek's movements. . . I'd taken that as a kind of brotherly protectiveness. But now other pieces fall into place as I realize that Philip loves Laek exactly the way I love Laek, and this realization crumbles any remaining resolve I have to keep our plans secret from him.

"Listen. There's something I need to tell you. . ."

As I explain, in carefully coded phrases, what we're planning to do and why, including what Laek thinks he saw on the newsfeed in the hospital, I watch Philip struggle not to cry again and my respect for him grows, because crying now would be for himself, not for Laek. Instead he swallows a lot and nods his head, even smiles slightly when I tell him the plan is to cross the border by bicycle.

"You're doing the right thing, Janie. Finding somewhere safe is what's most important."

"It might not be safe."

"If Laek's looked into this like you say he has. . . He's very sharp about politics. I'm not saying there isn't a risk, but. . . Look, most people stay on the path they're already on, even when it's a bad one. What you two are doing is smart and brave, and I'm proud to know you. I wish. . . I kind of wish I could join you there."

"You know you'd always be welcome. You're like family. We could raise our kids together." I look over at Simon chasing Kyla, then running ahead to make sure she doesn't get too far away. He seems more mature lately.

"Yeah, a tempting idea, only one little problem," Philip says, looking at the kids too. "Dana would never go along with me taking Kyla across the border."

I can't say I blame her. Especially with all the concerns about international travel these days. Suddenly I feel my own fears returning.

"Philip, aside from my friend Magda, you're the only one who knows about this."

"Thank you for trusting me. It means a lot. It would have been very. . . hard, not knowing this ahead of time."

"I understand."

I meet his eye and nod. He looks at me carefully, chewing on his lip, maybe wondering how much I do understand. After a moment, he breaks eye contact.

"Janie, can I keep visiting Laek in the meantime, even though it might be difficult for me to hide what I know? If he figures it out, will that make him nervous?"

"No, it's OK, he wanted to tell you. It's me who resisted. He trusts you completely."

"Good. Good. I'm glad to hear that."

"I should be getting back upstairs," I say. "I don't want to leave him too long."

We stand up, walk towards the middle of the room. Just then, Kyla comes flying into the back of Philip's legs from behind, giggling.

"Safe! Safe!" she cries, as Simon pretends to lunge at her.

"I think it's time to take you to the park." Philip lifts Kyla up and flies her around his head as she giggles in delight. Simon is watching with a sad, dreamy smile. Philip looks down at Simon and then at me, lifting his eyebrows. I shrug.

"Simon, would you like to come to the park with us?" Philip asks.

"Can I, Mommy?"

"Sure. I'll ask Henry's mom to pick you up later."

"OK, let's go, kids. I'll call you, Janie."

I watch Philip as he leans over and scoops Simon up in his free arm. Simon relaxes in Philip's hold, leaning his head against his shoulder. Yes, I did the right thing.

CHAPTER 20
LAEK

I wake up feeling rested for the first time in a long while. I take a deep breath. Stretch my arms over my head. It hurts but it's nothing I can't handle. It's time to be out of this place. Before that cop traces us here. Despite the false electronic trail that Dr. Metcalfe laid in the medical records. Leaving here means finishing with the drugs. Having a whole conversation about this isn't something I feel up to, so I simply pull the micro-infuser from my arm. Toss it to the floor. The machine beeps softly in inquiry. Then turns itself off.

Janie's waking up in the chair next to my bed. Maybe it's from the sound of the machine. Or maybe it's just this sixth sense she has that tells her I'm awake. She looks exhausted.

"How you doing, baby?" she asks, still yawning.

"Better. Hand me that hairbrush and come up here. I want to brush your hair."

"I look that bad, huh?"

"You look great. I just need to do something with my hands."

"You sure it's OK? I mean, won't it hurt?"

"I'll be careful with the tangles," I tease her. "Come on, don't make me beg you."

Janie climbs into bed carefully. I brush her hair. She seems to be enjoying it. But she's holding herself stiffly erect. Like she's worried about leaning back and hurting me.

"It's OK," I say softly into her ear. "Relax. I won't break, I promise."

I put the brush down and wrap my arms around her. Kiss her ear. She's shaking a little. I think she may be crying. I kiss her neck and gently pull her back against me. I nuzzle her, rub her nipples with my fingertips, feel myself get hard. "You see? I didn't break. Got harder, in fact."

Janie turns around to kiss me on the lips. "You know you're crazy."

Just then Dr. Metcalfe comes in. Janie slips off the bed, blushing but happy. The doctor looks pointedly at the infuser lying on the floor. I shrug and give him my best smile. He picks it up, checking the monitors.

"So how are you feeling this morning, Laek?"

"Better. I want to talk about going home."

He asks my permission before reaching over to examine my ribs, a courtesy I appreciate. Dr. Metcalfe not only saved my life but has been unfailingly kind to both me and Janie. So I don't understand why, when he places his hands lightly against my upper ribs, I suddenly feel so scared that I'm sick to my stomach.

I close my eyes. Concentrate on my breathing. There's a belief that some people can lay their hands on you and heal you. I visualize this, Dr. Metcalfe's hands on my rib cage, a cool blue light coming from his fingertips and knitting my bones together. And I do feel good now. My breath has slowed. I'm relaxed. I let myself feel his calloused fingertips on my skin, imagine I can smell the faint tobacco scent that's always there, from a smoking habit he tries to hide.

I suddenly realize he's been saying my name, gently but insistently.

"I'm here," I answer.

"Laek, stay with us now. I need you to open your eyes.

Otherwise, I'm not going to be able to complete this examination.

"OK." I open my eyes. The doctor's giving me a concerned look. "I'm fine."

"I was asking you to tell me when it hurt."

"I guess it didn't hurt. I feel good."

"Laek, can you tell me how many of your ribs I've checked?" He waits. "Or how long the examination has lasted so far?"

"Um. . . I'm not sure." I glance at the doctor for a clue and then at Janie. Janie's looking grim in her chair in the corner of the room.

"I'm sorry. I was just. . . thinking about something. I must have lost track of. . . of things. Let's try it again." I lift my arms and try to put them behind my head, but I'm shaking so badly I can't manage to lace my fingers together.

Janie jumps out of her chair and puts her arms around me. "Shh, it's OK, you can put your hands down."

I hold her. I'm fine again. "I'm sorry. I don't know what's the matter with me," I say.

"It's OK, Laek. Let's try this another way," Dr. Metcalfe replies.

The doctor helps me to a chair and instructs Janie to stand behind it and hold my arms up for me. With my hands in Janie's, it's easier to stay present. Still, the examination is more grueling than I'd expected. By the end, I'm sweating and shaky and short of temper. But when the doctor asks me how I'm doing, I tell him "fine." He then asks if I want to walk around a little. I'm eager to do anything that brings me one step closer to discharge.

We walk into the corridor and down the hall. I'm shocked at how weak I feel. How shaky and stiff. I don't want to admit how relieved I am to get back. The doctor suggests I sit in the chair instead of getting back into bed. I'm grateful for this. Even though I'm almost shaking with exhaustion, being in the chair instead of the bed makes me feel less defeated.

"I'm very pleased with the progress you've made over the past couple of weeks."

I smile. Maybe he'll send me home.

"But you need to understand that you've been through a lot. It's important not to push yourself too hard, to have unreasonable expectations."

"I'm not. I. . . I won't."

"It's not only your physical injury. When a person is injured as the result of any trauma, it's difficult enough. But when the injury is the result of an act of violence. . ."

My heart races as his words bring it all flooding back. I remember the shocking impact of the p-stick, the sick sound of my bones crunching, the taste of blood in my throat, and even before the excruciating pain, the terrible sense of wrongness in my body. I try to shake it off.

"How much do you know about post-traumatic stress disorder?" Dr. Metcalfe asks.

I shrug. Look out the window. Imagine being outside.

"Extreme anger, panic attacks," he begins. "If left untreated, things can get much worse. There can be memory loss, insomnia, anxiety, depression, even suicidal thoughts."

Janie squeezes my hand hard, but I concentrate on feeling nothing.

"And it can be worse for someone who may have experienced trauma in the past."

I look at him at this point, and then at Janie, wondering what he knows. He seems to have read my thoughts because he says: "I promise you, Janie has told me nothing about your past. But as you probably realize, your medical history is full of holes. That alone tells me something. Laek, the first step in treating the problem is acknowledging it."

He pauses again, waiting for me to reply, but I have nothing to say. He sighs. "I'll give Janie some references. For when you're ready. I understand that it's all a bit much right now."

"If there's more, say it now. I don't want to have this conversation twice."

"Alright. That thing you do, the way you can disappear inside yourself. I can see it's been an important survival mechanism for you. But I want you to understand that it's. . . It's really very scary. You may think you can control it, but—"

"Yeah, OK." If he's not going to let me go home, I just want him to leave now. I can't think about all this. Simply sitting has become a trial. I put my face in my hands. I know I should thank him or something. I pull my hands away. "Look, I appreciate everything you've done. But I just want to go home. I need to see my kids." I hear my voice catch because what I really need is to get my kids somewhere safe.

"Laek," he says gently. "I don't want you to feel you're a prisoner here. If you continue to improve, I won't try to talk you out of discharging yourself in a few days. But you'll still need lots of rest and care. Maybe when you're well, you could take a little vacation."

"That's exactly what we're planning," Janie says. "Next month, we're going up to Vermont to pick up Siri from camp and then we're off on a trip, all four of us."

"A change of scenery, a little adventure, that'll be just the thing," the doctor says.

As the two of them chat about traveling, I return to my earlier thoughts about natural healers. People can heal with words too. Because now I'm feeling lighter as I reframe our flight in terms of change and adventure. I'm also reminded that there are still so many good people in the world. People like Peter Metcalfe.

"Peter," I say, calling him by his first name like he's been asking. "I want to thank you for all you've done. I'll try to follow all your recommendations. Janie will give me those references. And when we're on our trip, we'll send you a real paper postcard." I put out my hand.

"I'd like that," he responds, clasping it in his own.

Two days later, as promised, we're on our way home.

CHAPTER 21
SIMON

've decided to kill the cop who hurt Daddy. After I broke Keri's nose, I'd decided not to, but I changed my mind today, when we finally took Daddy home. I'd visited Daddy in the hospital, so I knew how skinny he'd gotten and how tired he looked. But in the hospital, I couldn't see how much it hurt him to do normal stuff like yawn or cough. And the way Daddy looked around, real fast, when he got outside. It was like I used to do at school when I was scared of Keri. At Henry's, when I was imagining this day, I pictured jumping into Daddy's arms and him lifting me high into the sky. In real life, Daddy didn't try to lift me up. Instead, he hugged me softly. I left my arms sticking out, scared to hug him back.

I haven't figured out how to do it yet. I think maybe hacking into the police database or something would work. Then I could see which cops were with Daddy at the demo. After that, I could cross-examine them, like Mommy does. Henry says it don't matter anyways which cop I kill 'cause they're all guilty. One of theirs for one of ours. That's what Henry says. Especially if I narrow it down to who was at Battery Park. I saw the newsfeeds and the cops were all hitting and kicking and doing mean things.

Still, I don't know. I want to find the one who *actually* done it. I think it's important to be exact about stuff.

Daddy had said we'd play a game when we got home. But now Mommy says no. She says Daddy has to take a nap instead. I was hoping Daddy would argue but instead he asks if I want to nap with him. I'm too old for taking naps but Mommy says she'll lay down with us and tell a story. That settles it. I lay down between Mommy and Daddy, at least to listen to the story.

Mommy tells us about the Bicycling Family. There's something different about it, though. Like it's more real or something. Daddy's smiling, with me snuggled next to him. His eyes keep closing and opening again. He looks less bad lying down, just tired. I'm almost falling asleep too when I hear Mommy ask me something.

"What'd you say?" I ask.

"Do you think you'd like to go on a real Bicycling Family adventure?"

"For real?"

"Yes, for real."

"Where to?"

"Well, first you'll visit Grandma and Grandpa and then we'll take the train to Siri's camp. When we're all together, we'll continue north."

"Where exactly?"

"Daddy will have to show you on the map. He's in charge of the route."

"Like Ocean in the Bicycling Family." I look at Daddy. His eyes are open, watching me.

"Yes, like Ocean," Daddy says. "Do you want me to show you on a map, Simon?"

"Yes, please!"

"OK, but not now," Mommy says. "Daddy needs to sleep. We'll talk about it more later."

"Are we really for real going to go?" I ask.

"Do you want to, Simon? Do you like this idea?" Daddy asks me.

"Oh yes, oh yes!" It's like a dream come true.

Daddy smiles a big smile and suddenly he doesn't look so hurt anymore. "Good. Then I guess that's settled."

Daddy turns on his side carefully, putting his arm around me. Even though I didn't mean to, I end up falling asleep too. When I wake up, Mommy's on the other side of me. She puts her fingers to her lips and makes a motion to follow her. We go into the kitchen.

"Do you want to help me make some cookies for Daddy?" she asks.

"Yes! Can I lick the batter?"

"Sure, if you really help, you can."

Daddy comes out of the bedroom as the cookies are coming out of the oven. He's not wearing a shirt so I look to see if there are any broken parts of him showing. He looks pretty normal. Even though he's skinnier, he still has his muscles and stuff. He rubs his tummy.

"You sure you slept enough, Laek? You know what the doctor said."

"How can I sleep with those delicious smells floating into the bedroom?"

"Well, if you want any of these cookies that Simon and I made, put a shirt on. You could catch a chill that way."

"Janie, it's gotta be ninety degrees in this apartment, especially with the oven on."

Mommy just looks at him so he goes back into the bedroom and comes out wearing his old red Occupy t-shirt. If it were me, I would even put on a sweater if it meant Mommy wouldn't let me have cookies otherwise.

Daddy and I each have four cookies and a huge glass of oat milk.

"You have a milk mustache, Simon," he tells me.

"You have a real mustache, Daddy."

"That reminds me, Laek. I need to give you a haircut and a shave. Are you ready?"

"Yeah, I guess."

During the haircut, I get bored. "I thought we were going to play a game," I say.

"We are. We're playing barbershop," Mommy says.

"You and Daddy are maybe. I'm not playing anything. I want a haircut like Daddy's."

"OK, monsieur," Mommy says to me. "You're next."

"Missyer?"

"It's French, Simon," Daddy says. "That's what they speak in Quebec."

"But what does it mean?"

"Mister, or sir. It's like señor in Spanish."

After Mommy cuts my hair, me and Daddy look at ourselves in the mirror. We look alike. He looks younger than before and I look older. And he looks less messed-up than before too.

"Ready for a game?' Daddy asks me.

"Yes!"

"What'll it be? Geography? Prism? Class War? Chess? Analogue?"

"Scrabble!" I tell him.

After Scrabble, we eat dinner and watch a screen show about animals of the north. I'm so happy that Daddy is finally home, and now there's our adventure to think about.

"Hey, when are we leaving on our bike trip, Daddy?"

"In two weeks."

I wonder if this will be enough time for me to find and kill that cop. Probably not. I guess I can do it when we get back. It's not like it's an emergency or anything, with Daddy finally getting better. Yeah, it can wait till we get back.

CHAPTER 22
LAEK

"Get your sorry ass over here and taste this chili," I say to Philip as soon as he walks into the apartment. I'm wearing a white t-shirt with the sleeves cut off, an apron over it. Nothing like bubbling tomato sauce to make it look like there's been a massacre in the kitchen.

Philip comes over. I shove the spoon into his mouth.

"Whoa, hot!"

"I blew on it."

"Not that kind of hot—spicy."

"You like it?"

"Sure. I love food with a kick. Speaking of which, I brought you two something."

"Something recycled?" Janie asks, taking the scratched, thick-glassed bottle from him.

"You could say that. It's home brew. Is it OK for ...?" He indicates me with his chin, speaking directly to Janie like I can't be trusted to decide for myself.

"For fuck's sake, I can have a little drink. Look at you two mother hens." I stir the chili and add more dried red chili pepper when they're not looking.

Janie takes three small glasses down from the shelf. Philip

pours about an inch of clear liquid with a slight yellow tint into each of them. I down mine.

"What is it, urine?" I say.

Janie chokes, holding in a laugh.

"Well, I'll just bring it back home if you don't like it," Philip says.

"Oh no you don't." I grab the bottle and refill our glasses.

"Nice haircut." Philip musses my hair.

Janie answers. "Thanks, Philip, I cut it myself."

"Oh yeah? A woman of many talents."

"It makes me look about twelve years old," I complain.

"An innocent look is not the worst thing when you're trying to cross a national border." Philip punctuates this statement by swallowing down his second glass like medicine. The conversation stops dead in its tracks.

"Listen, I can finish up in the kitchen while you two hang out," Janie offers. "Why don't you go into the bedroom where you can have some privacy?"

"What are we eating?" Philip asks, lifting up pot lids.

"Aside from Laek's chili, there'll be collards, rice and peas, sweet potato soup, even homemade cornbread."

"That sounds amazing." Phil sneaks another taste of chili. "Whoa! Still adding spices?"

I pick up the spoon and mix some more.

"Gimme that." Janie takes the spoon out of my hand. Reaches around my waist to untie the apron. I kiss her while her hands are busy, trying to undo the knot.

"Why did you knot this instead of tying it in a bow?"

"So I could mess with you while you were busy with the knot." I try to bite her.

She turns me around and gets it untied. Then smacks me on the ass with it.

"Go. Out of the kitchen."

I walk into the bedroom. Philip follows me. I close the door behind him.

"Make yourself comfortable. I'm gonna stand. All those weeks laid up in bed. . ."

"I'll stand too, then."

Philip leans against the wall by the bedroom door. I walk to the window on the opposite wall. "Thanks for visiting me in the hospital. I know it wasn't much fun. But it made a big difference. I felt like I was going crazy in there sometimes."

"No problem. But how are you doing now?"

"Good. Fine. I mean, I'm still sore, but getting better every day."

"How about the other stuff? Anxiety? Um, depression?"

"No, I'm fine."

"Insomnia? Panic attacks?"

"How about rage? Like if you don't stop asking me these questions, I'll strangle you."

"Sorry. Just checking."

"I don't mean to give you a hard time. I'll admit I still get nightmares, but I'm fine."

"OK, good."

"So Phil, I guess you've been in touch with Erin."

"She asks about you all the time."

"What do you tell her?"

"That it's been a hard recovery but that you're doing better now. Of course she wonders why you don't call and why she can't see you."

"How much does she know about what happened?" I ask.

"Enough to tell me that she wouldn't bring Chris. But of course, Chris tried to help."

"I know, but somehow that only complicates things. Especially since I didn't. . . I couldn't take his warning. It's hard to explain."

"Erin might understand if you gave her a chance."

"She might, but I still couldn't tell her about our plans."

"No, I can see that," Philip concedes.

"I don't want to have to hide things from her. I don't have the strength right now. It's just about killing me that I can't say good-bye to my friends. You're the only one who knows. You and Janie's friend Magda. I guess you'll have to stand in for everyone. Think you can handle that?"

"Sure. The thing that's hard to handle. . ." Philip chews on his lip, looks down. "Just the thought of going back to school in the fall without you there. Listen, Laek, I need to tell you. . ."

"No you don't. You don't need to tell me anything."

"I think I do. Really."

"You don't. Trust me." I walk towards him.

"But. . ."

"How's this," I say. "A bet. If I can show you I understand, you have to promise to come to Montreal with Kyla. But if I'm wrong, then I have to come back to New York and visit you."

"Come back to New York? Are you crazy? How could you even consider that! I mean. . ."

I push him hard against the wall. Start kissing him. I keep it going for a good, long while, sliding my hands under his shirt and pulling him in close. It's not until he's shaking so badly that I feel sorry for him that I finally let go. I reach over and trace his upper lip with my index finger.

"I win," I say, smiling triumphantly.

"Yeah." His face seems flushed and he's breathing hard. I think he's still trembling. "Yeah, you absolutely win. But listen, Laek, do me a favor. Don't talk right now. Maybe. . . uh. . . go over there, to the other side of the room. I need to sit down for a few minutes."

"Whatever you say." I walk to the bed, but can't keep myself from laughing. The look on his face! I haven't had this much fun in a while. And I don't think I've ever won a bet so easily.

"Por favor, Laek. Shh! Have pity."

"OK, OK." I pick up Janie's screen. Open up the French learning program she loaded for me. Put the earpiece in. I've already reached a conversational level of French from the studying

I did in the hospital. Right now, I don't have the head for thinking about words or grammar. I close my eyes. Absorb the sound and rhythm of the language, the regional accent. The rises and falls remind me of mountains. The smooth liaisons of streams. It makes me think of our bike trip to Quebec. The thought is bittersweet.

After about five minutes have passed, I look over at Philip. He's sitting on the floor, his back to the wall. He seems calmer and his face has returned to its normal color.

"Can I come back now?" I ask.

"Yeah."

I sit down beside him on the floor. He turns to me.

"I'll find a way to come to Montreal even if I have to kidnap my own child."

"There must be another way to come over with Kyla. You'll think of something. Ask Janie to help if there's legal stuff."

"Janie?"

"Yeah, Janie. You remember her. My partner? The lawyer? The one who said, 'Why don't you guys go into the bedroom where you can have some privacy?' That Janie."

"Yes, understood. Absolutely."

"Listen, don't worry about all that right now. Just be here with me."

"OK." Phil puts his arm around my shoulder. I lean into him and he tries to pull me closer. I change position so I'm sitting with my back in front of him. He wraps the hand that was resting on my shoulder gently around my chest.

"Am I hurting you?"

"No. Hold me tighter."

He pulls me in closer as I lean back against him. I'm struggling to take my own advice. To not think about anything but the present moment. But my mind is flying backwards, remembering the night of the prom. I see myself standing under the night sky, leaning against Philip, and later, talking with him and Erin with my arms around their shoulders. Then I see Al and relive the whole stream of violent events that led up to and then flowed from that night.

"Tighter," I say. I'm thinking of next fall now. Of my school and Philip and Erin and all my other friends, going about their lives without me. What will I be doing? A refugee, maybe in hiding. No job, an uncertain future. How can I be dragging my family into this, uprooting them from their home? And Siri, at camp, innocent of everything that's happened this summer.

"Tighter. As tight as you can and don't let go."

He wraps both of his arms around me, enfolding me in his strong embrace. I'm conscious of his fingers on the bare skin of my shoulders, his forearm across my chest, my back snug against him. I close my eyes, fixing myself firmly to these physical sensations, past and future slipping away from my thoughts. I relax into that one continuous present moment: now, and now, and now. Nothing exists but the tightness of his grip, the warmth of him against my back. We stay this way, without moving or talking, for a timeless interval . . .

Janie calls us to supper. Philip presses his face gently against mine. Then releases me. We stand. Time starts moving forward again. I can tell from the bleak look on his face that Philip feels as I do. Yeah, this was good-bye. The rest of the evening will be a drawn-out process of moving away from each other. I feel the sadness expand up into my throat, but I don't cry.

I don't cry at supper either, as I watch Philip swallow his favorite foods like they were broken glass. And I don't cry after he's washed and dried every single one of our dishes, pots and pans. Even when I see him biting his lower lip like he does when he's upset, looking desolate as he searches the kitchen for something else he can wash, just to prolong his time with us. I don't even cry at the door when we cling to each other and I feel his hot, silent tears and the way he's trembling, not with pleasure this time but with pain.

It's when my face is pressed to the window glass, watching Philip disappear around the corner, that Janie starts crying, and this is what finally makes me let loose my own tears. I cry so long and so hard that I have to lie down on my side, holding my ribs against the racking pain. But it's nothing to the pain in my heart.

———

In the morning, I do a quick survey of my physical and mental state. Like I've done every morning since the day in the hospital when I decided I wanted to live. My ribs aren't any worse, despite my long crying jag. I feel rested. I'm not particularly anxious or depressed. I slip out of Janie's arms and out of bed. Re-cover her with the sheet. I stand by the window in the living room. The sun is rising.

I feel a cautious optimism this morning. I carefully let myself think of the friends we're leaving. Remember different moments with each of them. Some of this makes me smile.

As the sun begins to light the streets of Brooklyn, I'm thinking of the kids. My heart lifts when I remember Simon's excitement in the bicycling adventure we've planned, Siri's pride and pleasure when she learned we'll all be there for the end-of-summer game at her camp. I can see a sunny path stretched out before us, our bikes rolling down it, our shadows weaving and playing with each other. And Janie at my side, full of life and love, beautiful and clever and good.

Then I think about leaving Philip, like a tongue searching out a sore tooth. What comes to mind is his solidity and strength. The calm determination on his face when he made his promise. The depth of his love and courage. Whatever ends up happening, it will be alright somehow. I find I actually believe this.

CHAPTER 23
JANIE

Our last night in Brooklyn, I'm prowling from room to room, checking that everything's in order and reviewing our plans for the umpteenth time. Our bags are all packed—two overstuffed panniers for each of us, mostly containing clothes, with the extra pair of sandals, multi-purpose jacket, and rain gear on top. The sleeping bags I just bought, expensive but worth it for their lightness and durability, can be fastened to our racks. Despite his injury, Laek will carry the heaviest load—both tents as well as an assortment of tools, bike parts, and other items, in case of a breakdown on the road. As for me, I carry what's needed to prevent human breakdown— first-aid supplies, including emergency medication for Laek, extra sun block, snacks, chocolate, and energy drinks to supplement our water bottles. And my ukulele.

We'll take the train to Albany where Simon's waiting for us, visiting with my parents, and from there, another train to Siri's camp. For once, I'm grateful that Mom and Dad have a big car, able to take Simon's bike, four of the stuffed panniers, and all the kids' extra clothes. Simon didn't even notice I'd emptied their drawers, excited by the trip, but bored by laundry and packing. My parents will have to make a few trips to collect the rest of our things and store them in their house. Later, if all goes well, maybe they'll be able to gradually send certain items across the border.

Much will have to be left, of course. Hopefully, some of the larger items of furniture can be sold. Magda agreed to handle this. I've written out detailed instructions to both her and my parents, with real pen on paper, like in some cloak-and-dagger drama. I find myself talking and writing in thinly disguised code and euphemisms, referring to our "grand adventure," the "delivery of packages," "crossing the line," "green mountain country" and, of course, "New Metropolis." I feel cool and calculating, clear-headed and methodical, and deeply superstitious, all at once.

The apartment, without the kids and with everything packed, seems unnaturally neat and quiet. It's like we're already gone and I'm a ghost, haunting my own home as I pass our now-empty walls, drawers, and cabinets. The fact that Laek and I are still here fills me with a preternatural dread. I imagine someone coming for us during the night and dragging us away by our throats—maybe a federal cop or maybe our own ghosts.

I wander into the bedroom, the only room with some life in it. Laek is doing his pilates exercises. He's been at it for almost an hour. I lean against the wall and watch him, trying to calm myself. His movements are fluid and graceful, filled with energy and intention. He climbs onto the bed and drops to his hands and knees, arching his back and breathing deeply.

Whatever position he puts his body into, it's gorgeous. He lets me watch without missing a beat. This total lack of self-consciousness, it's one of the things that gives him that aura of childlike innocence. Or masculine self-confidence. One or the other. All I know is that watching him makes my heart beat strongly and quickens my breath. There's nothing more I can think of that needs doing. I get undressed.

He's resting now, kneeling in the middle of the bed, hands on thighs, eyes closed. He almost looks like he's praying. I fold my clothes and pack them away quickly, then climb up onto the bed and face him, my knees touching his. He opens his eyes.

"All done?" I ask.

"Yeah. Just waiting for you."

"How'd it go this time? You were careful not to overdo it?"

"It was fine. It's just. . . I'd hoped to be back to my full strength by now. You know, for the trip. I feel pretty good, but I still tire more quickly."

"Maybe it's not such a bad thing for you to see what it's like to actually have a limit to your energy, or to need eight hours of sleep a night, like the rest of the world. As for the trip, look at it this way: I won't have to feel so guilty all the time, like I'm holding you up, especially on those long climbs."

"Do I make you feel guilty, waiting for you on the tops of hills?"

"OK, maybe just inadequate. Now I'll tell myself I'm going slow for you, so you can rest waiting for me."

"Well right now I've waited long enough. Climb up here." He removes his underwear.

I do, mounting him in one swift motion and wrapping my arms around his shoulders. I still can't get past the idea that we're in a position of prayer, here in the middle of our bed. This bed, where years ago, I lay breast-feeding Siri. And where we conceived Simon. This bed, which will have to stay here in Brooklyn, too big for my parents to ever sneak across the border.

What is it that makes me feel so much like praying right now? I'm an atheist, but a non-practicing one, as I've often joked. Maybe I want to hedge my bets. I'll pray right here, on this bed, while I'm having sex. I think to myself: "If I believed in God, what would I pray for? And if I were that God, how would I bless this world?"

I feel Laek's arms around my waist and I hold him more tightly, the way I know he likes it. I feel his heart beating against me. Time holds its breath.

My thoughts are floating. I think back on our life here. It

doesn't distract me, not while my body is tightly connected to his. I try to visualize everything good we've struggled to do here, the individual gestures of kindness, the collective planning for social justice, the decisions we've made and stuck by, motivated by a desire to improve the world. I pray with all my heart that these acts be imbued with a force and a power all their own to bring good, however badly we failed in their execution, however mixed-up and confused were our ideas and intentions.

I also imagine everything I may have thought or done that was motivated by selfishness, by weakness, by bad faith. I pray that all of it be drained of power and forgotten, dissipating like a poorly created holo. And that we are pardoned. That our friends forgive us. And our children. Please forgive us. . . forgive me.

Laek rocks us slowly back and forth, my heart beating faster with his. I pray: Let all good intentions become actualized, incarnate in this world. May they all join together to have more power, more sway over the future. And let us continue to be a part of that, wherever we may be. I feel Laek inside me and squeeze him with all my strength, envisioning a spinning, glowing ball of hope and goodness grow huge and then explode, dripping down to fill the cracks in the world, the broken world of religious mysticism I've read about—a world that can only be healed by the good acts of living beings.

Laek's lips are pressed against my ear. I think I hear him say, "Amen".

BOOK TWO: CHANGING GEARS

Cycle tracks will abound in Utopia.

H.G. WELLS

CHAPTER 24
SIMON

t turns out I can see the borderline between the United America and Québec, even though it's supposed to be invisible. Daddy warned me not to expect it to be like on a map, where there's a thick black line between the two countries, but I didn't need Daddy to tell me that. I mean, all lines are invisible 'cause they only have one dimension—length. The thing you see on a map isn't a line at all but more like a long, very skinny rectangle.

If it wasn't for my super-powerful eyesight, I might've missed the invisible borderline. But there it is, sitting right between the Vermont pavement, which is darker, and the Québec pavement, which is lighter.

I wonder if crossing the border will change me—if, once I'm on the other side, I'll become different, like in a parallel universe. Maybe my bike will become even more powerful. I'm already going so fast that the rest of the family can hardly keep up with me.

The other thing I wonder is what the animals will be like on the other side. Can the animals sense the borderline somehow? Will they act different in Québec? Siri thinks I'm being stupid, that animals don't care about national boundaries and stuff. I know that. I'm not ignorant. But if people act different on the other side of the line, maybe that *influences* the animals or something.

Mommy says that we're all connected—people, animals, the earth, everything!

This is the greatest trip ever. We're on a real adventure, just like in a story, and anything can happen. I can't wait to meet the people and animals on the other side of the invisible line.

CHAPTER 25
SIRI

Mommy and Daddy are acting even weirder than usual. I noticed it the minute they got to my camp. Daddy's hyper-intense one minute and all spacey the next, and I keep catching Mommy watching me when she thinks I'm not looking. Plus they took my screen and won't let me use it without permission. I wonder if they know about me and Michael.

They're worried about something, that's for sure. I can always tell with the two of them, even though they do opposite things: Mommy can't stop talking and Daddy closes up completely, like a pistachio nut that you can't open with your fingernails. If you're hungry enough, you might bite down hard on it instead, but half time you end up with a mouthful of shells. So there's no way I'm gonna ask Daddy what's wrong. I could get it out of Mommy, though. She's terrible at keeping secrets. Anyway, I'm sure I'll figure it out myself eventually.

The bike ride has been pretty fun so far, even though Simon keeps trying to get ahead of everyone. Usually when we bike together, Daddy's in the lead, but this time, he seems to want to bike next to Mommy all the time. I thought that maybe he was still weak or something from his accident and being in the hospital and all, but then a few times he biked way ahead of everyone, very, very fast, and then all the way back. I guess he was scouting things out. Maybe he just doesn't want Mommy to feel like a slowpoke and that's why he mostly stays back with her.

Daddy's back from scouting again. He puts his hand up for us to stop.

"The border's ahead, around the bend. I need to pee."

He looks around, but there doesn't seem to be anywhere to go.

"Daddy, can't we wait until there's a rest stop or something? I gotta go too."

He doesn't answer. Doesn't he know that it's harder for me to pee in the middle of nowhere than it is for him? I can do it if I need to, but I'd rather wait for a real bathroom where I can sit on the toilet like a normal person and then wash my hands afterwards.

Daddy walks a little ways off and then stops and turns around in a circle, before walking most of the way back again. Is he going to pee right here, where everyone can see him? What's wrong with him?

"Daddy, are you OK?" I get off my bike.

"Stay with Simon, Siri," Mommy says, then walks over to him herself.

I turn around and look at Simon. He's staring up into the trees, like he's searching for birds or something. I look back at where Daddy and Mommy are and see the two of them kissing. I can tell that they're using their tongues. Even though there's still something disgusting about watching your parents kiss like that, I have to admit that the idea of tongue-kissing seems less gross now than it did at the beginning of the summer.

Daddy and Mommy come back to where Simon and I are. We get back on our bikes.

I'm excited about finally getting to the border. None of my friends have ever been in a different country. I crane my neck to try to see Québec. The border station has a building that looks just like a little white house with a surveillance window, but inside there's all this tech—big screens and mini-scanners and complicated controls. When I try to look past the house into the distance, the air looks all hazy and weird, like there's some kind of blurry barrier. Is it a distortion field or just the rain? It's been drizzling on and off, but now it seems like it might be stopping. How long will it take before they let us in?

This is getting hyper-boring, standing here in the middle of nowhere between two countries, especially since Daddy insists on speaking French, even though the border person can speak English. Blah, blah, blah, blah, blah. The woman who's the border person is very pretty and Daddy's giving her one of those smiles of his. Maybe he's feeling less worried now, or maybe his face just does those smiles automatically. Mommy doesn't seem to mind, though. She's even holding his hand. Maybe Daddy's nervous about the border crossing, though I don't know why. It's not like we're doing anything illegal, like smuggling stims or plotting terrorism or something.

CHAPTER 26
JANIE

The first thing I notice is that the border guard looks about twenty-two years old, max. I find myself staring at her hair, an unnatural shade of reddish-purple. Interesting, kind of. I must be nervous, paying attention to bullshit like hair. The important thing is that she seems nice, not suspicious or anally bureaucratic or power-crazy, although the niceness could simply be a way of catching us off guard.

Laek is standing there smiling and comfortably conversing with her in French. If you didn't know him like I do, you'd think he was enjoying himself, maybe even flirting. But there are certain telltale signs, something about the juxtaposition of his relaxed pose and warm smile with the hyper-alert look in his eyes and the way he's gripping the seat of his bike. I take his free hand and hold on tight.

I can't understand what she's saying. I thought I might be able to catch some of it, at least. There are similarities with Spanish, although if we're not talking about cucarachas and ratas or el pueblo unido, I'm pretty lost in Spanish too. I did study some French vocabulary in the hospital, but nothing sounds familiar. I try to listen more carefully but what I hear is something like

"Ooskavoo la la la ..." Yet, when Laek speaks, I can follow what he's saying a little bit. Is there some magic thing where you understand a foreign language better when it's spoken by your partner? I guess it's mostly the accent. I can tell that Laek's trying to mimic hers, but his vowels don't sound quite right—more like they're leaning in that direction.

I look around, noticing the flags. There are four of them. There's the Canadian flag with its innocuous maple leaf, making one think of forests rather than the rockets' red glare and bombs bursting in air. It's positioned highest of the four, but there's something that makes it seem less dominant. Maybe it's how thin and washed out it is compared to the blue and white one with the fleur-de-lys just below it. Or maybe it's the fact that the second flag is actually bigger even though it's lower down. There are two other flags nearby. I'm not sure what they represent. I ask the kids if they know.

"That's Canada and that's Québec." Simon says, pointing.

"Good job, Simon, but how about the one that has an 'H' inside a 'C'?"

Simon shrugs, but Siri smiles. "That's the hockey team. They're hyper. Too bad we're not here in the winter. We could see them play."

I don't say anything, but I dearly hope we'll be here in the winter. And that come winter, Siri will still feel this way.

Laek is looking over at me expectantly so I hand the woman Siri's screen, where I've beamed the eco-travel passes issued by the Québec government. I don't want to appear nervous, so I look over at the fourth flag. I concentrate on its image of a round globe, hands reaching across it to clasp one another in a symbol of international solidarity. This is the first time I've seen this flag somewhere other than at a demonstration, where it's usually a harbinger of increased police presence, as though the idea of abolishing borders were a direct threat to the State. Which, in a way, I suppose it is. Seeing the flag at this particular international border should be reassuring. Perhaps it's the irony of it, or perhaps just how it's associated in my memory with police violence and repression, but either way, the sight of this flag makes my heart race and my stomach clench. I'm not sure if its presence here is a good or bad sign.

CHAPTER 27
LAEK

At the border, I'm alert and in control. Janie comes over. Takes my hand. The woman at the border station is young. Very pretty. She says: "Bonjour/Hello?" I answer her the same way: "Bonjour. Hello." Smile broadly. She laughs. Asks me what language I would like to speak. I answer her in French and she seems hugely pleased by this.

There are fewer questions than I thought there'd be. Food, weapons, alcohol, drugs, smartech. I know all the vocabulary. Studied up on the usual inquiries at border crossings. I'm not thinking of what this conversation really means. I'm pretending it's one of my practice dialogues. A part of me, though, is sharply aware of what I'm actually doing here. That part of me is ready to jump in. To take over if necessary. Meanwhile, the Laek that's present in this conversation is paying attention to words, to grammar. A beautiful language. The woman sounds a lot like the voice on my learning program for Québecois French. Her voice is younger and warmer, though. And I can watch her lips and teeth and tongue as she makes the sounds. I'm in love with this language. I want to make my vowels sound like hers. I concentrate harder. She laughs. Asks me if I am understanding everything. Yes. Yes I am. Then she asks me if the purpose of our visit is business or pleasure. I think hard about pleasure. The pleasure of being on our bikes, of being free. Of being free from fear.

"I teach high school history in Brooklyn, in New York City. So definitely not business," I explain, laughing. She laughs with me. It's easy to make her laugh. But I don't let my guard down. I can see that she's also very sharp, very observant.

When she asks me about the length of our stay, I tell what grade each of our kids are in, and how school restarts after Labour Day. "But Québec doesn't celebrate Labour Day, does it? You have May Day, like in Europe, oui?" I ask.

"Très bien," she answers. "You have also done your studying."

I try for a grin which is pleased but also a little shy.

She finally asks for our travel docs. I turn to Janie. She catches on and hands Siri's screen to the woman. I let the student of French slip away. A tougher, colder me comes to the fore. My heartbeat quickens, but I keep my breathing slow and deep, my body relaxed, my brain clear and sharp. The woman scans the info. Waits. Her movements are deliberate, professional. She's staring at her screen as our images come up. And now stealing glances at each of us, one by one. When she looks at me, I smile again. Make sure the smile reaches my eyes, warms them, even though I feel like my heart is enveloped in ice. She finally speaks.

"C'est un mélange, je dirais."

"What's she saying?" Janie asks nervously. I don't answer, but I'm thinking: *Mélange* is mix. Mix up? Is she talking about my background data?

I force myself to stay calm. Maybe I can talk my way out of it. Maybe I should simply give myself up right now. Could I then make sure somehow that Janie and the kids get across?

"Your children," the woman responds and I feel like she's peered into my mind. But then she says: "I am looking to see of whom they resemble. Some of Maman, some of Papa, I would say. Beautiful children." She hands Siri's screen back to Janie.

"Thank you." Janie answers.

I swallow hard and hold myself very quiet.

Soon we're pedalling again, the children's first souvenirs—a holo sticker of a snowy owl riding a bicycle—adhering to their handlebars. Bienvenue, I think, my body weak with relief and gratitude.

For a long time, I just pedal. The kids' excited chatter is a warm background that's somehow very far from me. I'm feeling blank. I'm hoping it will pass. And not get worse. There's almost no one on the road. This is good. There are trees, sky, ground, dirt, insects, corn fields. I feel like I'm nowhere, but I know exactly where we are. I see a precise map of our location in my mind. I see us moving along our route. I shift my mind's eye upward and see the next few kilometres of the road. Up some more and I can see the town where I thought we'd stop. Higher still and I can see the border crossing behind us, Siri's camp in Vermont, Janie's folks' place in Albany. And behind all that, our lost home in Brooklyn. Far ahead I can see Montréal. I mean, I can see where it is on the map. But I can't see it. Not really. The people, the streets, the buildings, our lives. I just can't see it.

Panic pours through me. I'm shaking so badly I can't keep my bike straight. I stop. I feel like I need to do something, but I'm not sure what. Pee or shit or throw up or have sex or slit my throat. One of those things. The last one, I think. I try to push that thought away. I look around, desperate to fix onto something steady, something safe. I see the trees. Mumble to my family about needing to pee. I let go of my bike.

I walk into the woods. Get to a tree. Stop. I look back at Janie. She motions me further in. I walk more. See another tree. Stop. What am I doing here? Where am I going? My head is spinning, I can't think straight. Please, what have I done, what am I doing to my family? I'm sitting on the ground now. I steady myself against the tree with one hand. My other hand is in the dirt, digging a hole with my finger. I don't know where I am. I'm lost.

The next thing I know, Janie's beside me, holding me. I inhale her familiar scent, cupping her head in my palm. My fingers are in her hair, trying to hold on to reality. I'm still lost but no longer alone.

"It's OK, it's gonna be OK," she's saying.

"Oui, ça va aller," I hear myself reply. Janie looks at me in confusion. "Yeah, s'OK, I'm OK." I stand up with her.

"You sure?" She seems alarmed by my lapse into French.

"Yeah, it's passed. I'm fine."

Janie wraps her arms around my waist. "You were great at the border. I had no idea you'd become so fluent." She squeezes me tight, bringing me fully back into the world. When she tries to step back, I hold her against me. She pushes me away gently with her hand on my chest. "The kids are waiting. And if you speak more French to me later, in the tent, who knows?"

We walk over to where the kids are. Siri's looking worried, but Simon's in his own world.

"Hey, race you to the top of the hill!" I say.

I let the kids get a head start and wait while Janie struggles with her heavy, sturdy bicycle, a ton of luggage strapped on. I take off after her, standing to pedal hard towards the top of the hill. The sun's pushing aside some clouds to make its first appearance of the day. I see Simon in the lead, imagine him thinking "vroom, vroom, vroom" as he pulls out ahead. Siri's right behind, pedalling for all she's worth, "go, go, go, go," with her powerful, young legs and determined heart. And Janie, sweat darkening her curls, push, push, pushes up the hill, not even thinking of slowing down as I pump beside her. I'm careful not to get ahead.

Simon has made it to the top first and has stopped dead. He's staring up and out. Like he's transfixed. The rest of us stop too and then I see it. A double rainbow, stretched across the sky. Like the earth is a big, beautiful present that's being offered to us, gift wrapped and ready.

"Is it real?" Simon asks in a hushed voice.

"Of course it's real," Siri answers. "You think someone shot a giant holo into the sky or something?

"Hush," Janie says. "It's beautiful. I've never seen anything like it."

I drop my bike gently to the ground and join my family, standing behind Janie and pulling the three of them in close. I don't speak. I look from the background of sky, an almost unnaturally dark blue, to the perfection of the rainbow, to the brightening land, and back to the sky again. I have this sense that if I wasn't holding on to my family, I'd fly up into the air and my molecules would scatter everywhere.

CHAPTER 28
SIMON

One thing's for sure, there's less roadkill on the Québec side of the border. The first time we passed a dead animal in Vermont, I wanted to stop and bury it, but Mommy said no. Daddy looked sad and put his hand on my shoulder. I think he wanted to stop and bury the poor creature's body too. Today, I'm happy because there are alive animals all around—cows mostly, black and white or brown, just hanging out and chewing grass. I saw llamas too. I didn't know llamas lived in Québec. And there was a horse who raced me on my bike!

All of a sudden, I see something small and furry and orangey-brown. I hit my brakes.

"Hey, what the hell!" Siri yells at me. I turn around and see her bike skidded out sideways. "I could've smashed right into you!"

"What's going on?" Mommy's caught up to us now.

"I had to stop or I would've killed an animal," I explain.

"What animal? What are you talking about?" says Siri.

"There." I point to the little furry beastie crawling on the road in front of us.

"That's not an animal." Siri says. "That's an insect, a caterpillar."

"It's alive and it crawls, so that means it's an animal and I don't kill animals. Do you want to make it into roadkill?"

"Do you want to make me into roadkill?"

Daddy, who'd been up ahead, is squatting down in the road watching the caterpillar. He picks it up and lets it walk around on his hand. "I don't think Simon was choosing between you and the caterpillar, Siri. It was just instinct that made him brake."

"He hasn't even said he's sorry, Daddy!"

"I didn't do anything wrong!"

"Let's just keep going," Daddy says. He puts the caterpillar in some green leaves on the side of the road and walks back over to his bike.

"You *would* take his side," Siri says. And then she mumbles. "Probably did something stupid like that yourself when you got into your accident."

I look ahead to Daddy. He stops for a second but doesn't turn. Then he gets on his bike. Did he hear? Well, Mommy sure did. Now she's yelling at Siri. "What's the matter with you?"

"I'm tired of Simon cutting in front of me all the time. And then stopping so I almost run into him. He's hyper-annoying, and. . . and dangerous!" Mommy just looks at her. "And why can't I call Michael? Why aren't I allowed to use my screen?"

Daddy turns around. "Let her have her screen, Janie. I don't think there's any harm in it now. And Simon, let your sister go ahead for a change. You can switch back later. OK, let's go."

Siri still looks all grumbly even though she just got her way on two things and didn't even say thanks. She's been acting like she's mad at Daddy all day, but I don't know why.

I thought Siri might ask me about what happened to Daddy this summer. I'm not sure what I should tell her if she does. Daddy and Mommy still don't know that I know how he got hurt. If I tell Siri, maybe they'll find out somehow.

Siri's ahead now and I'm trying to bike slowly and peacefully. The roads are calm, sometimes straight and sometimes curvy. It's very quiet. There's hardly anyone around. The sky is big and blue and you can see it all around you. It makes me want to breathe in all the air I can. I've never seen a sky like this, but I know it's part of the same sky we have in Brooklyn. But the air smells different. It's heavy and tastes green. Sometimes it smells like poop, but not like a bathroom. I have this idea that if I got to look at this big sky and breathe its free air all the time, I'd never have an asthma attack again.

There's a sign up ahead. I read it in French first: "Vignoble biologique." Then I put on the magic glasses the tourist-office person gave us. The letters pop out at me, in English this time: "Organic vineyard." Purple and green grapes are dancing around the letters. Mommy bikes past me and catches up to Daddy. They talk to each other and then Daddy signals us to stop.

We walk inside the "vignoble." Bottles of wine are stacked everywhere. Daddy talks to the woman behind the counter in French and soon she's filling glasses with different wines. I walk around the room and look at everything. I see Mommy letting Siri have a taste of the wine, but I'm not interested. Wine is sour, like how this room smells. I see some bars of fancy chocolate, though, and look at Mommy and Daddy hopefully. They're drinking down their glasses of wine and laughing. They don't notice me and the chocolate. A kid wearing a red dress and plastic sandals comes in and sees me looking. They take a bar of the chocolate, which is square instead of rectangular, and ask me something. I say, "Je ne parle pas français," like Daddy taught me. The kid giggles and holds out the bar. I look around, shrug and take a piece. The chocolate is kind of bitter, like the wine maybe, but also good—not plasticky the way chocolate at the store tastes sometimes. I say "merci." The kid says another bunch of words and I shrug. They point to the door. They're probably like two years younger than me, but playing with them would be less boring than watching Mommy and Daddy drink wine.

"Mommy, Daddy, can I go outside?"

Daddy looks from me to the kid and smiles. It's Mommy who answers, though.

"Sure, sweetheart. Don't go far. We'll meet you outside in a little bit."

I follow the kid. It's amazing how much you can understand without talking. They bring me to see a dog and two cats. I pet the dog. One of the cats turns around and walks off, like they're bored of us and have something way better to do somewhere else. Soon Siri comes out too.

"Mommy and Daddy are getting drunk. I hope neither one of them falls off their bike. Especially Daddy. He already got hurt enough, right?"

I wait, but she doesn't ask me anything. Siri shrugs and starts picking up rocks and throwing them towards some trees. Siri can throw very far. I look at the kid. They're watching Siri and looking surprised but not mad or anything. Then they offer Siri a piece of chocolate, saying something that sounds excited. I think the kid is either impressed by Siri's arm or talking about how yummy the chocolate bar is. I wish I knew which, but my magic translation glasses don't work on people.

After a while, Mommy and Daddy come out and tell us it's time to go.

"Where are we going now?"

"On to Farnham," Daddy answers.

"Are we staying at a hotel there tonight?" Siri asks.

"No. We're camping out."

"Like the Bicycling Family?" I ask.

"Yep, except that you guys get your own tent," Mommy says.

I turn to the kid and say "Au revoir." They reach up on their tiptoes and kiss me once on each cheek, I don't mind too much, especially since now I can tell Henry I had my first kiss. Then the kid kisses Siri the same way. I wonder if it still counts.

CHAPTER 29
JANIE

There are bodies falling from the sky. It takes me a minute to connect them with the advertisement for "parachutisme" we passed a few minutes ago. When I first noticed the ad, I took it as a positive sign. A mystical message that we'd found our parachute, our daring escape. But watching these bodies plummet to earth, I'm not sure it's a good sign after all.

"Mommy, Daddy, look at that!" Simon shouts.

Siri is pedaling slowly, looking to where Simon's pointing with a smile of wonder on her face that quickly morphs, even as I watch it, into a condescending adolescent smirk.

As more and more parachutes unfold themselves in a rainbow of bright colours, my unease is replaced by awe. I strain my eyes to see the parachutists more clearly, to follow their progress in the sky. After a while, though, my view is blocked by trees and hills. I can't see where they land, and more importantly, if they land safely. So how will I know what kind of sign it really was?

"Mommy, when are you gonna give me back my screen? I need to make a call," Siri says as I pull up beside her.

"When you can remember what I told you. One, that you

have permission to send a text, not make a call, and two, that you can do it when we get to the campgrounds."

I know I'm nervous. Maybe I should apologize for biting her head off, but Siri's been prickly and unpleasant all day. It's getting on my nerves. Or is my grumpiness a cover for how guilty I feel? What we're planning is going to be hard enough on the kids, but to do it without prior discussion, without any warning? I don't even want to think about how that's gonna go down. And the call I made while in town did little to bolster my confidence about any of this.

Because my friend Roberto had a contact in Montréal, I allowed myself to believe that this plan of ours wasn't as insane as I'd feared. I reasoned that if there's an actual organization up here to help political refugees, that must mean something.

Laek wanted to wait until we were in Montréal, but I thought it'd be safe if I used Siri's screen and limited the conversation to less than a minute. Honestly, I don't have a fucking clue what is or isn't safe. Now that we're in Québec, in these peaceful surroundings, I'm having trouble wrapping my head around the idea that the government could still have any interest in going after a pacifist teacher, let alone in chasing him across the border. When I made the call earlier, trying to push aside my paranoia, it was in the hope that it would result in some concrete reason for optimism, but all I was able to establish during the brief conversation was the obvious skepticism this local activist had about our plan to demand asylum. Even though I tried to hide how upset I was, I'm sure it was written all over my face. I saw how Laek looked at me.

No, I shouldn't have made that call. We're supposed to be on vacation. This was what we told the kids and this is what we're telling ourselves, at least until we get to Montréal and file our application. Until then, Laek and I are not technically lying about anything. Not really. When vacation time is over and we need to take our next step, that's when we'll explain to the kids.

We arrive at the campsite and set up our tents. After a full day of biking and being out in nature, we've all worked up an appetite. I'm looking forward to the challenge of cooking on an open flame, but three minutes trying to get a fire going from scratch is enough to make me want to kick our kindling apart in frustration.

"Let me do this," Laek says, taking the kindling out of my hands.

"I don't know how they expect us to make a fire when they won't let us collect twigs and branches from the ground. I'm going to take a walk."

"Janie? Don't come back here with stolen timber from the woods. I'm not going to need it and I will absolutely not use it." He smiles to take the sting out but I see that he's serious.

"Can't a person take a nature walk without being accused of eco-terrorism?"

I decide to skip the walk and take out my ukulele instead. Each of us was allowed one comfort item on this trip, and this is mine. I tune it as I watch Laek patiently arrange the firewood. He uses a knife with a wicked-looking blade to cut and pry off smaller pieces of kindling from the logs we purchased at the general store. In practically the time it takes me to finish tuning my instrument, he has a strong fire going. I shake my head in admiration.

After supper, I let the kids roast marshmallows to make s'mores. I feel funny using local, organic, raw dark chocolate with cheap graham crackers and artificial marshmallows.

"Mommy, can I have my screen back now?"

"What are you going to do with it?"

"Just send a text."

"And who are you texting?"

"Why are you trying to control my life?"

Siri sounds furious. I answer her calmly.

"Not your life, I just want to know who you're texting."

"Who did you call before, using *my* screen?"

I don't answer her but feel Laek looking at me. I take a deep breath. I need to stop being so paranoid or Siri's going to suspect something. Sitting here in the middle of the woods, the idea that the government already has a close trace on even our kids' screens seems outlandish.

"Fine, you're right. You're entitled to your privacy. Here." I hand her the screen. "But text only." Siri grabs the screen. "Siri?"

"Yeah, OK Mommy, I heard you." She heads for her tent.

"Why don't you get ready for bed, Simon?" I start rooting around in our bags for his toothbrush and a towel. "Should we ask Daddy to go with you?" I turn to Laek and see him staring intently into the flames. Simon looks over at Laek as well.

"No, I can go by myself, Mommy. But I'll need our most powerful glowlight."

"OK, here you go." I watch our little explorer gear up for his intrepid foray to the bathroom. After Siri is done texting, the two of us join him. When we get back to our campsite, I notice that Laek has cleaned up and put out the fire. But he's nowhere to be seen. He must either be in the bathrooms himself or already in the tent. He must be. I resist the urge to check. I won't let him think that I don't trust him.

When the kids are both snug in their sleeping bags, I crawl into our tent to find Laek lying on his back playing with an object resting on his bare chest. I turn up the glowlight and see that the object is the knife with the scary blade I saw him using earlier. He's spinning it around on his chest, stopping it every so often to check which way the blade is facing. The spinning reminds me of something. Yes, a roulette wheel. Russian roulette? But that's played with a gun.

"Laek, what are you doing?"

"Nothing." He sounds sullen, like a small boy who's been caught in the act.

"Nothing?"

"I'm. . . I'm spinning my knife around."

"Yeah, OK."

He stops the spinning, wraps his hand tightly around the blade and closes his eyes.

"Do you want to see it?" He finally asks.

"Sure." I'm curious because I've never examined the knife close up. Philip had asked my permission before giving it to Laek. A courtesy, maybe. Or a second opinion.

Laek passes me the knife, handle first. It's ornately worked but worn around the grip, obviously well-used. It looks like a family heirloom.

"Beautiful." That is, if one is inclined to find beauty in a potential weapon.

"Philip gave it to me," he says quietly. "He. . . I think he wanted to show he trusted me. To take care of myself. To. . . to take care of my family."

I purposely hand the knife back to him blade first. He hesitates and then avoids the blade to reach instead for my hand that's wrapped around the handle. I leave my hand there for a few moments before gently slipping it out from under his. He brings the blade towards him and carefully closes it before putting it away.

Laek looks up through the tent roof. I lay my head on his chest, just where the knife had been resting, and gaze up too. Through the thin nylon of the tent, we can see bright twinkling lights above us. I watch as one of those lights seems to fall to the earth. A falling star or just a spark from a campfire? It's hard to tell. And if it were a shooting star, what would that even mean? A good sign or a bad sign?

CHAPTER 30
LAEK

This close to Montréal, it's hard to hold myself back. Not that I'm impatient to end this trip. I love the quiet, the beauty of the countryside. The freedom and simplicity of our days. It makes me feel calm. Though I've had a few bad moments. But as long as I can hold myself to the present, I'm OK.

I crest the hill, standing up on my pedals. Then settle back into my seat to race headlong down into the long, winding valley, cornfields waving me on. There's no one in front of me as far as I can see, and that is very far. I spread my arms and throw my head back, my chin cutting the wind into two fast streams of air. Flight seems as close as one revolution of my wheel.

Should we stay here instead of going on to the city? Live on a farm or in a campground? I read that Québec has a version of the right to roam. "Everyman's right". I repeat the words in French: Le droit de tout un chacun. If that's true, we could legally camp out on private as well as on public land. For one night, at least. We could be like Janie's "bicycling family." Pedalling from place to place. Having adventures that always end well. Winter might be tough, though.

As peaceful as the country is, I do miss being around more

people. Maybe I'm a city person. Though I wasn't born in a city. I think about being in the centre of a big crowd right now. All of us dancing and laughing. To lean against someone's shoulder. To have someone I don't even know brush by me and say "sorry," putting their hand on my back. Not that this is how it always goes down in New York City.

Where is my family?

I crest another hill. Stop. Turn around. I see them far off in the distance. I decide to bike all the way back to them. I'm actually desperate to do that. I speed towards them, pumping hard enough that it makes my ribs ache with the effort. I concentrate on watching for all of the landmarks I just passed. Studying them in reverse. Things look different coming the other way. Almost like I'm covering new ground. Since they're also biking towards me, our rendez-vous doesn't take long to arrive. I breathe out my relief, passing first Siri, then Simon and then Janie. I turn around again. Bike beside Janie.

"I feel like a wayward sheep," Janie says.

"What?"

"Like you're herding us. Next, you'll start nipping at my heels."

"Mmm, would you like that?"

"Gross! Can't you two save that for your bedroom?" Siri says.

I bike up parallel to her. "We have no bedroom right now, Siri. Just the great outdoors!"

"But we're going to have beds tonight, right?"

"Yes, we have a reservation at a small hotel."

"In Montréal?"

"Yeah, but we should try to get a move on if we want to get there before dark."

"How are we getting there?" asks Simon.

"What do you mean?" Janie replies. "On our bikes."

"But it's an island, right? So we need to get across the water somehow."

"Very good, Simon. Siri, you can choose. La navette or le pont Jacques-Cartier."

"No fair, Daddy," she complains. "I don't know what you're saying."

"Try to guess."

"That's stupid. How can I guess?"

"Come on, Siri. Just pick one," I tell her.

"Fine. The thing with Jack Cartier sounds like a history lesson. I pick the other one."

"OK, so it's the navette. That'll be fun." I bike off to the front again.

"But Daddy, what'd I choose?"

"You'll see." I feel something small hit me on my back and turn around. Siri's throwing pistachio-nut shells at me.

We arrive at the pier in Longueuil. When Janie and the kids see the ferry coming, churning the water up white and foamy, they're too pleased to be mad at me for not telling sooner. Janie is especially excited. She loves the water. She has such a beautiful smile on her face, I want to lean over and suck on her lips. But we have just enough time to buy our tickets and rush onto the boat. We roll our bikes across the ramp. Someone with a sunburn who looks like they're in their teens or early twenties directs us down to where the bikes are held. Now I'm the one with the big grin on my face. I've never seen so many bicycles parked together in one place. It's like a nest of bikes. Can this really be only the bikes of the people taking the ferry?

"Should we lock them together like we usually do, Daddy?" Siri asks.

"No. It's OK. No one else is."

"Come on, Laek. Get your bike settled and let's go up on deck. I want to feel that spray of water on my face."

"All those bikes. It's so amazing. Can I take a picture?" I ask.

"You're funny. We've seen a double rainbow, parachutists, covered bridges, trees carved with faces, a bike lane that runs through a sculpture garden, and a whole holographic jungle. But this is what you want to take a picture of?"

"Yes, Janie. Please give me a screen."

"Alright, sweetheart. Here's Siri's."

"How is it that both of you lost your screens?" Siri asks.

"Mine's just broken," Janie says. "I'll replace it in Montréal. Come on guys, I guess Daddy will meet us upstairs after he's taken in the sights down here in the bike storage area."

I eventually force myself to leave the bikes and the safety below to join Janie and the kids on the top deck. They're hanging over the rail. Craning their necks towards the shore. Simon's taken out his screen. He seems to be doing a credible job of pointing things out. I hear him try to pronounce "Île Notre-Dame" and "Parc Jean-Drapeau." Then read out some tourist info on the history of the Biosphere. Siri is mostly fixated on the roller coasters and zero-g cubes in the island's amusement park.

They motion me to come over. I take some steps towards them, towards the water. I'm stopped by a wave of nausea. Followed by a feeling of suffocation. I back up a few steps. Force the air into my lungs. I drop down onto a bench in the centre of the boat. Wave to my family. Smile carefully. Try not to think about water. About water being poured over my mouth and nose, water entering my lungs. Soon we'll be on land again.

I still have Siri's screen, so I call up a holo of Montréal's bike lanes. I raise the holo to the level of my eyes. Stretch the image horizontally and vertically with my hands. I trace a few routes. Pinch one between my fingers. Move it to another spot. I trace a route from the pier at Le Vieux Port to our hotel on rue St-Denis, turning it orange. I do the same for another route running from our hotel to 1010 St-Antoine Ouest. Where claims for asylum are made. No, it's too soon to think about that. I turn the route back to neutral green. Satisfied, I immerse myself in the map. Stroke its surface with my hand. It moves and undulates like the body of a lover.

"What are you doing, Daddy?" Siri asks.

"Looking at les pistes cyclables. The bike paths of Montréal."

"But why are you *petting* them?"

"Siri, Simon, have you ever seen so many bike paths in your life? It's just. . . it's just amazing. Janie, come and see too."

"Very nice. Which one are we going to ride on?"

"All of them! Let's ride on all of them!" I laugh a little. I know I'm getting a bit carried away. Even if Siri wasn't giving me that "Daddy's unhinged" look. Even if Janie didn't seem half amused and half worried. But I can't believe that in just a few minutes, we'll be in Montréal! "Look here. This path takes us to our hotel. Hey, let's get our bikes, we're almost there."

Once on the dock, we follow the stream of passengers towards the ramp that brings us to the Old Port. The ramp is very steep. I'm not sure if the kids are going to be able to push their bikes, reloaded with the luggage, all the way up themselves. Simon in particular. I hurry over to try to help him, but someone's already there. One of the crew, a person with spiky, black hair, is showing Simon how to place his wheel in a groove at the side of the ramp. The bike jerks twice, then starts moving its way up the ramp on its own. I see it's a pulley system. Operated by someone else up on top, pedalling a stationary bike.

"Look at that!" Simon says.

I place my bike behind Simon's. Race up to the top of the ramp ahead of him to help him disengage his wheels. When all four of us have ascended with our bikes, I walk over to the person operating the pulley. They seem about my age, maybe a little older. Long hair in a ponytail, two earrings on each ear. I try to offer a tip. They refuse. Insistent, but not offended either.

"C'est mon métier. Ma job, man. Quelle belle vie, eh?"

Yeah, a great job, great life. I want to stay and talk. See if they can use another pedaler. Part-time, maybe. But it's starting to get late and I know the kids are tired and hungry.

Just as we're getting to the bike path leading from the Old Port, I freeze in my tracks.

"Daddy? What is it?" Simon asks.

I shake my head. Don't understand what to think, what I'm seeing. Janie has come up beside me. Grips my arm tightly.

"What the fuck?" she asks.

What we see is a group of cops. On bikes. They're in uniform. Sort of. Wearing short-sleeved police shirts, badges, everything. But on the bottom, they're wearing fluorescent-pink bike shorts. But with all the normal gear. The police are forming a line on either side of the bike path. And on the path are a huge number of cyclists. Totally naked.

My heart is racing. Whether from fear or excitement, I'm not sure. One of the naked bikers approaches us. "Voulez-vous vous joindre à nous?" they ask. Before I can figure out an appropriate response to this, Janie answers. This is the first time she's taken charge of a conversation since we arrived in Québec. Odd that it's with a naked man.

"Um, parlez-vous anglais? I'm a tourist here," she says.

"Yes, but of course."

"I'm Janie, she/her. Can you tell me. . . what is all this?"

"I am Luc, he/him, and this is the vélorution! Every third Wednesday of the month. We ride to create together a more bike-friendly culture and society. More écologique, healthy, safe. Today we are trying to souligner, to. . . to underline the vulnerability of cyclists. That is why we wear no clothes. To have safer bike paths and traffic rules, to raise awareness of the drivers of cars."

"Yeah, but why are the cops wearing pink shorts?"

The man turns to me. "Your blonde, she thinks la police wearing pink is more strange than cyclists who are nude?"

"Why is he calling me your blond?" Janie whispers. "I'm not blond and. . ."

"It just means girlfriend. It has nothing to do with your hair colouring," the man answers.

"You say 'blond' for girlfriend, even if she's brunette? Even if she's *Black*?" Janie asks.

"You are very concerned about colour, I see."

"Well, we're from New York."

"Ah, I understand perfectly. Yes, all girlfriends are blondes, whatever is their actual colour. We do not discriminate. And I will answer your question about the pink too. The police, they are en grève, on strike. For better pay and work conditions."

"How is wearing pink being on strike?"

"The people notice, as you did. It bothers them. This brings attention to their issues."

"Are there, are there clashes here between the police and the demonstrators?"

"Clashes?"

"Yeah, like violence, forceful arrests. . ."

"Oh! Yes, of course, this sometimes happens, but not so much with the manifestations that are nude. The public is watching—this is a popular event. And there is our volontaire to be vulnerable. The police do not want to be seen as savage animals, not with all the camera drones streaming realtime."

"Vous êtes l'un des organisateurs, monsieur?" I ask.

"Mais pas besoin de me vouvoyer. You do not have to use "vous" with me. You can say the informal "tu." We are co-militants, cyclists. And, well, I am naked, after all."

"Merci. My name is Laek, and you have met Janie. These are our children, Siri and Simon."

"Laek, that sounds a lot like Luc. Is it a common name where you come from?"

"No, not at all. Maybe I'll call myself Luc here."

"And do the others want to change their names too? Janie, what do you say? Would you like to be Jeanne? Janine? Simon can stay with Simon, just a different pronunciation. Siri, I don't know. She will be more difficult."

"Well, we'll come up with something," I say.

"So, Laek who is also Luc, will you join our vélorution?"

I start taking off my shirt.

"Daddy, what are you doing?" Siri asks in an alarmed voice.

"Joining the vélorution!"

"Does vélorution mean getting naked? If so, I don't think we should join. Mommy, tell him to stop taking his clothes off. It's embarrassing!"

"There's a cadre for the children too. La vélorution d'enfants. But the children are with clothes," Luc explains. "Children are vulnerable already, even clothed, yes? The children ride in front, up there," he points.

"Will they be safe?" Janie asks.

"Parfaitement. Others of our group will be guarding them."

"Siri, Simon, do you want to bike up front with the other kids?" I ask.

"If Siri comes," answers Simon.

"OK. If it's a choice between that and having to look at your naked butts. . ." Siri answers.

"Good." I point to an intersection on the map on Siri's screen. "We'll meet there."

"OK, Daddy, but you better have your clothes back on by then. Otherwise I'm going to pretend I don't know you." Luc calls over a clothed person with long, black dreads who leads the kids to their part of the rally.

"What do you say, Janie?" I ask, unfastening my shorts. "Are you ready for your first demonstration in New Métropolis?"

She laughs. "Why not?"

I take Janie's hand. "OK, then. Bring on the vélorution."

CHAPTER 31
SIRI

"Mademoiselle Siri? You are called Siri Wolfe?"

"Yes, that's me."

"There is a package for you. We've put it in your room."

"A package? Hyper!" I run upstairs, Simon right behind me.

I like the way the people at the hotel don't treat me like a little kid. Plus, me and Simon have our own room, even if it's tiny and the bathroom is in the hall. Sure, the couch in the lobby is pretty worn out, but you can stare up at a real old-fashioned chandelier and the only way to go up to our rooms is by climbing a winding staircase!

At first I don't see any package, but then notice my camp duffel bag next to the wall.

"Hey, why was this sent here?"

"Maybe Mommy thought you needed more clothes," Simon answers.

I unzip the duffel. Everything seems to be there. I hear Daddy and Mommy coming up the stairs so I open our door. "Look what came, Mommy. My things from camp."

"Oh, yeah, great," Mommy says.

"But why did it get sent here and not home? Isn't our vacation almost over?"

"We may be staying longer," Daddy says. "Today, after the park, we're going to a government office to fill out an application."

"But school starts in just a few days." And then I'll get to be with Michael again.

"Since when are you so worried about missing school?" Mommy asks.

She sounds suspicious. Maybe they really do know about Michael and me. In case they're just trying to trap me into admitting it, I change the subject. "What did you get us?"

"Croissants. Chocolate and plain," Daddy answers. "Knock when you're finished eating."

Daddy walks out and Mommy quickly follows him, leaving us all the croissants.

"But wait, aren't some of these for you guys?"

"That's OK, Siri. I'm not hungry right now," Daddy says.

———

We're on a bike path with about a zillion other cyclists. Daddy's just ahead of me, talking over his shoulder. He's dressed up, wearing a clean, white shirt with brown three-quarter length pants and his nice sandals, like for school. Maybe that's why he's in his lecturing mode.

"This is one of the most famous of Montréal's bike paths. The 'Claire Morissette' path that runs along boulevard de Maisonneuve."

"Claire Morissette?"

"Yeah, a cycling and environmental activist. Founded two organizations, wrote books. . . She accomplished a lot in her lifetime."

"What happened to her?"

"She died of breast cancer in the year 2007."

That makes me think of my own breasts. I notice they're getting bigger, which I'm not so happy about. I know that even people with small breasts can get breast cancer but I still feel like the smaller they are, the less stuff that can turn into cancer. Plus, big breasts get in the way of sports.

"Daddy, do we *have to* go to the government office now?" Simon asks.

"Yeah, I'm sorry, love. Hopefully it won't take too long."

Then again, Michael really likes my boobs. But maybe I shouldn't have let him do what he did. I wonder if someone at camp saw us, if they told on us. Maybe that's why Mommy and Daddy are being so strict about using my screen to talk to Michael.

I look up in time to see another holo-flash of a bike fact. The path has a new one every kilometre. The last one was about the United America. It said that each year, more people are killed in car accidents there than all the soldiers who were killed in the Vietnam War of the twentieth century. Pretty intense, since the people in the accidents weren't even trying to kill each other!

Here comes the next one: "Le vélo permet d'apercevoir la beauté."

"What does that one mean, Laek?" asks Mommy.

"Just use your translation glasses, Mommy," Simon says.

"Daddy took mine away. Thought it would make me learn French. Instead I've decided to make Daddy be my translation glasses."

Simon laughs. "Tell us your translation, Daddy."

"You have your glasses," Daddy answers.

"C'mon. Let's see how good you are," I say.

"Well, OK, fine. The bicycle permits us to, to see the beauty."

"The translator says: The bicycle opens us up to the beauty of the world," I tell him.

"Yeah, that sounds better," Daddy admits.

We lock up our bikes and Daddy leads us to a building across the street. It's pretty dingy-looking for a government building.

The lobby is tiny, with just enough room for a broken-down elevator and a broken-down looking old person sitting on a metal stool and wearing a uniform. They have a name tag—M. Landry. I learned at the hotel that "M." means Monsieur, so "he" or "il" pronouns. The man says something in French and Daddy tells us to hand him our backpacks.

"Hey," says Simon. "That's the same kind of scanner they use in my school!"

"Ah, oui?" the man says, smiling, and all of a sudden he looks a lot less broken down. He seems nice, like someone's grandpa. "And where would your school be, mon petit bonhomme?"

"Brooklyn," says Simon.

"That's in New York City," I add, in case the man doesn't know.

"A pleasure to meet citizens of such a famous city." He turns to Daddy. "You are making an application, Monsieur?"

"Oui, pour l'asile. Mais les enfants ne savent pas."

"The elevator's here," Mommy says.

The elevator rattles as it goes up and then spits us out on our floor. Around the bend are a bunch of screens with instructions in French and English. Past that is a crowded room where people are speaking all different languages. So I guess my parents weren't the only ones who forgot to get a long enough permission slip for their vacation.

Mommy brings us to some seats towards the back of the room and tells us that she loaded new games and puzzles onto our screens. She joins Daddy at one of the service windows, so I start looking through the new games. After a few minutes I look up to see Daddy standing at a high counter, typing on one of their screens. Mommy's trying to peer around his shoulder. "Why are you doing this in French?" I hear her ask.

"It's best this way."

"But don't you think you could be more articulate in English?"

"No."

"Can I have a bit more detail with that 'no,' please?"

"The French puts some distance between me and what I'm writing. And I like French."

I tune out the rest of their argument. I know that tone of voice when my dad's not planning on giving in. Anyhow, Daddy's obsession with French will end when we're back in New York. And I have a lot to think about between now and then. Like about how I promised Michael that we'd go public as a couple in September. I wanted to keep it a secret, but Michael thought that meant I wasn't serious about him. Maybe that's why I let us go so far at camp, to show him he was wrong. Was it OK what we did? Will he tell other people? Will he still like me once we're back at school? Even though this vacation is kind of hyper, I wish I was home already so that I could talk to Michael face to face.

Maybe I can send him a quick text right now. I look to see if Mommy's watching me. Just then, we finally get called into one of the little rooms. The person asks me and Simon to say our names and ages. Then Mommy asks if the kids could wait outside and the person nods.

Simon and I play games for a while, but I'm distracted, thinking about Michael. I imagine us doing more of what we did on the last night of camp. I feel weird and wonder if people can tell what I'm thinking about. Daddy and Mommy are still in the room. Maybe I should talk to Mommy about what happened. When are they gonna finish in there?

I look around the ugly room. The ceiling is all stained and some of the tiles on the floor are broken. Bits of paint are chipping off of the walls. Most of the people who were here when we arrived have already left, but more people have come to take their places. Some people are looking at screens but most are just staring off into space. I make a funny face at a baby whose head is peeking over their parent's shoulder. The baby has huge, dark eyes that open even wider at me when I make the face. Simon wanders around the room and picks up a palm-sized news screen attached to a table.

"Stop pretending you can read French," I tell him.

"I can read some of it. Look, there's a whole bunch of words that are like English."

"Lemme see." I look at the article he's reading and see the word "condom" and then the word "CO2". I wonder what it could be about. I wonder if Michael has condoms.

"Simon, this news screen is too old for you. You should put it back."

"Is not."

"Oh yeah? Then tell me what the article's about."

"It's about *condoms* and carbon dioxide."

"So what's a condom?"

"It's a thingy. That you use for having sex. I'm not a baby, you know."

"Uh, huh. Use it how? And what's that got to do with CO2?"

"I don't know exactly. But I think the article's about global warming. See, it has the word 'planète' and 'climat'? What do you think condoms have to do with climate change, Siri?"

"Well. . . maybe when people are having sex they pant a lot and make carbon dioxide." I smile to myself. This is exactly the kind of thing that Simon doesn't want to know about.

"No, that can't be it. They wouldn't write that in a *news story*!" He moves the screen away, like it's gonna contaminate him or something, but then he says, "I know! Maybe the condoms let off carbon dioxide when they're in the landfill. I bet that's it. That's a lot less gross."

"You think a million gooey condoms sitting in the landfill is less gross than people panting because they're enjoying sex?"

"Shut up! Stop acting like you know about sex." Simon shouts.

"More than you!" I shout back.

"Why, 'cause you *made out* with Michael at baseball camp? What base did you get to?"

"Shut your face! You're so stupid!" I jump up, thinking about tackling my bratty little know-it-all brother and putting my hand over his mouth.

Mommy comes out of the room. "Quiet down! Where the hell do you think you are?"

"It's his fault. . ." I try to explain.

"I don't want to hear it! Not another word. If I can't count on you to behave in a government office. . . You see how people are staring at us?"

I'm about to point out that *she's* the reason they're looking at us, yelling even louder than me and Simon were, but I snap my mouth shut. Mommy looks furious, like if I say anything, she'll totally lose it. She gives a final warning look, then goes back into the room.

I take out my screen and ignore Simon, but after a while, I'm bored again. I look up at the door where Mommy and Daddy are and decide that maybe it would be alright if I sent a quick text to Michael. No one has specifically said I can't. I turn my back on Simon and start typing: *How r u? I am BORED. Almost cant w8 4 skool. Who do u have 4 HR? Miss u. -S*

Mommy walks out of the room with Daddy. I push "send" and hide my screen.

"Give me that, Siri," Mommy demands.

Did she see me send the message? She doesn't seem mad, though. She's smiling at Simon reading the news screen like it's the cutest thing. She uses my screen to take a photo. Suddenly one of the people who works here walks over to Mommy quickly and grabs the screen from her.

"C'est interdit de prendre des photos!"

"They're saying that taking photos is forbidden," Daddy tells Mommy.

"Yeah, I kind of got that, Laek, when they took my screen and deleted the picture."

"That's *my* screen," I remind them. The person hands it to

Mommy and Mommy hands it back to me. Close call. I'll delete the evidence of my text later.

We leave to eat some "pressed" cheese sandwiches and then come back for another interview. We're wasting so much time here, it's hardly even worth the few extra days of vacation we'll get. And I, for one, would rather just go home anyway, even though it's been pretty fun. I can't wait to tell Michael all about it! While Daddy's checking at the front desk to see if it's our turn, I take the opportunity to turn away from my parents to check my screen. Why hasn't Michael texted me back yet?

Daddy comes back to wait with us. Simon asks if we can play geography.

"OK," Daddy says, "But let's limit it to places in Montréal."

"That's not enough places, Daddy," I complain.

"How about I do just Montréal and the rest of you can also use other places in Canada?"

"I hate playing different rules for different people," Mommy says.

"Alright, we'll expand it to all of Canada for everyone."

"I'll start. Canada," says Simon.

"Youngest to oldest," I say, "Alberta."

"Ahuntsic," Daddy says.

"You go Mommy."

"Côte-des-neiges."

"What letter does that end in, Mommy?" Simon asks.

"An *s*," Mommy says.

After a while, I realize Daddy's just saying places in Montréal anyway. It's like he's cheating in reverse. Now Simon has a *t*.

"Trois-Rivières," he says, glancing up from his screen.

"You looked that up!" I tell him.

"It's OK," Daddy says. "This way he learns about new places."

"Saskatchewan." I stick my tongue out at Simon. Daddy's looking at the door of one of the little rooms where an official-looking person has just come out.

"Daddy, it looks like it's your turn."

He looks back at me like he's confused. "Yeah," he says.

"You have *n*, Daddy," Simon tells him.

"Right. . . *n*. . . New Metropolis." Daddy stands up, still watching the door, as the person motions to him with a very serious expression on their face.

"Where's New Métropolis, Daddy?" I ask.

"Nowhere. It's a made-up place. I lose."

Then Daddy gets up and slowly walks over to the room.

CHAPTER 32
JANIE

Laek emerges from the interview room looking shaky. I rush over. "What happened?"

"We'll have our hearing," he answers.

His eyes seem strange, a little too bright. "But?"

"It. . . it wasn't easy. It almost went the other way."

"Tell me what happened."

"Not out here."

"Madame, monsieur, le bureau ferme. We need to ask you to leave."

"Can we at least use the bathroom?" I ask. "Les toilettes?"

They show us where the bathrooms are and I ask the kids if they have to go. They shake their heads, but Siri looks like she wants to ask me something. I avoid her gaze and tell them to wait outside for us. Then I push Laek into the men's room, look around, and slip in behind him.

After confirming that we're alone I ask him again to tell me what happened.

"He asked a lot of difficult questions. Like about my group. Whether we broke the law. And if it would be considered a terrorist organization by the U.A. government."

"What did you tell him?"

"I tried to explain, but he just kept repeating that the U.A. is a 'safe country'. At least as far as the Canadian government is concerned."

"Did you tell him about the torture?"

"He kept talking about credibility and proof, and, and. . . scars and. . . I wanted to explain. About the scars. Where they were and how some torture doesn't leave scars. But when I tried, I couldn't think because I was in the room, I mean all of a sudden I was in The Room and. . ." Laek grabs hold of the sink, breathing hard.

"Easy, Laek, easy does it. Take a deep breath." I rub his back like I do with the kids when one of them has had a particularly terrifying nightmare. I wait until I feel him fill and empty his lungs a few times before letting him continue.

"I guess I panicked. I mean, I blanked for a few minutes. And when I came back, I was standing on a chair with my clothes off. I guess so he could see my scars for himself."

"God! What happened next?"

"He was very flustered. Kept asking me to please put my clothes back on. In both French and English. Much more politely than he'd been speaking to me before. I tried to get dressed. But my hands were shaking. So I just sort of covered myself with my clothes. Until I was more in control. I put them on while I faced the wall. After he turned around the other way."

"And then?"

"He said he'd schedule me for a hearing. Suggested I find a lawyer. . . and a therapist."

"Yes, a good idea. Ideas."

"I need to pee," Laek says abruptly, pulling away from me. He disappears into one of the stalls. After some long minutes, he comes out and washes his hands slowly.

"Are you OK?" I ask. When he doesn't answer, I try again. "Tell me how you feel, Laek."

He looks at himself in the mirror, then down at his hands

again. "I feel like damaged goods, that's how I feel. And that's what I am."

"No, that's not true."

"Yes. And it's time we faced it."

"Look, you've been damaged, OK. But you're not 'goods.' You're a human being who's been hurt, that's all. You need to be patient with yourself. And less stubborn. You should've let me go in there with you. We need to stick together."

"To watch that little spectacle I put on?"

"To be with you. And I've seen your naked body before. Even in public. Have you thought about the fact that this is the second time in a week you've taken your clothes off in a public place in this city?" This gets a small smile out of him. "I'll admit the first time was more fun. But things will start looking up again."

But then I remember that now it's time to tell the kids.

"Listen, I have an idea. I'll take Siri out to supper and tell her, and you go with Simon."

"What happened to the idea of sticking together?"

I don't answer, don't want to say that I think telling Siri is going to take more strength than he has to spare right now.

We walk out of the bathroom and down the hall. Simon's looking at another news screen, swiping from page to page with a dreamy expression on his face. Siri's all focus, looking at me expectantly. She looks like she's just on the threshold of an unpleasant adolescent moment. Laek looks from Simon to Siri and then back to me, relaxing his shoulders in defeat.

"Yeah, OK. Simon and I will meet the two of you back at the hotel later."

"What's up?" Siri asks.

"You and I are going to have a mother-daughter evening. What do you want to eat?"

CHAPTER 33
SIRI

Mommy orders avocado sushi and I get fruit sushi. It's very good, the apples juicy and the kiwis not too sweet. It goes great with the spicy wasabi. I'm waiting for Mommy to tell me why she brought me here. At first I thought that it had to do with Michael and me, that someone told her about us and that this is what she and Daddy keep whispering about. Now I'm not so sure. They both seemed more nervous than angry. Plus, all that time in the government office. . . I know travelling is tricky with hyper security and rules and everything, but when Daddy came out of the room before, he looked whacked out. Why would just getting a new permission slip be such a big deal?

"So I think you know I have something to tell you," Mommy begins.

"Did you and Daddy do something wrong?" I blurt out. "Are we in trouble?" It's hard to imagine this. Daddy and Mommy are hyper-honest about everything, like that time we were at a restaurant and we realized they forgot to charge us for something. Daddy went all the way back to pay the extra amount, even though we were almost home.

"We didn't do anything wrong. It's. . ."

"What? Is it about our permission slip?"

"Permission slip? What are you talking about?"

"You know. To visit Québec. I thought you said that we needed to get permission."

"Oh! No, it's not about our visitor's permit. It has to do with us staying here, though."

I wait, but Mommy still doesn't say anything. "Just tell me already."

"This isn't easy, Siri."

"Drawing it all out like this isn't helping, Mommy."

"I know. OK. Daddy and I. . . We've decided to *really* stay here. In Montréal."

"What do you mean?"

"I mean we want to live here. And we're asking the government for permission to stay. That's what today was all about, those forms, the interview. . ."

"What are you saying? Like move here?"

"Yes."

"I don't wanna move, Mommy." I drop my chopsticks onto my plate. Mommy's hands are squeezed between her knees and I see that she's hardly eaten any of her supper. "You're not serious, are you? We. . . we can't move!"

"Siri—"

"And why are we first talking about this now? Why did we leave from camp instead of going home first? When someone moves they, like, pack. And say good-bye to their friends and . . . We can't just stay here! We need to go home first, discuss it."

"Sweetheart, I understand your confusion. We couldn't do things in the normal way. We had to do this fast and in secret."

"Why?"

"Because Daddy was in trouble. With the government."

"I don't believe you. What did he do?"

"He didn't do anything. I mean, anything wrong."

"Then why?"

Mommy looks around at the other people in the restaurant, then leans across the table to speak more quietly. "It's political. You know that Daddy and I don't agree with the government. That's why we go to demos and participate in other. . . in other stuff."

"Yeah, so what? Other people do that and they're not moving away." I don't bother to lower my voice. People are laughing and speaking French and shovelling in their sushi. No one's paying any attention to us. I feel totally alone, even though there are people all around.

"Daddy's done more than just go to demos. When he was younger, before we met, he did other things. The people who did these other things, the government may be looking for them."

"What did he do?"

"Nothing bad."

"How do you know if you weren't even there? If the government is after him, maybe he did do something wrong."

"Your Daddy would never do anything bad, you know that. I can't give you all of the details, though. You just need to trust us."

"Trust you? After you lied to me?" Then I wonder about something else. "Does Simon know?"

"Daddy's having the same conversation with him that I'm having with you right now."

"Why aren't we having this conversation all together?"

"Siri, this has been extremely hard on your father and I knew how upset you'd be. . ."

"Why are you protecting him? This is all his fault, isn't it? Because he did some crazy, freaky thing and now he's in trouble with the government."

"Honey. . . a person has to stand up for what he or she believes is right."

"And this is right? To take me away from my friends? To ruin my life? " I can't believe this is happening to me. I have to go back home. I have to see Michael. We didn't even get to talk about what happened. I stand up. "Well fuck that!"

"Siri!" Mommy yells, sounding shocked.

"You're ruining my whole life and you're mad that I said 'fuck' in a restaurant? Well, FUCK, FUCK, FUCK, FUCK!" I say, standing up.

Everybody's looking at us now, but I don't care. I don't want to see any of these people ever again, anyway. I run out of the restaurant and down the street but I can't really go anywhere. I don't know this city and I don't speak French. I stop and lean against a building. I feel weird, dizzy and like something inside of me is beating a loud, angry drum. Some people look like they're about to come over and ask me if everything's OK. Why can't they mind their own business? If I were in New York, no one would bother me. I turn away from them and start walking back up the block. Maybe I can talk Mommy out of this crazy idea. I see her through the front window glass, standing up near our table, pulling bills out of her wallet and throwing them down on the table. She looks at them like they're random bills, like she doesn't know or care how much they're worth. And she wants to live here? She comes out, looking around for me frantically. I take a deep breath and try to act calm and logical.

"Mommy, please, you can't mean it. We need to go home. Talk this over. There must be something else we can do. Can't you get Daddy a lawyer or something?"

"I'm not sure it would help."

"What did he do?" Mommy doesn't answer me. I try another question. "What do Grandma and Grandpa say? Do they even know?"

"Yes. They're going to help. To try to bring some of our things over little by little."

Somehow, the fact that Grandma and Grandpa know makes this all more horribly real. It's not just some nightmare I'm gonna wake up from.

"Mommy, you can't do this to me. Please!"

"Sweetheart. . . We don't have a choice."

"We could go back, talk this over with your friends. Do Michael's parents know?"

"No."

"But they're your friends!"

"We couldn't tell anyone. It wasn't safe."

"You're choosing Daddy over us, that's what you're doing."

"No, don't look at it like that."

"Why not? This is all his fault and you're sticking up for him. Why couldn't I have had normal parents? You don't care about us at all, otherwise you wouldn't do these crazy things. Otherwise you wouldn't be ruining my life!"

"You're wrong. We're trying to give you a better life. That's what this is about. The politics, everything."

"By taking me away from all my friends?"

"Sweetheart, you'll make new friends. And you can keep in touch with the old ones."

"Can I go back soon, visit them?'

Mommy doesn't say anything right away. Just looks at me sadly. "No, my love. I'm sorry. We've applied for political asylum. That means we're saying it's not safe to go back. And it isn't. We'll have to wait this out and see what happens."

I just look at her. I can't believe it. Not go back home? Not go back to my school, my friends, Michael? They planned this whole thing and didn't say one word to me, never asked me what I thought. They didn't even warn me so I could say good-bye. I feel like I just fell into a big, black hole. No, that my parents pushed me into one.

"I will never, ever forgive you for this."

"Siri. . ."

Mommy tries to hug me, but I push her away. "Never!" I scream.

I cry the whole way back to the hotel. I only stop when we get to the lobby. I don't want people I already know to see me crying. I run up the stairs and into my room. Simon isn't back yet. I see my camp duffel, open it and put my face inside. It smells of grass, the camp laundry and baseball. And the end of summer. I just want to climb in and mail myself home.

CHAPTER 34
SIMON

"'m not five years old," Siri says, "and I don't need anyone to bring me to school."

She pushes her eggs around with her fork. I take another huge bite of my chocolate banana crepe. Maybe if Siri would've gotten one too, she'd be less grumpy.

"It's your first day at a new school. You don't know the neighbourhood," Daddy says.

"And whose fault is that?" Siri yells.

Daddy puts his fork down beside his blueberry crepe. "There's no use arguing about it."

"Yeah, I know you think I should have no say in my own life. Otherwise you wouldn't have kidnapped me away from my friends and sent me to school in French."

"Siri, Daddy's just trying to help. He knows high schools," Mommy says.

"Daddy being there will only make things worse."

"The letter from the school encouraged parents to come on the first day. Right, Laek?"

"Yeah," Daddy says, lifting his fork up and putting it down again.

"Daddy," I ask. "Can I have the rest of your crepe if you're not going to eat it?"

"Sure, Simon. Go for it."

Siri leaves for school before me. Daddy follows a few steps behind her, looking as sad as Henry's dog when Henry has to leave her at home. I wonder how Henry's first day of school will be. I'm a little scared about going to a new school. I don't know anybody or where anything is. What if I have to go to the bathroom and can't find it? What if everyone teases me because I can't speak French?

After I finish Daddy's crepe, Mommy and I walk down the big hill on St-Denis to the métro. I'm glad Mommy's coming with me to school. I zigzag down the block on a pretend magna board. In my backpack, I have my lunch, a student pass for the métro and a shiny new screen, just for school, with hyper-good tech. I pass about a gazillion spicy-smelling restaurants and one spicy-smelling store with a picture of a big, green leaf in the window.

The Berri-UQAM station has way more air than the subway stations I know in New York. In the middle of the station is a big, round bench where you can sit and watch everyone come in and out. There's art everywhere and musicians too. Right now there's someone playing an instrument I've never seen before under a big, silver holo of a harp. I watch someone who looks like a grandparent give a coin to a little kid, who runs over to toss the money into the musician's big, round velvet hat.

On the platform, the train going the other way comes first. I listen for the special Montréal train music. *Ba Da Daaa!*

"What *is* that music, Mommy?"

"It sounds like the first few notes of the song 'Fanfare for the Common Man'—an old piece of music by a famous musician named Aaron Copland."

"Why does the train play it?"

"I read about this. The music is to warn people when the doors are closing. But the more interesting question is, why *that* music? It turns out that in the old days, the train's motor used to make those sounds when it revved up."

"All by itself? A train making music?"

"Yep."

"Hyper!"

Now our train is pulling in too. The doors open and people come pouring out. We wait on the platform, not like in New York, where everyone starts pushing in right away. I'm still thinking about the type of train that can play music by itself when suddenly I realize that it must be a *magic* train.

Inside the train are vines with pink and orange and purple leaves winding around the poles and seats, but the poles have turned into trees filled with small, rainbow-coloured frogs and birds. There are monkeys too, and a waterfall, and a stream of bluish-white water rushing along the floor of the train right over our toes, only we're not getting wet from it. In the background, pixie music is playing, all sparkly like the sounds of stardust, and I also hear the monkeys making little sounds, and that's like music too, that and the gurgly sound of the stream and the fast sound of the waterfall. One monkey grabs a banana from a tree and offers it to me. I look at Mommy. She laughs, so I reach for the banana. My hand passes right through the holo, of course, but that's OK. I had enough bananas in my crepes this morning.

When we get to the school, I have to say good-bye to Mommy at the front door. A tall teacher wearing a big, red clown nose brings me to my class. Another teacher in the hallway is wearing a sorcerer's hat. And then, when I get to my classroom, my teacher—Madame Nathalie—has face paint on that makes her look like a leopard. Is today Halloween in Canada or some-thing? Or maybe in Québec. Daddy told me that Québec has some holidays that Canada doesn't.

I'm in a special class called the "classe d'accueil," the welcome class. Maybe this is the way they welcome people here, by dressing weird. But I like that my teacher looks like a leopard. It's serendipitous, since I'm Panther in the Bicycling Family stories. I wonder how to say "serendipitous" in French. I don't know how to say hardly anything. I feel so stupid.

We go around the room and each of us says where we're from and what language we speak. Some of the kids can speak two or even three languages. I say "anglais" and then add "espagnol." I don't know a lot of Spanish, but I feel embarrassed to say I only know English.

The teacher speaks to us in French. Daddy says this is the best way to learn. I guess she doesn't have a choice anyway, since everyone in the class speaks something different. She can't be expected to know every single language! So we'll all learn French and then there'll be one language we can speak together.

During the morning, I try to listen carefully. Some of the words sound like English words but some don't, and with them, I try to imagine my magic translation glasses turning them into English. It helps when Madame Nathalie puts words on the big screen and acts them out. After a while, though, my brain feels really tired, like when I sneak out of my room in the middle of the night to play my sim game and Mommy doesn't catch me until the morning. I decide that instead of translation glasses, I'll imagine Madame Nathalie beaming what she means directly into my brain. I hope my brain will turn bilingual soon. I don't like feeling so stupid.

In the afternoon, we do math. Madame Nathalie comes over to help me. She says my name like "Sea–mo," not pronouncing the "n" at the end, but it's like you know it's there anyway. She's showing me all kinds of different stuff about how things with numbers are done here. Like for temperature, I need to learn it in degrés Celsius instead of Fahrenheit. And to weigh in kilos, not pounds. Distance is kilometres, not miles, which I already know from our bike trip. I even need to learn to tell time all over again, using a 24-hour clock. Right now it's 13h24, not 1:24. And money, of course. This is French money. No wait, it's Canadian money, but the French way to tell the time. Sometimes I get confused between what's different because it's Canada and what's different because it's Québec and in French.

I finish all the problems Madame Nathalie has given me. I look up and she comes over.

"Est-ce que tu as une question, Simon? Une question?" she asks slowly.

No, not a question, but I don't know how to say this whole sentence.

"Non question. Fini!" I say, pointing to my screen.

"Ah, tu as terminé! Bravo! Tu es rapide!"

Yeah, I'm rapid, but now I guess she'll ask me how I got the answer, and I won't be able to tell her and she'll be mad. If I can't explain it in English, I sure won't be able to in French. But she doesn't ask me to "show my work," just gives me more problems to do. They're harder ones, but as long as I don't have to explain how I got my answer, they're not too hard for me. I think I'm going to like this school, even if Madame Nathalie doesn't dress up like a leopard every day.

CHAPTER 35
SIRI

On my way to school, I see that same group of kids I've seen every day in the skate park since the first week. I can smell what they're smoking from here. I take a quick sideways look at them. There are some kids from my class and some from higher grades too. I see Gabriel, that boy from Venezuela who's hyper-hot. He sees me too and motions me over.

"Tiens," Gabriel says, handing me a joint. I take it, trying to act like holding a joint is normal for me. He turns and says "Regarde!" to one of the older boys grinding his magna board a few feet away, then drops down and does ten one-handed push-ups. He jumps back up and walks over to the other boy, putting out his hand. The other boy looks annoyed but digs into his pocket and slaps a bill into Gabriel's palm. Then the same boy walks over to me.

"Câlisse, donne-moi le spliff. You're just letting it burn."

"Attends!" Gabriel says, then turns to me. "Veux-tu fumer de buzz, Mademoiselle Brooklyn?" He pronounces it "Broo-kleen," which makes it sound exotic.

"Sure." I put it to my lips and pull some smoke into my

mouth, only letting a little bit into the back of my throat. The rest I breathe out before handing it to the other boy.

"Don't waste good weed on this little girl. She doesn't even know how to inhale."

"Tabarnak!" I say, trying out a swear word I learned. "I know how to inhale. I'm from New York City." I grab the spliff back and breathe in a lungful of smoke. It burns the back of my throat and I start coughing.

Gabriel laughs and puts his finger under my chin. He's about five inches taller than me. Most of the kids in my school are bigger than me. Beginning high school with grade seven is such a stupid idea. Some of the boys in my grade haven't even started their growth spurts yet, and they're in school with guys who already have moustaches.

"So little Siri, why does a girl from *New York City* come to Montréal?"

I feel like he's teasing me a little, with the exaggerated way he says "New York City." My classe d'accueil is all immigrants, but I'm the only one from the United America, though a lot of kids speak English anyway. Since there are more grades in high school than there are classe d'accueils, there are a bunch of kids in my class who are one, two or even three years older than me. I figure Gabriel is at least fifteen. He's good-looking, with muscles on his arms. I'm surprised he's interested in talking to me. I better not let him think I'm less tough than he is.

"I was kidnapped. I had a boyfriend in Brooklyn. They broke us up."

"Vraiment? Who kidnapped you?"

"Mostly my father. He's a criminal, wanted by the government. He dragged me and my little brother here so he can hide out in Montréal. I don't even think he uses his real name. His first name, I think it's made up. And he uses my mom's last name."

Why am I saying this stuff? I can't seem to shut up. Suddenly

I feel hyper-paranoid. I stop myself from blabbing more by spitting on the ground.

"Do you have any gum?" I ask. "Wait, I do." I take a pack of gum out from my backpack and offer it around before shoving a piece into my own mouth.

"You're OK, little Siri. Don't worry. I can protect you from your father. Regarde!"

He takes off his shirt. He has tattoos on both his arms. On his right arm, it's a tattoo of a gun. He makes a muscle and the gun moves a little so you can imagine it firing. On his other arm, he has a tattoo of a string of barbed wire around his biceps. It reminds me of something. Oh yeah, the tattoo on Daddy's wrist.

"It's time to go to class," he says, and pushes me in the direction of the school.

"Aren't you coming?" I ask.

"I have to skip school today. For a small job. So I can earn some money for my mother and little sisters. My father's dead, you see, murdered by soldiers from your country."

"That's awful!" Maybe he blames me, since I'm from there. But that's kind of paranoid.

"You're good in math. Meet me after school with the homework." Gabriel says.

"OK. I can help you with the math, but not the French. I've decided I'm not gonna learn French at all. So my father'll have to send me back to New York."

Gabriel laughs. "Bon. Puis, à plus tard?"

"À plus tard." It's only when I get to school that I realize I'd answered him in French.

CHAPTER 36
JANIE

"Jane Wolfe, she/her," I say, reaching out my hand. I hope I haven't gotten it wrong and that this isn't another time I'm supposed to greet a relative stranger by kissing them on both cheeks.

"Pierre-Ryan Corcoran-Gagnon, he/him, at your service."

He shakes my hand firmly while I look him over: medium height, slightly paunchy, curly, light-brown hair, but what stands out most are his remarkably red cheeks. A cheerful-looking fellow, especially for a refugee lawyer.

"That's quite a name," I say.

"A mixture of French and Irish ancestry isn't uncommon here."

"And this is Laek, he/him."

"A pleasure," the lawyer says, shaking Laek's hand and ushering us towards two large wooden chairs. The chairs have the rough solidity of something manufactured in an earlier century. They inspire confidence, making me wonder if a parent or grandparent of Pierre-Ryan—a Corcoran or Gagnon perhaps —might have sat behind the same broad, scarred desk, reassuring refugees as they grasped the padded armrests, telling

their stories of persecution and escape. The flowery seat cush-
ions, on the other hand, seem a bit out of place.

"I'm going to tell you right off the bat that Laek prefers to
speak in French, but he's agreed to let us have this interview in
English for my sake," I tell him.

"I understood that you're both from the U.A. Is French your
first language, Monsieur?"

"No. Just my preferred language," Laek says.

"Ah! Well, let's get started with some preliminaries. Your full
name, nom de famille?"

"Laek. Laek Wolfe."

"So Laek and Jane Wolfe. I should mention that in Québec, by
law, a woman keeps her birth name."

"I didn't take Laek's name. He took mine."

"Oh! Well, that's unusual. The authorities will certainly ask if
there are any other names or aliases that you're known by,
Monsieur Wolfe. . ."

Laek remains silent. He looks like he's thinking. After a few
minutes, when he still hasn't answered, the lawyer says, "You
understand that whatever you tell me is confidential?"

Laek finally responds. "Yes, I understand. But I don't have
any other name. My mother named me Laek and that's it. Now
I'm thinking of going by Luc. If I'm allowed to stay here."

"Maybe we should wait on any name changes for now. One
legal issue at a time, no?"

"OK, d'accord," Laek answers, smiling shyly. I watch the
lawyer's expression soften as he looks from Laek to me. I feel a
familiar combination of wonder, mild frustration, and relief as I
realize that, without even trying, Laek has already managed to
win him over as a protector.

"So your intake form states that you have no income right
now. Is that correct?"

"That's right. I was a lawyer in New York, and Laek was a
teacher. I worked for legal services, actually. I never thought I'd

see myself on the other side of that desk. Frankly, I feel funny about this, like we shouldn't qualify for free legal help."

"We all find ourselves needing help on occasion."

I nod and he asks me if we have any other financial resources.

"Not much," I tell him. "Laek was badly hurt before we left the U.A. I had to use all of my sick time and a lot of vacation time too. I'm owed about five weeks pay, though. A friend's getting it for me. Unless you think that could be dangerous?"

"Why don't I hear your story first. Then we'll talk about safety."

"Laek's written an account of things right here." I hand him the refurbished screen we just purchased, feeling suddenly uncertain. Although I worked with Laek on the account, making sure it clearly showed how he meets the legal standards for protection as a refugee, I wonder if there's anything Laek wrote there that I don't know about.

"A lot of refugee-seekers find it easier to write about their experiences than talk about them," the lawyer says to Laek. "But you do understand that you'll need to speak of things at the hearing, answer questions and so forth?"

"Yes, bien compris."

"I see you've written it in French."

"Yeah. And I'd like the hearing to be in French too."

"Even though your first language is English? You risk not communicating your story as well as you could."

"There are other risks if I do it in English."

"What kinds of risks?"

"That I'll blank out."

The lawyer seems startled by the bluntness of Laek's response, but hardly misses a beat.

"Alright, I understand. But the hearing won't be right away, so you can make your final decision later. Meanwhile, I can direct you to some services. Therapy, support groups, food banks, temporary housing. . . Some resources are only open to

permanent residents and accepted refugees, but there are municipal programs, too. As well as less official help."

"The International Solidarity and Sanctuary network," I say.

"Good, you know about that. Let me take you two next door
to speak to my colleague, Mélissa, while I read what you've written. She can go through resources with you in detail."

When we come back to his office, the lawyer is looking a lot
less cheerful than before, although if anything, his cheeks are
redder. "It's a compelling story," he says.

"But what do you think about our chances . . . Can I call you
Pierre? Please call me Janie."

"Pierre or Pierre-Ryan is fine. What I think is that your case
for asylum poses some very. . ." I feel Laek go still beside me and
I take his hand, simultaneously trying to catch Pierre's eye. He
meets my gaze and nods slightly. "Some very *interesting* legal
challenges," he continues, even managing to sound enthusiastic
about these challenges.

"I know there will be a political problem. Canada's official
position is that the United America is a safe country," Laek says.

"Yes, that's probably our biggest challenge. But there's
some recognition of the fact that the U.A. uses torture in
certain contexts, like in military facilities and detention centres,
particularly with undocumented immigrants and political pris-
oners. And less officially, of course, in the criminal justice
system."

"What about the problem of my. . . my activities when I was
younger?" Laek asks.

"Unfortunately, if they decide that you were involved in
certain illegal activities or that you pose a security threat, you
can be denied refugee status on the grounds of exclusion. Even if
you can prove that you were tortured."

"How about the fact that Laek was so young? He was a
minor then, only fifteen."

"It's definitely an argument I plan to make."

"So you'll take our case?" I ask.

"Yes. But I don't want either of you to think it will be simple."

Now it's Pierre who's giving *me* the significant look.

"We understand," I say quickly. "But if we lose ...?"

"If you lose, there are other things we can try, but as a good friend of mine used to say, we'll burn that cross when we're nailed to it. In the meantime, the important thing is for you to get established here."

I know he's right, but it seems so overwhelming. Work, housing, French classes. . . where to start? And with the hearing hanging over us. "At least we found schools for the kids," I say.

"I see that your oldest is twelve. Neither one of you seems old enough to have a child that age! In any case, it's great that your children are already attending school. The next thing to concentrate on would be housing."

"Mélissa explained that without legal status, we're not eligible for government housing."

"There are low-income co-ops that are part of a certain réseau, that is, a network, who will accept undocumented immigrants who seem like good candidates. There's a large, relatively new one in Griffintown that's still looking for residents, and the subsidies are interesting."

"Griffintown? That doesn't sound very French. Where is it?" I ask.

"I can show you on a map," Laek says brightly. "It's not far from Simon's school, actually." This talk of maps and places suddenly has him sounding much more like himself.

"And the question of safety?" I ask, reluctant to change the mood, but needing to know.

"I think you made a good decision, coming to Montréal rather than to another Canadian city. Our sanctuary and solidarity movement. . . it means it would be harder for the U.A. government to recapture a political refugee here, notwithstanding our close proximity. They couldn't count on the cooperation of municipal authorities, not even the SCSVM—the police."

I smile at Laek. I wasn't so sure about his analysis of this. It's a relief to be wrong.

"What about contacting friends and relatives in the States?" I ask.

"That's harder to say. Clearly, they could track you if they were willing to expend the resources. It's a question of how badly they want you," Pierre concludes.

"There's also the danger of our friends being harassed. And of their safety too," Laek says, with a rare flash of anger. I put my hand on his arm.

Pierre seems unfazed. "Frankly, you're in a better position than I am to judge how far your government is willing to go in these cases. But what I can do is point you to some network groups that offer scrambled and anonymous communication services. They can still be traced on the other end, of course."

"And the money owed me from my job?" I ask. "Any reason not to pursue that?"

"Legal Services, where you worked, are they funded by the federal government?"

"Yes, in part."

"Hmm. Well, there's no harm in trying. It will be informative to see if you succeed in getting your pay. Let me know what happens. We'll talk again next week." He stands up and I understand that this is it for today. "Don't hesitate to call if you have any questions or concerns. Laek, Janie, my best advice to you right now is to concentrate on building a new life here. We'll meet the legal challenges a step at a time."

Once outside, I try to draw Laek out.

"How you doing, sweetheart? Did you like the lawyer?"

"He seemed nice."

"You OK?"

"Uh huh."

I'm not convinced. Understandably, his mood darkened

when the conversation moved from co-ops and maps to possible pursuit by the government. If only he'd talk to me about it!

"So what do you want to do now?" I ask him instead. "I'm thinking about trying to see what I can find out about my cheque."

"I'm gonna look for work."

"We don't even have our work permits yet."

"Something informal, maybe. I'll just look around. See what I can turn up."

"OK, but can you also contact that co-op in Griffintown?"

"I'll bike over in person if you like."

"That'd be great, love. You make a good impression, especially in person."

He doesn't say anything, just unlocks his bike. I walk over and rub his back.

"It's gonna be fine. Try not to worry too much."

He turns to me and I reach up to kiss him on both cheeks. He laughs and shakes his head.

"Janie, for me, it's the lips, not the cheeks. But if you want, you can kiss my lips *and* my cheeks. And anywhere else you can reach."

"Sorry." I feel embarrassed, my cheeks probably as red as Pierre's. How am I going to adapt to a new country if I can't even get straight when and where I'm supposed to kiss people?

"I'll see you at home," he says. "We'll practice kissing then."

He gives me a mischievous smile and I'm reassured. Not just by the smile but by the fact that he's referring to the hotel as "home." I feel the same way. Wherever we're together is home.

I grab a cup of coffee at a café and look through the information Mélissa gave us. One of the network groups mentioned is also located in Griffintown. If we end up finding an apartment in that area, it'll be good to know where the different community resources are. Plus, maybe I'll even run into Laek. I hop on my bike feeling upbeat as I head over to Griffintown.

Griffintown isn't far from the lawyer's office, so it doesn't take me long to get there. It's nothing like any of the areas we've been to up till now, more like a small town inside the city than a neighbourhood, and clearly very old, but developed in a hyper-modern way. I ride around to check it out, careful to remember the turns I've made so I can retrace my steps later.

I'm pedalling along rue Notre-Dame on a sweet little bike lane. It's elevated above the street level and protected from traffic by an artful barrier. The pavement is painted an almost psychedelic shade of yellow. I feel like I'm on my way to Oz.

Around me, the buildings are a rainbow of rich colours—azure, deep purple, forest green and tangerine—with murals or holo-art decorating the walls. On the rooftops, all kinds of vegetation is growing, flowers as well as vegetables. I can see giant sunflowers and rustling corn. The light rail system running through the neighbourhood passes right by the sky gardens. I stare up, imagining sinking my hands into the rich, fertile earth high above the city streets. I'm so mesmerized that I almost run into the cyclist ahead of me as they stop at a corner and dismount. I've been tailing them for a few kilometres, admiring their speed and fluidity.

"Attention!" the cyclist says.

"I smile sheepishly and motion up at the roofs.

"Ah, les jardins sur les toits!" I shrug my incomprehension. "Beautiful, aren't they?" the cyclist asks, switching to English.

"Yes, they are."

"And healthy too. Organic. To improve the health of both the people and mother earth."

And with that, the cyclist pulls off their helmet, letting loose thick, white-grey hair. Their wrinkled face seams with laughter as I react in surprise to their obvious age. Yes, I think I might like to raise my kids here, if this is the condition people are in when they're senior citizens.

At the community centre, with few preliminaries and even less bureaucracy, I'm led to a screen I can use. Text is less costly than voice, so I decide to go with that. Since I'm paying by the letter, I keep my message to Magda brief:

R u well? News on my cheque? Other news? We r fine. —J

I'm not even sure she's available, but she responds right away.

Where are you? Don't recognize message origin. We're fine. Life crazy, as usual. Bad news on cheque. Money not available. Pay frozen, "under investigation." Continue to try?

I stand up and push my chair back, suddenly so nervous I don't even want to touch the screen, as though someone's going to reach through the connection and grab me by the throat. Or worse, grab Laek. I feel almost violated, having them fuck with my paycheque like that. Five weeks of salary! If we were careful, with the lower housing costs here, we could have made that money last several months at least. Fuck them, those bastards! Well, they can have their goddamned money, as long as they leave Laek alone.

I sit back down, my temper up and my fear more or less pushed under that. I type.

Dont pursue $.

And now I'm worried that I may have gotten Magda into trouble. Or our other friends.

You OK? Other friends OK? I send the message and wait. She writes back.

No worries, everyone fine. Rebecca and David very upset tho. And Michael, of course. We all miss you.

Miss u too. Sending love.

I terminate the contact, thank the staff and leave the building, anxious to get as far away from it as possible, even knowing that this is irrational. I'd told myself that I never doubted Laek but had I secretly thought he was being a little paranoid? Why else would I feel so shocked right now? I think I finally have a glimpse of how it is to be Laek, thinking about being on the government's screen, with nowhere to flee that feels far enough from danger. Nowhere to flee but deeper inside himself.

CHAPTER 37
LAEK

The trees of the park frame the sky, and my head is filled with blue. I'm on my back. Grass tickles me through my t-shirt. I stroke a blade of it with my thumb. My other hand rests on my bike. I finger the spokes, spin my wheel. Yellow and burgundy leaves whirl and fall around me. What made me think I'd ever known autumn before?

I sit up slowly. Take account of my physical state. I don't mind the slight ache in my back from all the hours of raking. But I'm a little dizzy. Maybe it's the surreal colours of the leaves. Or maybe I'm just hungry. What did I eat today? Did I eat? I'm thirsty, that's for sure. I take a long drink from my water bottle. The coolness slides down my throat and into my stomach. It's flavoured with mint leaves from the community roof garden.

There's usually food at the support group meeting. But first I'll have to get through the counselling session. I'd rather spend my time looking for work. Or taking more French classes. But I promised Janie. I check my pocket. Eighty dollars. Not a lot for all that raking, but with it, we should have just enough to make November's rent. I feel lucky. The folks at the Griffintown co-op were nice to take us in. I walk by a group of high-school students, hanging off each other the way they do at that age, like my own students did back in Brooklyn. I turn away. Think some more about the colours of the leaves.

———

"We'll be breaking up into different language groups to facilitate communication. Many people have English as a common second tongue, so you can go with them," the group leader, Pascal, tells me. He's youngish, small in stature, his looks unremarkable, but he has a certain physical presence that inspires confidence.

I answer him in French. "J'veux pas ... I'd prefer not to speak English. Please. . ."

"None of the others will be speaking French for this exercise."

"How about Spanish? Yo hablo español. Can I go with the hispanophones?"

"Did you speak Spanish in New York? Well enough to express yourself?"

"My best friend is Latine; he teaches Spanish. We spoke it together sometimes."

"OK, go ahead and join the hispanophone group, then."

We're sitting in a loose, horseshoe-shape on rickety, wooden chairs. They look like they were borrowed from ancient classrooms. I'm the newest member of the group. Pascal has us introduce ourselves. Name the country we're from. Everyone seems friendly. They smile to hear a New Yorker speaking Spanish flavoured by that unmistakeable accent—half New York and half Puerto Rico.

Pascal asks us what we each miss most from our home countries.

Why think about this? There are so many amazing things here. The people in my group are mostly talking about food. I think the food in Montréal is exceptional. Much better than the food in the United America. Even than in New York. Except the pizza, anyway.

Now they're talking about the beauty of the natural environments they left behind. Mountains, forests, plant life. Yeah, right. I don't need to cry over that. Not where I come from. Should I miss the smell of garbage during the stifling summer months? Or maybe the hot blacktop, literally melting under my sandals? Giving off toxic odours. Speaking of toxins, maybe I should miss the pesticides they sprayed over everything one wet spring. They said it was to kill mosquitoes supposedly carrying a dangerous flu. Meanwhile, dozens of young and elderly asthmatics were killed when they over-dumped the stuff in some of the poorest neighbourhoods.

It's my turn now. They're all looking at me. What should I say I miss? I glance up at the ceiling, notice a trapezoidal-shaped water stain that reminds me of Prospect Park. I do love that park, but there are a lot of beautiful parks here, and none of them sprayed with pesticides.

For some reason, I talk about biking to work. The energy of the city during the morning rush. The smell of muffins. How if you stand on your pedals and look hard all the way down Thirteenth Street, you can see the sun lighting the river, illuminating everything in its path.

"That sounds beautiful," Pascal says.

"New York City is very ugly," I respond. "An ugly place."

"Tell us about something you loved from back home," he asks.

I shrug, unable to respond. I feel guilty, though. They're all looking at me, waiting for me to share a good memory, something that will help them bear their own losses more easily. It reminds me of being in front of the classroom again, of having all those eyes on me, full of expectation, so I say, "My job, my kids. I was a teacher. I. . . I miss the feeling of hope that things could be better for them. That I could be part of making it better."

"And were you? Did you help make things better?"

"I don't know," I answer. I think about Fari and Nina at the demo in Battery Park. "Not alone, anyway. There were my colleagues. My friends. Without them. . ." I remember Erin's hand on my arm that last night. And leaning against Philip's shoulder. No, I won't think about that.

"You had mentioned your best friend who teaches Spanish," Pascal says.

I want him to leave me alone. Isn't my turn over yet? Let's go back to talking about mountains, forests, safe things like that. But it's too late because now I see Philip's features on the face of every man in this room. And I can't stop thinking about his goodness, his sense of humour, his fierce loyalty, his strength when I leaned against him. And his hot tears on my neck the last time I saw him.

I find myself standing, shaking with fury, fists clenched. How can they have taken all this from me? My students, my friends, Philip? It's so unfair. I had a good life! I was happy! Janie and the kids were happy! I try to sit back down, to fade into the background, but something's wrong—my chair's missing. A wave of panic hits me as I realize that I've flung it across the room, where it now lies broken against the far wall.

Half the people in my group have jumped to their feet, some looking at me, others at the chair. Two start walking towards me. I stumble backwards, my heart beating in my ears. Pascal waves them off and approaches me himself with slow, cautious steps, his expression somewhere between fear and concern. I hear Philip's voice in my head, saying "Pull yourself the fuck together." Heat rushes to my cheeks as I wonder if the chair came close to hitting anyone.

"Lo siento. Lo siento mucho," I say, moving to recover the chair.

"It's OK," Pascal responds. "No need to apologize."

"Laisse moi, let me fix it." I'm having some linguistic confusion, switching between Spanish and French. I hold pieces of the chair in my hands. A leg, a wooden support. "I can fix this. I think I can."

"It's OK, Laek. Can I touch you?"

"What?" I ask.

"For some of the people who come here, a touch can be unsettling."

"Don't worry. I won't freak out. I just want to fix the chair."

"It's OK, we'd be happy to have you fix the chair. Just not right now. Come," Pascal says, putting his hand on my shoulder. "Come back to the group and sit down. I have another chair for you in the meantime."

I let him lead me back to the circle. His hand on my shoulder steadies me. I feel relieved by this. And I didn't blank out. Not exactly. I don't think I was conscious of throwing the chair, but I remember doing it now, when I think back on it. So I wasn't really gone.

I'm quiet for the rest of the meeting. Session. Whatever it is. I feel tired and ashamed as I listen to the others talking. With my chair-throwing incident, discussion has turned from food and environment to people. Those left behind. A woman talks about her elderly parents, how she may never see them again. And how sad this is for her, especially now that she's given birth to her first child. I feel for her. My own mother is dead—and I have no interest in ever seeing the man who's probably my father—but I hope Janie will be able to see her parents, that the kids will see their grandparents. I think they will, if things go well. Later, if we succeed in getting permanent residence. We're very lucky in this respect.

A man talks about leaving his lover behind. His husband, that is, if his country recognized same-sex marriage.

"Maybe you'll see him again," I hear myself saying. "Maybe you can bring him over."

He looks at me sadly. "He is in prison, amigo. He may never leave that place alive."

My heart twists inside me. I should have been paying more attention when he said where he was from. And now I should ask him, as Pascal asked me, if he minds being touched. But my body is moving on its own as I squat by his chair and squeeze his shoulder saying: "Don't give up hope, hermano. Every day you keep going, it's another small victory. And you're fighting for him too. You see that, don't you?" Maybe Janie will have an idea of how to help. I think about how, after this session, I can go home to Janie, lie down beside her, but how this man's bed will be cold and empty. I swallow hard to keep the tears back. Whisper that my partner is a lawyer, that I can introduce him to her and our own lawyer, an expert on asylum. Maybe there's something that can be done. After a moment he nods, squeezes my shoulder back.

At the end of the meeting, there's pizza. The one food that's better in New York. I find that as hungry as I'd been before, I don't have much of an appetite now. Pascal approaches me.

"You don't like pizza?"

"No, I like it fine. It's just that. . . I'm vegetarian. So the pepperoni doesn't work for me."

"That's a problem easily solved," he says, redistributing the round pieces of pepperoni from two of the slices onto others in the pie.

One of the men from the group is standing beside me, listening to this exchange.

"Good. More for us carnivores," he says, grabbing a slice heavily loaded with pepperoni.

Someone else comes over. Offers around a drink from their bottle. The liquid is clear, but it's definitely not water that's warming me now from the inside. I pick up one of the denuded slices. Take a bite. It's pretty good. Only a faint taste of smoky meat lodged in the mozzarella cheese. Hunger, as they say, is the best spice. That, and good company. I lean back against the wall and imagine I can feel Philip's hand on my shoulder.

CHAPTER 38
SIRI

It's "mardi en français," one of the two days during the week that my parents have ruled are French-only. I feel like I live in some kind of mind-control dictatorship. I've told my parents I can't speak French and I won't learn it. So I'm sitting at the kitchen table doing my homework, my math homework that is, and pretending I can't understand a word they're saying. Meanwhile, my head automatically translates everything into English.

"How many dollars did you gain?" Mommy asks.

Daddy pulls some bills out of his pocket and smoothes them out on the table.

"Not much, but every dollar helps."

"You seem very fatigued. Did you do much of, of *raking*?"

I notice that Mommy can't get through one sentence without using some English words.

"Yes, but I did some of it for free."

"Shit! Another time?"

"I had promised some seniors that I'd return when more leaves fell. They needed me. It's important to finish your work."

"Oh, Laek."

"And you? Did you search for your cheque today? For the catering that you did?"

"For what?"

"The *cooking*. That you did for those community events."

"Oh yes. I was paid. But the dollars were not a lot more than I paid. For the foods."

My parents don't know anything about how to earn a profit—Daddy raking for free and Mommy buying all organic, cooking fancy meals and charging almost nothing. Meanwhile, I earned a whole bunch of money with my garage sale and lemonade stand this weekend. Mommy tried to talk me into not asking for my allowance since I made so much, but why should I be punished for being enterprising? Anyhow, Gabriel and I have other uses for my money. Which reminds me, I better beam him my math homework.

Daddy is taking some stuff out of his sacoche now. Food, it looks like. Some fruits, vegetables, cheese, other stuff.

"But, it is something expensive that you have?" Mommy asks, in her broken French.

"I have vegetarian pâté, brie, Oka cheese. . ."

"How did you buy? Was many dollars?"

"No. Not really. I paid like nothing."

"Like nothing? What do you mean, 'like nothing'?"

"Nothing. I mean nothing. I paid nothing."

"Laek, what you have done? You have stole?"

Whoa, this conversation is getting interesting, but I can't let them know I understand French, so I keep looking down at my work.

"No. Of course not. It was free."

"Free? Where did you find? Say the truth to me."

"At the Jean-Talon Market. At the end of the day."

"Oh. Oh. Did you, did you *dumpster dive*?"

"Yeah. That is exact."

What! Daddy dumpster dived for this food? I have to say something, but I don't want them to know I understand French.

Wait, I can get away with it because Mommy used English when she said "dumpster dive."

"Do I have this straight? Are you saying you *dumpster dived*, Daddy?"

"Yes. It's OK. The food is good."

"Speak English. I don't speak French."

"At least make an effort, Siri."

"Je. Ne. Parle. Pas. Français!" I refuse to give in to their craziness.

"Siri, calme-toi."

"Did this food actually come from the garbage? I think I deserve to know that, even if I don't speak French!"

Mommy caves and talks to me in English. "There's nothing wrong with this food."

"Then why was it in the garbage?"

"Some of the items were expired."

"Expired? Like dead?"

"I mean the date stamped on the product. The stores aren't supposed to sell things when the date is expired. But it's still perfectly good, especially if we use it right away."

"The vegetables look like they're going rotten."

"We can just cut off the bad parts."

"I refuse to eat food from the garbage. It's gross."

"It would be a sin to let good food go to waste."

"A sin? You want me to eat it for religious reasons? You don't even believe in God."

"A crime, then. It's just wrong to waste food. One problem with a consumer society. . ."

"Oh, I get it. You want me to eat it for *political* reasons. Just like you took me from my friends and home and are forcing me to go to school in French for political reasons."

"Siri, stop being unreasonable. We're a bit short now and this food is perfectly good."

"So get yourselves real jobs. And if you can't find any here, let's go back home. You had good jobs there and didn't force Simon and me to eat garbage!"

Simon looks up sadly and then looks down again. He's reading a book on his school screen about whales and seals. While I'm pretending not to understand any French, Simon's pretending that he isn't even in the room.

"Ça suffit, Siri. If you don't want to eat this food, don't," Daddy says.

I pretend I can't understand him, but get up to leave anyway.

"You can't make me eat garbage!" I run into my room and slam the door behind me, throwing myself onto my bed.

I'd like to speak to Michael, but I'm not allowed to even text until the weekend. I can't wait to tell him about this newest type of child abuse my parents are doing to me. I go through my school bag. Yes! I thought there was the rest of a candy bar in there. After I finish eating it, I beam a message to Gabriel.

My parents r making me eat food from d garbage. I hate them. Can I come over?

I wait. No response.

I despise my school. Aside from Gabriel and a few others, the kids are either boring or annoying. There are no kids like my friends at home. And everyone in my class breaks up into little immigrant cliques—the Chinese kids sit in one place, the kids from Roumanie in another, the Russians in their own corner, whatever. The Chinese kids are good at math and the girls hide their mouths when they laugh. The kids from Roumanie speak French better than the rest of us and act superior. The kids from the Philippines are OK, I guess. Some of them play basketball well, even though they're short. But that's the other thing. Where are all the Black kids? There are hardly any in my class, and that feels weird. This whole place is way too white. And the few Black kids are mostly Haitian. They speak French, but in a weird way. Same with the Black kids who are from West or Central Africa. They don't sound like my friends at home. Their voices sound lower and. . . I don't know. At home, there are all kinds of kids, but they all seem like Brooklynites.

Gabriel finally beams me back. He says I can't come over but that he'll bring me something tomorrow. And he asks me to beam him the French homework too. So I sit down and do the French homework. It's pretty easy and doesn't take long. After I beam it to him, since I don't plan on handing in any French homework myself, I delete the original. Send it right into the trash. Let my parents dumpster dive for that.

CHAPTER 39
SIMON

I run inside our building with my jacket over my head when the rain starts. I hope the garlic we planted on the roof garden doesn't drown. More than anything though, I hope it stops raining so that we can go back outside to play street hockey. I was finally gonna get to play goalie. In Brooklyn, we'd never just go out with a bunch of kids and play on the street. All the stuff we did was scheduled way ahead of time on Mommy's screen. Here, kids just go out and play with each other when they feel like it, and all different ages play together.

I turn to ask Siri whether she thinks it might stop raining and realize that she's still outside. I stick my head out the door and call to her in French and then in English, but she doesn't come so I go out to get her. She looks at me and then at the trees and then at all the wet leaves on the ground and says, "I guess that's that." I don't know if she means there goes our hockey game or that's it for the leaves. I have the feeling it's something else, something I don't get. She seems hyper-upset for just a hockey game.

At suppertime, the rain has stopped but the wind is still blowing fierce, knocking the tree branches all around and sending the leaves flying. It makes me think of a shakedown. It's like the trees are being forced to let go of their leaves or get pushed to the ground. Maybe some trees will even fall or get killed. Then the rain comes back again, and any leaves that had been able to hang on against the wind now fall down with the weight of all that water.

Alone in my room at night, the wind sounds loud and scary, but it's when a banging noise starts inside my room that I really get spooked. It sounds like someone getting beaten with a phaser stick. I run into Siri's room. She tells me to go back to bed, that it's just the heat starting up in the radiator. I know she thinks I'm being a baby, but I'm still not used to sleeping in a room all by myself. Plus, she wasn't there this summer. She doesn't know what things were like.

In the morning, everything is calm and quiet. I hear small kitchen sounds and smell something delicious and chocolaty. For a second I think it's Saturday and Daddy's making crepes, but no, it's a weekday. Why hasn't Mommy come in to wake me up for school?

I walk over to my little window and pull back the curtain that Mommy sewed out of some blue material. I look out, expecting to see fallen leaves but instead there's a sparkling whiteness. Snow! Our first snowstorm! And it's still snowing hard! I run into Siri's room and try to wake her, but she puts her head under her pillow and ignores me. I run out into the kitchen. Daddy's eating breakfast and Mommy's looking at the screen.

"Looks like school's cancelled for you and Siri," she says. "There must be like three feet of snow out there already, and no sign of it letting up."

"Centimetres, Janie. Try to think in metres and centimetres," Daddy says while chewing.

"Um, what's the conversion again?" Mommy asks.

"If you would think in centimetres, you wouldn't need to do a conversion. Same issue with French. You have to think in it, not be translating in your head all the time."

"It's one inch to 2.54 centimetres, Mommy." I tell her. "That's. . ."

"Don't tell me! Um, that's like ninety-one and a half inches, I mean centimetres. OK, restart." Mommy puts on a fake excited voice. "Look, Simon, look Laek! There's approximately ninety-one centimetres of snow outside. Isn't that lovely!"

Daddy shakes his head like he can't believe Mommy's acting so silly, but he can't stop his lips from smiling. Mommy calls Siri into the kitchen.

"If school is cancelled, why are you making me get out of bed?" Siri asks Mommy.

"Daddy's working at the bike shop today and I have my French classes and then a rendez-vous with career planning. So you need to look after your brother."

"OK, fine. Can I go back to bed now?"

"Can't we go out and play?" I ask. "Please?"

"Alright, fine. We'll go out to the park or something."

"Come. I made everyone hot chocolate," Mommy says. "Lucky we got those boots for you guys last weekend. You should put on the long underwear, too. Laek, what about you? What do you have to wear on your feet?"

"I have my work boots."

"Will that be enough? And why are you wearing your jeans with the holes in them?"

"I'm wearing another pair of jeans underneath. See? That's why all you see is denim under the holes, instead of my flesh."

"What will we do in the park, Siri?" I ask.

"Hey, I have an idea," Daddy says, digging into his pocket. "Here, Siri, you can use this to buy something to glisser. . . to, to slide on the snow, down the hill."

"Do you mean 'sled,' Daddy?" Siri asks. "Have you forgotten how to speak English?"

"Yeah, sled, sleigh, whatever. . ."

Now Mommy gets into the act. "Laek, a sleigh has bells and

is drawn by horses." I think she's getting him back for the centimetres.

"A sled, then. Or one of those sliding things. Here." Daddy digs into his pocket again and gives Siri whatever he finds in there.

"Mais ... c'est tout l'argent que tu as." Mommy says this while looking around sneakily at me and Siri. I think she's using French to try to hide what she's saying from us, which makes no sense, considering I speak French way better than she does. Maybe she's just trying to hide it from Siri. I look into my hot chocolate and pretend not to be paying attention. I listen, though, as Daddy tells Mommy in French that it's OK, that he can walk to work and bring some food from home for his lunch, that he doesn't need any money. That he'd rather the kids have fun, and anyway, he'd like to go sledding too.

I'm not sure if I should say something. I want a sled, but maybe Daddy needs the money more. He did look happy when he talked about sledding, though. I look at Siri, forgetting for a second that she couldn't have understood what Mommy and Daddy said. She's watching Daddy get up and throw some stuff from the refrigerator into a cloth lunch bag. Siri puts her lips together and looks at me. I wonder. Could she have somehow understood?

Outside, the air tastes fresh and cold. Puffs of smoke are coming out of our mouths. I stick out my tongue, trying to catch the snowflakes. The world seems quiet, like the snow is cotton in my ears. It's coming down and down and down, soft but unstoppable.

Siri buys us a red plastic sled. The man is francophone but understands English. I say "merci" to be polite since Siri only talks to him in English. The sled is flat with a curled part in front, but it's long and light and slick. I just know it'll fly down the hill faster than anything.

Siri heads for the path into the park, but we decide to walk across the grass part. It's not grass now, of course, just a big field of snow, white and perfect. Nobody has walked there yet. We'll be the first, like explorers. We dive into the snow and flip onto our backs, like we're swimming. Siri grabs a handful of snow, trying to make a snowball. She throws it at me, but it falls apart. I feel bits of it on my cheeks. It's like she's thrown cold, white sand at me.

After a while, we find a hill. There are kids already there who came from the other side of the park. They're sledding down in all kinds of things, like tubes and rafts and saucers, plus real wooden sleds and toboggans, and even things that look like magna snowboards. No one's sliding down on metal garbage can lids, like we see sometimes in Prospect Park. But then again, it doesn't snow that much in New York. And when it does, there's usually rain right after, washing it all away. I hope it doesn't rain.

After going down the hill about a million times, I ask if we can go over to the playground.

"Why would you want to go to the playground? The equipment will be covered in snow."

"Maybe we can swing, anyway. Swing really high and jump off into the snow."

We walk towards where the playground should be. It's hard to find with all the snow. Everything looks different. I feel like an explorer again. I even see animal tracks.

"Look Siri! Paw prints! In the forest! We need to see where they lead."

I get down low and examine the tracks. The prints are small. Maybe of a rabbit or a fox. No, I know what it is. It's a miniature magical panther. I follow the tracks until I lose them in a big mess of human prints, sneakers and boots and stuff. I look up and see we've found the playground. There are a bunch of big kids leaning against the fence, smoking. Then I see the creature I've been tracking—a small dog with pointy ears and shaggy hair. I lean over to pet him or her as one of the biggest boys comes over.

"If it isn't little Siri," he says.

"Don't call me that," Siri answers, and then says hello to some of the other kids without walking over to them. "Let's go, Simon. We need to get home."

"I wanna pet the dog."

"You shouldn't pet strange dogs you don't know," Siri says.

"It's OK. I can tell it's a sweet doggy."

"C'est ton chum, ce petit fif?" the big boy says.

Siri answers in English."He's not my boyfriend, he's my brother. Let's go, Simon!"

"What's your rush, little Siri? Just because Gabriel isn't here? Let the little fif play with the dog. It's a bitch," he says to me. "Go on, pet her."

When I bend down, he kicks the dog towards me. The dog starts snapping and barking and I jump back. Then I'm on the kid in a second, kicking and punching him. What a mean thing to do to a little dog! But the kid is much bigger than me. He pushes me off easily and throws me into the snow. Before I can attack again, Siri grabs me from behind and pulls me back.

"Go get the sled," she orders me. "I mean it, Simon. You better do what I say."

I'm hyper-mad but I turn to get the sled which we left near a tree. As I'm walking away, I hear what sounds like Siri's voice cursing the kid out in French.

"Espèce de petite merde," she says. "If you ever fucking touch my little brother again, I'll take my father's hunting knife and cut your balls off. If you have any, which I doubt, since you pick on boys half your size. Fucking ostie de débile qui s'amuse à licher sa propre queue!"

Teenagers are weird. He doesn't get mad— just laughs and says he'll see Siri at school. We walk out of the park. I can't help feeling impressed by how Siri put him in his place. I'm not even sure of what one or two of the words she used means.

"Siri, what's débile?"

"It means, like, retard, idiot."

"And queue? I thought that meant tail. And what's a fif?"

"You're too young to know these words."

"And you're not supposed to know French at all."

She stops and looks at me, like she's trying to figure something out. Then she lets out a puff of air. "OK, fine. If you keep my secret from Daddy and Mommy, I'll tell you what the other words mean. But I'm serious. You have to swear not to tell about the French."

"I swear."

"Alright, then. Queue is a word that can be used to mean penis."

"And fif?"

She sighs before answering. "Fif is girlie, or, or gay."

"That's a stupid way to insult people."

"He's an asshole, just forget it."

"Un trou du cul, right?"

"Right."

"But why don't you want Daddy and Mommy to know that you can speak French? I know you're mad that we moved, but still. . ."

"Simon, you better not be thinking of going back on your word."

"No! I just want to know why."

"How about if you and I get a snack somewhere? We'll talk about it then, OK?"

"OK, d'accord." Now that I know she can speak French, I don't have to stick to English.

Siri takes me on the métro. Even though there's no school today, our free school métro passes still work. We sing out each stop as we go by, trying to match the exact accent and tone, like we used to do when we first got here: "Prochaine station, Sherbrooke ... Prochaine station, Mont Royal." A lot of grown-ups in the métro are smiling at us. Maybe they think what we're doing is funny, or maybe it's the big sled we're carrying. Or maybe they have off work because of the snow and are happy too.

We go into a small restaurant. It's hot and steamy inside, the windows all fogged up. We walk up to the counter and Siri orders two "queues de castor." It's the first time I've gone into a place with Siri and heard her talk in French. But what's she ordering? I whisper to her.

"Siri, we can't eat that! We're vegetarians."

"This *is* vegetarian," she answers.

"Beaver tails? That's meat, not vegetable!"

Siri laughs. "It's not an actual beaver tail."

An even more horrible thought hits me as I remember the other meaning of "queue."

"Siri, no! We can't eat the. . . the thingies of beavers. That's even worse!"

Now she's laughing so hard she can hardly talk.

"Trust me, little brother, you're going to like this. It is not at all what you think."

It's true the restaurant smells more like cinnamon and chocolate than meat. And when we get our orders and sit down, I can see it's not shaped like a penis, although it does look a little like a beaver tail. I take a small, cautious bite.

"Hey, it tastes like fried dough. Like what we get in Little Italy back in New York."

"Yep, it's just like that."

"Only it's better. It has gobs of Nutella on it, my favourite."

"I am so sick of all of you talking about how everything is *so much better* here."

"Well, lots of things are." Though even while I'm saying this, I realize I might be wrong about certain things. Up until today, I'd thought there weren't any bullies in Montréal.

"Don't you miss Brooklyn? Don't you miss your old friends and school?" Siri asks.

"I miss Henry, but Mommy says maybe he can visit if everything works out. Otherwise, I don't miss New York that much. At first I did, but now I'm used to being here."

"Well I miss. . . everything. My friends, my neighbourhood,

my school, baseball, the way people talk, the way they act. I just can't believe Daddy and Mommy did this to us."

"They had to. They said. About how Daddy was in danger."

"And you believe all that?"

"Sure. Don't you?"

"Why should I? I mean, maybe if they had told me about it sooner, explained, showed me evidence or something. Now, it's like they're just using it as an excuse to do what they want."

"But. . ." Maybe I should tell Siri about what really happened this summer. About my finding out how Daddy was beaten with a phaser stick, by that cop, about how he almost died. But this is a secret, right? Otherwise, Mommy and Daddy would have told. And if I tell, Siri will think I can't keep secrets and won't ever tell me anything. So I decide not to tell her. I try to think of something else to say, something convincing.

"There may be stuff we don't know about. You know, like maybe terrorists were after us. At least there aren't terrorists here."

"What makes you say that?"

"Back in New York, we had to watch out for terrorists all the time. They talked about them on the newsfeeds and they were always issuing those warnings. You know: 'Code Amber' or 'If you see something, say something.' Our school had to be checked for bombs and viruses and stuff. I never hear about that in Montréal."

"Just because people somewhere talk about terrorists, it doesn't mean there are any. Did you ever run into any terrorists?"

"No, but. . ."

"And just because you don't hear about terrorists somewhere else, it doesn't mean there aren't any there. Maybe there's a terrorist in this restaurant right now."

"I'm done with my queue du castor. We should go home now," I say, a little nervous.

"OK. But don't forget, not a word about this to Daddy or Mommy."

"Don't worry, I can keep a secret."

That night, right before bedtime, we hear all these loud noises on the street—beeps and scraping sounds and big, powerful motors. Siri and I kneel on the couch in front of the big window facing the street. Outside, there are like seven different trucks. They're driving around with attachments that scoop and dip and grab. One truck has a huge tube that looks like it's for shooting missiles. A mini-vehicle drives hyper-fast onto the sidewalk like it's a getaway car. A neighbour walking her dog jumps out of the way just in the nick of time. Everywhere, lights are flashing, like some major sweep-up operation back in New York. Only, I don't see the police. Just the assailants. And what they're doing is they're stealing all our snow.

Mommy and Daddy are talking quietly in the kitchen, but I can hear them anyway. Daddy has just told Mommy that his job at the bike shop is over.

"You've been there for only a month. I thought. . . " Mommy says.

"They hardly have enough work for themselves during the year, with all the improvements in the free bike system. And now that a real snowfall has come early. . ."

"You'll find something else, sweetheart, don't worry."

"Daddy, Mommy, come here," I yell.

Mommy comes and kneels next to me. There isn't enough room for Daddy to squeeze in like that too, so he comes up behind Mommy and wraps his arms around her waist.

"Papa," I whisper, "Are they terrorists?"

Daddy puts his arm around my shoulder. "No, they're just city workers."

"But why are they stealing all the snow? I like the snow."

"I do too."

"Even though it means your job is over?"

"So you heard that? Yeah, even though it means my job is

over. Snow is beautiful. And like Mommy said, I'll find something else. Don't worry. And don't worry about terrorists either."

"D'accord, Papa."

I look at Siri. She's still staring straight ahead like she doesn't understand. But she does.

"Goodnight, Siri. And thanks for the. . . for the beaver tails. And everything."

"I love you, Simon," she answers.

CHAPTER 40
JANIE

"Des études montrent qui 81% des femmes sont comblées," reads the headline. I start looking up the English translation for the word "comblée" but then remember Laek's scolding and bring up the French-to-French dictionary instead. OK, "combler" means "satisfaire". Satisfied about what? I find another definition: "remplir un trou," to fill a hole. A pothole? I don't get it. I read further on in the article, get to the word "sexualité." Oh, *that* kind of hole. So according to this article, eighty-one percent of women in Montréal are sexually satisfied. What I still don't get is how this constitutes serious headline news. I suppose it's my own fault for choosing such a lowest-common-denominator news source instead of the more intellectual screen journal that Laek reads. But shit, if I read that, I'd get through maybe one story a day.

I scan some more articles, and learn that seventy-three percent of Montréalais are friendly with at least half their neighbours, that ninety-one percent of local university students think there'll be a global catastrophic climate event in their lifetime, and that the popularity of the latest non-tobacco cigarettes has forced the government to install 424 new ashtrays in public spaces throughout the city.

What is this obsession with figures? I'm beginning to hate numbers. Yesterday in class, I was called on to read aloud and was doing just fine until I came to "1999," forcing me to do a whole string of calculations. Mille, neuf-cent, quatre-vingt-dix-neuf—a thousand, nine hundred, and four twenties plus ten and nine. Next, we'll be singing about four-and-twenty blackbirds baked in a pie. Ridiculous!

Simon comes into the kitchen. "Can I have an omelette?" he asks.

"Would you mind just getting some cereal? I have to do my French homework."

"Mommy, you should not have left it to the last minute like this. Madame Nathalie says the best time to do your homework is right before supper."

"That's a great idea. Only problem is that right before supper, I'm cooking supper."

"Oh yeah. OK, I'll make my own breakfast."

"Where's your sister?"

"I don't need breakfast. I'm gonna eat at school," Siri says, coming into the kitchen.

"Take something at least. You shouldn't go to school without eating."

"There's nothing good to eat here, anyway."

I take a deep breath, trying to control my temper. Every cent we have is used to provide the kids with healthy food and the things they need. Laek doesn't even have a decent winter coat.

"Siri, there's plenty of good food here. There's bread, there's cereal, there's yogurt. There's even some left-over quiche from supper."

"I'm tired of cereal and you know I don't like vegan yogurt. You just told Simon you didn't even have time to make an omelette."

"Quiche is like a fancy omelette pie."

"Do I have to eat last night's supper for breakfast? Do I have to eat the same thing for breakfast, lunch and dinner, like in prison or something?"

"Eat what you want, Siri, but eat something. Meanwhile, we need to talk about your grades. I don't understand how you can be failing French but acing math."

"Would you rather I be failing math too?"

"Of course not, but don't you need to understand French to do the math?"

"Not really. Listen, Mommy, I'm gonna be late. Can we talk about this some other time?"

"Yeah, we'll talk about it tonight. Here, catch." I throw her a cereal bar. She snatches it out of the air and stuffs it into her pocket.

"OK, thanks. See you later, Simon."

I continue scanning articles at our small kitchen table, trying to choose one for my essay. Well, one thing's for sure. You may not need French for math, but you sure as hell seem to need math for French. Maybe one of the sexual statistics articles would be fun. There seem to be no shortage of them. Aside from the one I just saw, there's another that says forty-seven percent of the men surveyed wait for their female partners to achieve orgasm before having one themselves. And there was that other one. . . here: "Statistics show that 39% of women fake their orgasms." OK, so if forty-seven percent of the men wait, but thirty-nine percent of the women are faking it, how many women with male partners are really getting their orgasms first? And are eighty-one percent of them actually feeling sexually satisfied this way?

My eye falls upon another article, also with statistics. It shows how many refugees have been accepted by Canada in the past five years. The percentages vary between fifteen and twenty-five percent. Not great. It's organized by country of origin, with the countries having the most accepted applicants listed on top. I can't even find the United America on the list.

Laek comes up behind me and kisses me on the neck. I pass

my hand quickly in front of the screen to blank it. "Hey, you shouldn't do that," I complain.

"What, kiss you on the neck?"

"No, sneak up on me."

"I just came down to walk Simon to school. T'es prêt, mon grand?"

"Oui, Papa."

"Oh shit! What time is it? I gotta go. I'm gonna be late for class!"

I throw on coat, hat, gloves, boots, and scarf, and burst outside to start jogging to the community centre. Suddenly, I find myself flat on my ass. I stand and my footing slips again. What the fuck? Someone seems to have turned the sidewalk into a skating rink overnight. I get up more slowly and look around. Block after block of white and grey and black ice, smooth or wavy or textured, but equally frozen solid.

One thing you have to say about the weather here, it keeps life interesting. First, all those weeks where it snowed every single day, the milky sun distant and ephemeral in the grey sky. Then a break in the routine, with temperatures climbing well above freezing, so relatively balmy that we were all leaving hats and gloves at home, our coats flapping open. Next came the rain, turning streets and sidewalks into icy lakes. My winter boots that had withstood mounds of snow were defeated by thick, soupy puddles. I brought extra socks to class, leaving the drenched pair on the radiator, guarded by my dripping boots. And now this, the freezing overnight temperatures giving every-thing a hard, unforgiving surface. The seven-block walk to my class has become an arduous trek, fraught with danger. How the hell am I going to get to class without breaking my neck, let alone on time?

Simon and Laek come out. "Careful!" I yell. Laek takes Simon by the hand, sharing a mischievous smile. Then the two of them take a running start and glide several feet down the block on their boots, laughing and whooping the whole time. Simon glances up at Laek with a look of adoration on his face.

I take a few old-person steps in the opposite direction. At this rate, I'll miss the whole first part of my class. I try to move with more confidence and keep this up for a good half block, until I arrive at a driveway, and the downward slope brings me to my knees. Slipping and sliding, I get down and crawl until I'm clear of the driveway. Laek ought to be proud of my dedication— crawling to my French class. I finally figure something out that I should have thought of at once, as a cycling advocate and partici- pant in so many "take-back-the-street" campaigns. I get up and walk to the centre of the roadway, where it's clear of ice and snow, and continue my commute from there. Sure, there'll be some traf- fic, but I calculate that the risk of getting hit by a car is statistically less than that of my falling and fracturing a bone on the sidewalk.

The first half of our "francisation class" is taken up by a lesson from our monitrice, a young woman from Québec City who's here to teach us about culture as well as language, to help us "integrate." For today's discussion, she asks us to talk about what we find here that is most different from home. This should be fun, judging from other discussions of culture shock we've had. A man begins:

"Why do persons here wait on line to enter upon the bus? Why do they act like sheep?"

Next, a woman says, "I don't understand why to buy prod- ucts that are equitable. They are more expensive and not supe- rior. Are the people who buy these things, are they ignorant? Or does the government force them?"

I smile at the young teaching aid as she tries to answer these questions. She does a reasonably good job, although I'm not sure if the responding nods from the questioners show understanding or merely politeness and respect for the instructor. She calls on me next. I ask something that's been bugging me even more than French numbers.

"I find it bizarre that ordinary objects can be masculine or feminine. And countries. How can a country be male or female? And why do countries have different names in French and English? Shouldn't there be just one name, like whatever the name is in the language of that country? And, and. . ." But then I stop myself, seeing the put-upon expression on the poor teaching aid's face.

"You must not look for logic in these things, Madame," she answers. "Of course words do not have real gender attributes. There are also rules in your own language that are not logical, such as English spelling, which seems to be a way to confound non-English–speakers."

"It confounds some English-speakers too," I admit. I feel bad about my little diatribe. I think she was counting on me, as a fellow North American, to understand things here better.

A woman in the back raises her hand.

"Here is my question, or my surprise. Why do people here make a riot during your hockey games, but do not protest when your politicians accept that the U.A. government should dictate Canada's foreign policy and domestic security measures?"

Now there's a good question.

During the afternoon, we work on our essays. After that last comment, I decide to choose a political article, like the one on refugee acceptance rates. I wish I knew more about what's behind those figures. I scan through the journal that Laek reads. They, too, have an article on Canada's refugee policy. I adjust my screen and begin to read.

On my way home, I navigate the ice slowly—not because I'm afraid of slipping, but to give myself time to absorb what I read. In fact, they've sprinkled something on the ice to give the surface more traction. It's not salt or gravel but a type of sugar, supposedly much less harsh on the environment. Certainly it's more attractive— neon purple grains, glowing softly now as the sun sets. I look up at the sky, marbled blue and grey and white, dissolving into an expanding rim of pink. The trees are sparkling, their branches trimmed in a thin layer of ice.

Each day, I walk to class with the sun coming up behind me, then return home with it sinking down at my back. When I imagined winter here, I wasn't bothered by the idea of cold and snow. I never considered the shortness of the day, though, the depressing absence of sunlight this far north. Yet I find that there's something about the darkness of the season that makes me feel my life more intensely, like every minute counts, like every bit of light and warmth is precious. I think I'm beginning to fall in love with this city. But will they let us stay?

The temperature, already very cold, begins to plummet further with the setting of the sun. A gust of icy wind smacks me in the face as I think about what will happen to Laek if we lose the refugee hearing. Tears fill my eyes and begin to wet my lashes. Just before they overflow, the water thickens and begins to solidify. My tears are turning to ice! My eyelashes are frozen! I briefly wonder if this is dangerous.

When I get to the apartment, Laek is there waiting for me. I wrap my arms around him. He bends over and kisses my mouth, the tip of my nose and both of my eyes, warming each place his lips touch. My eyelashes defrost and my tears recede for the moment, along with the coldness of the world.

CHAPTER 41
LAEK

dig my nails into the flesh of my wrist. Janie pulls my hand away. "Stop that," she says.

"Sorry. Just checking if I'm awake."

"You're awake. Just a little nervous."

"No."

"Yes. It's only that you're not letting yourself feel it."

What I feel is blank, but there's no point in arguing. I lean back against the wall. Close my eyes. If only I could summon up a little anxiety, some concern for the future. The problem is, I can't even imagine anything beyond the trial.

I start to drift off. The sound of Pierre-Ryan's voice brings me back. I open my eyes.

"Nervous, Laek?" he asks.

"No," I say, answering honestly.

Janie laughs and shakes her head. Pierre-Ryan smiles at her, then turns to me.

"Like I've explained, you won't be expected to tell your whole story. They should already have read your written submissions."

"I understand," I tell him. "They'll just be asking me questions."

"That's right. The Crown Officer will do most of the questioning."

"Et la Protectrice des demandeurs d'asile du Québec?"

"If the Québec Protectrice has anything to ask, she'll generally wait until the Officer is done. Whoever's asking the questions, just answer honestly, but as we've discussed, try not to say more than necessary. The Immigration and Review Board member will make a decision after consulting both the Officer and the Protectrice. Do you have any questions?"

"No. I don't think so."

"Janie?"

"I have a couple. If I end up testifying, are you sure it's OK if it's in English?"

"Absolutely. Everyone involved in the hearing is completely bilingual."

"And if we lose—"

"Let's concentrate on today. The Board member has a lot of discretion—more than you're used to from trying cases in front of courtroom judges. So our testimony today is key."

"It's less different than you think. But Pierre, did I tell you I'd like to follow in your footsteps? Become a refugee lawyer? Once I've gotten my French up to speed, that is. And if all goes well here," Janie adds, smoothing the front of the dark blue sweater she chose for me.

"All the more reason for me to work hard today. Ah, they're calling us in. Ready, Laek?"

Janie jumps up and starts smoothing her own clothes—a maroon-coloured skirt and pants combo and a top with flowing sleeves. I'm thinking about what Janie just told Pierre-Ryan. It's the first time I've heard her speak so enthusiastically about her own plans for the future here. It makes me happy. Then I think of what needs to happen today in order for her plans to move forward. My mouth goes dry. I nod and let myself be led down the hall.

Before crossing the threshold, I scan the room for possible

exits. An old habit that's come back. The only door is the one we're entering from the hallway. There's a single small window behind the broad platform desk where the Board member sits. It doesn't look like it can be easily opened. On his desk is a small Christmas cactus, its flowers spilling like blood from the sharp, green leaves. Beside the plant is a gavel that looks heavy enough to bludgeon someone to death with. Built into the desk module are scanning and recording devices as well as other tech. I imagine myself vaulting onto the table. Using the gavel to smash the window. Even so, I don't think my shoulders would clear the frame. I could probably push Janie through, though. And then I could use one of the shards of glass to slit my throat.

Someone is attaching a patch to my wrist. And the side of my neck. I hold very still and will myself not to tremble. *Take deep breaths,* I hear Al's voice telling me. Just keep breathing.

I look at Janie to measure her against the size of the window frame again. Janie looks back and narrows her eyes, taking my face between her two small hands. She kisses me tenderly on the lips. "It's OK," she whispers, "Just answer as best you can." It's then I realize I'm seated at the table facing the Board member, cameras and scanners trained to catch every nuance and bodily response, and that the questioning has already begun.

"Now that we've gone through some general information, I'd like to turn to some specifics. Beginning with the more recent incidents included in your submission. For instance, the beating you received at the demonstration. . . Did you know the police officer who struck you with the. . . the *phaser stick*?"

The Crown Officer, like the other functionaries in the room, is wearing a black suit with a white ceremonial collar. Her hair is pulled back and I think she's in her fifties, though up until this question, her face was perfectly smooth. Now it's puckered with a sour look of distaste. I'm not sure if it's just the idea of these brutal phaser sticks that aren't even legal here. If so, that would be encouraging. But my feeling is that she's put out by *me*, by my claims, my whole story. That it's somehow my fault she's being forced to consider such unpleasant things happening, not that far from her own home. I find myself wanting to soften the facts. So she won't be upset. I resist, trying instead to explain what I think she needs to understand.

"New York's a very large city. It's extremely unlikely you'd end up confronting a police officer you knew. There are just too many of them."

"Unless, perhaps, they were out to get you."

"Even so. That wouldn't mean you'd know the police officer. It's an anonymous place, New York. Not at all like Montréal."

"But you have no reason to believe those police officers knew about your past, your political activities. You ran at them in an aggressive manner. Isn't that why you were struck?"

"I was trying to draw their fire. Away from my students, so they could escape. But even so, I wouldn't have been hit if I hadn't been participating in the demonstration. Yeah, it could have been *other* police officers swinging phaser sticks, or *other* demonstrators on the receiving end of those blows. But it couldn't have been just anybody."

Janie's whispering in my ear. About the Terror Squad cop.

"There was an officer present with whom I'd had. . . a run-in. It's in my account." I swallow. "The one who'd sexually assaulted me a few months earlier."

"So you *are* saying it wasn't a coincidence."

I look at Janie.

"Please answer my question without consulting your partner."

"At the time, I didn't know he was there. It was only later, watching footage from the manif, that I saw him. I thought. . ." I stop, not sure what to say about that moment when I saw the cop on the newsfeed and thought about sleeping and never waking up.

The Officer interrupts my thoughts. "Monsieur Wolfe? Please tell us what you believe was going on and also if you have any evidence for this belief."

"I. . . I don't know." I pull myself away from memories of my time in the hospital and focus on her question about the cop. "I have no proof he was gunning for me," I say. "Just a general skepticism about coincidence."

"There must be coincidence sometimes," the Officer says. "Even in a big city like New York. But let's move on to that earlier. . . incident you mention. The sexual assault. You'd been pulled over for going through a red light."

"But I hadn't. Gone through a red light."

"Yes, well. But concerning that incident, do you have. . . is there any evidence that you were being persecuted for your political beliefs? That you were being personally targeted?"

Personally targeted. It certainly felt personal. "At the time, again, I didn't think so. I believed I'd been stopped for being a cyclist. Cyclists in New York City. . . it's practically a war between us and the motorists. And the authorities. Again, not at all like in Montréal. Here it's. . . it's like a bicycle utopia in comparison."

The Québec Protectrice smiles at me. The Officer continues her questioning.

"So then you *don't* think you were stopped because of your political beliefs."

"Being for cyclists' rights *is* a political belief. But I understand what you're asking. No, I didn't think I was being stopped because of my past. But if not for my past, my beliefs, I wouldn't have. . . I wouldn't have felt so trapped. I would have been able to react differently. And he knew this. He sensed this power he had over me. Knew what threats to make. So in the end, he was able to. . . to do that to me, and to get away with it, because of my past, because of my political beliefs and activities. And again, the fact that he resurfaced at the demonstration, at the time of the other incident. . ." Janie moves closer to me. I realize I'm shaking.

The Protectrice steps in.

"I can certainly see where that must have been extremely frightening. And you say in your account that when you saw this same officer in the newsfeed, looking in the direction of Madame Wolfe, you believed that he might target her. That you feared for her safety and for the safety of your children."

"Yes," I say gratefully. "Yes, that is exactly correct."

Janie takes my hand in hers and squeezes.

The Crown Officer takes up the questioning, seeming a little put off. "Let's move on to the main series of events that you speak of in your application. Your participation in—let's just call it a group for now—and your eventual arrest. Your lawyer has already provided medical and psychiatric reports, both from here and New York, to substantiate your claims of torture and post-traumatic stress disorder." She nods towards Pierre-Ryan. "We also reviewed the research you provided to document the use of torture by the United America government and law enforcement agencies. Very. . . thorough."

I'm proud of Janie, who did that research herself under Pierre-Ryan's supervision.

"So my questions are not about that, but rather, about your own activities. You understand that even if you prove that you meet the criteria for protection as a refugee under the Act, you can still be excluded from Canada if it's found that you committed certain types of crimes?"

"Yes. My lawyer explained this," I say.

"Then I ask you to tell me now, in your own words, the reason you were arrested."

Pierre-Ryan has prepared me for this question. And Janie long ago taught me what every trial lawyer knows—that if you're not sure of an answer, don't guess. It's better to simply admit that you don't know.

"I don't know why I was arrested," I say.

"You must have some idea. . ."

"It could have been for certain of our activities. Or just because they were trying to shut down political groups like ours. Or for reasons of their own. I can't speak to that. In all the time I was in custody, they never told me why I was being held."

"Why don't you describe your group's activities. Did you break the law?"

"We planned acts of civil disobedience. Engaged in some level of. . . of disruption."

"Disruption?" she asks, raising her eyebrows.

"Disruption of government projects we believed were harmful. Like the propaganda ads they used to justify the military invasions. Or to encourage people to turn in their neighbours. We replaced them with our own ads. And we did some sabotage. . ."

"What kind of sabotage?"

"Digital sabotage. Hacking. You know."

"Assume I don't know," the Officer says, with a look of encouragement.

"We hacked into some databases. Like the weather experiments. And later, leaked info to show that they were using this research to create weather-based weapons. To threaten coastal countries that wouldn't go along with their trade and economic treaties."

Pierre-Ryan stands up, pulling on his ear—a nervous habit he has.

"My client has carefully outlined the various activities of his political group, to the extent that he understood them, in his submission."

"It's instructive to hear about some of it in his own words. But I can ask a more specific question." She turns to me again. "What did you do to ensure that the actions you took were the least extreme possible? Why not just demonstrate peacefully? Engage in voting campaigns?"

I feel more confident now, talking about politics, about

history. "In U.A. elections, the winners are already bought and paid for. Even before the '*Electoral Freedom and Financing Act.*' Historically, third or independent parties have never been allowed to gain a foothold there. And demonstrations had simply become staging areas where government and law enforcement could test out their latest crowd-control weapons and techniques. Or get better footage of political dissidents for their dossiers. So some people chose to go underground."

"But destruction of data, couldn't that cause greater harm? You wrote that your group tried to compromise the Unified National Identity Chip system. But this system is used for crime prevention and anti-terrorism measures."

"More for harassment of political activists. As well as apprehension and torture of undocumented immigrants and so-called border terrorists. Other than that, the main thing the Uni system does is help mega-business organize their money-making activities by connecting biometric data with financial info and purchasing histories."

I can see she doesn't buy it, but there seems little point in engaging in a political debate. I just wait for the next question.

"You used physical sabotage as well," she says.

"Yes. Sometimes."

"And what did you do to guard against harm to individuals or property?"

"We did research. Made sure buildings or sights were empty. We were always careful." This is true, I tell myself. We did our best.

"But even so, there's always a risk when violence is used. Accidents can happen."

"Yes." I say, refusing to look down. But I can feel my own heartbeat accelerate, feel the sweat begin to dampen my armpits. Is she monitoring the sensor feed right now? Is that why she's looking at me so closely? I feel like an animal in a lab.

"Was there ever any loss of life or physical injury as a result of one of your actions?"

I know this would be the wrong moment to look at Pierre-Ryan. Or at Janie. Or even to hesitate. "I don't know," I say. That's the right answer, isn't it? When you're not sure, you say you don't know. Like before. And I *don't* know. Not really. But why, then, do I feel a darkness descending on me? Like I'm drowning. Like I'm back in that room, and they're drowning me again. I take Janie's hand. *Look at me. Please look at me, Janie.* She turns her head towards me and smiles encouragingly. But her eyes are filled with fear.

I turn towards Pierre-Ryan. He glances at me quickly and then addresses the tribunal.

"We need to keep in mind that Laek was only a child when he participated in these activities. Of course he wouldn't know everything that happened."

"Monsieur Wolfe," the Protectrice du Québec asks. "How old were you when you first became involved in this group? And when you were arrested?"

I turn towards her, relieved at the change of subject. The Protectrice is probably ten years older than the Officer, but she's dyed her hair a lively red and her clothes are much more contemporary. At the same time, unlike the Officer, the Protectrice's face doesn't appear to have received any anti-wrinkle therapy, let alone surgery.

"I was fourteen when I joined. Fifteen when I was arrested."

"The others in this group, what were their ages?"

"Some were in their twenties. Others in their thirties. One who was older than the rest."

"What was your relationship with these others in your group? Were you close?"

"Yes. They were like family. My brothers and sisters." *Even me?* Al asks, in my head.

"And your real family? They were. . ."

I'm confused for a second, so she repeats the question.

"I'd run off. My mother was in a cult. It was. . . I . . . Do I need to tell you about that too?"

"No, that's sufficient. But your father?"

I see the cult leader standing over me. With my hair and eyes. But his face like stone.

"I don't know for sure who my father was."

"Can you describe your relationship with the older person in your group?"

"We were close. This person was. . . like a mentor, I guess. Or . . . I don't know."

"Like a parent, perhaps? Might you have regarded this person in such a way?"

"I suppose," I say, though this doesn't feel quite right.

"This person, the whole group, they must have had a lot of influence on you."

I know where she's going with this. And it's good of her. But it's also wrong.

"The beliefs I had, that I have, they're my own. I wasn't brainwashed. If you want to talk about brainwashing, we can talk about my mother's cult. Like I said, I left that."

"But the actions your group took, did you plan them? Or were they mostly planned by the others—the older members of your group?"

"Mostly the others," I admitted. "But I participated of my own free will."

"Would it have been hard to say no, perhaps?" the Protectrice asks me in a gentle voice.

"I could have left. I could always have done that. I didn't want to. You are very kind. But I need to be clear about this. I was young, yes, but I wasn't forced by anyone. If anything, they tried to keep me out of danger as much as possible. To protect me."

"You *were* very young, though. Perhaps, had you been an adult, had you the opportunity to decide again, you might have chosen differently."

"Maybe. Is there anyone who wouldn't do things differently if given a second chance? But I need to be clear about this. I do not disavow my activities with this group. And I won't let my old friends take responsibility for my actions. That would be wrong. I'm sorry."

The Protectrice looks like she wants to argue, but the Crown Officer clears her throat.

"Let's return to my last question. Whether people may have been hurt. Were you arrested because someone had been harmed in one of your. . . actions?"

"No. No one was ever hurt in any of our actions before the arrest."

"What about after? In your account, you don't talk about what happened after your arrest. Or even how or when you were released."

Had I known what was coming? Is this why I couldn't think beyond the hearing?

"I was told that my release was secured by a children's rights NGO. Though I don't know if this is actually true. After I was freed, another group from my organization took me in."

I'd known most of them already, from previous mass actions. I think of Imani, who shared her bed with me most nights. But she only let me make love with her once. Said she was too uncomfortable with how young I was. I stayed with her anyway, even though a couple of the guys in our group would've slept with me. Imani, only twenty-one herself, was wise and quiet and strong. I thought she was beautiful. And I liked the way she smelled. She made me think of the rich earth and fragrant flowers in our backyard where she'd started an organic garden. She and I worked there most days.

"You didn't mention this other group. What did you do with them?" the Officer asks.

I clench my jaw against an assault of sensory memory. A hand on my shoulder. The smell of boiled lentils. Of blood and soil. High-pitched laughter, a deep voice reading an old screen novel. I push it away. Focus on the question.

"We didn't have a chance to do much of anything. Less than

two months after I joined them, there was another raid. They were all taken."

"What about you? What happened?"

I close my eyes and just let the words come. "I was out when the Terror. . . when the Anti-Terrorist Squadron arrived. It was. . . it was devastating. I now believed I'd been released only so they could use me to find others from my organization."

"What did you do?"

"I don't know. I felt numb, blank. I think I wandered around the house for a while. It smelled musty. It was very empty. I thought about running. They might come back, take me too, torture me again. But I couldn't bring myself to leave."

I feel Janie's eyes on me, Pierre-Ryan's as well. I know they're both feeling derailed by this. A lawyer's worst nightmare. Testimony that's not only unrehearsed, but about events that weren't even previously discussed. I rub my eyes with my fist. I'm so tired. I've been having those nightmares again. Little by little, memories of the event I'd long ago buried have come back. I stayed awake last night to avoid dreaming about it.

"Go on," the Crown Officer prompts. "Tell us what happened next."

"I went into the backyard of the house. To the garden. We had a garden. Some days, I'd stay out there from sun-up until sundown. Weeding, planting."

And during the night, I'd dream of pulling weeds, of my hands in the dark soil. . . I stop, confused. I feel Janie's hand on my shoulder. Holding on tight.

"Monsieur Wolfe? Are you alright? Can you go on?"

"I .. I went out to the garden. We'd used old bricks to section off plots. I saw that the Terror. . . that they'd been back here. Destroyed everything. Shards of smashed bricks against the back of the house. The plants dug up, trampled. It just undid me, seeing that. . ."

"What did you do?"

"I picked up one of the broken bricks. Sat down in the middle of the yard. Where our garden had been. Thought about my friends who'd been taken. Thought about them being tortured, like I'd been. I thought about the Terror Squad coming back for me too. Then I used the brick to open up my wrist."

I remember the rough feel of it against my skin, how I kept digging and tearing at my wrist until I had a nice flow going. Just the one wrist, though. I wasn't in a hurry. I watched the blood go into the soil. I felt OK watching that. Good, almost. I imagined my body returning to the earth. I lay on my side, watching the dirt become dark and wet with my blood.

I've stopped talking. Maybe I've said enough. Maybe I can finally sleep. I hear Pierre-Ryan asking for a recess. An adjournment until tomorrow is proposed. I can't go through this again. I push myself to my feet.

"I can continue. Please, I. . . I want to finish."

The IRB member, the judge, speaks from his place in the front.

"We will let the applicant continue his account."

I sit back down, relieved but shaky.

"I don't know how long I lay there. A long time, I think. Someone eventually found me."

"The. . . the Anti-Terrorism Squadron?" the Québec Protectrice asks.

"No. Someone from my group. The previous one. The older person I'd mentioned. I woke up in the back of this person's vehicle. A recreational vehicle. I was on a bed or couch, covered in blankets, my wrist bandaged up. Getting a blood transfusion."

I hope they don't ask me how this was all managed. I can't answer that. All I know is that Al has his resources. He always did. I continue.

"This person nursed me back to health. And when I was strong again, asked me to participate in an action. Just this person and I would be involved. I couldn't. . . I didn't refuse."

"What were you asked to do?"

"Enter a complex. In the midwestern drylands. Do some

physical sabotage. I thought it was an important target, hidden away like that. I didn't know what it was, though. Still don't. I had an idea it was related to the weather-based weapons research. But maybe that was because of all the dry lightning that night. I may have confused it in my mind. I. . . I wanted to help my friends. I thought this was related somehow. I wasn't very lucid maybe. . ."

I realize I'm babbling and stop.

"But you were asked to do this by your. . . friend?"

"This is what I was good at. Getting in and out of set-ups. Memorizing long strings of code, seeing the complete physical layout of a place in my head. All this came naturally to me. And with the right tools and intel, it would be fast. So I. . . I didn't really mind."

Am I talking too much? I look up and see everyone watching me, listening closely. The Québec Protectrice looks a little sad and I feel bad for her. The judge seems troubled. Pierre-Ryan is very alert, but looking at me as though from a great distance. Like I'm sliding down a mountainside and he's trying to reach out to me but can't. I won't look at Janie right now, but I feel her iron grip on my arm. Instead, I turn to my questioner. She has an avid expression on her face. She sees me looking at her and smiles with encouragement. I go on.

"I got in without a problem."

Despite the mantraps, timed lockouts, numerous coded entry points. A Sirius-cloud–type security set-up, but I had all the non-biometric pass codes. Tricks for bypassing the others.

"I placed all the charges as instructed. The idea was to set off a series of linked explosions that would destroy outright certain key tech and cause massive flooding in other targeted areas. I had plenty of time to leave the complex before it became danger-ous. But on my way out I saw there was someone in one of the rooms. No one was supposed to be there."

The man hadn't seen me. To be in the building in the middle of the night, it had to be someone high level. Or an intruder like me. I could easily have just slipped out. But there was a charge set to explode on the other side of the wall. Right behind his head.

"I warned him that he needed to leave. Immediately."

I close my eyes and it's like a graphic screen novel, the colours too bright. I see him pull a disrupter gun on me. Fire it. I duck behind the entranceway as soon as I see the gun. The charge flies past me. But the man still isn't leaving. I shout at him that an explosion is due to go off right behind him in three minutes. "Who the hell are you?" he asks me. I don't answer. I just run.

"Then I took off down the hall, hoping he'd get out too. He came after me."

Shooting at me down the hall. He clips me in the back of the shoulder and I fall with the impact. I lie there on my stomach like I'm unconscious. When he sees I'm not moving, he kneels down and turns me over. "Shit, you're just a kid," he says. I punch him hard, right in the face.

"He caught up to me. We struggled."

I kick the gun out of his hand. It spins down the hall. We trade blows. He's bigger than me, but less used to fighting with his fists. But the disrupter burn is starting to hurt badly. When the explosions start, he grabs me by the shirt and flings me against the wall. "Who the hell are you?" he repeats. "Who sent you here?" The pain in my shoulder makes red spots in front of my eyes. I keep fighting him. And keep trying to move us further away from the explosions. Water is beginning to flow in from the walls and ceiling. As we approach another mantrap, he pulls us both inside. Grabs a derma mask.

"He managed to pull us into a. . . a room. That had an airlock. He put a mask on and started the process for evacuating the air. I began to feel dizzy."

He keeps hitting me while asking who had sent me. After a while, I can't get up any more but I still refuse to answer. He makes to leave the room. I hold onto his leg. He kicks at me but I don't let go. I'm getting very groggy, losing consciousness. I feel him grab me under the arms.

"A few minutes later, I came to, choking, on the floor of a small room. My face was underwater. The room was flooding. The water level rising fast. The man was gone. I tried the door, but it was locked. I knew that if I didn't get out, I'd eventually drown in there."

I begin to panic, thinking about drowning. All that time in prison, the drowning torture. It was just practice for this. That's what I'm thinking when Al bursts into the room.

"My friend must have gotten worried when I didn't come out as scheduled. He came in after me. Found the room I was in. Broke the lock on the door and rescued me."

Al's pushing the other man ahead of him. Holding a knife to his throat. He gives me his other knife and tells me to tie the man to a chair. When I've done this, he tells me it's time to go. The water is up to our knees now. "But he'll drown!" I say. "Use the knife then," he answers. "If you think it's less cruel that way." I shake my head. Not believing he's serious. He explains that the man knows him, that leaving him alive will put us and others in jeopardy. That he's involved in a higher level of operations and that I could be too, with time. That I could stay with him and he'd look after me and teach me until I'm old enough to be on my own. But only if this operation is ended appropriately. Only if I'm willing to trust him.

"I was worried about the man I'd encountered earlier. I wanted to make sure he got out too. I didn't want anybody to die."

Al carefully checks the man's bindings. I feel cold. I tell Al I can't leave a man to die, but Al says: "He left you." The man protests, "No, I was coming back. Your friend. . . I don't know what name you know him by, but don't listen to him. He's not who you think he is. He's a liar. A traitor. I was coming back for you. I swear it." I don't know what to think. Why did the man drag me out of the airlock if he meant to let me die? But I would have died in that room if Al hadn't come for me. How is it that Al always arrived at these moments?

"Before we reached the exit to the complex, I decided to go back and look for the man."

We're halfway to the exit when I tell Al I'm going back. That I'd rather use the knife than think of him drowning. I find the man. Give him the knife. After cutting through enough of the rope myself that he'll have time to escape but not catch up to us. I find Al and tell him we can go now. But Al knows me too well. Asks me where the knife is. When I won't answer him, he says he's going back. Orders me to leave the complex and not re-enter it. I beg him to leave with me, to not do what he's planning. "You have no fucking clue what I'm planning," he tells me. He looks so angry. I don't know what to do, so I do what I'm told.

"I wasn't able to make sure that the man escaped. Then, my friend decided to go back himself. He'd left something important. And I think he wanted to look for the man too. I exited the complex and waited for him outside. All night. But he never came out."

For hours, I scan the complex's exits while lightning lights the sky. I watch for them even as I crouch on the ground, dry heaving, sick with anxiety. Over and over, I play out the most likely scenarios. I imagine the man cutting through the rest of his bonds and getting loose. Armed and dangerous when Al arrives. Killing Al with the knife I'd given him. I also imagine the reverse. Al killing the man with his other knife. Or the two of them fighting, killing each other. Or drowning, drowning in the waters I'd loosed. At dawn, I decide there's no point in waiting any longer. I leave the vehicle for Al. Just in case he's somehow alive. I don't believe he is, but still. I have my magna skates. I take some water and food. I skate east and don't look back.

"What did you do then?" the Crown Officer asks.

"I left."

"But your friend. What happened. . ."

"I left," I repeat. "I didn't look back!" I'm gripping the table with both hands to keep from slamming my fists against it. Doesn't she get it yet?

"Can you tell us more about your friend who may have died?"

I let go of the table, slump down in my chair. "No. I'm sorry. I can't."

"Even some basic information? Name, gender, a brief physical description?"

"I'm done. I'm done talking now."

I lay my head down on the tabletop in front of me. I just want to sleep. But then Pierre-Ryan puts his hand on my shoulder and asks me if I need to take a short break. I shake my head. He tells me that I need to sit up then. To be prepared to answer any questions that are asked of me. So I sit up. Wait to see if there are more questions. But there aren't.

Pierre-Ryan consults briefly with Janie. Now she's standing up to testify. And in French, despite what she'd said before the hearing. I watch her struggle to find the right words.

"I know Laek for seventeen years. I have never encountered anyone who is more gentle, sweet. More. . . more good. He is a dedicated pacifist. He avoids at all times any violence, to not make an, an injury. Please believe me, he would not pose a danger to security here. And he loves our new home so much. He loves Montréal. Please let him be saved here, to be secure. If you return him to the United America. . . Please. Give our lawyer's words every. . . every consideration. Thank you very much."

When Janie comes back to her seat, she lets me lean against her. I think Pierre-Ryan would like me to sit up. But just being in this room is about as much as I can take. I listen to the closing remarks but know that the hearing is already over. My trial was long ago and I lost.

CHAPTER 42
JANIE

"Stop saying you're sorry," I tell Laek. "You didn't do anything wrong."

Stupid, maybe, but not wrong. Laek turns to Pierre. He and I have positioned ourselves on either side of Laek, as though to offer him physical protection and support as we ride the métro back to the law office.

"I'm sorry, Pierre-Ryan," Laek says.

"There's certainly no need to apologize to me."

"I messed up your case."

"It's not my case. It's your case."

Exactly. And maybe stupid isn't the right word either. Self-destructive is more precise, which is what's bothering me about all this apologizing. It's like he's apologizing for hurting himself, as though the only thing that bothers him about being self-destructive is the effect it has on others. Not an encouraging attitude, mental health–wise. Although finally airing those painful memories is a good thing for Laek's mental health. I just would have preferred this to happen in front of his therapist instead of at our asylum hearing.

Meanwhile, my brain is carefully shying away from any

thoughts of the actual testimony, of Laek's blood in the garden, of Al's knife in his hand.

"In any case," Pierre says, "You made at least one friend in there, Laek."

Laek doesn't respond.

"Yeah, the Québec rep," I acknowledge. "But how much influence does she have?"

"Her influence is not insignificant, if she chooses to use it. It's a delicate balance here between federal and provincial power. You understand that Québec's role in the immigration process is unique?"

"Yes. Laek explained a lot of the history to me. How the separatist movement regained power as the federal government got more and more conservative. And how the voting patterns of Québec kept diverging from the other provinces. Laek said that what tipped the balance was when the traditional Québec nationalists were joined by the anglophone progressives. And the. . . what's the word for people who speak something other than French or English?"

"Allophones," Pierre says. I look over at Laek, hoping to get him engaged. Normally, this type of conversation would have him jumping up and gesticulating while he explains all the historical factors leading up to this fascinating political moment. Instead, he's just sitting quietly, leaning a little against me, and gazing straight ahead. Yet the only thing in his field of vision is an elderly man sitting erect in his seat, the holo of the métro map projected just above his head.

Pierre looks Laek's way too, then continues. "So what we have is not quite sovereignty, not yet anyway, but some fairly radical compromises by the federal government. Autonomy in certain areas. And let's not forget a bigger tax transfer."

"Is that why there's free daycare and a free university system here?" I ask, still hoping to get Laek into the conversation, or at least to distract him.

"In part. Also our own regimes for welfare, underemployment and pensions. But immigration is trickier. Québec wants control over choosing and integrating its own immigrants, but Canada, for obvious reasons, wants final say on refugee status and national security risks."

"So the compromise is to have the participation of the Québec Protectrice."

"Among other things. But the role of the Protectrice is still limited. She has to choose her battles. And when it comes to a question of exclusion. . ."

"Yeah. I get it. That's where Canada wants most to stay in control."

"That's right. In any case, there's little point in speculation right now. They said we'd have a decision by the end of the day."

"Thank you for letting us come back with you. Waiting at home would have been hard."

"It's fine. I'd already cleared my schedule, not knowing how long the hearing would last. And this way, whatever happens, we can react immediately. . . Our stop, Laek."

Pierre takes Laek by the arm. We follow the underground network to Pierre's office.

———

"It's coming in now," Pierre says, looking at his screen.

I stand, leaning over his desk. He tilts the screen so I can read it too. Laek remains seated.

"Scroll down to the bottom," I say. This is what I always do when I receive a decision.

Pierre is shaking his head. "It's not necessary. Look. There's no discussion, no analysis at all. Just the decision. Only the few lines you see."

I re-read the decision, desperate to find that I'd misunderstood—but no. We've been denied refugee status. I grip the side of Pierre's desk as a wave of panic weakens my knees.

"Our demand was refused, wasn't it?" Laek says.

"Yeah," I say, my voice sounding small. "I don't understand."

"I do. I don't deserve asylum. They're right."

"They're not!" I say, righteous anger pushing away the fear. "You never hurt anyone."

"I didn't tell everything. I know you think I spilled my guts, but I left things out."

"I know that. I'm not stupid. You were talking about. . ." I look over at Pierre and then at Laek. "I know who you were talking about, so I know you left things out. I also know that what you left out wasn't to protect yourself. It was to protect *him*. To. . . to protect Al."

I look at Laek defiantly, wondering how he'll react to my mention of Al's name. Mostly I'm past caring, though. I'm too angry at this man who would take a loyal, idealistic child and use him like that. A lonely, fatherless child, no less, who looked up to him. And yes, I'm frustrated with Laek too, for his pointless loyalty and his total disregard for his own interests. And what about me? What about the kids? Does he think it doesn't hurt us when he hurts himself?

"It doesn't matter, Janie. It's not as though that was his real name. Nothing matters."

Was. He's saying "was" even though we both know Al's still alive. But it's the "nothing matters" that chills me. I open my mouth to argue, but Pierre says: "Listen, I'm thinking about how this decision's been crafted. We're all assuming that the denial is based on exclusion and I'm sure it is, but it's not what the decision says."

"What do you mean?" Laek asks.

"All the decision says is that you haven't met the criteria for protection under the *Act*. There's nothing about you being a security risk or criminal acts or anything like that."

"It's true. They would normally have spelled it out. So why didn't they?" I ask.

"I think that this is where Laek's favourable impression on

the Québec Protectrice came into play. She negotiated for a decision that doesn't mention exclusion."

"But how does that help us?"

"It could clear the way for an application for permanent residence on humanitarian and compassionate grounds. It's Québec
who will process that application. Only. . ."

"Only what?" Laek asks. Pierre hesitates, but Laek answers
the question himself. "The Canadian Border Protection Bureau.
You're thinking about them."

"Yes. They could still decide that you present a security risk
and block the application."

"When would they decide this?" I ask.

"It could be at any point in the process, but. . . We could ask
for an expedited decision on the security question. It would be
based on the claim that returning you to the U.A. would present
a well-founded fear of torture or persecution. But we'd need to
file right away—within twenty-four hours of receiving the negative decision on the refugee claim."

"What's the down side?" I ask.

"First of all, we couldn't add anything to the file. They'd
make the security determination based solely on the written
application and the hearing testimony. And on their own
dossiers, of course. If we waited, we could submit more
evidence. Also, well, the longer it takes them to decide, the
longer you have to. . . to make back-up plans."

By back-up plans, I assume he means going into hiding to
avoid deportation. Living underground has always been an
unspoken possibility. We chose Montréal because it's a sanctuary
city, part of the international solidarity network, so this is an
option. It would be a precarious, marginal life, though, not a life
I'd choose for my children. It's also the worst type of life for
someone who's suffering from post-traumatic stress disorder.
Laek needs safety and security if he's ever going to completely
heal.

"What do you think we should do?"

"I don't know. You've had two lucky breaks. First, when the Officer who interviewed Laek at 1010 St-Antoine allowed the application to move to the next phase instead of flagging it as a security risk. And now, with nothing written in the decision about exclusion. Without those red flags, maybe, if we push for a quick determination, they'll be more cursory in their examination of the file and just pass you through."

"How likely is that, really? They have the hearing testimony and they have their own sources of information," I point out.

"I can't answer that, except to say that they're a mysterious agency. Secretive and difficult to gauge. I've seen them act in cases where I was shocked that my client was even on their grid, and then pass on cases of well-known political operators."

"And if we wait?"

"They'll do a security evaluation in any case, but we'd have the opportunity to present more evidence, which could be useful. If you had more to say, Laek, for instance, about extenuating circumstances in the events you describe. . ."

Pierre looks up questioningly, but Laek seems lost in his own thoughts. I'm afraid he hasn't even been following the conversation, but then he meets Pierre's gaze and says firmly, "Let's file now. There's nothing more I have to say. We gotta just go for it."

Pierre hesitates only a moment. "Alright, perfect. I already completed most of the application before the hearing, just in case. I'll add some finishing touches and send it off."

Laek asks if we're needed right now, and if not, whether there's somewhere he can lie down. Pierre directs him to a couch in the corner of the room that he uses when he's having a late night. I stay where I am in case Pierre could use my help. We spend a few minutes checking the application. After a few small additions, I watch him submit it.

"Well, that's done," he says.

"What do you really think's going to happen?" I whisper, once Laek is asleep.

"I don't like to make predictions, and the truth is, I have no confidence in my powers of divination, particularly in this case. But. . ." He looks over at Laek curled up on his couch, his chest expanding and contracting in a slow, peaceful rhythm. "I'll admit I'm nervous about this."

"Yeah. Listen, I'm going to leave you alone now so you can get some other work done."

"Don't worry about it, Janie."

"It's OK. I think I'd like to sit with Laek for a while."

"Alright. In that case, I do have some messages I should return."

I walk over to the couch where Laek is sleeping and carefully lift his head so I can slip underneath. I cover him with his jacket. He stirs only a little as he finds a comfortable position on my lap. After a few minutes, I start drifting off too. . .

I don't think much time has passed, but I feel like something's shifted. I look around and see Pierre working quietly at his desk where I left him. Laek is still sleeping, his head resting on my thigh, but his breathing is different—more rapid—and his eyelids are twitching. I put my hand on his cheek, hoping to calm him. When that doesn't do the trick, I stroke his hair, murmuring that it's OK. He settles down and even seems to smile in his sleep. But then he's suddenly awake and sitting up, shaking his head as though to clear it.

"I had a dream," he says. "About Al and—"

Laek stops abruptly and pats his jacket. He fishes out his screen and peers at it, calling up a message. I push myself up, a feeling of déjà vu creeping over me, as I read Laek's screen.

You have kept faith with us. We have done what we could. The rest is up to you. —A

A moment later, the screen explodes in brightness, like a thousand tiny stars bursting at once, the letters from the message dancing over the screen and then seeming to break free into the air. The screen goes dark and blips out. Laek passes his hand over it gently, like the head of a small, faithful dog. He looks up.

"I think my screen is dead."

Just then Pierre says: "I've just received word. You've passed the security check. Now your application can move forward."

"Already? Is it normal to get an answer so fast?" I've blurted this question out in my surprise, but on second thought, I'm not really sure I want the answer. Not if it confirms my suspicion about who's behind this quick decision. "Never mind," I say.

Pierre purses his lips, as though thinking about answering me anyway, then turns to Laek.

"Even though you're not home free yet, this is excellent news. Now, all we need to do is convince the Québec Ministère d'Immigration to let you remain here. You have a number of important factors in your favour. The children attending school, hopefully doing well. . ."

Well, one out of two, anyway.

"... and your community involvement. The fact that your French is good is also a big positive. You seem to be doing well now with your French too, Janie."

"Thank you."

"I can add supplementary information to the application. Like Janie's plans to go to school in the fall. Other things could strengthen your case."

"Like if I had a regular job," says Laek.

"Yes, that would be very helpful. Or if Janie did."

"But Janie's going to school. It's up to me." As Laek says this, I see him unconsciously rubbing the screen against his chest.

"What are you going to do with that?" I ask him.

"We need to get rid of it," Laek answers.

"Well, it's been a long, full day," says Pierre.

"Yes. It's time we were going," I say, gathering our things. "I don't know how to thank you for all you've done for us so far."

I remember the first time we came to his office and I wasn't sure whether to kiss or shake hands. This time I just hug him. Laek does as well. "Thank you, Pierre-Ryan," he says gravely.

"Take care of yourself, Laek."

As we leave Pierre's office, Laek takes my hand and leads me up to the street, instead of through the underground network to the métro. I don't ask where we're going, just follow along. When we've reached a small park, he takes me in his arms and kisses me.

"Janie, I have a favour to ask."

"What is it, baby?"

"Can you get rid of my screen for me? Take it to an éco-quartier. Where they can recycle the parts. But not the éco-quartier in our neighbourhood, OK?"

"OK. But you're going to need a new screen."

"I'll buy a used one. But I have another favour to ask. Turn all our screens off tonight."

"Why are you asking me this? Where will you be?"

"I'm going to walk around the city a little."

"I think you should come home with me. I don't think walking around alone is a good idea. It's been a rough day for you. You need to rest."

"What I need to do is to take some time alone to think about what's happened. And what needs to happen next. Please, Janie. I won't be able to relax or sleep or anything right now."

"But why do I have to turn off the screens?"

"So you don't wait for me to call. I'm not gonna call. I'll just walk around for a while and come home when I'm done. If the screens are off, you can relax. And I won't have to think about you sitting by the screen all night waiting for me to get in touch."

This is one of those things that Laek will say that has the form of logic, but when you probe it, even a little, it collapses into utter nonsense.

"Laek, picture me doing whatever it is you want to picture me doing, but the last thing that's going to make me relax is being disconnected from you right now."

"We won't be disconnected. Not in the way that counts. I'll be thinking about you all the time I'm walking around. And you can think about me. We'll be connected that way."

I shake my head, not at all happy about this. We're in the centre of the park now, near a set of benches. Laek pushes the snow off one of them with his arm and sits down, pulling me onto his lap. For a few minutes we just sit there, his face buried in my hair, his warm breath against my neck. I look at a statue in the middle of the park, formless under soft mounds of snow.

"Listen. When I was sleeping on the couch in Pierre-Ryan's office, I had a dream. Or. . . or a memory. I saw that night, with Al, the dry lightning all around. What I was most afraid of was that Al was dead. And that it was my fault for not killing the other man. You see, Al had given me a knife. But I couldn't do it, even though Al said that, otherwise, he'd be in danger. Worse, I gave Al's knife to the other man, so he could escape. Maybe he used it to kill Al instead."

"But you know that's not true. Al didn't die."

"What did happen, though? After I saw Al that night in Red Hook, I began to think about it again. Since Al was alive, did that mean that he'd killed the man? That he was a killer? I hadn't seen the other man come out."

"You hadn't seen Al come out either." I say this to be fair, though I have no desire whatsoever to protect Al from Laek's judgment.

"I don't know what to think, Janie. You saw that message. You know what it implies."

"What it implies scares me."

"Me too. And now, when I think about my time with Al, I realize just how far out of my depth I was. Maybe everything I did. . ."

"You were just trying to do right. Regardless of what Al was up to."

"I just want to understand. When you can't make sense of the past, how can you know how to act in the future? Maybe that's why I try so hard to live in the present. But living that way. . . It can be like walking a tightrope, sometimes."

I sigh and lean back as he wraps me more tightly in his arms.

It's starting to get dark and colder. It's time to go home. Thinking about this, I realize I've decided to let him go, because even though the idea of Laek wandering the city alone in this mental state alarms me, the kids need me too, and I can't force Laek to remain within four walls. I can see how it would be—him, agitated, pacing, full of desperate energy, even though he is, in fact, very, very tired. I can almost imagine how he feels, though all I want to do right now is to go home where it's warm, cook a nice dinner, and talk about school and everyday things with Siri and Simon. And then make love with Laek. But that part's going to have to wait until he's ready to come inside.

CHAPTER 43
LAEK

The city's too quiet. I need it loud. Loud enough to drown out the voices in my head. It was OK in the store where they had the music pumped up. I stayed longer than I had to, looking at the refurbished mini-screens that all cost more than I could afford. The middle-aged woman who owns the place introduced herself, then followed me around. Explained the advantages of each model. I watched the beautiful, fluid movements of her hands. Finally selected a screen. The young clerk in retro clothes was swaying to the music as I paid. I asked to borrow some tools and removed the GPS chip. Handed it back then left the store reluctantly. The smell of coffee and hashish is still lingering in my nostrils, but the music has faded from my memory.

I pull up my collar. Keep walking. I haven't worked out yet what to do. *The rest is up to you.* Al's words. Even the simplest meaning of this sentence weighs on me. We're so close now, so close to being safe here. But I know Pierre-Ryan is worried. If only I could find a job.

At the encampment for unhoused people near Champs de Mars, the nearby court and government buildings stand like sentinels. The hospital parking lot in the distance backlights the scene. There aren't many people out tonight. They've mostly gone inside. To a shelter or, if they're lucky, some other place where they can crash. I remember the time I spent living on the street after coming east to New York. When it was cold and I was feeling lonely, I'd be looking for someone who'd let me stay the night. It'd usually be someone older. Someone living alone. After the sex, they'd want to hold me. If I fell asleep, sometimes they couldn't bring themselves to kick me out and I'd get to stay until morning. I was good at finding someone kind. Usually, anyway. There was that one bad mistake. My mind shies away from the memory. And in the space that's left, Al slips in again. *The rest is up to you. Up to you, Laek. . .*

At Parc Émilie-Gamelin, people are partying. I lean against a tree, imagining the rush of some good drug hitting my system. That feeling of warmth and well-being. I force myself to keep walking. A group of people are drinking from bottles wrapped in plasticized opaque bags. They're laughing, seemingly oblivious to the dropping temperature. Someone calls out to me half-heartedly. I smile but keep going.

I'm tired and hungry but still keyed up. I enter a dépanneur, thinking about coffee and maybe a sac of mushroom jerky. It's self-serve, so I make it half oat milk, half coffee. That'll fill my belly better. At the counter, a kid, maybe eighteen years old, is buying a big sack of dog food. I stand behind them. I see they're probably closer to fifteen or sixteen. The dark rings under their eyes made them look older. The kid's counting out coins, to the obvious impatience of the cashier. I look at the figure cashed up and then at the money on the counter. Not enough.

"Je peux payer le montant qui reste demain. Ou même ce soir," the kid says.

"No credit here," the cashier answers. Or maybe they're the owner.

"It's for a sick dog. Like I said, I'll come back with the rest tonight, later on."

"Take your sous," they answer, pushing the coins away in

disgust. "You and your types not clean. I don't want dirty money."

The kid runs out of the store, leaving the dog food behind. The merchant moves to put the dog food back, but I put my hand on the bag. Return the jerky to the rack. Hand them the money for the dog food and my coffee. I then hoist the bag of dog food onto my shoulder and hurry after the kid. I find them about a block away, looking more angry than upset.

"Voilà," I say. "The merchant gave it to me."

"I don't need their maudit hand-outs. Or yours."

"It's not for you. It's for the dog."

They look me over. "You like dogs?"

"I like all animals."

"Even cockroaches?"

"Well, they're not my favourites. But I won't put out poison for the mice. My neighbours aren't happy about that, but I have my own methods."

"What do you do?"

"I catch them using peanut butter as bait and bring them to the park."

"I like that. OK, I'll take the dog food," they say.

We stop in front of a group of street kids sprawled along the sidewalk. Keeping company with two dogs. An old screen-board with a message asking for money is propped up near an extra dog food bowl. There are some coins inside.

"This is Blatte," the kid says, pouring dog food into a bowl.

Blatte! So now I understand the question about the roaches. I kneel down, hands open, in front of the dog. A mixture of German shepherd and something else, and not yet full-grown.

"There are nicer names for a dog," I say.

"He's not my dog, really. He's Trevor's."

"I'm Laek, he/him."

"Lila, she/her.

I hold the dog's head in my hands and scratch behind his ears. He seems a bit listless.

"If Blatte is sick, maybe you should take him to the animal clinic," I say.

"Not my dog," she says again, looking over at one of the other kids. "'Cause if he were *my* dog, he'd have good food and clean water and a warm blanket. And I would take him to the vet."

The kid says, "Ta gueule," and the two of them start arguing. The scene depresses me, and my presence is causing tension. I say good-bye and walk further east.

I find myself at the Jacques Cartier bridge. This is the bridge we would have crossed to enter Montréal if Siri hadn't chosen the ferry. The bike and pedestrian path is closed now. Locked and gated, too icy to be safe. I climb over the fence. Start walking along the slippery metal walkway. I think about my family. How I've dragged them all here. Messed up their lives. The least I could do is find a fucking job.

At the centre of the bridge, I stop. It's nothing like the solid, familiar Brooklyn Bridge. This bridge is vast, cold. I shiver, wrapping my arms around my chest. Why did I ever think I could do good in this world? That anyone could? The only way to have an impact is to do evil.

I lean over the side. Ignore the sick feeling in my stomach. The St. Lawrence River is frozen around the edges, but wild and ferocious in the middle, white caps below where I'm hanging over the railing. I hear a roaring in my head. I let my terror of the water build. Force myself to continue staring down into the depths. The wind is very strong. I imagine myself plummeting over the side, drowning in those frigid waters.

I let go with one hand. Try to bring myself to the point where I'm as scared as I was that night with Al, thinking I might drown. When Al ordered me out of the building and I complied, was it because of this fear? Or was it my fear of Al's disapproval, of losing his love? If I let a man die, I'd at least like to know why.

The wind is buffeting me around. A gust pushes me hard. My gloved hand nearly slips on the metal rail. I think about

Janie and grab on with my other hand too, pulling myself back. I suddenly remember that it was windy that night too. The hot gusts blew sand into my face. A desert hamsin. I was blinded for a few minutes. After that, I saw a flash of light. I'd originally taken it for dry lightening, but in my dream today, it was different. I saw the whole scene from an adult's perspective. Unclouded by the emotions of my fifteen-year-old self—terrified, uncertain, wanting to please, wanting to do right, filled with guilt and self-hate. In the dream, when I skated away from the scene, there was a second small flash of light. Too low to be lightening. Possibly the glint of a knife. Two knives, yeah, is what I think I saw. Two knives moving away from each other.

A car goes by and beeps its horn. It sounds like an expression of alarm. I start walking back along the narrow path. I don't think I killed that man. If he was killed that night, it was Al who did it, not me. But maybe Al didn't kill him either. But then. . . No. I can't be sure what happened. I need to just accept this. Move on. Plan for the future. Like Al said: *The rest is up to you.* If I could do just one good thing tonight, maybe I could face going home.

I walk all the way back to where I first saw the group with the dogs. No one's there now. These streets are too empty. I wander towards an area where I know there'll be some action.

Looking for a date? Aimeriez-vous faire le party? Any plans for tonight, honey?

I recognize a voice among them. The girl with the dog.

"Salut," I greet her, walking closer to the light where she can see me. I smile.

"It's you, the animal lover."

"It's me," I agree.

"J'peux t'faire une pipe pour quarante. Because you were so nice about the dog."

"That's—that's generous of you, but. . . Would you like to go get something to eat instead, maybe? I'm hungry and. . . I can't promise you anything too grand but it'll be nice to get inside for a bit."

She looks around at the empty streets. Shrugs and follows me.

I find a diner I know around here. Cheap and a little greasy but with tasty, generous portions. We're served coffees and we both pour in plenty of oat cream. I laugh. Shake my head when she asks me why. She's shy about ordering, so I order first—a veggie burger with fries and a side salad. She orders the same but with poutine instead of the fries.

"Have you been on the street long?" I ask, once she's eaten about half her burger.

"Long enough to know my way around," she responds, a little sharply, to warn me away from those kinds of questions.

"OK." I won't push her.

"Are you a vegetarian?" she asks me.

"Yes, but I don't mind if people around me eat meat."

"I like veggie burgers. Maybe I'll become vegetarian too."

I smile. "Listen, since you know your way around and I'm new here, maybe you could tell me about Montréal. Things they wouldn't include in the government info texts."

I finish my food, listening to her talk about the city with animated gestures, choosing more and more obscure facts as she gauges my knowledge. I'm surprised at how observant she is for her age. I try to draw her out about herself but she's closed pretty tight. The only thing I manage to learn is that, along with loving animals, she also loves music.

"You know, I can see you working for the Ministry of Tourism." I finally say.

"Really? But that would be boring, anyway."

"How about being in charge of one of those summer music festivals? That's tourism too."

"You think I could do that?"

"Sure. Why not? You're smart, know the city and love music. And you're good with people, too. You'd need some more schooling, of course. I saw an interesting program that was being offered. Look here, I can find it." I call up the info on my new screen and show her.

"Yeah, I heard of them but I have a lot going on right now. There's the dog, and my friends and. . . and stuff. Hey, are we going somewhere after this? I can still show you a good time."

I take all of my money out of my pockets, coins and no bills.

"I think I have just enough for a milkshake."

"Don't worry about the money. If you have somewhere we could go. . ."

"No. Listen. . . even if I did, I couldn't. I'm a high school teacher. Was one, anyway. And you're probably not much older than some of my students were. I'm sorry. I'm sorry if I've wasted your time."

"A teacher. So that's why you said those things. To try to push me back into school."

"No. I'm not trying to push you anywhere. I'd've been pissed off too if someone did that when I was your age and living the way you're living."

"You were on the street too? And. . ."

"Yeah. It wasn't such a bad life. I liked the freedom and I met a lot of people. But it was more dangerous than I'd thought."

"I'm careful. Besides, I can take care of myself," she says sharply.

"Yeah, I'm sure you can. But you can still make mistakes about people. Like I did. For instance, did you guess I was a teacher? Or that I'd been a street kid?"

She doesn't say anything. Just seems angry and closed off.

"Had you guessed I was carrying a knife?" I start reaching into my jacket.

She stands up, her eyes wide. "A. . . a knife?"

"Sit. It's OK. I'll leave it in my pocket. Unless you'd like to see it?"

"No. That's OK. I have to go now, anyway."

"Please, stay. I'll go. Stay and have that milkshake. I need to be outside now. I'm sorry."

I get up and walk towards the door, leaving all the money on the table.

Sometime later, I'm regretting having eaten all that food. I think it's slowed down my thinking. And I've used up all my money. I don't even have métro fare. How can I go home? Broke and no closer to figuring out how to make sure our application is accepted. No good to myself, no good to my family, no good to that kid, no good even to one sick dog.

My legs take me towards the bridge. I need to look at the water again. Need it badly. It would calm me, I think, or give me some peace. Weird, because the waters were anything but peaceful. Wild, dangerous even. Yeah, dangerous. Why is thinking about danger making me feel calm? This doesn't seem like a good sign. I stop walking. Lean against a building. No, I'm not thinking clearly. I'm too tired. I slide down to the ground and huddle against the brick, arms in my sleeves and head against my knees. Maybe I'll rest a little and walk home later.

———

I must have dozed off. I open my eyes, shivering and disoriented. I don't feel fully awake. Fractured tendrils from my dream are still embedded in my senses. The smell of mint. My fingers in Janie's damp curls. White clouds, the crack of a bat hitting a ball. Warm things, summer things. Janie was telling me something. That I have to wake up and make a call. *Call you?* I had asked. *No*, she said, *my screen's off, remember? Call Philip instead.*

I rub at my eyes with my gloved knuckles. Fish out my mini-screen. Speak the number and put the piece in my ear. I hear the call going through. It rings only once.

"Hello?" Philip's voice sounds rusty with sleep.

"Philip," I say.

"Laek? Laek, is that you?"

"It's me."

"Are you OK? What time is it?"

"I don't know."

"Wait, let me get a light on. . . It's two-thirty in the morning. Where are you?"

"I'm in Montréal, Philip."

"I know that, I mean. . . Have you been drinking? Did you take something?"

"I don't think so."

"You don't think so? You sound strange. What's the matter?"

I wrap my arms around my knees, shivering. "They refused us. For asylum."

"Oh, Laek. I'm really sorry. But listen, you knew this might happen. You have a back-up plan. The other application for permanent residence."

"I. . . I don't have a job. "

"Don't worry, you'll find one. You'll see."

"I'm just. . . I'm just so tired."

"It's late. That's why you're tired. Sleep now. Things will look brighter in the morning."

"I was sleeping before, I think. But I had a dream. And Janie told me to call you."

"That's funny, because Janie was in *my* dream. She said she needed my help, and then I woke up. That's why I answered the phone so quickly. I was already awake."

"Philip, am I awake now? Or do you think I'm still asleep?"

"You're awake but. . . you do sound strange. Can you put Janie on?"

"She's not here."

"Where is she?"

"She's at home."

"At home. But then where are you?"

I look around. I see mounds of snow, closed stores, a small empty park. "Outside."

"Outside? Outside where?"

"Outside. . . don't know. Near a wall. It's brick."

"Laek, you need to go home. Janie must be sick with worry."

"I can't. I don't have any money."

"Go into the subway and jump a turnstile. It's OK. Just make sure no one sees you."

"The métro doesn't run this late. It's not 24/7, like New York. I could. . . I could try to find a night bus, but they don't have turnstiles." I crane my neck but don't see any buses.

"What are you talking about? Never mind, I have a better idea. Call Janie and ask her to come get you. Or tell me where you are. I'll call her myself."

"Didn't she say in the dream? Her screen's off. I made her shut it off. So she wouldn't worry, waiting for me to call. It's OK. I'll just go back to sleep." I press my face against my knees.

"I don't think that's a good idea. It must be cold out and you don't sound right. Look at your screen and tell me what the temperature is."

I lift my head up to look. "It's, it's twenty-five degrees."

"That's pretty cold, below freezing. But wait. . . don't you use Celsius there?"

"Yeah."

"Then that doesn't make sense. Twenty-five degrees Celsius is warm, not cold. Check it again. What does it say?"

"Twenty-five. Negative twenty-five."

"Get up, Laek. Get up right now!"

"I'm tired. I want to go back to sleep."

"Get up right now or I swear I'm getting into my car, crossing the border and finding you, and when I do, I'll kick your ass all the way to the North Pole."

"OK, OK," I say, stumbling to my feet. "But stop yelling at me. It's hurting my ears."

"Your ears hurt? Are you wearing a hat?"

"No." I put my hands on my head. "Wait, yes. It's there. I'm wearing my tuque."

"What's that? Is that a hat?"

"Yeah, I'm wearing a cotton cap."

"Cotton. Are you wearing a scarf?"

"No, but I have a bandana around my neck."

"Take the bandana and wrap it around your ears. Then put your hat on over that."

"I can't."

"Why not?"

"My hands aren't working. Something's wrong."

"What? What's wrong? Aren't you wearing gloves?"

"Yeah, but I can't feel my fingers."

"OK, put your hands in your coat pockets."

"My coat doesn't have any."

"You're not wearing that brown flannel thing you had in New York, are you?"

"Yes. That's my jacket."

"Laek, that's not nearly warm enough. What else are you wearing?"

I look down. "Um, my jeans, a sweater."

"Jeans. Alright, then put your hands in the pockets of your jeans or under your arm pits. Anywhere, I don't care, just get them out of the cold air."

"OK." I cross my arms over my chest and stuff my hands under my armpits.

"Now walk. Walk to the corner, and when you get there, tell me what the intersection is."

"OK. . ." My limbs feel awkward, my feet, somehow far away from the rest of me.

"Are you walking?"

"Yeah."

"Did you get to the corner yet?"

"I'm there now."

"Tell me where you are."

The black letters of the sign seem to sharpen. "The corner of Ontario and Champlain."

"Fine. One second. OK, there's a shelter of some kind nine blocks west of where you are. We just need to figure out what direction you're walking. One more block will tell us that."

"I'm walking west."

"Are you sure?"

"Of course I'm sure. West is towards home."

"A few minutes ago, all you knew was that you were outside near a brick wall, so forgive me for double checking."

"Yeah, sorry. I think I had brain freeze or something."

"I thought you got that from ice cream."

"Different kind." I pause, press my gloved hand against the window of a café I'd noticed earlier. I keep walking. "Listen, Philip, I've been thinking. Should we just come back to Brooklyn? Or maybe at least Janie and the kids could come back. Siri, I worry about her. She doesn't seem happy. She's still so angry about being here."

"No, absolutely not. As far as Siri goes, isn't being furious with your parents a normal state for a twelve-year-old girl? Anyway, look, I should tell you. People have come by the school. Asking questions about you. And Janie's friend Magda got in touch with me. Apparently they've been snooping around Janie's office too."

"Oh. Did. . . Are you all OK? Did anything happen?"

"Everyone's fine. Don't worry about us. In any case, this was some months back."

"Some months back? Why didn't you tell me sooner?"

"I didn't want to worry you."

"But Philip, don't you think this was something we needed to know? It could have affected decisions we were making."

"Janie knew."

"From Magda, you mean?"

"Yeah. . . And from me too. I spoke to her."

I stop. A car flies through the intersection. "You spoke to Janie yourself about it?"

"Yeah. I call her sometimes. I find we see things in a similar way. We have some common, um, interests and such. That OK with you?"

I cross the street. "Yeah. I'm pleased about it actually. But why didn't you tell me too?"

"Like I said, I didn't want to worry you. You had enough on your plate at that moment."

"And Janie didn't?"

"Janie's different. She's solid as a rock."

"And I'm not, I guess."

"Is an ocean solid? It's deep and powerful and beautiful and wild, but solid doesn't apply. Laek, don't be upset. I'm telling you now, aren't I?"

"Yeah. And I suppose my taking a nap in negative 25 temperature doesn't exactly inspire confidence. Listen, we've been on a while, so I'd better terminate the call."

"I'd rather keep talking until you get there."

"We've been through this. About using the screen too much, about you being tracked. Maybe you think I'm being paranoid. . ."

"No. I've taken all the precautions you suggested. I got another reconstituted screen just last week and had it cleaned and reprogrammed by your people. Right now I'm more worried about getting you to shelter than about our conversation being tracked."

"Don't worry so much about me, Phil. If I can't stay there, I'll figure something else out."

"Telling me not to worry doesn't make me stop worrying any more than telling Janie to turn her screen off means she'll sleep peacefully without hearing from you. . . Listen, Laek, you need to stop doing this."

"Doing what?"

"Crazy things. Dangerous things. Putting people who love you through hell, worrying about you. How to put this? You have this ability to. . . to disassociate. From fear, from pain, which I get, but also from reality and responsibility sometimes.

And other people, we just can't do that, alright? You're incredibly brave and good, but looking at things another way, there's an aspect to your actions which is just. . . just. . . breathtakingly insensitive!"

"I don't mean to. . ."

"I know. That's why I said 'insensitive' and not 'cruel.' Just as an exercise, put yourself in the place of someone who loves you. In Janie's place, say. How would you feel right now?"

"Worried, I guess."

"Good start."

I think some more. "And angry, maybe."

"You think?"

"OK, very angry. Totally pissed off." It's not at all difficult to imagine this, once I give it three seconds of serious thought. Then I think of something else.

"Phil?"

"What?"

"Are *you* angry? Are you angry with me, too?"

"I don't want to talk about that right now. What I'd like is to eventually sleep some more tonight, so please say you'll call me again when you know what you're doing."

"OK, I'll call you back."

I think about our conversation. Consider simply running home to Janie as fast as my legs can carry me. But when I get to the door of the shelter, I realize where I am. It's a youth shelter. Run by that organization for street kids where I'd referred Lila earlier. I volunteered here a few times after losing my job at the bike shop. Now there's a sign on the door. Not a regular sign but one of Janie's "good signs." It's a posting for a teaching job at their alternative high school for street kids. I think Janie will forgive me if I delay my return just a little longer.

Forty-five minutes later, I'm walking out the door feeling my good fortune as keenly as I've ever felt the reverse, and promising never to take either one for granted. I remember my bandana. Tie it around my ears as Philip suggested. Pull my hat over that.

Once outside, I call Philip back.

"Philip? You won't believe it."

"What? Wouldn't they let you stay?"

"No, forget that. I think I may have found a job."

"Wait. Go back. Tell me what happened."

As I walk, I explain everything to him—that the director of the organization was supervising a night shift, the on-the-spot interview disguised as a conversation, how impressed she was with my experience and that I speak three languages, and the teacher's certification program they offer in cooperation with the Ministry of Immigration. I even tell him about Lila and kids like her who might attend such a school.

"So will you be one of my references?" I ask him.

"Of course! But she'll probably want someone more local. . ."

"I gave her six or seven local references too. I've met loads of people through our neighbourhood community centre and the solidarity network."

"I bet you have. But what are your chances? Did she say anything?"

"I can't be sure, but it felt right. She kept smiling and nodding her head and was careful to check that I had all the right coordinates for where to send the application. She scheduled an interview for tomorrow evening and. . . It just felt right."

"That's amazing. Let me know what happens. But you still need to find shelter."

"I'm going home."

"It's too cold to be out right now, Laek."

"Our apartment's only about four kilometres from here. I'll run to keep warm. And I tied the bandana like you said. And I'll keep my hands in my pockets."

"Alright, if you're sure. But listen. When you get home, you need to warm yourself up, right away. Take off any wet clothes. Maybe get into a bath. But warm, not hot, you got that?"

"OK."

"And one other thing. Make love with Janie. Can you do that for me?"

"For you? Sure, no problem. Is there a position or style you'd prefer?"

I can feel his smile come all the way through the connection. "No. Whatever turns you on. The important thing is getting your body temperature up."

"Whatever you say. Anything else?"

"No, I think that about covers it."

"OK, then. I'll be thinking of you."

"That's sweet. Um, Laek can ... can we speak again soon?"

"If it's safe."

"Alright. Until then."

I jog the whole way home. Barely feel the cold. Janie is up and waiting for me when I get to the apartment. I tell her about the girl, the dog, the job, talking to Philip. The words spill out, one on top of the other, but Janie seems to follow everything. I put my hands under warm water in the sink as Janie runs a bath. Ironically, it's only now, when I'm inside, that I begin to feel cold. And my hands hurt so much that the pain makes me nauseous.

The bath is ready. I strip off my clothes. My legs under my jeans are bright red from the cold. All the way from thigh to mid-calf, where my wool socks began. I lower myself into the bath. Sigh with pleasure. I look up to see Janie watching me with her lips pressed together, her eyes bloodshot, her shoulders drooping. I think about my conversation with Philip.

"I'm sorry that I worried you tonight. And other times too. I know. . . I can only imagine how hard it must be sometimes, being with me. I promise you, I'm going to try my best not to do those kinds of things anymore."

Janie doesn't say anything. I try to read her expression, but I can't. All at once, I'm as scared as I've ever been in my life. What if she can't forgive me? What if she decides she doesn't want to be with me anymore? The water in the bathtub seems chilly now.

I shiver. Janie leans over and turns on the hot tap, using her cupped hand to mix the fresh water in. I wait, anxious and immobile, for her answer. Finally, she withdraws her pink, wet hand and gently touches my cheek with it. I reach for her, but she moves away.

"You'd best keep that promise, Laek, because if you ever do anything like that again, I'll kick your ass so hard that, that. . ."

She's moved closer to me again, so I grab her wrist and pull her to the edge of the bath. "Come in here with me and you can kick my ass all you want. Please."

"There's no room for me in there," she answers, pulling her wrist out of my grasp and folding her arms across her chest.

"There's a perfect spot right here," I say, spreading my legs apart.

Her cheeks are flushed now, pinker than her fist. She bites her lip but it escapes into her rosebud smile. "Fine," she says, sounding exasperated, but I focus on her hands tugging on sleeves and pant legs. Once undressed, she steps into the bath and settles down. Takes a quick intake of breath. "Fuck! Are you trying to kill me? Your legs are like ice."

"You can help me defrost. And I can wash your hair. Hand me the shampoo."

She dunks her hair under the water and I start to lather it up. Her curls are soft and wet and covered with suds. I play with them, trying to make her have rabbit ears and other weird hair shapes. Janie is rubbing the cold out of my legs. She keeps on adding more hot water. When I'm done with her hair, I reach for the soap and wash her back. It doesn't take long. It's so small. I start washing other places.

"Yeah, I'm really dirty down there," she says, laughing a low, throaty laugh.

My hands move all over her body. I want to touch every inch of her. "You smell good, Janie. And you're so. . . slippery. So warm and, and so slippery." She shifts and I slip myself inside her. I'm heating up now from both within and without. It feels like paradise. I'm transported by the wet warmth and fragrant soapy smell. I make it last as long as I can.

Janie has climbed out of the tub. As she leans over the side to open the drain and add more hot water, I kiss her soft curls.

"You smell like spring," I say. "Do you think spring's coming?"

"Spring? What's spring? I think I have some distant memory. . ."

"I can tell by the light. We still have a good stretch of winter to go, but it's coming."

"It's minus fucking twenty-five degrees outside."

"I'd go out naked into that cold every day if this is what I got when I came back inside."

"Put that idea out of your head. I'm not going to enable that type of crazy behaviour."

"You're very. . . solid and reasonable, Janie, you know that?"

"Is that a compliment or what?"

"Yes, a compliment. And me? What am I?"

"You're fucking crazy. But also gorgeous and wild."

"What else? Do you think I'm deep?"

"You're complicated, anyway."

"I love you, Janie."

"I love you, too. And thank you for saying you'll try to change. You are very, very good, and that's the real reason I love you."

I lift my knees up, sliding forward so that I can put my whole head under the surface. I lie like that for a while, ears and eyes under, only my nose and lips peeking out. My mind drifts in warmth and happiness. I find I'm falling asleep. That's when I realize I've finally gotten over my fear of water.

CHAPTER 44
JANIE

"Are you wearing your long johns, Laek?" I ask, walking into our bedroom.

"Janie, you have two kids, not three. But if you want, put your hands down my pants and you'll see what kind of underwear I have on."

"Ew!" Siri yells from her bedroom.

I step closer to Laek so I can whisper. "Does she have super-human hearing?"

"Yeah, maybe." He speaks more quietly too. "She seems more her old self lately. What do you think, Janie? Does she seem happier to you?"

"She's made a lot of friends, which helps. Though I wish she'd bring them around more."

"I'm also worried about her problem with French."

"Yeah, I mean to talk to her about that again. Maybe today."

Simon bursts into the room. "Come on, already! All the queues de castor will be gone!"

We head out the door. "Daddy," Siri says. "Where's your new jacket?"

Laek pats himself. "Oh yeah." He goes back and puts it on. "I would've remembered it if Mommy hadn't gotten me all worked up about my underwear."

"Two kids, huh?" I say. "Let's go, Siri. We'll let 'les boys' bring up the rear."

At the park, we go into a round glass building to rent skates. We store our shoes in small built-in wooden boxes that double as seats, warmed from below by some geothermal system. Stumbling down to the ice, I nearly wipe out on the rubber matting. This does not bode well. Laek is the first to push himself out onto the smaller rink reserved for less-experienced skaters, first checking that Siri and Simon are making out OK. He looks over to me and I wave him on. I plan on taking my time.

"Look, Mommy," Simon says.

Laek is circling the ice in smooth, fluid movements. He comes to a stop in front of us.

"Daddy, how did you do that? Mommy said you've never ice skated before."

"I guess it's because I know how to magna skate."

"You can *magna* skate, Daddy?" Siri's voice is between incredulity and awe.

"Yeah. It's something that came in handy when I was a teenager. Come on, kids. I'll take you both around with me. I'll come back for you, Janie."

"Don't worry about me. I'll be fine." I catch myself again before I almost fall.

I manage to complete only one circuit in the time it takes Laek to go around several times, with Simon holding his right hand, and Siri, his left. I wonder if I could get away with just stopping now. But no. Laek looks down at me with a mischievous smile and offers his arm.

"Don't touch me!" I say to Laek. "I can do this myself."

"C'mon, Janie. At this rate you'll never see the other side of the lake."

The kids are watching me. I guess I have no choice. I let Laek lead me out onto the ice.

"Laek, Laek, wait! We're going too fast; my legs are shorter than yours!"

"Your legs aren't any shorter than the kids' legs and I was going twice as fast with them."

"I'm gonna fall, I know I'm gonna fall."

"You're not going to fall. How could you fall, with me holding you up?"

"I'll pull you down too."

"Don't be ridiculous. You hardly weigh anything."

"I weigh plenty. Plus it's like. . . like a force of nature, the world's desire to see me on my ass stronger than your ability to stay on your feet."

"Janie," he says, stopping.

"What?"

"It's not. It's not what the world wants." I look up at him. He has a surprisingly serious expression on his face. "And please don't underestimate my ability to stay on my feet."

I don't say anything, suddenly finding myself in the middle of a conversation I didn't know I was having. But just as suddenly, Laek smiles.

"I know how to solve your problem."

"I don't have a problem. I just don't like skating."

He continues as though I hadn't spoken. "Here's what you need to do. You need to fall."

"But that's what I'm trying to avoid!"

"Exactly. And you're so focused on it, you can't even skate. So fall. Right now. Get it over with. Come on, Janie. Trust me."

"OK, OK, I trust you."

I let go of Laek and let myself fall.

"How do you feel now?"

"Well, that wasn't exactly pleasurable, but I think I'll live."

"Good. Now that you've experienced falling and see that it's not the end of the world, you can concentrate on skating."

Laek puts his hand out and I pull myself up. He draws me in close. "Just relax."

He leans over and starts kissing me. I kiss him back, forgetting about my feet for a moment. While we're still kissing, Laek starts skating. He pulls me around with him and it's more like we're dancing. Lean, glide, back and forth, his arm tight around my waist. The park is lovely—an open, rolling expanse with stands of tall, bluish evergreens scattered at different points. The air is fresh and clean and exhilarating. Maybe this isn't so bad after all.

After we've gone around a few times, we find Siri and Simon waiting for us.

"Can I have my hot chocolate now? And my queue de castor?" Simon asks.

"Sure," I say, stepping off the ice.

"And you, Siri?" Laek asks. "Do you want to take a break now or would you like to skate some more? Maybe go out onto the big lake and skate really fast?"

"Yeah! Let's do it."

Simon and I bring our hot chocolates out to a small, low bench next to the ice. I look for Laek and Siri and spot them right away. Laek is unmistakeable, a tall, dark, athletic form. I admire the way his black jeans look with his sleek black jacket. His dark hair has grown out again and spills out of the bright headband he's wearing under his old tuque. Siri is striking too, tall and athletic, but with her own form.

They finally stop in front of us, Siri's face flushed and her eyes sparkling. "That was amazing. I can't believe how hyperfast we were going. It was like flying! And you gotta see those ice sculptures out on the lake, Simon. They are epic."

"Daddy, would you take me out to the lake, too? I want to go fast and see the sculptures."

"Sure. But to see the sculptures well, it would be better not to go too, too fast. Come on."

Siri settles down next to me.

"Do you want any hot chocolate, Siri? Here, have some of mine."

"Yum. Mommy, you can't believe how fast we were going. It was hyper, really hyper. I can't believe Daddy magna skated. Did you know about that? Did you ever see him?"

"No. You know, Siri, there's a lot about your Daddy that you don't know. There are even things I don't know. It's why. . . Listen, I'd like to talk to you. Is that OK?"

"I guess so."

"We probably should've had this conversation a long time ago, but I didn't think you were ready to listen. And maybe I wasn't ready either."

Between the stress of preparing for the refugee hearing and trying to get by on very little money, I've hardly had the energy for anything but day-to-day survival. But now, Laek's got a job, the rest of us are in school, and our permanent residence application seems to be moving along. Plus, there's an openness in Siri's expression that I haven't seen in a while.

"Siri, I want you to know that you had a right to be angry about how we moved the family to Montréal so suddenly. Even though we had no choice."

"If only you had told me first."

"Would that have made it OK? If we'd told you, but made you keep it a secret, even from Michael? Would you have still enjoyed camp? Been happy about the move?"

Siri looks down. I don't know if she's thinking about my questions, or just trying to figure out how to "win" our argument. But I'm not trying to win an argument or even have an argument. I just want to talk to her.

"I don't understand. I have a right to be angry, but you didn't do anything wrong?"

"I guess I'm just trying to say that I love you and. . . that I wish so much we hadn't had to do something you feel has hurt you. Even though I can't change what's happened, maybe there's something I can do to try to make up for it a little."

"What?"

"I don't know. Or what I mean is, that it's up to you. What if we say I owe you something. A big favour, or a wish. And that I have to grant it, like a fairy godmother."

"Could it be anything? Anything at all?"

"Yeah, pretty much. I mean, within reason. I'm not going to murder your little brother, for instance, no matter how annoying you find him."

"Speaking of Simon. . ."

I look up to see him skating towards us, Laek right beside him.

"The sculptures are hyper-awesome! And there's an artists' atelier where we can make our own ice sculptures. Can we go over there? It's at the other side of the lake."

"Sure. That sounds like fun," I tell Simon.

"Janie, would you mind if I skated around a bit by myself while you guys do that?"

"No, go ahead." I watch Laek take off.

We skate over together, Siri holding my hand and Simon on the other side of me, talking my ear off about the sculptures he saw and what he's thinking of making. I'm surer on my feet than I was earlier, but Siri is already so much better than I am, pulling me along with her smooth, confident glides. How suddenly this creeps up on you. One day, you're holding your toddler's hand as she takes small, unsteady steps, and then all of a sudden, without warning, she's holding your hand and supporting you.

"Maybe you should go out for hockey, Siri. You seem to have caught on to this skating."

"Maybe."

"Daddy would probably hate the idea, of course. . ." I look up at her slyly, thinking that if anything might motivate her, it's the idea of Laek disapproving of hockey. "But it would be a good way for you to better integrate here, in your own special way."

I don't like buzzwords like "integrate," but still, it's descriptive of what we need to do now, both for ourselves and to ensure that our application for permanent residency is granted.

"I don't want to play hockey," Simon blurts out. "It looks

more like fighting than playing to me. There's even *blood* on the ice sometimes!'

"You don't have to play hockey, Simon. There are other ways for you to integrate."

"Like ice-sculpturing, right?"

"Right," I say, as we arrive.

Once Simon's settled with tools and a block of ice, I resume my conversation with Siri.

"There's something else I want to talk to you about," I say, sitting down on the bench.

"If you're going to give me a hard time about my French grades again. . ."

"It's not your grades I'm concerned about. It's your refusal to learn and speak French. Maybe you think that if you don't learn French, you won't have to stay here. Or maybe it's just your way of punishing us. But Siri, cutting off your nose to spite your face is never a good idea."

"I don't know what you mean."

"Trying to hurt us by hurting yourself. And it does hurt us when you do that. But in the end, it's still yourself that you're hurting."

"I'm not trying to hurt myself. It just makes me mad, being forced to speak French."

"So don't do it because you're being forced. Do it for your own reasons. To become bilingual. To open up doors that might otherwise be closed—Québécois music, francophone friends, interesting job opportunities. These are the reasons to learn French."

"And otherwise you won't give me that present, that wish you promised."

"One has nothing to do with the other. You have that wish no matter what. Even if you end up failing French. But I'd rather you didn't. For your own sake."

"Alright, Mommy. I'll work harder and try to pass French.

And speak more French at school. But I don't want to speak it at home. Especially not with Daddy."

"I hope you'll change your mind about that at some point, but for now. . ."

"I was hoping you would change *your* minds, after you lost the refugee hearing."

"Just because we lost the hearing doesn't mean it's safe for us to go back. The reason we lost. . . it's complicated, but it's not because the things we said weren't true."

Siri looks at me sceptically, but I don't know what to say. We made a decision to protect the kids from details that might be frightening or traumatic. Even if I thought it was better that Siri understand more about what happened to her father, it's Laek's story to tell, not mine.

"Don't you like being here even a little better than before?" I ask her.

"Yeah, I guess. But I still miss my friends. I don't understand why I can't see them."

"Maybe someday, but right now things are still uncertain. We have no legal status here."

"Mommy, Siri, come look at what I made!"

We walk over to take a look. "Excellent, Simon. It's a black panther, right?"

"Don't be silly, Mommy. It's an *ice* panther."

"It's great," Siri says. "Mommy, could me and Simon go tubing now?

"Sure. You guys go ahead. Why don't you return your skates. I'll wait here for Daddy."

The kids skate back towards the main building. Once they've gotten off the ice, I look for Laek. My eyes find him right away, not just because of the figure he cuts but because of how fucking fast he's going. His right hand is behind his back, like a speed skater, and his left hand is resting on his thigh. As he goes around the lake again and again, I notice that I'm not the only person watching him. There's a group on the shore pointing and a number of skaters on the ice simply staring at him. This worries me for some reason, but it's not like he's breaking the law or anything. Still, I'm glad when he finally spots me sitting alone and makes a dramatic stop right in front of me, the sound of his skates sharp as they dig into the ice.

"Hi," he says, with a huge grin on his face.

"Hi, yourself. Are you having fun?"

"Yeah. But I'm ready to do something else, if you want. Where are the kids?"

"They've gone over to the hill for some tubing. I wouldn't mind trying that myself."

"Sounds good. I can return our skates."

I let Laek lead me back across the ice to a bench. He kneels down in front of me and unlaces my skates, slipping my feet out and rubbing them gently. There's something deeply erotic about how he does this. It feels wonderful.

"Don't go anywhere. I'll be right back," he says, as he stands up with my skates in hand.

"Where would I go without any shoes?"

He heads towards the building as I pull my feet up. Before long, he's back with my boots. I put them on and we walk towards the hill where everyone is tubing. I look up, trying to find the kids. I see Simon first, his head thrown back as his tube spins down the hill.

"Do you see Siri anywhere?"

Laek doesn't answer at first. When he does, his voice sounds a bit strained.

"Yeah. Coming down on the far left. See her? She's with someone." I finally spot her, going down on a giant tube in a boy's lap. "Do you know that kid, Janie? Is it Gabriel?"

"I think so. How do you know him? You weren't even home the times he's come by."

"I saw him on the first day of school. When I took Siri."

"And you remember him from way back then?"

"Yeah."

"And?"

"You tell me."

"I don't know, Laek. He doesn't talk much to me. He's polite, though. That can be nice, but I can't say I'm a big one for politeness. It's too much of a surface thing. I'm more interested in what's beneath that, what a person is really feeling or thinking. And you? You can't form a fair impression from just one encounter."

"No."

"But?"

"I don't trust him. And I think he's too old for Siri."

"Well, they're just friends."

"Uh huh."

"It's true that Siri's fond of him."

We stand there for a few more minutes.

"So are we going to go over there?" I ask.

"I'd like to go home now, I think. I'm cold. Is that OK?"

"Sure. I'll get the kids," I say.

"I'll wait here for you. You can take a ride or two down the hill while you're there. Maybe Siri or Simon will share a tube with you."

"OK. Meet you back here?" I ask.

"No, back by the main building."

But as I walk up towards the kids, I see that Laek hasn't moved a muscle. He's still gazing intently up the hill.

CHAPTER 45
SIRI

"And then the fucking bitch threw a chair at me. Grosse vache. She's lucky I didn't kick her fat ass." Lilliana finishes by taking a long hit off the vape. I push myself up from the dusty, grey couch under the stairs in Javier's basement. I've already heard the chair story twice. Plus, I was there when it happened so I also know what Lilliana had said to our math teacher right before. Lilliana never tells that part, though.

"I mean we all knew that Madame V was ready to snap," I say. "All she needed was a push."

"Are you saying I pushed her to throw that chair at me?" Lilliana gets up from the couch too. There's a saggy indentation in the shape of her butt where she'd been sitting.

"No. But you should've known she'd lose it when you called her an ugly freak."

Lilliana turns to the others. "I knew Siri would take her side. Little teacher's pet."

"It's not my fault I'm good at math. I'm failing French, you know." Wow, that sounded stupid. To make up for it, I grab the vape from where it's leaning against the couch, almost hidden in the shaggy blue carpet. I breathe in some liquorice-flavoured smoke, hoping nobody notices that I'm not totally inhaling.

"Siri's not a teacher's pet." Good, Gabriel's defending me. "She's just. . . young."

"I'm not *that* young," I protest. "I'll be thirteen soon."

Gabriel reaches his hand out. I hand the vape to him. I watch his chest expand under his tight shirt as he slowly fills his lungs with the smoke. After he exhales, he turns to me.

"I'm not saying thirteen's young. Some thirteen-year-old girls are already out earning money, or are even mothers. Kids from the United America, though, are more, you know, naive."

"You're being prejudiced."

Gabriel doesn't answer. He just looks at me like I'm acting naive. Like I'm just proving his point. That's not fair. How can I win the argument if he won't even argue with me? He stands up like everything's settled and turns to the rest of the group.

"Let's play something."

"How about a screen game?" Anton says.

Lilliana rolls her eyes. "Only boys like screen games."

I sort of like screen games, but I don't say anything.

"How about poker?" Gabriel says.

Anton shakes his head. "Poker's boring, unless we play for money."

Gabriel turns to me. "Do you have any money, Siri?"

I shake my head. I already told Gabriel that, when he wanted to buy more weed.

"Well," he says. "There are other stakes we can play for. Who wants to play strip poker?"

Anton immediately says he's in. Javier shrugs as though to say "whatever." I look at Lilliana and then at Gabriel. I have this feeling I'm being tested.

"Sure." I say. I'm a pretty good poker player.

We walk across to the other side of the basement where there's a small, square table and four folding chairs propped under the dirty glass window. Javier and Anton set up the table while Gabriel and I unfold the chairs and drag over a crate. Then Javier takes the deck of cards from the corner of the wobbly blue bookshelf and begins to shuffle, but Gabriel smiles and reaches over to take the deck from his hands. "I'll deal," he says, and as usual, everyone goes along.

At first, I'm winning. Then Gabriel lights up a blunt and we switch to smoking the old-fashioned way, which goes with poker and hand-held cards. Somehow, the blunt keeps coming around to me, and if I don't take a toke each time, Gabriel looks at me as though I'm acting like a baby. He's watching me so carefully that I even have to inhale. I get this flash of an idea. Maybe the reason I always win at poker is because I'm usually less stoned than everyone else.

Javier and Anton both have their shirts off now. Anton's skin is very white and his nipples are all puckered with cold since the basement has no heat. I don't know why he didn't take off his jeans instead—I can see that he's wearing long underwear. That makes me think about how cis boys have an unfair advantage in strip poker. They can take more stuff off without showing their private parts. When I complain about this, Javier says he has an idea. He pulls over an old, worn box covered in cobwebs. He opens the box and pulls out different hats.

Javier throws a straw hat with fake red cherries at Lilliana. She wrinkles up her nose but puts it on anyway. Next he tosses me an antique Montréal Expos cap that's a soft, faded blue and too big. I turn it around so that the bill faces backwards. Gabriel tells Javier that he wants a hat too. Javier hesitates, then gives him a grey cap that makes him like an old-time gangsta. Gabriel gives me a look, like he knows he's hot in his boxers and black tank and cap. I feel myself blushing so I turn away and watch Anton pull a hat with furry flaps over his ears. Javier bows his head and puts on something that looks like a sleek, black magician's hat. Then we all start talking in funny voices while pretending to be screen stars or other famous people, only stoned. I decide not to be mad that the boys got hats too.

There's a cloud of smoke around our heads and everything is kind of hazy, but I also feel hyper-focused, like nothing's more important than these four people I'm sitting with while slapping down cards on the little folding table. It's exciting, too, with everyone half dressed and trying not to shiver, red and black kings and queens deciding who has to strip.

I think the pot may be affecting my brain because I'm not winning like I usually do. Maybe the difference is that I'm a good bluffer and there's no way to bluff in strip poker. Merde, I lost again! I'm down to only three pieces of clothing—my underpants, my bra and my t-shirt. I don't want to be wearing less than everyone else, especially Lilliana. It's no fair because she started out wearing more layers.

"So what's it gonna be, little Siri? What will you take off?" Gabriel asks.

There's no way I'm taking off my underpants. If I take off my t-shirt, I guess it wouldn't be too bad, like I was wearing a bikini bathing suit. But I have another idea.

"I'll take off my bra." I undo the back of my bra and slip the straps off one arm at a time, with my arms still inside the shirt. Like this, I'm able to take off my bra without showing anything. I look over at Gabriel with a big smile on my face, but he doesn't smile back.

Lilliana looks at her cards. She's wearing black leggings, underpants and a black bra with lacy straps. I'm glad I decided to keep my shirt on since my bra isn't all fancy like hers. Gabriel deals Lilliana another card, face down. She peeks at it. Then she throws her cards on the table and announces that she has to go home, that she promised to help with dinner. She puts her clothes on so fast, you'd think she practices taking them off and putting them on again all the time.

Anton stands up. "I have to go too." He grabs the rest of his clothes and hurries up the stairs after Lilliana. Anton has a huge crush on her.

"I better go lock up after them," Javier says as he pulls on his sweater.

I get dressed, beginning with my pants. I put on my socks and sneakers, looking around for my bra. Gabriel walks over with a weird smile on his face, my bra in his hand.

"Gimme that," I say, but he just lifts it up higher, way above my head.

"What's your problem?" I say. "I have to get dressed."

"What will you give me for this bra, little Siri?"

"Nothing. It's mine. And stop calling me that."

"If you don't want me to call you little Siri then you should stop acting like a child."

He's standing very close to me now. "I'll tell you what. I'll take off my shirt and you take off yours," he says, pulling his shirt over his head.

Usually I like seeing Gabriel without his shirt on, but right now, I don't. It reminds me that he's much stronger than I am. I back up, but Gabriel follows me. My back is against the wall.

"Don't worry, Siri, I'll help you take it off." Before I have a chance to say anything, he pushes my shirt up and is squeezing my breasts. I don't like how it feels. I want to go home. I think about how he's supposed to be my friend, and I get so mad that I kick him as hard as I can.

"Ow!"

"You leave me alone or I'll kick you somewhere else too," I yell.

Just then, Javier comes back downstairs. "Uh, désolé. Didn't mean to interrupt. . ."

I grab the bra from Gabriel's hand and run upstairs. I put on my coat, stuffing the bra in my pocket. Javier comes upstairs, followed by Gabriel.

"Wait, I'll get the door," Javier says. "Are you OK?" he asks me quietly.

I look over at Gabriel, who says, "See you in school tomorrow?"

I don't answer, just walk out the door. Once I'm around the corner, I take off down the block. All I want is to be alone in my own room. It's raining and there are huge puddles on the sidewalk surrounded by slush. Where the snow has melted, you can see dog poop and bits of garbage that the snow had hidden up until now. It wouldn't be so bad if it meant that spring was coming, but the forecast calls for snow again tomorrow. From one day to the next, you never know what to wear. I like the winter and the snow, but this freeze-and-melt, freeze-and-melt thing is getting old already. It's been going on for, like, six months. If I were in Brooklyn, we'd already be playing baseball and I'd have photos of my new teammates on my screen.

Two blocks from my apartment building, I'm looking at a huge puddle in the street and trying to figure out where I should jump over it. Just as I'm ready to leap off the curb, a car goes by and splashes me with dirty, slushy water. My throat gets all tight as I look down at my soaked jeans. Tears come into my eyes. There's a big chunk of ice right in front of me. I kick it as hard as I can to the other side of the street, where it sinks into the next puddle.

When I get home, the apartment is quiet, except for the sound of pots being moved around in the kitchen. I don't see Simon's boots on the little wooden shoe rack by the door, and Daddy's bike helmet isn't hanging from its usual hook. I walk quickly down the hall towards my room, but as I pass the kitchen, Mommy calls out to me.

"Where are you going, Siri? Hang your coat up and take off your sneakers. You're tracking dirty water all over the apartment."

I go back down the hall, take off my sneakers and hang my coat on one of the hooks, stuffing my bra into the pocket of my jeans. I try to go into my room again.

"Wait, Siri. Come over here. I need you to taste this."

Mommy's standing in the doorway of the kitchen with a towel over her shoulder and her hair tied back with a red and purple striped cloth that looks like it came from the circus or something. She's holding a wooden spoon out to me so I have no choice. I step into the kitchen. It's warm and steamy and smells delicious. I taste what's on the spoon, some white, creamy sauce.

"Good, it's fine." I try to leave but she stops me again.

"Siri, is everything alright? What's that in your pocket?"

"Everything's fine. I need to do my homework."

"Since when are you in such a rush to do homework? And I asked you what was in your pocket." She reaches over and pulls the bra out.

"Give that back to me! It's mine!" I yell. Then I start crying. Why is everyone trying to take my bra away?

"Siri, what's the matter? Take it, of course it's yours. But why aren't you wearing it?"

I don't say anything.

"Siri, please tell me what happened. You're starting to scare me a little."

"OK, we were playing strip poker. That's all. And. . . and I lost."

"What do you mean, you lost? What did you have to do?"

"Nothing."

"But your bra?"

"I took it off under my shirt. Nothing showed."

"But something happened. Tell me. Please."

"Just leave me alone."

"Who were you playing with? Were you the only girl?"

"No. Lilliana was there."

"I don't like that girl."

"You don't know her."

"I don't know any of your friends well. I'd like to. What about Gabriel? Was he there?"

"Yeah. And Anton and Javier."

"I've met Javier. He seems nice."

"He was upstairs when. . ."

"When what?"

"When. . . when the others had to leave."

"So you were downstairs alone with Gabriel. What did he do? Did he touch you?"

"He already thinks I'm a baby. And if I tell you. . . "

"This has nothing to do with being a baby. Did he touch you, Siri? Please, sweetheart. I won't be mad at you. And I won't do anything without talking to you about it first. I promise."

I feel trapped here in the kitchen with my mom and all her questions. Maybe if I tell her what happened, she'll feel bad for me and finally let me go to my room. So I tell her. She doesn't speak for a moment. Then she says, "Good for you." I must look confused because she adds, "For kicking him. For standing up for yourself."

I feel a tiny bit better when she says that, but Mommy keeps talking. "I want you to stay away from Gabriel from now on."

"No! He didn't mean anything bad. He just. . . He wasn't totally himself."

"That's no excuse."

"You don't understand, Mommy."

"What is it that you think I don't understand? That he was high?"

"How did . . ."

"It's obvious you've been smoking pot. Do you think I can't see your eyes? Smell it on your clothes? I'm not as clueless as you think, Siri. Actually, parents usually aren't. Maybe you should bear that in mind."

I think about this and wonder what else she knows.

"We need to address what happened," Mommy says. "I want to speak to his mother."

"No! You can't!"

"He shouldn't get away with what he did."

"He didn't. I kicked him."

"What if he tries something else?"

"He won't."

"I don't want you to spend any time alone with him. I don't trust him."

"Stop trying to control me! Gabriel's my best friend. At least, ever since you ruined my life by making us move here." Mommy opens her mouth to argue, but I don't let her. "You don't know him. He just made a mistake. He won't do anything like that again."

"I don't agree. You need to think this through."

"And you need to stop telling me what to think!"

"Siri. . ."

"I just want to be alone right now!"

"OK, fine. We'll talk about this later, when Daddy's home."

Once behind my closed door, I immediately feel relieved. Sometimes when I'm with my mom, when I'm with any of my family, I feel like I can't think straight. All their ideas, all the things they want me to be and do, it's like it crowds me out.

I won't let Mommy tell me what to think. She doesn't even know Gabriel. Maybe what he did shows that he likes me. I like him too, but that doesn't mean I wanted him to touch me like that. But maybe it's my fault for giving him the wrong idea or something. He's been a good friend to me, stuck by me all year, even the times I was in a shitty mood and didn't act very nice. And even though all his other friends are, like, two years older than me. It's true I sometimes give him some money or lend him my school work, but he has a really hard life. His family is poor and sometimes he has to work instead of going to school. And he always shares whatever he has with me. But why did he act like that, even when I told him to stop? I was scared of him. But my heart tells me not to be, that I can trust him deep down.

I press my face into my pillow so Mommy won't hear me crying. In Brooklyn, with Michael, everything seemed simpler. But Michael's my own age. Is that the difference? Or maybe Gabriel is just more complicated. Or maybe. . . I don't know. I just feel so wrecked inside.

After a while, I take out my screen to write Michael a message. Of course, I can't say what happened, but I can tell him I had a fight with one of my friends and my parents won't let us hang out any more. This is pretty much what happened. The real story would mess his head up too much. Michael's smart and stuff, but I don't think he's as mature as I am. Maybe kids in the U.A. really are more naive.

CHAPTER 46
LAEK

'm perched on top of the high ramp in the skate park. I've been here since dawn, watching the dark shape of Siri's school grow sharp against the lightening sky. From the ramp, I can see anyone who approaches the park. Whether on foot or by vehicle.

I don't think about the confrontation I'm about to have. I'd rather just follow my instincts. Instead, I'm thinking about confrontations from my past. Other ways they might have played out. Where would I be now if I'd acted differently? Where would my kids be? Would things be better or worse?

I finally see him. Arm clutching his backpack, peering around, hoping for a few sales. It's not the first time I've watched this park. Nor his comings and goings. Siri would be mortified if she knew. I jump down from the ramp. He's startled but tries not to show it. I give him a signal I've seen others use, then duck behind the small brick building containing the public toilets and supply room. He obeys my summons. I'm almost disappointed by how trusting he is.

"Gabriel." I pronounce his name in the Spanish way. He's thrown off for a minute. Answers in French. When I don't respond immediately, he switches to English.

"Do I know you?" he asks.

I decide, for once, to stick with English. I don't know why. It's a visceral decision.

"I know *you*. I'm Siri's father."

"Siri who?" he says, but his lie is obvious. His eyes shift quickly sideways, searching for an escape. I don't give him the opportunity. I use his surprise to push him ahead of me into the men's room. I close the metal door tightly behind us. Stand in front of it to block his exit.

"What the hell! Lemme out of here. You got no right."

"I just want to talk to you," I say calmly.

"Fuck that. I'm outta here."

He makes a dive for the door. I catch him by the shoulders and shove him, hard. He stumbles but keeps on his feet. He seems wary, not yet afraid, studying his environment carefully. I look only at him. I already know the layout of the room. Two stalls and a urinal on one side, metal sinks on the adjacent wall to my right, a broom, rake, and mop in the far corner, and opposite, some kind of cleaning device with a long plastic hose. Gabriel's gaze returns to the door. The only exit is through me. I watch him decide to try to talk his way out.

"I didn't do nothing."

"You and I both know you did something."

"I didn't do nothing *wrong*."

"Siri's twelve years old. And you are. . . fifteen? Sixteen?"

"Fifteen. Siri's almost thirteen. Anyhow, no one's forcing her to hang out with me."

"That doesn't mean you get to touch her."

"She likes me."

"Yeah. She did. But that makes what you did worse, not better."

"I didn't hurt her."

I take a step towards him. Think about Siri's tears when Janie snatched the bra out of her pocket. The look of naked betrayal on her face last night when she thought no one was looking.

"You didn't hurt her?" I repeat.

He backs up. I follow. He's up against the wall now, with me practically on top of him. He's lean and muscular, like I was at that age, but I'm taller and have a physical solidity he won't match for years. He tries to pull away but I pin him to the wall. I can feel the beat of my pulse, but I also feel very calm. I place my hand on his cheek. Stroke it gently with my fingers. He's old enough to have some stubble, but just barely.

"Gabriel, you can do better than that," I say softly, almost tenderly.

He tries to push me away but there's no room to do anything but grapple with me.

"Leave me alone. Don't touch me."

"But I'm not *hurting* you. I'm being real sweet with you. I can be a lot rougher," I add.

"Let go, just let me go. Please!" I feel him tremble and can smell his sweat.

"OK. Since you're asking so nicely."

I remove my hand. Take a step back. He rubs his cheek hard. Edges away sideways.

"Let's start again, Gabriel. And listen carefully because I don't want to repeat myself. If a girl says 'no' or 'stop it' or squirms away from you, or anything like that, it means you leave her be. The same goes for a boy, by the way."

"I'm not. . ."

"Shut up." I stop. Wait to be sure I have his undivided attention. "Do you understand?"

"Yeah. OK. But Siri. . ."

"Yeah, about Siri. She's a straightforward person. If she ever wants something like that from you, she'll let you know. Unless and until that happens, you don't touch her. Understood?"

He doesn't answer.

"Is that understood, Gabriel?"

"Yeah, whatever," he answers, recovering some of his bravado.

"Because otherwise, you will be very, very sorry."

Saying these words, I feel this strange detachment. Like I'm reciting a script. I take another step back, thinking about this. He moves even further away from me. From this more comfortable distance, he gives me a defiant look.

"You watch yourself too. Siri told me everything. I could tell the government about you. *Your* government. And they'll come after you and kill you. Like they killed my father."

For a moment, I have a pang of conscience, listening to the empty threats of this child trying to be a man. Thinking to intimidate me with the spectre of his own father's death. There's something very sad about this. But then I remember Siri's face last night when I looked in on her. Like her best friend had stabbed her in the back.

"Do your worst. But if you hurt Siri, whatever happens, I'll find you. Like I did today."

"You don't scare me."

"No. Maybe you're still too stupid to be scared. When I was your age, I wasn't scared of anything either. But then the same government that killed your father arrested me and my friends. I was held for six months. Tortured and. . ." I swallow hard as I watch his eyes widen. "Yeah, when I was fifteen, I thought I was pretty tough too. We were both wrong."

"Are we done talking? I. . . I have to go to school."

"Sure. You can go."

I move aside and let him leave. Follow him outside. The morning's grey but dry. Gabriel walks away, towards his school. I lean against the building, arms folded over my chest. He turns around once. Sees me watching him. Walks a little faster. I watch until he's out of sight. Then l slide down to the ground and press my head to my knees. I don't want to think about what I just did. I feel like I need a shower. I rub my eyes hard with the heels of my hands until all I can see are rough smears of colour and light moving in front of my retinas, blocking all other images.

When I get home from work at suppertime, Siri's waiting for

me, a look of fury on her face. I sit down at the kitchen table next to Janie and across from Simon.

"What did you do? Tell me, Daddy. What did you do to Gabriel?"

"I thought you weren't going to school today." I look at Janie.

"She decided to go after all. She didn't want it to seem like she was scared or ashamed."

"Tell me what you did to Gabriel, Daddy."

"I didn't do anything to him. We just had a talk."

"You must have done something. He wouldn't even look at me. He acted like. . . like he was scared of me or something."

"Well, I'd rather he be scared of you than the other way around."

"I'm not scared of him. He won't try anything like that again with me."

"No, he won't," I say and pour myself a glass of water from a reused wine bottle.

"I thought we could still be friends. Once he realized what he did was wrong. After we talked it out or something. But now he won't even speak to me!"

"Didn't he say anything, Siri?" Janie asks, putting some left-over vegetable stew on my rice. I take the serving spoon from her hand.

"Yeah. He told me he was too old for me. That I should hang with kids my own age. And one more thing. He told me my father was crazy. But I guess I knew that already."

Siri shoots me another angry look. I keep silent. Let Janie handle this.

It's been a while since I've heard Siri go off about how we ruined her life by moving here. This time, there's a tone of tired hopelessness in her voice when she adds that I've driven away all her new friends, too. Just in time for her thirteenth birthday. She asks Janie why we don't just kill her instead. I know all about adolescent drama, but her words still make me flinch. I put my fork down. Notice that Simon isn't eating either.

"You usually like my veggie stew, Simon. Do you want some cheese on top?" I ask.

"It's fine, Papa. I'm just not so hungry today." He looks up at me and something changes his mind. "Sure. Cheese would be great."

I return to the table with a block of parmesan and the metal grater. Janie's suggesting different ideas to Siri for celebrating her birthday. Meanwhile, Siri is working herself up to a tirade. Something I've seen Janie do when she's upset but would rather be angry. Siri turns to me. I brace myself. She stops, closes her mouth. Turns all her attention on Janie.

"Maybe there is one thing that might make me feel better. You remember the promise you made, Mommy? About granting me a special wish?"

"Yeah. . ."

"Well I know what I want to ask for. . . I want to invite Michael here for my birthday."

"I don't know, Siri. This idea worries me. We still don't have our permanent resident status. Our interview is in two, three weeks. Would you be willing to wait until then?"

"My birthday is next week. Please, Mommy. You promised."

Janie catches my eye, but I'm not sure how to respond.

"I'm going to have to think about this. Discuss it with Daddy. I want to say yes, but. . . Let's sleep on it, OK? I'll give you an answer in the morning."

I watch Siri pick at her food. Every so often she steals a quick glance in my direction. Like she's trying to figure something out. Maybe whether I'll veto her request to see Michael. Or what happened between me and Gabriel. Or maybe something else. Like who I really am, this man who's her father. Who's always been gentle with her. Who hates violence and even competitive sports. But who somehow, some way, managed to scare the shit out of her very tough friend.

I can see Janie wondering the same thing. She's watching me as I do the supper dishes. Bubbling with impatience to ask me things. I wash the dishes slowly, trying to think it through. It's probably driving her crazy how slowly I'm washing. I try to go faster. End up breaking a glass and cutting myself. I keep washing anyway. I'm almost done.

"Shit, Laek. Stop. You're bleeding on the silverware. I'll finish up. Go take care of your hand and I'll meet you in the bedroom."

When Janie comes in, I'm sitting up in bed in my shorts, the cut cleaned and bandaged, teeth brushed, face washed. And still unsure what we should do.

"So what happened with Gabriel?" she asks me.

"I waited for him. We talked. I explained that his behaviour was unacceptable."

"Uh huh. And?"

"And what?"

"Laek, you know what I'm asking you. Don't make me spell it out."

"I was somewhat forceful in my explanations, if that's what you want to know."

"What did you do?"

I shrug.

"Did you hit him?"

"No, I didn't hit him."

Janie lets out a sigh of relief. "I didn't think you'd do that, but even so. . . Do you think you might have gone too far?"

"I don't know. Maybe."

"It could be you're identifying too much with the situation."

"You mean because he reminds me of myself at that age?"

"No. I wasn't thinking that at all. Kind of the opposite, actually. That you were identifying with Siri."

"Oh."

"But the thing is, you and Siri, your experiences. . . They're very different. Thankfully."

"Yeah. Thankfully. But still. I don't know."

"I don't know either. I wasn't there. But I trust your judgment."

Hearing Janie say these words makes me feel lighter. "Hey, come here." I pull her in close, her hair tickling my bare chest.

"Aren't you cold that way?"

"No. Listen, Janie, what do you think we should do about Siri's request?"

"I don't know. I'm ambivalent. I feel like I promised, and I'd hate to let her down. On the other hand, I'm nervous, even about him coming here. But I'm not sure that's totally rational."

I'm also nervous about the idea. Extremely uneasy. I close my eyes for a minute. Janie's hair feels soft on my skin. I'm thinking about Siri, and suddenly I'm remembering a moment with her, when she was just an infant. It was three in the morning. Siri was lying on my bare chest. I was in the living room of our two-room Brooklyn apartment, Janie sleeping in the bedroom, ragged and desperate with exhaustion. Siri was never a good sleeper. Not as a baby, and not now either. I suppose it didn't help that Janie and I both immediately sprang to her side the moment she made even the smallest murmur. I was all of twenty years old at the time. Barely grown up myself. I had no clue how to care for an infant.

I remember the warmth of Siri's soft, round, baby head lying against me. Her sweet smell. Her little fists pushing against my chest. I had no milk for her, no breasts. She'd nursed not more than half an hour earlier. Could she really be hungry again? At the time, I wore my hair long, a section on the right side plaited into a thin braid. Siri grabbed hold of it and tugged. Was she mad at me for not having milk? She tugged again, harder. And started laughing. Her laugh was like warm sunlight in late autumn. My sweet child. She wasn't hungry at all. She just wanted to play.

What I wouldn't give to hear that laugh right now. To see her smile.

"Let's do it, Janie. Let's just say yes. It's her birthday and. . . I want to make her happy."

"OK. Good. Do you think she's still awake? I can't wait to tell her."

"Yeah, probably. She's never been a big one for sleeping."

"Reminds me of someone. Do you want to come with me to give her the good news?"

"No. You go. You were the one who promised her. And anyway, I think she's pretty mad at me. I don't want to spoil the mood."

Janie walks down the hall to Siri's bedroom. I close my eyes to better picture my daughter's smile.

CHAPTER 47
SIRI

Michael beams me when they're outside the building. I whip open the apartment door. As soon as I see them, I run down the hallway and throw my arms around Michael, dancing him around in a circle. "I can't believe you guys are here! I can't believe it!"

Mommy's waiting for us with the door held open. She leans over to kiss Rebecca on both cheeks, but Rebecca moves back like she's surprised. I guess Mommy forgot that this isn't how people say hello in New York.

"Did you have trouble finding our place?" Mommy asks.

"With all the French, it wasn't easy. But once we found the building, we were able to come right up. There's no security at all. Doesn't that worry you, Janie?" Rebecca asks.

"No. Why should it?"

"You know they don't care about that, Rebecca. Even in Brooklyn, they didn't live in a gated community," David says.

"Well, bienvenue. That means welcome. Excuse the mess, I'd expected you a little later. You must have made good time. Any problems at the border?"

Mommy steps aside to let them in, but they just stay in the doorway. I want to grab Michael and bring him into my room, but Rebecca has her hand on his shoulder like she doesn't even want him to take off his coat.

"Is Laek home?" David asks, looking around.

"No. He's doing the late shift at work today. And Simon's at a friend's. Are you hungry?"

"We're tired from the drive. We were thinking of just eating at the hotel and then relaxing. But maybe Siri would like to come with us. The hotel has a pool on the roof," Rebecca adds, turning to me. "Would you like to go swimming?"

"That would be great! Could I, Mommy?"

"Yeah, I guess so. You sure you don't want to hang out a little, Rebecca? David? I was going to put out some wine and cheese. Or I could give you a tour of the city."

"We don't want to put you to any trouble," Rebecca says. "I know your budget is tight. You, back in school after being a lawyer all these years and Laek working these weird hours."

Mommy looks like she wants to argue, but then shrugs. "Whatever Siri wants. But sweetheart, I'm not sure your bathing suit still fits you. You've grown since last summer."

I blush, thinking about where I've actually grown. My mom can be so embarrassing!

"That's no problem," Rebecca says. "We'll just pick up a new one for her."

"Oh, you don't have to do that," Mommy replies.

"It's no trouble. It's her birthday, after all."

After swimming, we go to a restaurant for supper. Michael and his parents get confused because they think "entrée" means main course instead of appetizer. I forgot I used to think that too. But of course an entrée being an appetizer makes more sense: like *entering* the meal. I try to explain this, but Rebecca gets all annoyed. I guess they're tired. Anyhow, Michael likes that I know these things. He whispers into my ear, "You're so sophisticated now. Like a French girl."

I walk them back to their hotel room. They've gotten a suite with a giant wall screen and holo-board. This place must have cost them a lot of money. It's nothing like the hotel where Daddy and Mommy and Simon and I stayed when we first came here, when I thought we were tourists instead of refugees. Even though I still feel mad about that, I have this warm feeling when I think of our little hotel. It was cozy and fun. Montréal is a pretty hyper city. I realize I feel disappointed that Rebecca and David don't want us to show them around. Well, there's always tomorrow. My birthday! I can't wait.

"So I guess I'd better get going," I tell them.

"Oh," Rebecca says, looking at David. "Listen, Siri. David and I are exhausted. It's a long drive from New York. . ."

"That's OK," I say. "You don't have to drive me back. I can take the métro."

"No, no," Rebecca says quickly. "We wouldn't hear of it. I have another idea. Maybe you could stay over with us in the hotel tonight. There's plenty of room."

"But tomorrow's Friday. I have school."

"It's your birthday. And it's not every day that somebody crosses a border to visit you."

"Please, Siri? It'd be fun," Michael says.

"Well, I guess I could ask my mom."

When I ask Mommy, she says no at first, but I can tell I'm gonna be able to talk her into it. Mommy always lets me argue with her. Lots of times I can either convince her or wear her down. Today, I have at least eight good arguments. She finally caves when I agree to beam my homework to my teacher.

In the morning, I send in my homework like I promised. I watch Michael's parents pack.

"I thought you'd be staying for the weekend," I say.

"I have work," David answers, closing up his bag.

"And we had to leave Sara and Benny and Georgie with David's mother," Rebecca adds.

"Yeah. I understand. It's just that I'd hoped to spend more time together."

"We've missed you too, Siri. Michael especially, of course, but all of us."

"The baseball team isn't the same without you," David says, touching the bill of his cap.

"I've missed you guys too. You were like a second family."

"We feel like you're a part of our family, too. Maybe you will be some day," Rebecca says, looking at Michael. I feel hyper-embarrassed. "I know this has been very difficult for you, Siri. For Michael, too. And the messages he's gotten from you. . . We've been worried."

"I'm fine. It's OK."

"You don't have to be brave. I've known you since you were practically a baby."

"It's OK," I repeat, wishing I hadn't made Montréal out to be such a bad place. Even so, maybe I can still convince them to stay another day.

Rebecca tells me that she and David have a surprise for my birthday, but that we need to drive there. I tell them great, since Mommy's letting me miss school today. And this will also give me more time to convince them to stay longer. Maybe they'll come with us to the garden restaurant tonight and we can have supper together for my birthday.

We drive away from centre-ville and I eventually see signs for the bridge. Since we're four people, we get to pay the smallest toll amount. I've hardly left Montréal at all since coming here. Crossing the bridge with the sun shining down on the water and with Michael sitting next to me makes my heart feel big inside my chest. It's great to be able to laugh and talk face to face after all this time. After a while, though, I get too curious about where they're taking me. I finally make them at least give me a hint.

"What's your favourite restaurant in Brooklyn?" Rebecca asks.

"Pizza and Boots, I guess. We had my tenth birthday party there, remember Michael?"

"Sure. They let us make our own pizzas. You made one with a smiley face."

"Yeah, black olive eyes, a mushroom nose and a red pepper slice for the mouth."

"How would you like to go there for supper tonight, Siri?" Rebecca asks.

"Are they a chain or something? They have one here too?"

"No, I mean in Brooklyn. We can be eating their pizza in less than five hours."

"Four hours," David says, "Once we get out of Québec and their ridiculous speed limits."

"But. . . how could we do that? I don't even have a travel pass or anything."

"No worries," David says. "I have a family pass. You're around Sara's age."

"You really think it's OK?"

"We're just a family on holiday. You know I travel a lot for my job with the government, right? Believe me. They won't give us any trouble."

I turn to Michael. He has a pleading look in his eyes. I know Mommy and Daddy wouldn't approve of this, but they can be so paranoid sometimes. I think back on all the misery they caused me. They never even gave me a chance to say good-bye to my friends. And it's Daddy's fault that my birthday was ruined. Going home for my birthday would make up for that a little. And Michael's parents would never do something that could get us in trouble.

"If you really think it's OK. . . yeah. Let's do it! I'm gonna need to call my mom, though."

"What time does she get home again?" Rebecca asks.

"Four or four thirty."

"That's fine. We'll be at the restaurant by then."

When we finally get to Brooklyn, I'm practically jumping out of my seat. We get out of the car and I can't stop looking around at everyone and everything. I'm surprised by how crowded the streets are, and loud and dirty, too. It's not how I remembered it. At the same time, there's all this stuff that's hyper-familiar, like how the air smells and feels, and the look of the stores, and the way people talk to each other—not just their accents, but the rhythms in their sentences. I never noticed this stuff while I was living here. The other thing that's weird is how it feels like just yesterday that I was in Brooklyn, but at the same time, it's like a whole lifetime has gone by. I can't decide if I feel like everything or nothing has changed.

When I finally call my mom, she flips out.

"Please tell me you're joking. You couldn't have really crossed the border."

"The border wasn't a problem. David works for the government and everything."

"I can't fucking believe this. Put Rebecca on. How the hell are you getting home?"

"I guess the same way. We didn't talk about that."

"I said put Rebecca on. Now."

I give the call to Rebecca. "She wants to talk to you. She's hyper-pissed."

I can't hear what my mom is saying, but I can imagine a lot of it from Rebecca's responses. I listen to her end of the conversation while pretending to be interested in my food.

"Because I thought it would be nice for her birthday. . ."

"No, I didn't think it would be a problem. . ."

"How should I know that? If you'd told me about it before just disappearing. . ."

"Aren't you being a little dramatic?"

"Janie, if you're going to scream at me, I'm hanging up."

"We're exhausted from all that driving already."

"No. There's no point. . . No. I'll call you tomorrow."

Rebecca blanks the screen and puts it in her pocket.

"My mom didn't want to talk to me again?"

"You know your mother when she loses her temper. We'll talk to her tomorrow."

The next day, I ask David when he'll be driving me home. He tells me there's a baseball practice today and asks me if I'd like to come. It's still the weekend, so I guess there's no big rush. My mom can't complain as long as I'm home for school on Monday.

Being in Prospect Park is great. David lets me practice with his team. It's sunny and much warmer out than in Montréal. I touch fists with a bunch of kids I knew from last year. Some of them didn't even realize that I don't live here anymore. They only saw me during baseball season. A few kids who are from my school, though, ask me where I've been. I don't know what I should tell them. I finally say we've been living up in Canada but haven't decided yet if we're staying. No one seems to know much about Canada so their questions don't make a lot of sense. One kid asks me if the U.A. president is president of Canada too, and another kid asks if there are igloos.

I call Mommy when we get back. She asks me right away when David is driving me home. I tell her I don't know and that he's not here right now, but I figure it'll probably be tomorrow since it's already pretty late. I tell her about baseball and she listens without saying much. Then she asks me to put Rebecca on, but Rebecca says she's busy right now and she'll call back. Mommy then asks me to please try to convince David to bring me home today. I tell her fine but I don't see what the big deal is. My mom's always in code red for no reason.

When David finally gets home, I ask him when he'll be driving me back. He asks me if I had fun at practice today and would I want to go again tomorrow? I say OK, but we should leave right after that because my mom is getting all hyper. Then Michael and I go out for a walk. With little Benny and Georgie always following us around, we've hardly had any time to ourselves.

We walk around the condo complex. Hardly anyone's out, even though it's a beautiful spring night. There are guards patrolling, though. One comes over. After Michael shows his resident ID, the guard asks who I am. I'd forgotten how much security there is here. Michael explains that I'm a good friend of the family. I'm glad he didn't say I was his girlfriend, but then the guard starts looking me up and down. Michael usually acts calm but now he looks hyper-angry. I hope he isn't going to talk back or anything. I feel a little nervous. When the guard finally walks away, I ask Michael if there's somewhere we could go where no one will bother us.

Michael takes me to a different part of the complex. He pulls me into a small area in between two of the buildings. There's a ledge where we can sit. It's dirty, with beer cans and cigarette butts and candy wrappers, but it's private at least.

"It's so great that you're here, Siri."

"Yeah. It was nice of your parents to plan this surprise for my birthday. I'm worried, though, about *my* parents. I think they're pretty upset."

"After what they did to you, why are you so worried about them?"

"What they did to me was wrong but—"

"Siri, they dragged you away from home. They didn't even let you pack or say good-bye. They wouldn't let you visit. You have to sneak around to even call me. They make you eat garbage and punish you for speaking English. They won't even let you hang out with the new friends you've made. When I told my parents about all that—"

"You told your parents?"

"Of course. They care about you. Even if your parents don't."

"My parents care about me. It's just that they're a little crazy. I wish you hadn't told. That was supposed to be between you and me."

"Sorry. I thought maybe they could help. You know how I feel about you."

Michael leans over like he's gonna kiss me, but just then someone starts yelling at us.

"Hey, you kids! Outta there. No loitering on the property."

"We're not loitering," Michael answers him.

"I know exactly what you're doing, Romeo. And if you don't get the hell out from between those two buildings, I'll write you up. So what'll it be? Either show me your ID or show me the backs of you, walking yourselves home."

"We're not doing anything wrong. I live here. . ."

"Michael, please, let's just go back. I don't want to get into trouble."

"Listen to your little girlfriend."

"Fine. We're going. Come on, Siri."

When we get to the condo, Rebecca's talking on the screen. She hangs up when she sees us. I ask if she was talking to my mom. She tells me yes but that she already hung up and that it's late and we should get to bed.

The next day, I go to practice but it's less fun than on Saturday. The first baseman keeps looking at me, and making little signs to the second baseman and laughing. I finally ask him what's so funny.

"It's just that every time you throw to first, your tits jiggle so much it makes me dizzy."

"Well, maybe you should sit down and put your head between your knees. That way, you can suck on your own dick."

"Hey, stop horsing around out there," the coach yells from behind the backstop. I can't believe he didn't hear what the first baseman said to me, but maybe he doesn't care, since I'm not really part of the team.

After practice, David says he has to go to a meeting. Michael and I go home alone. When we walk in the door, I hear Rebecca talking in an angry voice.

"Do you ever think about anyone besides yourself? Do you know what this did to my son? But why would you care about him when you don't even care about your own daughter."

When Rebecca sees us, she turns her back and walks into her bedroom. Her voice is muffled, but I can still make out some of what she's saying.

"... can't just drop everything and drive all those hours. . . you're delusional. . . no. . . she's not here. . . no. . . later."

Michael goes into the kitchen with Sara. I knock on Rebecca's door.

"One minute," she calls out. She opens the door and asks me about the baseball practice.

"It was OK. Was that my mom?"

"She couldn't talk. Listen, Siri, would you be a dear and help Michael babysit tonight?"

"I thought David was going to drive me back today. I have school tomorrow."

"I'm sorry, sweetie. David is under a lot of pressure at work right now. Would it be a big problem if you missed one day of school? You hardly even needed to study when you lived here—Michael was always a little jealous about how you were able to ace your exams anyway."

"It's harder when you're studying in a second language."

"Yes, you haven't been doing well in school there, have you? It's a shame, a bright girl like you. Listen, I have a great idea. How would you like to go with Michael to your *old* school? That way, it would be like you aren't even missing class tomorrow."

It would be pretty hyper to see my old school and friends, and I guess staying here one more night isn't that big a deal. I tell Rebecca OK, but I'm beginning to wonder when they plan on taking me home. I decide that whatever happens, I'll make David bring me back tomorrow.

In the morning, Rebecca drives us all to school. Michael and his sister, Sara, go off to their classes, but I have to wait while Rebecca talks to the director. They close the door to her office, but I can see them looking at me through the poly plastic. When they come out, everyone has big smiles. There's something weird about it. It's like I have some kind of terminal disease, but no one wants to tell me about it. They bring me to Michael's class and everyone is staring at me. Maybe I look different. They do too. Raun even has a thin moustache.

I spend the day doing the same stuff as everyone else. The class work is easy, boring actually. The math we're doing in Montréal is more advanced, but it takes me a little while to get used to the signs and operational symbols they use here, even though they used to be normal for me. Spanish class is a joke. Everyone's still memorizing lists of vocabulary—colours, animals, foods. They have no clue how to teach a second language here. The only two subjects that are interesting are English and history. And, of course, gym.

After school, Rebecca is waiting for us in her car. She ends the call on the screen. She seems angry. I figure it must be my mother again, but when I ask her, she says that it was Magda.

"Magda? But it sounded like you were talking about me."

"We were. It's not enough that your mother calls all the time. Now she's having Magda call too. If she wants you back so badly, maybe she should just come up and get you herself."

"Down."

"What?"

"Come down and get me. New York is down from Montréal, not up."

"You sound just like your father. Maybe *he* should come down and get you. I have four kids and David has a very demanding job. And I thought you might enjoy being back home."

"It's been great. I appreciate everything you've done for me." She's gone out of her way to make my birthday special. I don't want her to feel bad. Or be angry and not take me home.

"I'm sorry, Siri. I know you do. You're such a good girl. When I think of all you've been through. Here comes Sara. Let's all go pick up some ice cream for dessert on the way home."

From this I guess that David's not driving me home today either.

Mommy calls again during supper. Rebecca and David both look up but neither one of them answers. I stand up to get it, but Rebecca waves me off.

"Let's call her back after supper."

But after supper she and David go into the bedroom. I hear them arguing. I want to listen, but baby Georgie hears them too and starts bawling. I pick him up and try to figure out what to do. Sara's on the couch helping Benny with something on his school screen. Michael's gone into his room. I cuddle Georgie in my arms until he quiets down.

After a while, Michael's parents both come out. Rebecca looks like she's been crying. Then another call from Mommy comes in. I look at Rebecca and David tells me to answer it.

"Sweetheart! I'm so glad you answered. How are you?" Mommy asks.

"Great. I got to see my old school today. How are you and Daddy and Simon?"

"We're all very worried about you."

"Why? I'm fine."

"When are you coming home?"

I look at Rebecca but she just shrugs.

"Mommy, David has been busy with work and Rebecca can't just drive all that way with the kids. Maybe you or Daddy are gonna need to come down and get me."

Mommy doesn't answer right away. I feel like Rebecca is holding her breath.

"Siri. . . you know we can't. Daddy especially. We talked about this. It wouldn't be safe."

"If you say so. But you'll have to wait then. Until David has time. Meanwhile, I guess I can just keep living here and going to my old school."

"But we have our interview next week. For permanent residency. If you're not home. . ."

Nothing about missing me, just about how I'm going to screw up their application.

"You don't need me. You and Daddy. . . You never really thought about me when you made your plans. If it's so important for me to be there, I guess you'll come and get me yourselves." I wait but she doesn't say anything. "I gotta go now, Mommy."

I look up to see Rebecca smiling at me. She looks relieved, satisfied. For some reason, this makes me angry. I turn and look at Michael. He's smiling too, but it's a nice smile. Who cares why Rebecca looks satisfied, why David seems angry, or about Mommy and Daddy and their craziness. At least Michael and I get to be together for now.

CHAPTER 48
SIMON

Last night I had a terrible nightmare. We were on our bikes, like the Bicycling Family, when suddenly everything became horrible and wrong. All around us was broken glass and sharp pieces of twisted-up metal. The air felt heavy and thick and tasted like it was filled with poison chemicals. Up ahead, I could see that things were nice, with sun and grass and flowers and animals, but no matter how fast I biked, I couldn't get there. Then I realized that Siri wasn't with us anymore. I tried to call her, but she was too far away. Mommy and Daddy were way ahead and didn't realize that Siri had fallen behind. I didn't know whether to go back for Siri or forward to get Mommy and Daddy. Before I could decide, I saw that we were all trapped. The road was twisting up and around like a Mobius strip and there were huge chunks of pavement flying through the air. We were being shot at by robo-riot cops armed with giant phaser guns. I tried to scream but I couldn't get enough air. Then I woke up.

When I pushed my way into Mommy and Daddy's room, I thought I was having an asthma attack. Mommy ran to get my medicine while Daddy held me. Once my heart slowed down, I realized I could breathe again. So instead, Mommy just rubbed my back until I fell asleep. This morning, I remembered the last time I slept with Mommy and Daddy. It was after Daddy got out of the hospital, just before we moved here.

All day while I'm at school, I think of last summer and how awful it was. I don't feel like playing soccer with my friends, or even drawing. I just keep thinking about stuff. Maybe I did something wrong and I'm being punished and that's why bad things keep happening to my family. Violence is wrong, but I hit Keri anyway and really hurt him. But that happened *after* Daddy was in the hospital. Could something that happens after something else still cause it?

What if Siri had been home instead of at camp last summer? Should I tell her what happened? But Mommy and Daddy didn't want us to know. They must've had a good reason. And it's bad to tell secrets, to be a tattletale. Everyone says so, Siri especially. If I tell her the secret now, for sure I'll be doing the wrong thing, one way or another. Either I shouldn't ever tell, or I should've told a long time ago.

I try to think of what Mommy and Daddy would want me to do. One thing they're always saying is that you can't control what happens, but you can still try to choose good over bad. And each day brings new choices. So doing something bad yesterday doesn't mean you can't do something good today. You can try to do better, and even if that doesn't erase the bad thing, it still adds good to the world.

After supper, Daddy kisses us good-bye to go to work. He turns to Mommy again.

"Are you sure it's OK I'm going in tonight? I could explain. . ."

"It's OK. Your job's important. We'll be fine."

Daddy still seems like he's not sure, but Mommy kisses him good-bye again and pushes him out the door. After he's gone, I ask Mommy if we can call Siri 'cause I need to talk to her.

"What do you want to tell her?" Mommy asks.

"It's private. Please?"

"We can try, sweetheart, but Rebecca and David don't always pick up my calls."

"If I do a holo-call they'll see it's only me."

"I guess there's no harm in trying. I'll wait in the bedroom."

I go to the screen and activate *holo-call*. Mommy and Daddy always only use voice. Then I tell the screen to call not Rebecca and David, but Michael. Michael picks up.

"Hello? Simon?"

"I need to talk to Siri."

"She's here, but. . ."

"Please, I need Siri's help with something."

Michael winks and tells me to wait a sec. He was always one of my sister's nicest friends.

"Hi Simon. How are you?"

"I miss you."

"I miss you too, but we may have to wait a while to see each other again. When David's work is less busy or when Daddy or Mommy decide they can come get me."

"But they can't. It would be dangerous."

"It's OK if you want to believe Daddy and Mommy, but. . ."

"Mommy cries all the time. I hear her at night, crying and saying your name. And Daddy. . . his eyes are so sad. Sometimes he even looks all weird and spacey like. . . like when. . ."

"Like when what?"

"Listen, I wanna tell you something." I hear a voice in the background. A grown-up voice, I think. "Are you still just with Michael?"

"No."

"Can you do me a favour? But first, I want you to know I never told. About the French, I mean. I never told Daddy or Mommy or anyone that you could speak French."

"I know, Simon. You're a good little brother."

"But now I need to ask you to speak French with me. So we can be private."

There's a pause and then she says, "D'accord."

I switch to French as well. "Cet été, quand tu étais au camp de *baseball* ..." and I tell her everything that happened.

"Mais, ils nous ont dit que ...

"Je le sais. They wanted us to think it was an accident, but it wasn't. A cop broke Daddy's bones with a phaser stick on purpose. Daddy almost died. He was in the hospital for the whole summer. From the day you left for camp until two weeks before we picked you up. And even when he came home, he wasn't all better. He was thin and could hardly walk around. I never seen Daddy so tired and. . . I don't know. Like beaten down."

"Comment tu t'en es rendu compte? Wait, hold on Simon."

I hear her talking to someone as she turns away from the screen.

"Simon needs help with his homework. . . Yeah. Just a few more minutes."

"OK, Simon. J'suis là."

"I found out what really happened from Henry," I tell her in French. "He heard his mom talking about it with his dad. Me and Henry, we had it all planned. We were gonna kill the cop who almost killed Daddy."

"Oh, Simon."

"But then Daddy and Mommy and I left on the train, for the bike trip. So I never got to. I thought we'd do it when I got back to New York."

"So you didn't know either? That they planned to never go back?"

"No. But when Daddy told me, I couldn't be mad. Not after what happened this summer."

"Why didn't you tell me?"

"It was a secret. Daddy and Mommy didn't want us to know. At first, I thought knowing might be dangerous. And then I thought maybe they just didn't want us to feel bad or scared or anything. I don't know. But one thing I do know is not to tell secrets. I learned that at school and I learned that from Henry and I learned that from you."

I hear voices in the background. Siri blanks the screen. Then she's talking to me again.

"Écoute, Simon. Thanks for telling me. But I still don't know what I can do. David. . ." Even though she's still speaking in French she lowers her voice. "He's probably the only one who can take me back, if Daddy or Mommy can't come. But I'm beginning to think maybe Michael's parents planned this all along."

"You have to escape somehow, Siri. Or maybe we can rescue you. . ."

I turn. Daddy's standing in the doorway watching me. I never even heard him come in.

"Simon? Are you still there?"

"Yeah. I'm here."

"I have to hang up now. But I'll do my best to convince David to take me. Tell Mommy and Daddy that I love them. And that I'll try to get home as soon as I can."

When I hang up, Mommy comes out of the bedroom. Daddy walks towards me too.

"Why aren't you at work?" Mommy asks Daddy.

"It's OK. They said they could get by without me today. I wanted to be with my family."

Mommy hugs me and Daddy kisses the top of my head. He wraps his arms around Mommy, with me still in the middle. He hugs us both so tight I can hardly breathe, but I'm not scared. It doesn't feel anything like an asthma attack.

CHAPTER 49
JANIE

'm preparing my arguments. I think of all the times I've done this for a client, even when the case was hopeless. Some people imagine that emotion has no role to play in argumentation. This is bullshit, as anyone with a flair for winning arguments knows. Logic, consistency, and accurate information are important, but true passion has no peer in sharpening your rhetoric.

At least, I tell myself this as my body trembles, and tears threaten to close up my throat. Somehow I have to convince Rebecca to do the right thing and send Siri home.

"I know you think you're helping," I say. "I can imagine the kinds of things Siri told Michael. But remember, she's an adolescent. Exaggeration and drama are normal for her age."

"Michael doesn't do those things. And they're the same age."

"He's a boy."

"I thought you were so non-sexist."

"There are developmental differences. Wait until he's fifteen or sixteen and talk to me."

"You're just making excuses, Janie. You need to accept the fact that Siri *wants* to be here. She was happy to come with us to Brooklyn."

"Of course she's missed her friends, but she told you she wants to come home now."

"She was pressured to say that. Besides, if you really cared, you'd get her yourself."

"We've been through this. I know you don't want to believe. . ."

"Don't start with that again. Has Laek actually gotten you to swallow his crazy, paranoid fantasies? Sometimes I think he's cast a spell on you. I never trusted him. He's too slick. David agrees with me. Any man who doesn't like baseball. . ."

OK, maybe it's time to forget logic. There must be some way to reach her.

"Rebecca, please. For the sake of our friendship. . ."

"A true friend wouldn't have left like you did, without so much as a good-bye."

"It was necessary. My other friends understood, why can't you?"

"You told Magda, though."

"I had to tell one person. Maybe I did the wrong thing, but I never meant to hurt you."

"But you did. You deserted us, me and my family, like we were nothing."

"I'm sorry! It's not what I wanted. But please, as a mother, how can you do this to me?"

"As a mother? I asked myself the same question a million times. How you, as a mother, could do this to Michael and Siri. Knowing they were in love."

"In love? They were just twelve years old!"

"Michael's been depressed and heartbroken all year. His grades are slipping. And David and I are fighting again."

"You can't lay all that on me. You and David already had problems. Before Georgie. . ."

"Shut up! If I'd have listened to you, Georgie would never have been born. Sometimes you have to. . . to do things to keep a man."

"Is that what this is about? Another new child in the household? A crisis to pull the two of you together? You can't use a child like that. And Siri's not even your child!"

"Maybe not, but it's me who has her best interests at heart. You never acted like normal parents. Letting them ride the subway, living on a public street. . ."

"Rebecca, this isn't about Siri riding the subway or not living in a gated community. This isn't about her at all. You've essentially kidnapped my child for your own reasons."

"Kidnapped? How dare you! But if that's what you think, call the police. Or just come and get her. But you won't do either of these things, will you? You'd rather hold on to that fantasy about Laek being in danger. Well just go back to him now, your beautiful perfect partner, and live your delusional little life together. But you'll have to do it without Siri."

"You've really lost it. What you're doing, it's. . . it's crazy, wrong."

"Is it? You know I saw the two of you that night in the park."

"What?"

"The night of the concert. The night that Michael and Siri had their first kiss. David and I had argued, but then Michael came and gave us the good news. He was so happy. I went to look for you, to tell you. I'd always hoped that some day we'd be one big family."

"I. . . I don't remember seeing you that night."

"No, you and Laek were too busy rutting like animals in the middle of the park."

"Fuck you," I say, immediately wishing I could take it back. "I'm sorry, but. . ."

"Don't apologize, it's classic Janie. And a perfect way to end this pointless conversation."

"No, not until we resolve this. You need to send Siri back. If you don't. . ."

"Don't threaten me. You're forgetting that David works for

the government. So you'd better just stay on your side of the border. And don't call me again."

"Rebecca, wait. . ."

But she's already terminated the call. I stare at the screen, unwilling to believe that it's over. In court, I'd have a chance to present a rebuttal at least. It can't end like this! It just can't!

Laek comes up from behind me and wraps me in his arms.

"Is Simon asleep?" I ask.

"Yeah. I told him a story. Like one of your stories. With rescues and reconciliations and happily-ever-afters."

"That's good because I'm fresh out of stories. Oh Laek, I fucked that up badly."

"There's nothing you could've said that would've made a difference."

"I've always thought that if you could find the right words, if you put your heart and soul into communicating, that. . . I should call her back." I try to pull away but Laek holds me fast.

"Janie, stop. You're shaking. And it doesn't matter how eloquent you are, or how right. The person you're talking to still has to be listening. And sane."

"What are we going to do?"

"I'm gonna bring her back."

"No, Laek, no." I pull myself out of his grip. "Please, you can't. It's too dangerous."

"I can do this. It's the only way."

"There has to be another way. I'll go. I'll go and get her."

"Tell me how you're gonna do that, Janie. Cross the border on your Uni? They'll have you in a second. You'll be detained and then. . . who knows what. You'll sure never make it to Brooklyn. No. This is something I need to do my own way."

"Please, I'm scared. I can't. . . I can't lose you both."

I start crying, thinking of the morning in Brooklyn when Laek left for the demonstration, after seeing Al, after our argument. If only I had done something to keep him from going. I knew it would be dangerous, that it was a bad decision. I should have thrown myself in front of the apartment door, anything to stop him!

Laek presses my face against his chest. "Shh, it's OK." he murmurs. "I'm not planning to do something irrational or hopeless. I promise you. I can do this, Janie. I'll bring her home."

I think again of when he left for that demonstration. That day he was angry. Angry and scared. But now? He seems calm, confident. All I feel is his strength, his determination. I let myself relax in his arms, thinking how much he's healed from his traumas since we've been living here. This new place has been so good for him. But we've lost Siri. What have I done? Was Siri right, the night I told her we wouldn't be returning to Brooklyn? Was I sacrificing her, choosing Laek over my own children? Fresh tears fill my eyes as I think about this.

"Siri," I sob. "My poor baby. My poor baby."

"Please, Janie, please. Don't cry. I love you so much. I can't bear it. Please trust me."

I rub my eyes and try to stop crying. "What are you thinking of doing?"

"I have an idea. Part of a plan. I'm still working out the details, but I'll need help. From a lot of people. Can I count on your parents? Your brother?"

"They'll do whatever's needed."

"Good. And Philip. He'll coordinate everything in New York. And I'll need Magda. And. . . and Erin. Actually, Chris. And. . ."

"What?"

"I'll need Al. For the border."

I grab his arms. "No, Laek, no. Not Al. I don't trust him."

"I can trust him for this. I can. I wouldn't risk it otherwise."

I don't answer. I just start crying again.

"Janie, listen." He lifts me up in his arms. "Let me tell you a story. Once upon a time, there was a lonely boy. Lonely and scared and filled with pain. One day someone came and took him into her heart and made him her family. The boy moved away from the pain and the loneliness and the fear, because deep down, he was a person who loved life and was filled with hope. So the boy, now a man, made the girl, the woman, a promise. He promised that he'd never throw his life away. Because he loved her and his children so much. And because she'd helped him love life again. Together, they worked to heal the world and make it a better place."

"And then what happened?"

"And then? Well he took her, and laid her down. . ."

As he says this, he carries me over to our bed and gently puts me there.

"... and he undressed her carefully, never taking his eyes off her. . ."

I watch Laek as he watches me, mesmerized.

"... and then he made love to her, very, very slowly."

Much later, I wake up to find him gone from our bed. It's three in the morning. I get up quickly and walk into the living room. He's seated in front of the big screen, with the image split to show a moving aerial view of a road on one side, and a listing of border crossings on the other. To the left of the screen is a holo of a map that Laek is manipulating with his left hand, while touching his ear piece with his right, appearing to flip between two conversations.

I watch him for a while. He sees me watching but doesn't look up at me until he's done with the calls. I make him go through every detail of the plan with me. I ask my questions. Make some suggestions. When I'm satisfied, I nod my head and go back to bed.

In the morning, I wake to feel his warm body curled behind mine. As I'm wondering how much of last night was a dream, he brings his lips to my ear, his voice low and soft.

"And the story isn't over yet. Far, far from it. . ."

CHAPTER 50
SIRI

pitch the practice baseball into the corner of Michael's bedroom where his two blue walls meet the wooden floor. The ball makes a satisfying bang before bouncing back. I adjust my pitching stance, thinking about how it's been three days since I spoke to Simon and two since Rebecca and my mom had their big argument. I'm still no closer to getting home.

"What are you doing?" Michael asks me.

"I'm practicing my pitching," I tell him in my *what-the-f-does-it-look-like* voice.

Bang! I crouch down and scoop the ball up into my glove.

"Maybe it would be better to practice outside. I could catch for you."

I squeeze the rubbery ball in my hand. "Why? Afraid it's gonna bother your parents? Then let them take me home."

Ba-bang!

"I asked them to take you home. I even begged them, but they wouldn't listen to me. They kept saying it was for your own good."

"You never should have told them all those things I told you."

"You never should have told *me* all those things if they weren't really true."

Ba-bang! I chase the ball down to where it's ricocheted.

"Shit! Ball two. Notice how when I don't hit dead centre, it makes a different sound?"

"Siri, listen. Maybe if we wait a few days until my mom calms down, we could reason with her. But with that banging every two seconds, she's gonna come in here and. . ."

"Your mom isn't going to come in here and do anything. She's afraid to face me."

"My dad, then."

Ba-Bang!

Michael sighs and turns his back on me to look for something in his closet.

Bang! Bang!

"Siri! Stop already!" Michael says over his shoulder.

"That wasn't me!"

"Oh! Maybe it's the door. But I didn't hear the visitor screen ping."

We both rush out of his room to go downstairs. I'm a couple of steps down when Rebecca opens the door to two cops. I stop dead and back up the stairs quietly, gripping the ball in my glove harder, like I do during a big game that we may be about to lose. Michael backs up too and spreads his arms out, like he's trying to hide me.

I get down on my hands and knees in the hallway near the top of the stairs so that I'm out of sight, but can still hear them. Michael stays standing, but pressed back against the wall. One of the cops says, "We're looking for a thirteen-year-old girl named Siri Wolfe."

I crawl backwards farther down the hall towards Michael's room. Should I hide? Try to escape? My heart is beating fast. I feel a little sick. At the same time I feel hyper-awake, like all my senses are sharper than normal.

I hear Rebecca ask the cops what's going on. A voice answers her, saying something about a complaint. The voice sounds familiar. I crawl back to the end of the hall and peer around the corner. One of the cops has a shaved head and looks angry and tough. The other has dark brown bangs and a ponytail and is just a little shorter than the other cop. While Rebecca calls David over, the shorter cop lifts their head and looks up the stairs in our direction. I quickly pull back again, but this time I get a clear look at their whole face. Now I know who the cop reminds me of —Daddy's friend Erin. But Erin's a teacher, not a cop.

I hear David's voice. "There must be some mistake. Siri is a close family friend."

"Is she here?" the bald cop asks.

Someone says something I can't make out, but Rebecca's answer is high and loud.

"Kidnapping, that's crazy! Who would say such a thing? David, tell them!"

"Officer, who made this. . . this absurd complaint? It couldn't have been Siri's parents."

I peer around the corner again, too curious not to look. The Erin look-alike is reading a screen. "It was the grandparents. The parents of Jane Wolfe."

"I don't know what would make them say such an awful thing, but shouldn't an allegation like that come directly from the parents?" David asks.

"The grandparents have been granted legal custody. The documents were beamed this morning from. . . from a Magda Diaz, Esq. of Legal Aid Services," the Erin cop says.

"I ask you again, is the child here?" the other cop asks, sounding angry. They look up, right in our direction, and I realize that they must know we're upstairs, that they probably saw us from the start. The cop continues looking towards our hiding place, rubbing their finger along the top of their lip. It seems like a strange place to have an itch. All of a sudden, I'm picturing a moustache there and now I think I know him too. He looks like

Erin's husband, who actually *is* a cop, but with his moustache and hair shaved off. I've only seen him a few times, and never with his cop uniform on, but it definitely could be him. What the hell?

"Come down here, kids," David says. "We need to clear up a little misunderstanding."

Michael starts walking down the stairs but I don't move. What if this is some kind of trap? When I don't come down, Erin —or the cop who looks just like her—opens the front door. In walks a tall person with big shoulders. Another cop? They look up in our direction. No, it's Philip! I make a decision and follow Michael. When I get downstairs, I squeeze my baseball in my left hand for courage and say, "I'm Siri Wolfe."

Philip nods and gives me a big smile, then turns to the cops. "That's her."

I'm still kind of confused because if this really is Erin and her husband—Chris, that's his name—then why does Philip have to tell them it's me? Erin for sure knows what I look like. But Erin's not a cop anyway, so none of this makes sense. I decide to play along and follow what Philip does. The idea that Daddy might have sent him makes me feel happy and way less nervous. But then I notice that Philip seems nervous, so I go back to being on my guard.

"Siri," the Erin-cop says, "We need to ask you some questions."

Before I even have time to open my mouth, David is talking. "This is a complicated situation. More complicated than you may realize. Officers, can I speak with you in private?"

"No you may not," Philip says.

"Who is this man, officer?" David asks.

"I recognize him." Rebecca says to David. "He's a friend of Laek's."

"We are asking the questions here, not you." Chris says to David.

"I apologize. I understand your position because I work for

the government too, for the federal OPIM. And there's something that you need to know. It's about the girl's father—"

"Shut the fuck up, you miserable, soulless prick," Philip says, slamming David against the wall. David's screen, which he'd been reaching for while he was talking to Chris and Erin, slips out of his hand and onto the floor. Philip stomps on it, hard. Rebecca jumps back with her hand over her mouth.

"Are you going to just stand there and let this man assault me?" David shouts.

"The NYPD doesn't appreciate people who kidnap young girls. I suggest you take this person's advice and shut up." Chris then nods to Erin.

"Siri, are you being held here against your will?" she asks.

Rebecca is swinging her head back and forth between me and David. Her eyes look wild and her hands are shaking. I almost feel sorry for her. I need to figure out the right thing to say, the thing that will get me home without getting anyone in trouble.

"Wait!" David says, bent over his ruined screen. "I need. . . I need to make a call. This will be cleared up in a minute. Michael, give me your screen."

Michael looks to me to give him a sign, just like he does when he's pitcher and I'm catcher during a game. I think hard, then give him the sign for a curveball.

"Sorry, Dad, I can't find it," Michael says, making a big show of searching his pockets. "I may have left it on the ball field after practice."

"You've got to be kidding! Rebecca, where's yours? Never mind, you're both useless."

He stomps off towards the living room, where the younger kids are watching a fantasy clip. I hear him order them to their rooms so he can use the house screen. Little Georgie starts crying and I feel my face get hot.

Erin and Chris look at each other, but Philip stares up at the ceiling like he's searching for something. I follow his eyes and see them stop at the house transponder at the opposite corner where the two walls meet the ceiling. I squeeze the baseball in my hand and realize what I need to do. I focus on my target. Not that different from the corner of Michael's bedroom, just higher. I wind up and pitch, my anger making my throw hard and sure. The ball hits it dead on with a satisfying bang that turns my anger into exhilaration. Everyone stares, not saying anything, as pieces of the hardware fall to the carpet. I scream into the sudden silence, "I want to go home!"

Philip goes down on one knee and I run to him. He wraps his arms around me. "Don't worry, chica. I'll take you home."

The younger kids have all come in from the living room. Sara is trying to shush Benny, who's talking about the hyper clip they were watching when the screen went dead. Little Georgie is holding on to Rebecca's legs and crying, but she's ignoring him.

"Why are you lying to Siri?" she says to Philip. "You know you can't take her home."

Philip doesn't answer, so I ask him straight out. He doesn't say anything at first. Then he shakes his head. "I'm sorry, Siri. She's right. I can't take you home. But I can take you out of here and to my place right now, and to your grandparents Friday night. How would that be?"

"OK," I say, feeling very tired.

"David!" Rebecca says. "Why are you just standing there? Go next door and use their screen. We could—"

"Be quiet, Rebecca. It's enough. Siri knows she's welcome here, but if she wants to go to her grandparents, that's up to her."

"But—"

"I told you to be quiet!"

The expression on Michael's face as he watches his parents argue drains any remaining feeling of exhilaration from me. "What's gonna happen to Rebecca and David?" I ask. "I don't want them to get into trouble. Or anyone else either," I add, looking from David to Michael.

"If they cooperate, your grandparents will probably agree

that it was just a big misunderstanding and withdraw the complaint. In that case, the charges would probably be dropped too, right?" Philip asks.

Chris and Erin nod, then tell me to go upstairs and get my things. I walk up the stairs slowly. Everyone seems frozen in place, just waiting. Everyone but Michael, who follows me up. I start putting my stuff together as Michael watches. I don't want to look at him, because I'm afraid I'll start crying. Finally, I just throw myself into his arms and he holds me without talking. When I finally look at his face, he's smiling, not sad.

"That was some pitch, Siri," he says, laughing. "You totally shut them down!"

I laugh with him, a little of my happiness coming back. "I'm just glad we're still on the same team," I say, and kiss him right on the lips.

———

Philip and I don't talk much after leaving Rebecca and David. He just holds my hand tight, my bag on his shoulder, and brings me to his car. I fall asleep on the ride to his apartment in Queens. I wake up as we cross the Whitestone Bridge, its lights like blurry, bright jewels to my sleepy eyes. I drift off again, thinking that something isn't right. Then it hits me. The Whitestone Bridge doesn't go from Brooklyn to Queens. It goes from Queens to the Bronx.

The next time I open my eyes we're on a fast highway and are no longer in the City. I rub my eyes and sit up.

"Where are we, Philip?"

"Almost to your grandparents."

"But I thought we weren't going there until the weekend."

"No, we're going there now."

"But you said. . ."

"I lied."

I'm happy that I'll get to see Grandma and Grandpa right

away, but why did Philip lie like that? And then something else occurs to me. If he lied about this, maybe he lied about the other thing too. I turn to Philip and he winks at me.

"You're gonna do it, aren't you? You're gonna get me across the border!" I shout.

"Make sure you get some rest tonight, because tomorrow's another adventure. Then we'll see how good a closer you really are."

CHAPTER 51
LAEK

leave at dawn, pedal all morning. I'm not nervous, but my bike flies. My progress is marked by a terrain that changes from grey to yellow, to greens that lighten as the sun swings higher in the sky. By the end of the ride, there aren't more than a handful of cars sharing the road. Almost no one but cyclists take this particular route. And then only to access bike paths used by locals, far from the highway. I stop 2.7 kilometres short of the border and dismount. I cut across a field, finding the path that runs to the farm road. It's pitted with muddy holes and overgrown clumps of grass. The path dries as it smoothes out. Dust tickles my neck and cheeks.

I leave my bike leaning against an old info sign. Walk the final hundred metres to the border, kicking up more dust on the shoulder of the road. There's a little, white customs house just behind the crossing. It has a diagonal roof sloping down to my right, and two metal bathroom doors embedded in the side. There's a flag, a drive-through window, an overhang extending above the path. The structure is small enough to look like the entrance to a provincial park—the place where you pay your fee and they beam you the map of the campsites. It's innocuous-looking too. If not for the distortion field. I watch as the air seems to pinch and waver. Then Philip emerges, walking towards me. I go still. He veers towards the bathrooms, an over-sized metal key dangling from his big hand. I move parallel with him, my own hands clutching at air.

Philip uses the key to enter the bathroom furthest from the road. He emerges less than a minute later, shoving a metal object that looks like the key, but isn't, into his pants pocket. "Laek," he says, planting himself a few feet in front of me. "You're a sight for sore eyes."

"Siri?" I ask.

"She's fine. You should start seeing her just. . . about. . . now."

I look to my left as Siri appears on her bike on the circular path in front of the border station, less than ten metres from us. My heart leaps and I have to stop myself from running to her. I hold myself back and watch her intently instead. Blue jeans, sky-blue t-shirt, sunglasses, bike helmet. She crosses the border, then quickly loops around and crosses back. She has a look of fierce determination on her face, but when she sees me watching her, she smiles. The whole world seems suddenly brighter.

I turn to Philip as she disappears up the path again. Move towards him.

"Wait, Laek. Don't come any closer."

"It's just an imaginary line."

"No. No, it's not. It may be random, but it's real."

"But if it's random, what difference can a metre or two make?"

"Mira, you and Janie entrusted this task to me and I'm not going to let you down. But we need to do things my way."

I tilt my head slightly. What happened to my shy, insecure friend? I have to admit that I like what I see. The confidence and control.

"How did things go in Brooklyn?" I ask, watching for Siri to reappear.

Philip pulls the device from his pocket and checks it before answering. Some kind of scrambler? Or maybe a drone detector. "They went fine."

"Your mouth looks tight, Phil."

"Alright, we had words. Michael's parents and I."

"You weren't even supposed to be there."

"I changed the plan."

I wait, but he leaves it at that. "And Siri?"

"She was perfect. Smart, resilient, adaptable. . . She's some kid. On the ride up to Janie's folks, she mostly slept, but when we got there, she had a nice long talk with her grandparents. It seems to have helped her sort things out. And on the way up this morning, she and I had an opportunity to chat too. Don't be too hard on her."

I watch Siri loop around the circular path again. "I don't plan on being hard on her at all."

"She realizes that she messed up."

"I think we're the ones who messed up. Me, particularly."

"What could you have done differently?"

"Been honest about everything from the beginning. We thought we were protecting her. I don't know. Sometimes I think I shouldn't have had kids so young. How could I have known what I was doing? I still don't sometimes."

"None of us do. But your kids are great. You two must be doing something right."

"How's Kyla?"

"She's the light of my life. I told you I have joint custody of her now, fifty/fifty? But I have a feeling Dana might agree to even give me more than that. She's with this new guy now. He's not too keen on raising someone else's kid. And. . . well, she's pregnant too. I just found out recently."

"How do you feel about that?"

"It feels like the end of a chapter, which is sad in a way. But I also feel like I've been freed. That I have the freedom to do what I want. For me and Kyla both."

I nod. "How long do we have here, Philip?" Siri crosses the border again, then loops back to the U.A. side.

"We have some time. I want to get as much footage as possible so I'm sure to have all the angles I need to fix the recording. After that, it'll be easy, no different than editing a music clip."

"How did it go with Al? Did you end up meeting him in the flesh?"

"We met face to face once. It's not an experience I'd care to repeat. He looked me over pretty carefully. He's a very scary person."

"But did you feel you could trust him?" My eyes go to Siri, then search the sky for camera drones. Philip checks his device again.

"I trusted that he'd do what he promised, and he has. Everything at the border has gone exactly as he said it would. Al came through for you, Laek. For whatever that's worth."

Quite a lot, I'm thinking. He's given me back my life, my child. Whatever happened in our past, I feel it's finally been put to rest. All debts paid or cancelled.

"What will they see, if someone were to look at the clip?"

"No one's going to, that's the beauty of what Al's arranged. But if someone were to randomly review the recording of this time period, they'd see exactly what we're seeing. A girl, not recognizable because of her helmet and sunglasses, biking back and forth across the border. Only the clip will show that she started on the Québec side rather than in New York."

"But the border guards. . . What story did we end up using?"

"They think we're shooting an art film about illegal migrants. One of those post-wave things, with repetitive images interspersed with slash scenes. That it's filmed at a real border crossing is supposedly giving it some kind of edgy cachet. And as long as the cameraperson is the required distance behind the distortion field, it's all perfectly legal. With the permits and bribes all paid, of course."

"You're kidding me."

"No, I'm serious. We have a real cinematographer using a long-distance micro recorder. I think you'll remember her, actually."

"Who?"

"Nina—she was in your class, couple of years ago. She's studying film at NYU now. One or two of our former students are there. I asked for a volunteer. Didn't say what it was for, just that it was to help you out, and that it could be dangerous. Nina nearly begged me to take her."

I crane my neck, trying to see her, even though I know it's impossible with her so far away and well behind the distortion field. Could Philip know about what happened at Battery Park the day of the demonstration with her and Fari? After a minute I give up. Watch Siri instead. She looks confident on the new bike that Janie's brother bought for her birthday and personally delivered to Philip's apartment in Queens. So many people had a hand in this plan. And everyone has done exactly what was needed of them. A huge wave of gratitude engulfs me.

"A film, huh? Philip, what do you think would happen if I put my hand up like this, right at the borderline, and then you put your hand up against mine from your side."

"I suppose it'd be like in one of those old sci-fi flicks where matter and anti-matter come into contact. There'd be this *zzzzp* sound and then, well, the world would come to an end."

"Yeah, that's what I figured too. Wanna try it?"

He hesitates for only a moment. "Sure. Why not?"

I put my hand up about shoulder height in the air. Like it's resting against an invisible force field. Philip puts his hand flat against mine. His hand and my hand are just about the same length. Philip's is only a little bigger, wider palm, fingers less slender. I press my hand firmly against his. Then tilt my head like I'm listening. "So do you sense anything, Phil?"

"Yeah, I feel an electrical charge or something."

"I think we've been flung into an alternative universe."

"New space-time continuum."

"Phil, maybe reality has shifted and all the rules have changed."

I lace my fingers between his and squeeze hard.

"I don't know, Laek."

"Yeah."

I tug his hand towards my side of the border. He resists at first. Then gives in. I pull his arm all the way across to me. Swing it around like a trophy.

"Look, Phil, I've got your arm on my side. I think it's turned into anti-matter."

He smiles at me. But it's a little forced. He pulls his hand out of my grasp. Places it gently on my face. With the side of his thumb, he slowly caresses my cheek. I want to make another joke, but I can't get it past the lump in my throat.

"I miss you so," he says, his voice low and rough. Like sand-paper over an open wound.

"But, Phil, I'm right here. I'm right here in front of you! Please. . ." I start bending towards him. He lets his hand fall from my cheek to my shoulder. Holds me still.

Please. I only want. . . I just wish. . . What? That reality had actually been transformed? Yeah. Maybe into a world where watching the news didn't make me cry. Or where love didn't sometimes hurt as much as hate. But no, I won't give in to despair. Not when I've been so lucky. Not when my heart is so full. But it's my heart that makes me need to do something. Something for Philip. My whole body is aching with that need.

"What did you promise Janie? Tell me," I demand.

"That I wouldn't let you cross the border. Even if things went wrong. And. . . and me too. That I wouldn't put myself into unnecessary danger."

"What else?"

"Nothing else. Only that I'd keep you and Siri safe."

I look for Siri again as she makes her turn. "Well you have," I whisper, looking down.

"Maybe. . . maybe I could just lean over," Philip says.

He reaches across the border and wraps his arms around me. I pull his head down onto my shoulder and stroke his hair. Put my mouth close to his ear so I can talk softly.

"See. That wasn't so hard. Just hold onto me. Let me keep you safe for a little bit."

"Oh, Laek, that's not what's hard. It's letting go. How am I ever gonna let go of you?"

He leans farther over, holding me tighter. Farther and farther, until his whole weight is on me. Until he's leaning so far, he'd topple over if I wasn't holding him up. All I'd need to do is give a small tug and I'd have his whole body in Québec with me.

"Hey, Phil, do you know that ninety percent of your body is already in Québec? You've practically immigrated. Look, even your knees are in Québec."

"It's OK," he says into my shoulder. "My feet are still behind the line."

"Your feet. Your fucking feet behind the line. Is that how you think it works?"

"That's how it works in basketball. When you're at the free throw line."

"You think this is like fucking basketball. You and my daughter and your sports."

I feel him turn his head. Glance at the micro-screen strapped to his wrist. Lever himself up. This tells me our time is running out. I watch Siri start a new loop when I hear something high above. I lift my head. See the drone. I try to push Philip away, to the safety of the border house, so I can run to Siri. Philip holds me tightly, wrapping his arms around my head.

"Don't move," he says calmly. "Just keep still and don't look up."

"Siri," I say, my face pressed to his neck, his arms protecting and hiding me.

"She's fine." He checks his device. "It's leaving. Just another minute."

My body is trembling with the effort of not running, but Phil's arms around me help. Then he lets go. My eyes search for my daughter. I see her rounding the path. Phil and I stand silently, one on either side of the border, watching her progress. The sky is clear. I hear birdsong. The only evidence of the drone is my sweat-soaked body and rapid heartbeat.

"Phil, listen. Janie asked me to tell you. . . She sends her love."

"Tell her thanks. Give her a hug and kiss from me."

"And. . . and I love you too. I never got to tell you. Before we left."

There's a look of pleased surprise on Phil's face, which changes to mock outrage.

"*You* never got to tell *me*? Is that the revisionist history you've created? Because if I recall correctly what happened—and I think I do— it was *me* who was prevented from saying those words. Forcibly prevented."

"*Forcibly* prevented?"

"Yeah, forcibly. By the force of. . . of your lips. If I remember correctly—and again, I think I do—I was unable to speak or, or even breath, for a good long while afterwards!"

I smile. "Yeah, well. I just took you by surprise is all. If something like that were to happen again and if you were, say, prepared this time, it wouldn't have the same effect."

"Is that what you think? Well I beg to differ. In fact, I'm sure you're wrong."

"How sure are you?"

"It sounds like you're proposing another bet. OK, Laek. Another bet it is. And this time, it's me who's going to win."

"OK, then. Fine. Another bet."

No stakes are mentioned. We both know the stakes anyway.

I think about our other bet, that last night together in Brooklyn, and everything that's happened between then and now. It's like a path leading to this moment. To a place where Simon is happy, thriving. To where Janie is excited and hopeful about the future. And Siri, too. I can almost see it. Just around the bend. But beyond that, it's harder to see. Then why this shift in me? This certitude that a different world, a better world, is not as far away as I thought?

I watch his lips enter Québec. Feel his tongue cross the border into my mouth. I pull him in close, imagining myself, imagining everyone, closing the gap that separates us. I feel the heaviness in my heart. I feel my despair. I feel it all melt, as I watch my child cycle back and forth between two nations. Like an insane parody of border control. Crossing over that invisible line separating people and peoples. I imagine each crossover like a stitch. Stitching the world together. Stitching the tear in my heart. I imagine a raw wound closing up, healing. The flesh pressing itself together like two lips. My lips soft against his. If only I could translate the feeling in my heart into something tangible. Something I can hang onto, something transformative. At least until the next crossing.

Philip releases me. I open my mouth to speak, to ask how much more time we have, but he puts his two fingers on my lips. Shakes his head. Then places the same fingers on his own lips. Shakes his head again. As though to say he can't speak. Then he takes a long, shuddery breath. As though breathing is also difficult. *You win, Philip*, I say silently, smiling.

He looks over at Siri. Checks his micro-screen again, this time with a certain finality. He puts his hands on my shoulders and turns me around. Pulls me back snug against him, holding me tight with his right arm while he counts down the seconds with his left. At one, his lips brush me on the neck. I shudder in the late morning sun. Then he pushes me gently but firmly forward. Towards my bike and home.

I mount and start to ride. My eyes fill with tears. But then I hear his voice, even and firm: "Au revoir," and I understand that he doesn't mean good-bye, but the more literal meaning of the words: "To the next time we see each other again." For now, this is enough.

I feel a warmth against my back. A trace of Philip. The springtime sunshine. And Siri, biking right behind me.

CHAPTER 52
SIRI

Daddy still hasn't spoken to me. If it were Mommy, this would mean she was mad, but with Daddy, it could just mean he doesn't feel like talking. But *I* do. The whole car ride from Grandma and Grandpa's house, I kept on imagining what I would say to Daddy when I finally saw him. I had it all planned out. But now, I keep thinking about what I saw at the border—how Daddy and Philip were kissing. Did they mean for me to see them? I feel totally freaked out. I want to ask, why were you kissing? But I don't want to sound like I'm three years old.

There's hardly any traffic. The road has dusty little pebbles all over it and doesn't even look like a place where a car would want to ride. It's wide enough for a car though, and more than wide enough for two people to bike side by side. I speed up to be next to Daddy.

"Daddy?"

"Hmm?"

"Do you. . . do you still love Mommy?"

Daddy slows down and turns to me. "There's no one in the world I love more than Mommy. I love Mommy. . ." He smiles. "I love her infinity."

I smile back. We're both remembering when I was jealous of my baby brother. I would ask how much they loved each of us and they would both answer 'infinity.' I didn't want them to tell me that they loved me the best, I just wanted to know that they didn't love Simon more.

"And how much do you love Simon?" I laugh.

Daddy smiles. "I love him infinity."

"And. . . and Philip?"

Daddy doesn't stop smiling, but his smile looks different. Like the smile has a shadow on top of it or something.

"Yeah. Him too. Infinity."

I don't know what to think about this.

"Does Mommy mind?" I ask. "I mean, that you love so many people?"

"No. Mommy loves a lot of people too. Mostly the same ones. Listen Siri, there are a lot of things you must be worrying about right now. This should absolutely not be one of them."

"OK. I believe you." And I do. But I'm thinking about something else, about how hard it was to be separated from Michael and how a lot of how mad I was at Daddy and Mommy had to do with that. I couldn't think of any reason for moving that would've been good enough to take me away from Michael and all of my friends.

"But Daddy, if you really love Philip so much, how could you have left him behind? He looked so, so sad."

Daddy doesn't answer me. After a minute, I look over at him and see that he's crying. I didn't realize right away because he's not making any sound, but I can see streaks from the tears running down his cheeks. That's how dusty his face is. He sees me looking and tries to wipe his face with his arm, but this only makes things worse. I have this urge to find a washcloth and wipe the dirt and dust off his face, like he was a little kid or something. Then it occurs to me how fast he must have biked to get all the way to the border from Montréal this early. I think of all I've put Daddy and Mommy through.

"Daddy? Do you still love me?"

"Oh, Siri, I love you infinity infinities. Forever and ever and ever. And. . . and I'm gonna answer your question. And other questions you may have about all that happened. But just not right now, OK? We can talk tonight. There's a campsite I'd like us to get to, but it'll take some pretty hard cycling to be there before dark. Are you ready to go fast? Because if there's anyone in the family who can keep up with me, it's you. What do you say, sunshine?"

"Yeah, let's go hyper-fast, Daddy."

This is exactly what I want to do right now. I want to bike away from the disaster that going to Brooklyn turned out to be, and from the whole, complicated mess. The fact that Daddy doesn't seem to be mad at me makes me feel light and free, so I stand on my pedals and pump my way up to the top of the hill, then fly down it after Daddy, the wind and sunshine helping to speed me along. Each time I whiz past a tree or a scratchy patch of grass or a group of cows, I think about being one step closer to Mommy and Simon and home.

At the campsite, Daddy finishes getting ready for bed before me. When I crawl into the tent, he's already lying on his sleeping bag with mine all set up next to his. On my side of the tent, Daddy's left a glowlight on. There's a screen on top of my pillow.

"Daddy, you left your screen on my sleeping bag."

Daddy turns his head and looks at the screen and then at me. He doesn't say anything, just closes his eyes and curls up on his side with his back facing me. I pick up the screen and see it's open to a story. No, not a story exactly. I read the first line, scan forward and figure out what this must be. It's Daddy's application for asylum. Does he mean for me to read it?

"Daddy, this is in French."

Daddy looks over his shoulder at me, but doesn't answer. I remember something Mommy said recently—that your parents aren't as stupid as you think they are. I begin to read from Daddy's screen.

I don't have much trouble understanding the French. Here and there are some words I don't know, but it's not hard to guess what they mean from the sentence. There is one word I can't figure out. It's "waterboarding." It doesn't even sound like a French word. It sounds like some kind of sport, maybe using a surfboard. I look it up on the screen. It isn't a French word. And it's not a sport. It's a type of torture. A drowning torture.

I stop reading, thinking about how Daddy doesn't like swimming or being near water. I remember that time when we were on a boat and Daddy had to go down below to throw up. I remember teasing him for it. Now I feel sick to my stomach. Do I have to read the rest?

The screen is on my lap, all backlit. I could easily read it without the glowlight that Daddy left on, but I don't turn it off. I want there to be another light in this tent, aside from the light behind these awful words. Even though I don't want to keep reading, I do anyway. I read about other ways that Daddy was tortured. I look away from the screen again. I can see Daddy's back, including the part lower down near the top of his shorts. By the light of the glow lamp, I can see the little round rings there. I always thought they were birthmarks or something, but now I know they're cigarette burns.

I make myself read about how he was raped. I knew that boys could be raped too, but I'd never thought about it much. I wonder about the details, trying to picture it, and Daddy, as a teenager, having that happen to him. I don't want to picture this. So now I try *not* to picture it, but my brain won't listen to me. It's going ahead and imagining all these details while I try to close eyes that are inside my head.

When I'm finished reading, I go back and read some parts again, thinking maybe it will sound less bad or make more sense the second time. It doesn't. I shut off the screen. Daddy's not asleep. I can tell by the way he's breathing, or maybe that his body seems all tense.

"I'm done, Daddy. Here, take the screen back." I can't believe how calm my voice sounds. Inside, I feel jumpy and weird.

He puts the screen away and then turns to me. I think he's waiting to see if I have any questions. I do, but I don't think I'll ask them tonight. Daddy looks so tired. He also looks very young. He *is* much younger than any of my friends' parents. Plus, he looks even younger than he is. And tonight, for some reason, he looks especially young. Maybe it's just me thinking about Daddy back then when he was Gabriel's age, not much older than I am now.

Daddy's face seems sad, lonely maybe. I reach over and take his hand, like he was one of my friends. I think this was the right thing to do, because he seems to relax right away. Before too long, his breathing becomes deep and steady and I feel his fingers loosen around mine. He looks just like Simon does when Mommy's told him a scary story, but given it a happy ending.

In the morning, we get up very early. I can't wait to see Mommy and Simon, and I can tell Daddy feels the same way. He seems more like his usual self, too, but I'm still not ready to ask him about what I read. I decide, instead, to talk to him about something else that's on my mind.

"Daddy, you and Mommy must be pretty pissed off at Michael's parents. Even Philip acted like he wanted to bash their heads in."

Daddy laughs but doesn't say anything.

"But what about Michael? Do you think I should be mad at him?"

"I don't think you kids should be blamed for any of this."

"It's true that Michael didn't plan what happened, but he went along with it. Although after I told him I wanted to go home, he did try to convince his parents to take me back to Montréal. But when they wouldn't, he didn't do anything much about it."

"What do you think he should have done?"

"Not given up. Maybe he could have gone on a homework strike, or even a hunger strike. Or just yelled and argued with them more. That's what I would have done."

"So are you mad at Michael, then?"

"Maybe just disappointed. I still like him, but. . . I don't know. The thing is, Daddy, you may not be happy about this, but I still kind of like Gabriel too."

Daddy presses his lips together but doesn't say anything right away. Then he sighs.

"Well, I'm certainly not going to tell you who you should or shouldn't like, or that you can't like more than one boy at the same time. But after what Gabriel did. . ."

"Let me ask you something, Daddy. What happened to you. . . the bad things. . . is that normal? I mean, is it unusual that bad things like that happen in the world?"

"It's not so rare, no. Unfortunately, there's a lot of bad in the world. Even worse things than what happened to me."

"I had a feeling you were gonna say that. So why do you and Mommy bother? Why do you work so hard for social justice and stuff? Why not just give up on the world, if it's so bad?"

"There's a lot of good in the world, too. Beauty and love and all kinds of amazing things."

"Is there more good or more bad?"

"I don't know. I really don't know. But it doesn't matter. You can't give up on the world, or on life. You gotta keep trying to make things better, to love instead of hate, and to spread that love as much as you can."

"But don't you see, Daddy? You don't want to give up on the world, even though it's filled with evil. But there's way more evil in the world than there is in Gabriel. So why do you think I should give up on him, when there's so much good in him too?"

I can see Daddy thinking carefully about what I just said. It's like he's turning it around and around in his head, to see how it looks from all angles. He must like what he sees, because finally, a big smile lights up his face. It's that smile he has that I've never seen on anyone else—like a smile you might have if you lived in utopia or something.

Later, when we're almost to Montréal, Daddy has us pull over so we can look at the view of the city, Mont Royal popping up in the distance. There's something kind of exciting about living in a city with a mountain in the middle. But it's also an island, like Manhattan.

I'm remembering when we first came to Montréal, how Daddy asked me whether I wanted to take the ferry or the bridge, and I chose the ferry, not knowing at the time what either word meant in French.

"La navette or le pont?" I ask Daddy now, and I see that he remembers too.

"You choose," he answers, grinning at me from over his handlebars.

"OK, this time I choose the bridge!" I take off. "Meet you on the other side!"

EPILOGUE

SIRI

After I got back home, I found out a lot of my friends had been looking for me. I didn't realize that they cared so much. I guess I was too busy being angry and upset about everything. Even Gabriel had stopped by. He left me a birthday gift—a plant with purple flowers.

I still didn't know what to do about him, but I was so busy at school, trying to catch up and get a decent grade in French, that I didn't have time to worry about it. And we had our interview for permanent residence status, too. I spoke a lot to the government guy, telling him about how great it is when a new country welcomes you, how many friends Simon and I have made and how we both like school. I did it all in French, of course, and Mommy and Daddy looked so happy, it was like they were glowing.

The greatest thing is that Mommy found a baseball league that has a competitive travel team. When we went to register, they asked us to beam a photo of me. Mommy had some old photos from Brooklyn on her screen, but I wanted her to use something more recent. I look a lot different now, more grown up. So she came up with this photo of me from the winter. It was during that first big storm and showed me throwing a snowball at my brother. The guy who was registering us looked at the picture for a long time. Then he turned to me and asked, "Have you ever pitched? You have a perfect stance."

I started to explain how I wasn't good enough yet, but Mommy interrupted and said, "Siri is an extremely experienced ballplayer. She can play any position and she has an excellent arm."

Well, the long and short of it is that they tried me out and now I'm starting pitcher on the house league and I'm on the travel team too, where they sometimes put me in as the closer. The pitching coach of the travel team told me that I don't throw quite hard enough yet to be a starter at this level, but that there's no cooler, smarter, and more controlled pitcher than I am, which is just what you need for the end game.

SIMON

A few days ago, Daddy took me out to Crèmerie Sansregret for ice cream. It was beautiful and warm out, and plus, they have the best homemade ice cream in the world, so I guess that's why all the bike parking was taken. I looked around and saw a pole where I thought we could lock up. Only problem was that the pole had a "No Parking" sign on it. I went over there anyway, but then all of a sudden, I saw two cops walking towards us. I thought about Daddy and I guess I panicked. I was in such a hurry to get away from the No Parking pole that I tripped on the curb. One of the cops caught hold of my bike while the other caught hold of me. I tried to pull away but they held on.

"Calme-toi, c'est correct," they said to me.

It turns out that when I fell, I had cut my knee and it was bleeding. The cop got out a first aid kit and took care of it. Daddy stood close by me and watched, but he didn't say anything.

When we got inside the ice cream shop, the two cops came in too. I ordered a double chocolate fudge cone, but Daddy said he couldn't decide what he wanted, so he let the two cops go ahead. The cop who fixed my knee ordered vanille-cassis and the other cop, who had caught my bicycle, ordered the same flavour as I did. After the two cops left, Daddy ordered coffee bean almond.

Daddy and I sat down outside to eat our cones. I wanted to eat it slowly and make it last, but it was too good. Plus it melts fast in the sun. Daddy says that's because it's good-quality ice cream, which means mostly cream and not mostly ice.

"Papa, I didn't know cops liked ice cream."

"Of course they do. They have tongues and taste buds and stomachs, don't they? And they feel the heat just like we do."

"I was thinking it was because they were young cops, cadets. Maybe that's why they were nice, too."

Daddy didn't say anything. We sat there for a long time, not talking much, just thinking about stuff.

What I've been wondering is what if we had stayed in New York and I had killed that cop who hurt Daddy? Sometimes I think that it's too bad I didn't have a chance to do that. Maybe it would save other people from getting beaten up or killed by that same cop. But now I'm wondering what that cop is really like. Do they have kids? Are they sorry for what they did? Maybe that cop likes ice cream and animals and biking, just like I do. Maybe the cop felt so horrible about how much they hurt Daddy that they promised to never do anything like that again, like how I felt when I broke Keri's nose. Or maybe they even quit the police and found a new job where they didn't have to hurt people who didn't agree with the government. If I had killed the cop, they'd never have had a chance to be good from then on. There's no way of knowing for sure, but all in all, I've decided it's better that we didn't kill them after all, just in case. I guess moving to Montréal saved me from being a murderer. Me and Henry both. I'm going to tell Henry this when I see him this summer.

JANIE

I told the kids that each of us gets to invite one guest to visit us this summer, and along with that, we each get to have any type of party we want. I let Simon go first. Predictably, he chose Henry. For the type of party, he said he'd have to ask Henry what he thought, but he'd probably want either a pizza party or a game party. I told him not to worry, he could have a pizza-and-game party. I've already spoken with Henry's mom and she's willing to come with Henry, though neither one of them has ever left New York, let alone the United America.

Siri had a harder time of it, since she's loyal enough to still want it to be Michael, but she realizes that this is unlikely to work out. If Michael can't come, Siri said in her usual resourceful, opportunistic way, she wants to have two friends at the same time, arguing that she shouldn't have to choose between her two next-best friends from Brooklyn, and that their parents are more likely to say yes this way. Of course I let myself be talked into it. The more the merrier. As for type of party, she naturally chose two things as well—sports and music—because Simon got to have a double theme too.

Then I went out of strict reverse-age order to go next, so I could beat out Laek. I told my family that I wanted Philip as my guest. Simon remarked, "I thought he was Daddy's friend." I told him that he was my friend too. Then Simon looked at Siri, and Siri looked at Laek, and Laek just smiled his sexiest smile and asked me, "What kind of party?"

LAEK

Janie once told me there's no such thing as utopia. If this is true, then the comforting corollary would be that there's no such thing as dystopia either. But I'm not as sure as she is about this. I'm not even sure which truth would be preferable. A world without pain would be a very sweet thing. Might I be willing to pay for this first with a world that's filled with pain?

One thing I do know is there's such a thing as hope. Just as there's such a thing as despair. And the conditions that give rise to each.

I've been following events in the U.A. Through the news-feeds, but primarily through my friends and comrades who've continued the struggle there. They're trying to duplicate some of our successes in Montréal. For instance, the quiet, creative and unrelentingly stubborn occupation by the people of all the critical institutions of our society. Hospitals, schools, food banks, parks, credit unions. . . People are coming to understand that these things belong to the community. Meanwhile, my experience as an activist from the U.A. has been of greater interest here than I would've thought. Yeah, getting an outside view on your society can be useful. And being useful has given me a great deal of satisfaction.

Seeing how our struggles, our successes, and our momentum can pass from one community to another has lifted my heart. They can spy on us. Jam our communications. Arrest and punish us. They can try to divide and isolate us. But they just can't keep us apart. Our solidarity and love slip right across their borders. Like those lines aren't even real.

IL ÉTAIT UNE FOIS ...

"Tell us about the Bicycling Family."

"That old story?"

"Ouais, ouais! Tell about when they went on a new adventure!"

"D'accord. So one day the Bicycling Family left on a new adventure."

"Was everyone there? All of us?"

"Everyone."

"Grandma and Grandpa and Grandpa?"

"Yes."

"Aunt Kyla?"

"Yes."

"Even little Annie? And Jérémie? And Zak?"

"Them too, but they were in bike seats."

"But did they find what they were looking for? Did they get asylum?"

"Yeah, tell us about New Métropolis. Did they finally find utopia?"

"It's not about finding utopia, it's about creating utopia."

"But did they? Create utopia? And live happily ever after?"

"Of course! But lots of things happened along the road. I

can't finish the story because it's not over yet. It keeps going round and round and round."

"Like the wheels of a bicycle?"

"Yes, exactly."

The end

ACKNOWLEDGMENTS

My deepest gratitude to Dave Dufour of Flame and Arrow Publishing, whose vision is giving this story a second life at this needful time.

Thank you to Ian Shaw and Deux Voiliers Publishing, who published this book in its first incarnation, *Cycling to Asylum*.

This novel would never have existed without the selfless efforts of my first readers and the members of my writers' groups who served as editors, motivators, correctors, brainstormers, and most of all, my community. Special love and gratitude to Sharon Lax, Cora Siré, Ahmar Husain, Maya Merrick, and Daniel Minsky, who were there at the very beginning. Thanks also to the Quebec Writers' Federation.

Thanks to my mother, Carol Kay Sokol, who has always loved and supported me unreservedly, and to my brother, Scott Sokol, who has read and offered feedback on all my manuscripts.

Deepest gratitude and love to Glenn M. Rubenstein, my partner in life and in crossing borders, who has served as a sounding board, proofreader and an ethical model, and to our children Mara and Joshua, whom I love with all my heart and who continue to inspire me.

ABOUT THE AUTHOR

Credit: Rachel Karp

Su J Sokol is a social rights activist and a writer of speculative and interstitial fiction. Xe is the author of three novels: *Cycling to Asylum*, which was long-listed for the Sunburst Award for Excellence in Canadian Literature of the Fantastic; *Run J Run*; and *Zee*, a finalist for the Janet Savage Blachford Prize for Children's and Young Adult Literature. Su's short fiction and essays have appeared in various magazines and anthologies. Originally from Brooklyn where xe worked as a housing rights lawyer, Sokol has made xyr home in Montréal/Tiohtià:ke since 2004.

www.ingramcontent.com/pod-product-compliance
Lightning Source LLC
Jackson TN
JSHW032126060725
87113JS00001B/7